Tough Month
for a
Ranger

Center Point
Large Print

Also by James J. Griffin and available from
Center Point Large Print:

Death Stalks the Rangers
Death Rides the Rails
Ranger's Revenge
Texas Jeopardy
Blood Ties
Renegade Ranger
Fight for Freedom

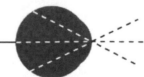

**This Large Print Book carries the
Seal of Approval of N.A.V.H.**

Tough Month for a Ranger

A Texas Ranger
James C. Blawcyzk Novel

James J. Griffin

CENTER POINT LARGE PRINT
THORNDIKE, MAINE

Dedicated to Texas Ranger Bruce Sherman,
his wife Kelle, and their sons,
Marshall and Wyatt.

1

"I sure hope we're not wasting our time, sittin' out here in the middle of the brush in the middle of the night in this middle-of-nowhere part of Blanco County, Copper," sixth generation Texas Ranger James C. Blawcyzk said softly to his paint gelding. "It's awfully dang cold out here. The temperature's gotta be below fifty degrees."

Copper responded with a soft nicker and a nuzzle to Jim's shoulder, then went back to cropping at the sparse, sun dried grass.

"I reckon you don't care, horse, as long as you've got grazin'," Jim said, slapping Copper's neck. He unscrewed the cap of his thermos bottle, took a swallow of the bitter, black coffee it held, then spit it out.

"Damn, even my coffee's cold. If there's one thing I can't stand, it's cold coffee."

Jim looked up at the myriad of stars pinpricking the inky curtain of the night sky. There was a new moon, so those stars provided the only illumination. A strong cold front had blown through two days previously, sweeping out the typical late August heat and humidity, leaving behind unusually clear and chilly weather, so, with no city lights to pollute the sky here in this remote location, even the Milky Way was visible, a filmy curtain covering a good portion of the heavens.

Jim pulled his eyes back down to gaze into his campfire, but only briefly. If the men he was expecting did indeed show up, having to take the time to allow his vision to adjust to the dark could easily prove fatal. He thought about stretching out on his back, which would be far more comfortable than squatting under the junipers and mesquite he was using for cover, and which also hid Copper from any prying eyes, but didn't dare take the chance. As the night wore on, the odds would become greater he'd grow drowsy, inadvertently drift off to sleep, and miss his quarry, should they finally show up. Or, if he slept too soundly and they spotted him, they could easily send him to his eternal slumber.

Time seemed to drag as the stars made their slow pinwheel around the sky.

"Reckon we guessed wrong, Copper," Jim muttered. "It doesn't seem like those *hombres* are gonna make an appearance, at least not here."

Copper snorted, and shook his head.

"All right, *I* guessed wrong," Jim said, grinning. "Tell you what. We'll give it another hour, then if nothing happens, we'll head for home. At least, that way you'll get to spend part of the night in your warm stall, and I'll spend the rest of it in my nice soft bed, with Kim alongside me to chase the chill out of my bones."

The words had no sooner left his lips when Copper lifted his head and pricked his ears sharply forward. His nostrils flared, then he started to give a low whicker.

"Shh. Quiet, boy," Jim warned him, with a pat to the big gelding's muzzle. "You hear somethin' movin' out there? Whatever or whoever it is, we sure don't want them to discover us. Lemme try and pick up whatever sound's got your attention."

Jim strained to hear, or smell, whatever Copper, with his far keener senses of hearing and smell, had heard or scented. After less than a couple of minutes, a soft sound also came to his ears.

"I guess our boys have shown up after all," he whispered to the horse. "You stay real still while we wait and see what they're gonna do."

Moving carefully, he picked up his Bushmaster .223 caliber rifle from where it lay on the ground alongside him. The hoof beats of several approaching horses could now be heard clearly on the stiff night breeze.

"You stay quiet, pard," Jim again warned Copper. "We're damn lucky we're downwind from those *hombres*. With the wind in our faces, odds are they won't hear us, and their horses won't catch your scent. Let's just wait and see what those ol' boys are gonna do."

Copper nudged Jim's shoulder, then stamped his foot.

"You're right. We'd better see how many of 'em

9

are out there, too," Jim said, with a soft chuckle. "Seems like I'm thinkin' backwards tonight. If a shootin' scrape breaks out, here's hopin' I don't turn my gun backwards and plug myself in the belly. That'd hurt somethin' awful. Be kind of hard to explain, too. Shh. They're getting close."

A minute later, four horsemen appeared from behind the brush, off to Jim's left. They stopped short when they spotted his campfire. One of them said something Jim couldn't quite catch, and another answered. A moment later, the answer was clear. One of the men lifted a rifle from its scabbard, aimed it at Jim's blankets, and fired three times. The blankets jerked at the bullets' impact, and Jim's hat flew several feet when one of the slugs tore through its crown.

The horsemen sat unmoving for several minutes, then, apparently satisfied the bullets had hit their mark and killed their sleeping quarry, the rifleman shoved his weapon back in its scabbard, and the men moved on.

"We'll give 'em a couple of minutes to put some space between us, Copper," Jim whispered. "I'm sure glad I wasn't actually *sleepin'* under those blankets. I'd've had two holes blown through my back and another through my head, if I had been. Seems like my trick worked. That decoy I set up with my bedroll and old hat sure fooled those *hombres*. I'd imagine they thought

I was just a cowboy keepin' night guard, who dozed off."

Jim waited until the four men disappeared down a slight slope, and the sound of cattle, bawling in protest at being disturbed from their dozing or grazing, came to him.

"Time to get movin'," he said to his horse. He tossed aside the end of the rope he held, which he'd tied to his hat, to tug at it when the bullets hit. "We'll pick up those blankets and my old hat later, after we're finished with our work. Damn, I sure hate to leave that fire burning, but I can't chance one of those *hombres* spotting it goin' out, then getting curious and comin' back to see why. I cleared enough brush and grass from around it and dug the hole deep enough I'm not worried it'll spread. It's dyin' down, anyway. Let's get to work. We'll follow those boys and see where they lead us."

Jim eased into his saddle, then put Copper into a slow walk. The sounds of the bawling cattle, the hoof beats and occasional whinnies of the horses, even the shouts of the horsemen as they drove the cattle, were clear in the night. The smell of cigarette smoke mixed with that of disturbed dirt and dust.

"We can stay well behind, so there won't be a chance one of 'em looks back and sees us, until we hear them stop, Copper. They're makin' it real easy for us to trail 'em. At least a couple

11

of those *hombres* are smokin', so that'll help us keep track of 'em, too. You just make certain you don't decide to call out to their horses and give us away. That's one reason you make a good Ranger's mount. You're not generally the talkative type."

The land in this section was level to gently rolling, so it was easy enough for Jim to keep track of the horsemen's and cattle's direction from a safe distance, by the sounds they made, plus occasional glimpses he had of them when they topped a rise, or when they had dropped down into a wash or low area and he stood Copper above them, making certain to stay behind whatever brush or trees were available, not wishing to skylight himself against the horizon while on top of a ridge. Between the men concentrating on their work keeping the herd bunched, and what little light there was from the stars obscured even more by the dust the herd threw up, it was unlikely any of them would happen to look back and see they were being followed, anyway. However, it made no sense for Jim to take unnecessary chances, either.

"Seems like they're headed for Ranch 1323, right where Smith West Ranch Road comes into it, Copper," Jim said to his horse, about thirty minutes later. "Four men, and about fifty cows, plus they probably have a lookout somewhere down on 1323 or Smith West Ranch, wherever they parked their rigs. Most likely a driver, too. Those sure ain't the best odds for us.

"I'd bet my hat they're aimin' for the sand pit, there. That'd be an ideal spot to hide an eighteen-wheeler. They can load up those stolen cows and be long gone before anyone's the wiser. Might could be one of 'em is even a worker at that pit.

"One thing's for certain, they're smart enough not to head north. That'd bring 'em way too near the West Ranch or its airport. Too close to the Smith or Cooper spreads, too. They'd most likely be spotted by one of the ranch hands if they tried takin' that route. We'll just mosey along behind 'em for a bit more, until I'm certain where they're planning on getting rid of that herd."

Still hanging well back, Jim continued following the apparent rustlers, until they reached the destination he'd suspected, an active sand pit off of Smith West Ranch Road, close by its junction with Ranch Road 1323.

"Just as I said, Copper. They've gotta have a cattle truck hidden in the diggin's. In this light, to anyone drivin' by, it'd look like just another piece of equipment, except when the cows are bein' loaded, and out here at this time of night—or, I guess I should say mornin'—the odds anyone'd be passing by are mighty slim. Time to call in the cavalry for some help, pard," Jim said. He reined Copper to a halt, then pulled his cell phone from its holster on his belt, and hit the speed dial for the Blanco County Sheriff's Office. He punched 0 to bypass the voice menu.

"Blanco County Sheriff's Office Dispatch. How may I help you?" the person on the other end answered.

"Dispatch, this is Texas Ranger Jim Blawcyzk. I need some assistance at the sand pit off Smith West Ranch Road, at its junction with Ranch 1323. I'm trailing a bunch of apparent cattle thieves. There's four of 'em that I know of, pushing about fifty cows. They're on horseback. So am I. I figure they've got an eighteen-wheeler hidden in the pit waitin' to load the herd, then boogie real quick. I can't say whether or not there are more, or if they've got a lookout either at the pit's entrance or at Smith West and 1323."

"10-4, Ranger. How many units would you like to respond?"

"Three, if they're available, but I'll take however many you've got."

"10-4. Stand by."

On his phone, Jim could hear the dispatcher as she radioed several Blanco County deputies. It only took a moment for her to return to the line.

"Ranger Blawcyzk, I have two units and three deputies available, one approximately thirty minutes away, the other approximately forty."

"*Bueno*. Have them approach from Ranch 1323. No lights or sirens. If they can arrive without headlights that would be more helpful. Have the

14

nearest unit wait on the side of 1323, far enough from Smith West the *hombres* I'm trailing won't be likely to see 'em, until the second is on scene. Tell them to come in the main entrance to the pit. If they come across a lookout, have one unit take care of him, and the other continue until they see me. I'll wait as long as I can, but if necessary, I'll move in to make the arrests before your units arrive."

"Understood, Ranger. Do you want me to advise when they are in position?"

"No, I don't want to chance these rustlers possibly hearing my phone ring. I'll call you back in twenty minutes, or sooner if I have to make my move. Just emphasize to your units, *no lights or sirens!*"

"Clear on that, Ranger."

"Appreciate your assistance, Dispatch. Clear for now."

"10-4, Ranger."

Jim slid his phone back in its holster, then removed his badge from his left breast pocket and pinned it to his shirt.

"It won't be long now, Copper," he said, lifting the reins to ease the paint into a walk, once again.

Jim found a place where he was well-hidden, behind a large mound of sand and rubble, while he waited for the Blanco County deputies to arrive. From here, he could observe the rustlers,

15

but was pretty well screened from their view, unless one just happened to turn and look directly at the top of the quarry waste. He left Copper ground hitched at the base of the sand pile, where the horse could graze on bunch grass and live oak leaves, until Jim needed him.

Jim watched and took pictures while waiting for his backup, shielding the camera with his hat to avoid one of the men spotting a glint from its indicator light. As he had suspected, there was a fifth man, the driver of the big rig. To tip the odds even more in the rustlers' favor, there was also a sixth man, apparently a co-driver. The men had the trailer backed up to a pile of sand and gravel that formed a rough ramp. Sections of portable corral fencing had been set up at the bottom and alongside the makeshift ramp to funnel the rustled cows into the trailer.

As the rustlers began loading the cattle, he glanced at his watch, then took a deep breath. These men were clearly practiced at handling cattle, for they were having little trouble keeping the cows bunched and moving. At this rate, they would have them on the trailer and be ready to pull out before the deputies arrived. Jim looked at his watch again.

"Jim Blawcyzk, you're a damn fool," he muttered to himself. "How the hell do you think you're gonna be able to hold four men on horseback, plus the truck drivers, single-handed?" He shook his head, then redialed the sheriff's office.

"Blanco County Sheriff's Office Dispatch."

"Dispatch, Ranger Blawcyzk. Forget what I said before. I still don't want your deputies using lights or sirens, but I need them to get here quick as they can. Tell 'em to step on it. These rustlers are loadin' the cows lots faster'n I expected. I've got to make my move right now."

"10-4, Ranger. Understood."

"Obliged."

Jim hung up, then pulled his rifle from its scabbard and sighed.

"Chances are I'll never be able to round up these *hombres* on my own," he muttered, then shook his head at his own bad joke. "No sense in puttin' this off any longer. Let's go, Copper."

He nudged the horse into a slow, shuffling walk, the quietest gait possible. Once he was around the sand pile, there was no cover until he reached where the cows were being loaded. He murmured a silent prayer none of the men would see him until he was almost at their backs. He patted Copper's shoulder as a reminder to keep quiet, and not whinny to the other horses.

Luck was with him, for, with the noise and dust of the bawling cows and the rumble of their hooves as they loaded into the trailer, none of the rustlers were aware of his presence until he was only about twenty yards away. If he drew any nearer, it would be too close to keep all of them covered. He reined Copper to a halt.

"All right, boys, you can stop right where you are," Jim ordered. "Texas Ranger. Keep your hands where I can see 'em. Y'all are under arrest for cattle rustlin'."

One of the men eased his hand toward the pistol on his hip. Without even seeming to move, Jim shifted his rifle, so it was pointed directly at the man's chest.

"Uh-uh. I wouldn't do that if I were you," Jim said. "Unless you think you can keep on breathin' with a big ol' hole blown clean through your lungs."

Reluctantly, the man lifted his hand away from the weapon.

"That's better," Jim said. "You two on the ground. Get in front of the others where I can see you."

The men did as ordered.

"You can't keep all of us covered, Ranger," the man who'd started for his pistol said, with a scowl. "You just bit off a helluva lot more than you can chew."

"Maybe so," Jim said, with a shrug. "But that's not your worry, because if any of you or your partners try somethin' stupid, you'll be the first to take a bullet. I can guarantee I'll take at least two or three of you with me before I go down. Any of you want to take that chance, that you'll still be standin' upright after I hit the ground?"

None of the men answered, nor made a move. Even their horses stood quietly, except for a stamping of hoof or swishing of tail at a pestering mosquito. The rustlers realized that, while they had the Ranger outnumbered, and could no doubt overwhelm and kill him, at least some of them would be certain to die in the attempt. Looking into the barrel of that menacing rifle held by the determined lawman on the big paint horse, not one of them was willing to risk being the first to take a bullet.

"I didn't think so," Jim said. "You just follow my orders and there's no need for anyone to get hurt. You two not on horseback, drop to your bellies and get your hands behind your backs. *Now!*" he snapped, when they hesitated. "The rest of you, take the pistols out of your holsters, with just two fingers, and drop 'em to the dirt. Then do the same with your rifles."

He waited while the men obeyed his commands.

"You that tried for your gun," he continued. "Get down off your horse, slow and easy, then take your rope, cut off some lengths, and tie your friends' wrists. Make certain you stay where I can see you. Don't even think about duckin' behind your horse. I can pick off a man at five hundred yards with this rifle, easy, so at this range I can't hardly miss if you try anything stupid."

Jim kept his rifle aimed at the suspect as he

slowly got off his horse. Making certain none of his actions could be misconstrued, he lifted his rope from the saddle horn, then hesitated a minute when he took his knife from its sheath on his belt.

"Uh-uh. Tryin' to get me with that knife would be a real mistake . . . and the last one you'd ever make in this life," Jim warned him.

The rustler shrugged, then he uncoiled a length of rope and cut off a piece. He proceeded to tie his nearest partner's wrists together, then the next man.

"You're doin' just fine," Jim told him, as the man secured the second truck driver. "The *hombre* closest to your pal, get off your horse, slow and easy, then lie on your belly with your hands behind your back. Soon as he's done that, mister, tie him like you did the others. You other two, stay in your saddles, then get down, one at a time, as soon as your friend finishes tyin' the man before you."

There was only one rustler left in his saddle when two Blanco County sheriff's units came speeding into the sand pit. Whether it was spooked by the sudden appearance of the vehicles, or goaded by its rider taking advantage of the unexpected distraction, the man's horse pitched into a fit of bucking, then took off at a gallop. His partner on the ground seized this opportunity. He took off on the run, scooped up his pistol from where he had dropped it, and raced for the edge of the sand pit.

"Aw, hell!" Jim exclaimed. "Let's get 'em, Copper!" He dug his boot heels into the big paint's ribs, sending him leaping into a dead run.

Copper quickly gained ground on the running cow thief. Hearing the horse's rapidly approaching hoof beats, the man turned and fired one errant shot, which came nowhere near his target. Before he could fire again, Jim was on top of him. He slammed Copper's right shoulder into the rustler, sending him sprawling. Knowing the man had the wind knocked out of him, at the very least, Jim didn't bother to look back. He urged Copper to an even faster pace. Always eager for a run, excited by the prospect of a chase, the big paint snorted, then stretched out his legs, increasing his speed even more.

As they drew nearer the fleeing rustler, Jim lifted his lariat from the saddle horn, shook out a loop, and twirled the rope over his head. Once Copper overtook their quarry, Jim threw the rope, which settled neatly over the rustler. A trained cow pony, Copper instantly planted his hooves and came to a stop, tightening the rope around the rustler, pinning his arms to his sides and yanking him out of the saddle. The man hit the ground hard. Copper kept the rope taut as Jim jumped out of the saddle and ran up to the rustler.

Despite being tied, the rustler rolled toward Jim's horse to put some slack in the rope, then scrambled to his feet just as Jim reached him, and planted his foot squarely in the pit of the Ranger's stomach, doubling him over. Copper pulled back on the rope and yanked the rustler off his feet yet again. Jim grabbed the rustler's left arm, rolled him onto his belly, and drove a knee into the small of his back. He then pulled the man's hands behind his back. He took his handcuffs from their leather pouch on his belt and secured the man's wrists.

"You still feelin' frisky, mister?" he asked.

"No . . . no. Can't catch . . . my breath."

"Good, 'cause neither am I, thanks to that kick in the gut you gave me. Let's get back to your partners."

Jim pulled the man to his feet, lifted the rope from around him, and, with Copper and the rustler's horse following, went back to where the others were now being held by three sheriff's deputies. He recognized only one of them.

"Damn, Jim, I ain't never seen anything like that, except at a rodeo," Earl Tuttle, one of the deputies said. "It looked like somethin' straight out of the old West. You all right?"

"I will be," Jim answered. "My gut's gonna be hurtin' for a while, though. Far as what happened, in the old days I could've just shot him in the back and been done with it. Would've been

22

simpler. How about the *hombre* I bowled over with my horse?"

"If the rancher who owns these cows hadn't gotten to that *hombre* first, and swung him from the nearest stout tree, before you had the chance to shoot him," Tuttle said. "The *hombre* your horse got is pretty banged up, but he'll live. I assume you'll want to take care of the legal stuff. Oh, before I forget, these are Deputies Linda Everly and Fred Haymes. I don't believe you've met them."

"Yeah, I reckon I'd better," Jim answered. He nodded to the other two deputies. "Did they have a lookout posted?"

"None that we saw," Tuttle said. "Just the *hombres* you'd already rounded up."

"Okay, let's get this over with," Jim said. "Listen up, y'all. You're under arrest for livestock theft. The two of you who tried to take off will also be charged with attempting to evade arrest. And you who tried to put your boot clean through my belly is also facing charges of resisting arrest, and assault on a law officer."

"You might want to throw in trespassing, too, Ranger," Everly said. "Unless one of these jokers happens to own this gravel pit."

"Y'know, that's not a bad idea," Jim agreed. "Trespassing, also. You have the right to remain silent . . ." He proceeded to give the suspects their Miranda rights. When he finished, one of them, the man he'd roped off his horse, finally spoke up.

"You're makin' a big mistake, Ranger. I bought these here cows, fair and square, from their owner."

"What's your name?" Jim asked.

"Burl. Burl Ivey."

"Mighty funny time of the night to be movin' cattle, Mr. Ivey," Jim said. "Not to mention a mighty funny place to be loadin' 'em, too. I don't suppose you've got a bill of sale for them?"

"It's in the truck," Ivey said.

"Do you mind if one of the deputies gets it so I can look it over? Or do I need to get a search warrant?"

"No, I don't mind," Ivey said. "I want to see the egg on your face. It's over the passenger side sun visor."

"I'll get it, Ranger," Haymes offered.

"Obliged, Deputy."

"While he's doing that, Mr. Ivey, would you mind telling me the name of the man who owns these cows?" Jim asked.

"Sure. Tom Price."

"Name of his ranch? His brand?"

"I . . . I'm not certain."

"Well, I don't suppose you'd mind if I called Mr. Price to ask him if he sold you those cows, and knew you were planning on moving them in the middle of the night, would you?"

"He's—um, he's not home, Ranger. He took off on a trip with his wife, right after I gave him the money. That's why he sold these cows, so he could have the money to take her on a vacation. But you'll see his signature on the Bill of Sale."

"You really expect me to believe that?"

Ivey just shrugged his shoulders.

"Don't matter none if you believe me or not. Price's signature is on the Bill of Sale, and that's all the proof I need."

"Ranger, I happen to know Tom Price real well," Everly said. "In fact, I saw him and his wife just this morning, at the convenience store a couple of miles from here. They didn't say anything about taking a vacation. I can tell you those are his cows, though. They're wearin' a Circle TP brand. That's Tom's."

"That's a real interesting development, wouldn't you say, Mr. Ivey?"

"I'm not sayin' another word."

"That's your right," Jim answered. "In fact, if I were you, I'd keep my mouth shut, too. You're just diggin' yourself and your partners in deeper. Well, here comes the deputy with the papers. It should be interesting to see what they show."

"Here you go, Ranger," Haymes said, when he got back to Jim and handed him the Bill of Sale.

Jim was able to read the paper in the headlights of the Blanco County units.

"Mr. Ivey, you're right. These do appear to be

in order," he said. "As soon as I can reach Mr. Price, I'm certain we can get this entire matter straightened out. Deputy, since you know the Prices, you wouldn't happen to have their phone number, would you?"

"I sure do," Everly answered. "However, if you'll let me see that Bill of Sale, I can tell you if the signature is legitimate, or a forgery. I've bought several horses from Tom over the years, so I know his signature as well as my own."

"Sure. That'll make things easier, and save us some time."

Jim handed Everly the paper. She only glanced at it before handing it back to him.

"That's not Tom's signature. Not even close."

"I guess that settles things," Jim said. "Now I can add forgery to the charges, too. You boys are all on your way to the county lockup. Deputy Everly, if you wouldn't mind calling Mr. Price, let him know he can come get his stock. He *will* have to keep this herd in a separate pasture until the case comes to trial, since they're now evidence. I'd say he'll be real surprised to find he had a bunch of his cows driven off. Deputy Haymes, I'd appreciate it if you'd find the judge who's on call tonight. We'll need a court order so we can impound this rig, and a search warrant so we can go through it. Also, call county animal control, since we'll be seizing these horses, so they'll have to be taken to the county ranch or the county humane society, whichever has room. Earl, while they're doin' that, you and I will start processing these *hombres*, and getting them ready for transport. It's been a long night already, and it just got a lot longer."

It took the rest of the night and well into the morning before Jim retrieved his truck and horse trailer, the stolen cattle were back on the Circle TP Ranch, the rustlers' horses taken to the county humane society, their eighteen-wheeler towed to the county impound lot, and the men themselves booked and ensconced in the Blanco County jail.

"Damn," Jim exclaimed, when he looked at his watch. "I've got to be in Boerne to testify at trial in less than an hour."

"You'll never make it," Tuttle said. "You'd best call and ask for a delay."

"Not with Judge Hardy on the bench. She'll never grant it. She's a stickler for punctuality. Actually, she's a complete pain in the butt. I have to say she is fair, though. At least, I can give her that much."

"Even if you can get to Boerne that quick, you sure can't go looking the way you are," Tuttle pointed out. "Your pants are torn, showing one of your butt cheeks hanging out, your shirt's all muddy, and you need a shower and shave, real bad."

"I knew I felt a breeze back there, but cleaning up's not a problem," Jim answered. "I've got a change of clothes in my truck, along with a razor. Ranger regulations. We always have to carry a clean set of clothes. Heaven forbid we should talk to the media without a clean shirt, tie, and pressed pants on. I'll duck in the men's room once I get to the courthouse, throw some water on my face, shave, and change my duds. Best I can do."

"There's no need for that, Jim. You can take a quick hot shower right here, in our locker room," Tuttle said. "While you do that, I'll run across the street to Clancy's Quik-Mart and pick up some coffee and doughnuts. You can be on your way in less than ten minutes. You won't be cuttin' it much closer than you already are."

"That's a good idea, Earl. I'm obliged."

"No problem. There's plenty of soap in the dispensers, and extra washcloths and towels in the drawers under the sinks, so all you need from your truck is your clothes and razor. By the time you're finished washing up, I'll be back with your breakfast."

Ten minutes later, Jim had showered, shaved, and donned clean clothes. He grabbed his coffee and doughnuts from Earl Tuttle's desk, left the sheriff's office at a trot, got into his Tahoe, fired up the engine, then hit the lights and siren as he stomped on the accelerator. He had forty-four minutes to cover the sixty miles of winding two lane roads between Johnson City and Boerne.

Once he reached the Kendall County Courthouse and pulled into the parking lot, Jim swiftly unloaded Copper and tied him to his trailer. He secured two buckets of water, one with two quarts of grain, and a hay bag filled to overflowing within Copper's reach.

"Sorry, pal," he told the horse, with a pat to his shoulder and a peppermint. "I'll make this up to you tonight. Right now, I've gotta rush." He grabbed his laptop and briefcase from the front seat of his truck, and hurried inside. As he'd feared, court had already been in session for twenty minutes.

"Ranger Blawcyzk. How kind of you to honor us with your presence," Judge Mary Hardy said sarcastically, from the bench. "I was about to dismiss the charges against Mrs. Delavance. I assume you have a legitimate excuse for your tardiness."

"I apologize, Your Honor, and I do. I did telephone the prosecutor's office to let them know I was *en route*, but was delayed slightly due to processing the arrests I made last night. I needed to clean up before appearing, and also had to let my horse out of his trailer, and leave him feed and water. It's too hot for him to stand in a horse trailer all day long. Do you want the entire story now, or afterwards?"

"I am well aware of why you are late, Ranger. However, as you are also well aware, justice delayed is justice denied, even if for only a short time. You can provide me the full explanation after court is done for the day. Just don't let this happen again."

She turned her attention to the prosecuting attorney.

"Mr. Horton, now that Ranger Blawcyzk has finally arrived, you may call your first witness."

Jim finally arrived home just before seven o'clock that evening. As always, when he pulled up to the barn, Frostie, the family's tan Wheaten/Cairn terrier mix, came bounding up to meet him, his tail waving wildly.

"Howdy, Frostie," Jim greeted the dog. "I'm sure glad to see you, too. It's been a real long day. Let me just get Copper unloaded and fed, then this trailer cleaned out and unhitched, and we'll head inside for some chow."

As much as we wanted to just go into the house, have a quick supper, then take a nice, long, hot soak before hitting his mattress, Jim had to get his chores done first.

He let Copper out of the trailer, then turned him into his corral, where he fed him. While the horse ate, Jim groomed him thoroughly, including cleaning out his feet and checking his shoes, then gave him a final peppermint and a good night kiss on the nose.

After that, he backed the trailer to the manure pile, where he swept it out. He then moved the trailer to its parking place, leaving the doors and windows open to air it out. He would have preferred not to take the time to unhitch the trailer from his Tahoe, but he never knew when a call might come in, and the few minutes it took to unhitch the trailer now could literally save someone's life later. Once that was done, he parked the Tahoe and went inside, with Frostie at his heels.

"Kim, I'm finally home," he called.

"I'm in the living room, Jim," she answered. He went to the front room. Kim was sitting on the couch, working on her laptop, with their seven-month-old son, Joshua, peacefully sleeping in his cradle alongside her. Jim gave the baby, then his wife, a kiss on the cheek.

"I'm sorry I'm so late, honey," he said. "That damn Judge Hardy has got to run the slowest courtroom in the world."

"I've gotten used to it," Kim answered. "You warned me about what I was getting into, marrying a Ranger. But I loved you so much I went in with my eyes wide open. I still do. And as you can see, I've also been working late."

Jim's wife, Kimberly Tavares Blawcyzk, ran

her own successful consulting business, helping new startups, especially those owned by women or minorities, navigate the hazards of opening a business. She also helped business owners who wanted to trade with Mexico through the regulations and red tape required for that. While she was taller than average, that was the only way she resembled her blonde, blue-eyed husband. Kim came from a line of Spanish ancestors that went back to well before Texas's secession from Mexico. Her black hair and dark features contrasted with Jim's fair looks.

"If you don't mind, I'm just gonna grab something to eat quick, then take a shower and hit the sack," Jim said. "It's been one helluva day. I spent most of the night waiting for the rustlers I've been after to show up. They finally did, and everything was going smoothly, until a deputy sheriff's car showed up and spooked one of their horses. That gave two of 'em the chance to take off runnin'. I used Copper to knock one off his feet and roped the other out of his saddle. He managed to give me a good kick in the gut before I got him hogtied. Then it took the rest of the night to get those hombres locked up and booked, the cattle back to their owner, and their horses to the Humane Society. After that, I still had to go down to Boerne to give my testimony. Needless to say, I was late, and that ticked off Judge Hardy. She didn't want to hear why

I was late, just gave me a real dressing down."

"I don't mind at all. As soon as I finish this application, I'm planning on turning in early myself," Kim answered. "There's chicken, quinoa, and green beans keeping warm in the oven for you."

Jim started chuckling, for no reason that his wife could see.

"What's so funny?" Kim asked, puzzled.

"Nothing really," Jim answered. "Just a thought that crossed my mind when you mentioned quinoa."

"Well, are you going to share it, or keep it from me?"

"I'll share it, as long as you promise not to hit me."

"I'll probably regret this, but I promise I won't hit you."

"You see, there's this old song from the 1950s my grandpa used to listen to, all the time. It's titled *The Green Door*. I heard it so much I've never forgotten it, since I kinda like it, too. The refrain goes 'Green door, what's that secret you're keepin'?' All I hear in my head right now is 'Quinoa, what's that secret you're keepin'?' Ow! You said you wouldn't hit me."

Kim had given Jim a solid slap on his butt.

"I lied," Kim said, chuckling softly herself, despite trying to keep a straight face. "Actually, I didn't, but that was so bad you needed a slap.

I just told you I went into our marriage with my eyes open, but I must have had my ears plugged. You must be more worn out than you realize, to come up with that."

"I reckon I deserved the slap," Jim conceded. "I'd better head for the kitchen before you swat me again."

"Jim, I know you're exhausted, but don't you want to see yourself on television first?"

"What?"

"You made the news. I already know everything that happened last night."

"I couldn't have. I haven't seen a reporter all day."

"See for yourself."

Kim picked up the remote and turned on the DVR. The logo for KEYE's, the CBS affiliate out of Austin, five o'clock news appeared on the screen, then the station's two anchorpersons.

"Good evening. I'm Jane Humphries."

"And I'm Blake Carlson. Here is our lead story. Texas may have some of the most populous, most sophisticated cities in the country; however, much of the state is still not all that far removed from its Wild West roots."

Humphries picked up the narrative.

"The six men whose police photographs and names you see on the monitor behind us were arrested last night for alleged cattle rustling, which unfortunately is still all too common a

34

crime in the rural areas of the state. However, the arrests in this case were anything but routine. Our Doris Monroe is standing outside the Blanco County Sheriff's Office in Johnson City with the details. Doris . . ."

"Good evening, Jane, Blake. According to a spokesperson from the Blanco County Sheriff's Department, who spoke on condition of anonymity, late last night their department was asked to assist a Texas Ranger in the apprehension of some alleged livestock thieves. This took place near the intersection of Smith West Ranch Road and Ranch Road 1323. When three sheriff's deputies arrived on scene, the Ranger who requested assistance, and whose name neither the sheriff's department nor the Texas Rangers has released, already had the suspects in custody, with four of them secured. However, the arrival of the first Blanco County unit apparently spooked one of the suspect's horses. The man riding that horse, as well as one on foot, then attempted to elude capture. What happened next was recorded on the deputies' body and dash cams. Here are those images now."

The screen cut away from the reporter to video of Jim chasing the two men, including his bowling one over with Copper, then roping the other man out of his saddle, along with the ensuing brief fight.

"Damn," Jim muttered, as the reporter's image appeared back on the screen.

"As you can see, the Ranger captured two fleeing suspects in a manner befitting any old West sheriff or Ranger," Monroe said. "We have John Tierney, from our sister station KWTX in Waco, live at Texas Ranger Company F Headquarters in that city, where he attempted to obtain more information. John . . ."

"Thank you, Doris. Company F's territory includes Blanco County, so I came here to its headquarters on the grounds of the Texas Ranger Hall of Fame and Museum, to try and obtain more information about last night's incident. No one from Company F would consent to an interview, nor to appearing on camera. However, they did provide us the following written statement:

'Last night, a Ranger from Company F, with the assistance of the Blanco County Sheriff's Department, interrupted six suspects during an apparent attempted livestock theft. As it is still early in the investigation, and none of the officers involved have completed their reports at this time, we will not be releasing the name of the Ranger involved, the deputies, nor the name of the person who owns the cattle which were allegedly being stolen. We can tell you all six suspects have been charged with theft of livestock, plus trespass. In addition, one of the two suspects who attempted to flee has been charged with attempt to evade arrest, and the other faces the same charge, plus resisting arrest and assault on a law officer. There is also a charge of forgery pending against one of the men.

As the footage from the Blanco County deputies' cameras shows, the method our officer used to apprehend the suspects was a bit out of the ordinary, for this day and age. However, as all Texans know, the Rangers will use any and all legal methods necessary to apprehend a suspected criminal. Many areas of the state are still isolated and rugged enough that using what might be considered outdated procedures, including horseback, is often required.

In addition, the Blanco County Sheriff's Office released the footage without first notifying the Rangers, nor asking our permission. The release of the footage was not authorized by anyone from the Texas Rangers. That said, as Blanco County deputies recorded this incident, their Department is well within its rights to release the footage. Also, a preliminary examination of the images appears to show no improper actions on the part of our officer. We will, of course, be reviewing the footage more closely, as well as interviewing the Ranger, and all Blanco County officers involved. We will update the media, and the public, further as our investigation continues.'

"That is the only statement we have received from the Texas Rangers," Tierney continued, after reading the statement. "They still have not provided us the name of the Ranger involved. However, according to the personnel records of the Rangers, the man who covers Blanco County is Ranger James C. Blawcyzk, who is stationed at Buda. I am still attempting to confirm that Ranger Blawcyzk is the officer in those videos. For now, John Tierney, reporting from Waco. Back to you, Doris."

"Thank you, John."

"Blake, Jane, that's the latest information we have for our viewers," Monroe concluded. "We, of course, will stay on top of this developing story, and provide any new information as soon as it is available. Back to you."

"Thank you, Doris," Carlson said. "It seems the Rangers are still true to their traditions, even in the 21st century. In other news . . ."

Kim clicked off the DVR.

"The images are kind of dark and grainy, but

anyone who knows you, or your horse, can see it was you, Jim," she said.

"This is just great!" Jim exclaimed. "Those deputies never told me they'd gotten video of the whole thing. Talk about bein' blindsided."

"You didn't do anything wrong, did you?"

"Not at all."

"Then you have nothing to worry about. Why don't you do what you said you were going to? Eat your supper, take a shower, and get some rest. I hate to say this, but you look worn out."

"I pretty much am," Jim admitted. "C'mon, Frostie, let's go attack that chicken."

As he headed for the kitchen, Jim began singing.

"There's an old piano and they play it hot behind the quinoa. Don't know what they're doin' but they laugh a lot behind the quinoa. Wish they'd let me in so I can find out what's behind the quinoa."

"Jim . . ."

"What, Kim?"

"Keep that up and you *won't* find out what's behind *any* door, ever again, except perhaps the door to Hell."

"You mean to Heaven, don't you?"

"Probably not. At the very least, you'll spend a long time in Purgatory before St. Peter lets you through the Pearly Gates, if you keep coming up with jokes like that. Confessions are every

Saturday at three o'clock. I suggest you go, and hope the priest doesn't give you too severe a penance. You might not want to tell him exactly how bad your weird sense of humor is."

"Actually, all the priests at our parish are already aware of that."

"Then I wouldn't remind whichever one's hearing confessions, if I were you."

"All right, I'll shut up and be good."

"If only," Kim retorted, laughing. "If only."

Jim made quick work of his supper. After eating, he headed to clean up. Once in the bathroom, he eyed the whirlpool tub longingly. He'd like nothing better than a long, hot soak to ease his aching muscles, particularly his bruised abdomen. The imprint of Burl Ivey's boot was plain to see in the ugly black and blue mark that stretched across most of his belly.

However, Jim realized if he laid back to relax in that tub, he'd fall asleep, and either turn into a prune or drown himself. So, he undressed, then stepped into the shower stall instead. He quickly washed, toweled off, then stumbled into the bedroom and collapsed face down across the bed, asleep before he hit the mattress. He never stirred when Kim came to bed an hour later, never realized she turned him gently so his head was on his pillow and his feet at the bottom of the mattress, pulled a sheet over him, and laid alongside him, giving him a good night kiss. He slumbered, undisturbed, until the phone on his nightstand rang. Groggily, he reached for the receiver and picked it up. The bedside clock read 1:37 A.M.

"Howdy?" he mumbled into the mouthpiece.

"Ranger Blawcyzk?"

"Yup, this is Ranger Blawcyzk."

"D.P.S. Dispatch, Ranger Blawcyzk. We have a request for assistance from the Hays County Sheriff's Office. Evidently, they couldn't reach you directly. There's been an apparent double homicide."

Those words jolted Jim fully awake. He grabbed the pad and pencil next to the phone.

"What's the location?"

"On Fischer Store Road, that's County 181, south of Ranch Road 2325, at the bridge over the Blanco River. The Hays County units will meet you there."

Jim scribbled down the location.

"10-4. I'm on my way. ETA 40 minutes."

Kim stirred sleepily when Jim rolled out of bed.

"Where are you going?"

"Hays County's got a double murder. I'm sorry, honey, but I've got to hurry."

"Jim, you're exhausted. Can't someone else cover for you?"

"You already know the answer to that."

"I do. Just please, be careful, will you?"

"I always am," Jim assured her. He hurriedly dressed, then gave Kim a quick kiss.

"I'll be home soon as I can. Kiss Josh for me when he wakes up."

Five minutes after the call, Jim was on his way.

2

A Hays County sheriff's deputy had blocked Fischer Store Road at its intersection with Ranch 2325. When Jim approached, she waved him past the roadblock. The bridge over the Blanco River was a little more than two miles from that intersection, so Jim arrived at the crime scene slightly more than a minute later. A large area along the left side of the road was brightly illuminated with portable floodlights. Three more county sheriffs' Dodge Chargers were there, along with a Wimberley fire truck, rescue unit, and ambulance. Also parked on the side of the road was an unmarked black Ford Econoline with darkened windows, the county coroner's van. Jim pulled in behind that. As he got out of his truck, Hays County Sheriff Mark Flanders walked over from his car. He took a final puff on the cigarette dangling from his lips, then tossed the butt into the dirt and ground it out with his bootheel.

"Howdy, Jim," he said. "Glad you were able to get here so quickly."

"Howdy, Mark. What have you got?"

"Two Cattle Raisers' Association brand inspectors. It looks like they were shot dead, probably while checking out a truck load of cows. The bodies are just off the road, over here. Their

43

truck is down in the river, underneath the bridge. It appears whoever shot those boys dragged 'em out of sight of the road, then rolled their truck into the water, hopin' no one'd find them for a while. But someone must've seen it happen, or caught a glimpse of something suspicious, and called it in."

"Any idea who?"

Flanders shook his head.

"Nope. It was an anonymous call, came in just before one o'clock. You'll find this hard to believe, but it was placed from what has to be damn near the last pay phone left in Texas, outside the Fischer Store. There's no possible way to figure out who made that call, unless someone saw them. At this time of the morning, way out here, the odds of winning the lottery are better.

"Also no way to tell whether the person who made the call saw the actual murders, or came across the scene afterwards, and somethin' that didn't look right just caught their eye. I've already had the phone dusted for prints, but I doubt we'll get anything useful. Of course, there's no security cameras at that tiny store, either, so no help there. I figured with two dead men on our hands, we needed to get those prints before they got smudged or erased, so the hell with jurisdiction.

"I've already called Sheriff Parker over to

Comal County to let him know we came into one of his towns. He spluttered a bit, but then calmed down."

"If Ben Parker gives you any trouble, just tell him to talk to me, and I'll straighten him out. You did the right thing. Did your deputies touch anything?"

"Not yet. They've been photographing the scene—and, of course, checked the bodies to make certain the men were dead. As you can see, the medical examiner's already here, but I ordered him, and my people, not to disturb anything until you showed up."

"I appreciate that, Mark. Well, let me get my stuff, and I'll start to work."

Jim took his evidence gathering kit from the back of his Tahoe, then rejoined the sheriff.

"I'll give you a quick overview while I walk you down to the bodies," Flanders said. He pointed to a set of tire tracks embedded in the damp, sandy soil of the road's shoulder. "You can see right here those tire treads are from a big rig, along with some splatters of cow manure. I'm certain the tread marks behind those will prove to be from the inspectors' pickup."

"No other tire tracks?" Jim asked.

"None that we've found," Flanders answered.

"Which means whoever called this in most likely didn't stop. If they had any sense, they sure wouldn't have pulled over in the middle of the

45

road to see exactly what was happening. If they had done that, we'd probably have at least one more body on our hands."

"I've got to agree with you there, Jim. Just ahead is where it appears the two men were shot."

A deputy was standing alongside a spot-lit patch of disturbed ground. Several yellow, numbered markers were scattered around the area.

"Jim, I believe you know Deputy Thorne," Flanders said. "He was the first officer on scene."

"I sure do," Jim answered. "Casey's worked with me on more than one occasion. What'd you find, Casey?"

"This is just preliminary, but you can see that two people fell here. There's impressions in the dirt, and I've marked where I found shell casings, also a pistol, which must have belonged to one of the victims. From here, you can follow drag marks along this dirt trail to where I found the bodies."

"Could you identify the deceased by sight?"

"Sure. They've both been workin' this county for quite a spell. One is Bobby Lee Garland. Just a young man, has a wife and two little ones at home. Damn, but I dread having to bring her this news. The other's Joe Baldwin. He's been a brand inspector for nigh onto thirty years, I'd say. Since his wife died, and both his kids moved to California, his job has pretty much been his whole life. You must know the two of 'em."

Jim nodded and sighed before answering.

"Damn right I do. Bobby Lee was only on the job for a couple of years, but he was a sharp kid. Joe was a tough old buzzard, who had most every brand in the state memorized. He could spot an altered brand or earbob from a hundred yards away. Neither one of 'em was likely to walk into an ambush, or get caught with his pants down."

"You're right, but something sure went wrong," Flanders said. "They're both just ahead."

Flanders indicated where another deputy stood guard over two prone, unmoving forms.

"Ranger Blawcyzk, howdy," the deputy said. "It's been a while. I sure didn't expect to meet you again so soon, especially under these circumstances."

"Evenin', Karen," Jim answered. "Yeah, it's not the best of circumstances, you've got that right. What you can tell me, from your first look-see?"

"Not a whole lot," Karen Munson-Lopez said. "The bodies haven't been covered, so as not to disturb them or contaminate any evidence. They were both shot, I can't tell you how many times yet. There's something else you need to see, but I'll let that wait until you've examined the deceased."

"Appreciate that, Karen. Good work."

"You might want to show Jim what you

mentioned first, Karen," Flanders said. "He probably has a better chance of figuring out what it might mean than we've done."

"If you say so, Sheriff. Ranger Blawcyzk, this way."

Munson-Lopez led Jim past the first body, to where the second lay face-down, right arm outstretched, its light tan cowboy hat askew.

"This is Bobby Lee Garland," she said. "From how it appears, his killer or killers must have believed he was dead, but evidently he wasn't—although, I don't imagine he lasted long. It looks like he attempted to scratch out a message in the dirt before he died. However, what he wrote doesn't make any sense to me, nor to Sheriff Flanders. We're hoping you can figure it out."

She shone her flashlight on a patch of sand just above Garland's right hand. The light revealed a series of cryptic, seemingly meaningless letters and numbers, crudely scratched out by Garland's finger. Jim pulled his own flashlight from its holder on his belt, then hunkered on his heels to study the writing more closely.

"D-M-N-M," he read aloud. "Then somethin' that looks like an R. Then an 8, maybe a 2 or a Z. Hard to tell. And this here looks like an O, a zero, or maybe a circle."

"The one that looks like an R could be a P or a Q," Munson-Lopez pointed out. "The squiggly

48

line might just be something Garland's finger traced inadvertently, as he grew weaker."

"Could be," Jim agreed. He studied the writing for a couple more minutes, taking pictures from all angles.

"I think I might have something," he said. "Look here."

He used his index finger to extend the diagonal leg of the R up through its loop.

"Slash P. You mean that's a brand?" Flanders said.

"I've got a strong hunch it is," Jim answered. "Also, that the N and M stand for New Mexico. If it does, that means our suspects could be headed that way."

"Or came from there," Flanders said.

"It's possible, but I doubt it," Jim answered. "It'd be a lot easier to get rid of a load of stolen Texas beef in New Mexico than a load of rustled New Mexican beef in Texas. Lots more cows to steal in Texas, too. Let's take a look."

Jim opened his laptop and turned it on. He entered the website for the State of New Mexico Department of Agriculture, then clicked the link for registered brands in that state. He scrolled down the list, looking closely at several, then discarding them, until he came up with a possible match.

"Here we are," he exclaimed. "The Slash P Ranch in Luna County, New Mexico, address given as 10917 New Mexico State Route 9, Deming. That road runs right along the border with old Mexico. It'd be the perfect spot for smuggling rustled cattle down into Chihuahua. D-M-N-M. That's gotta mean Deming, New Mexico. Also, it's hard to see, but if you look real close at the circle, there's what appears to be a dot inside it. The Circle Dot Ranch is about ten miles northeast of here. Mark, I'll need you to send one of your deputies up there, and see if they're missing any cows."

"They probably won't be able to get a count until daylight, Jim."

"I'm aware of that, but I need it as soon as possible."

"Okay, I'll radio in and have a man sent there."

"Bueno." Jim glanced at his watch. "If I'm figuring right, those *hombres* have about a four-hour start." He hit the speed dial on his cell phone for D.P.S. dispatch.

"Texas Department of Public Service Dispatch."

"Dispatch, this is Ranger Unit 810, Company F. I need a roadblock set up on I10 westbound, just past the junction with I20. I'll also need one on U.S. 190 at Iraan, and another on U.S. 90 at Sanderson. They'll need to stop all cattle rigs heading west toward New Mexico. Suspect vehicle is wanted in connection with the homicide of two brand inspectors near Fischer. License plate possibly has an 8, 2, and/or Z as in zebra in its sequence. Vehicle will probably be carrying a load of Circle Dot branded cows, and will possibly have papers showing cattle consigned to Slash P Ranch in Luna County, New Mexico. Cows are most likely stolen, and papers forgeries.

"Also have all state, county, and local units between Hays and Comal Counties and El Paso to be on the lookout for any vehicle possibly matching the description. Suspects are most likely past Fort Stockton by now, but I want every available law officer in the region looking for the suspect vehicle. Unknown how many persons are in vehicle, but they should be considered armed and extremely dangerous. Anyone seeing a vehicle matching the description should approach with extreme caution. Repeat, approach with extreme caution, waiting for backup first, if at all possible. Do you have that?"

"10-4, Ranger 810. I'll put that out immediately."

"*Gracias*, dispatch. Once you've done that, I need the New Mexican authorities contacted. Have them check every cattle truck coming through their Ports of Entry on I10, New Mexico 273, 178, and 9. Also notify U.S. Customs and the Border Patrol to watch all border crossings for suspect vehicle, particularly around El Paso, and the crossings at New Mexico 138 and Mexico

Federal Highway 2, and between Columbus and Puerto Palomas, Chihuahua."

"Will do, Ranger."

"Good. I'll also need the Luna County Sheriff's Office contacted. I'm going to ask them to have a search warrant issued for the Slash P Ranch in their county. Once you reach them, patch them through to my phone."

"10-4, Ranger. Is there anything else?"

"That will do for now. Get back to me to confirm roadblocks are being set, all departments have been notified of situation, then put me in touch with Luna County, as quickly as possible."

"10-4, Ranger 810. Dispatch, out."

"Ranger 810, out."

Jim hung up.

"Now, let's get a closer look at what we have here," he said. "Mark, there's a carton of dental stone in the back of my truck. If you can have Deputy Thorne get that and make casts of the tire tracks and any footprints, plus photos of course, that would be helpful. I also want a cast of those letters Garland scratched in the dirt. Also, have the M.E. join us."

"I'll get him right on it. Karen, if you would do that . . ."

"Right away, Sheriff."

"Good. Thanks, Deputy," Jim said. "Mark, I'll also need a couple of your people to question everyone who lives in the houses on the closest

52

side streets, to find out if they heard or saw anything. Also, checkpoints at the junctions of 2325 and 32. I want every vehicle passing by stopped, and the occupants questioned, on the off chance they saw something, anything, no matter how small or insignificant."

"It'll be done right now, Jim. What else would you like me to see to?"

"Soon as you're done, stay with me while I see what else these bodies can tell us," Jim answered. He waited a few minutes while Flanders relayed his instructions to the deputies, and for the county medical examiner, Floyd Simmons, to meet him.

"Jim, some day we've got to meet when we're not looking at bodies," Simmons said, once he came down from his van, and shook Jim's hand.

"Floyd, we probably wouldn't recognize each other if we *weren't* looking at a corpse," Jim answered. "Now that you're here, I'll get to work."

After pulling on two pairs of nitrile gloves and turning on his digital recorder, Jim dictated the case number, date, time, and location into the machine. After that, he took several photos of Garland's remains, then lifted the outstretched arm.

"All right. Texas Ranger James C. Blawcyzk of Company F, assisted by Hays County Sheriff Mark Flanders and Hays County Chief Medical Examiner Floyd Simmons, investigating the apparent homicides of two men at the Fischer Store Road Bridge near Wimberly, Hays County. This is the preliminary examination of victim one, identified by the Hays County Sheriff's Department as Texas and Southwest Cattle Raisers Association Brand Inspector Bobby Lee Garland. Victim is a male Caucasian. Mid-twenties to early thirties. Rigor mortis has begun, but is not yet set. No wounds are apparent to the victim's back, nor any signs of injury to the skull, or the visible flesh."

Jim paused while he rolled Garland onto his back, then opened the dead man's shirt, taking more photographs of the deceased brand inspector.

"Victim has one gunshot wound, to the center of his abdomen. Apparent extensive bleeding from wound, as well as bleeding from nose and mouth, along with minimal presence of livor mortis, indicates victim remained alive for some time after being shot. In addition, victim was apparently able to scratch out a message in the dirt before expiring. Distention of abdomen, as well as bleeding from mouth and nose, points to heavy internal hemorrhaging. The autopsy by the county medical examiner will be necessary to confirm this, but it appears death may have been caused by loss of blood, in addition to the gunshot wound itself. Rough estimate of time of death, again which will need to be confirmed by the medical examiner, would be four to six hours previously. Since there is no exit wound, the bullet is apparently still in the victim. Once that is recovered by the medical examiner, it will be processed for ballistics testing. Aside from the single gunshot wound, there are no other signs of injury to the victim."

Jim paused his recorder, while he finished his examination of Garland's body. Once done, he turned the recorder back on to make one final observation.

"Victim's holster is empty. Upon examination of a pistol, which I assume to be Garland's, found several yards from both victims, determination will be made as to whether Garland fired any shots before sustaining his fatal wound. I am now going to examine the body of the second victim, identified by the Hays County Sheriff's Department as Texas and Southwest Cattle Raisers Association Brand Inspector Joseph Baldwin, also a male Caucasian age approximately fifty-five to sixty."

Jim went over to where Baldwin had fallen. Unlike Garland's, the backs of Baldwin's shirt and pants were covered with blood. After taking his photographs, Jim lifted Baldwin's shirt and lowered his khaki trousers, then took more photographs before proceeding.

"Victim has two gunshot wounds to his back, one in the lower right quadrant, the other below the waistline, in the left hip, just above the buttocks. The bullet which entered the lower back possibly penetrated the abdominal cavity, passed through the victim and exited from the front. The bullet which struck the hip most likely fragmented when it hit bone. As in the previous victim, rigor mortis has begun, but has not set. No livor mortis is present on the back of the body. There are no signs of injury, other than the gunshot wounds. Victim's gun is still in its holster."

Jim stopped when his cell phone rang. A glance at the screen showed it was D.P.S. Dispatch calling him back.

"Ranger Unit 810."

"Dispatch, Ranger 810. Confirming all requested roadblocks are being put in place. Also, all law enforcement agencies in the search area have been notified. In addition, Ranger Company E has been contacted. They will have a Ranger at each roadblock."

"Thank you, Dispatch. That's excellent work. What about the New Mexican and Federal authorities?"

"They have also been contacted. Luna County advises they will call back as soon as they reach the sheriff, probably within forty-five minutes. I'll put him through as soon as he calls."

"I'm obliged for the assistance, Dispatch. Ranger 810, out."

"10-4, Ranger 810. Dispatch, out."

Jim hung up and returned to examining Baldwin's corpse. He rolled the dead man onto his back, again taking more photographs, then opening Baldwin's shirt.

"Victim has an exit wound from the lower left abdomen, indicating the bullet which struck him in the back traversed the abdominal cavity diagonally before exiting. There is an additional bullet wound, this one to the right side of the abdomen, about four inches above the waistline. As no exit wound is present in the back, this bullet is apparently still inside the victim. Minimal bleeding from mouth and nose. Livor mortis is present but not completely set, with pooling in the abdomen, and minor indications of livor mortis in the lower chest. Time of death would be approximately the same as the other victim. After checking both victims' clothing for any possible further evidence, I will release the bodies to Floyd Simmons, Comal County chief medical examiner, for a complete post-mortem and forensics report."

Jim clicked off his recorder and stood up, arching his back to remove a kink.

"Floyd, as soon as I go through their clothes for anything that might be useful, I'll turn these poor *hombres* over to you. I don't need to give you the drill. Bag everything, and recover all the bullet fragments you can. I want to know if these boys were killed by the same gun, or different weapons. My gut tells me there was more than one shooter. I've still got to try and put things together, but my hunch is Baldwin was shot first. He took the two bullets in the back, then he probably twisted around as he was going down and took the third one in his belly. Garland heard the shots, but before he could do much more than pull his gun he got hit. Dead center in the gut, right through the fourth button of his shirt. Whoever got him is a damn good shot. Just do me a favor. It'd save some time if you could outline the bodies for me. Soon as there's enough daylight I want to try'n figure out how this went down, the positions where everyone was at, the directions and angles the bullets came from, all that."

"I'll give it everything I can, Jim."

"I know you will."

Jim spent several minutes going through the dead men's pockets, removing and bagging their wallets and personal possessions, but finding nothing which would help in his investigation.

"Floyd, they're all yours," he said. "Mark, I want to check that pistol."

He and the sheriff went over to where Garland's pistol lay in the dirt. Jim slid a pencil through the trigger guard to lift the gun. He put the muzzle close to his nose and took a sniff.

"It's been fired," he said. "Garland got off at

least one shot." He slid the pistol into a plastic bag and sealed that shut, then stood up.

"Let's take a look in that direction. Some of that brush seems to have been broken."

Jim led the sheriff to where several bushes had been flattened, some of their branches snapped off.

"Blood," he said, indicating some damp, rust-colored patches in the light-colored sand. "It looks like Garland hit one of those bastards. He went down here. I can't tell for certain how hard he was hit, but bad enough he got knocked down, plus he was bleedin' quite a bit. I'm gonna take some samples, but first, I've gotta make another call. Wait, hold on one second. Looks like a piece of cloth here."

Using tweezers, Jim pulled a small scrap of green-checked cloth off the broken branch of a small mesquite, and placed it in a baggie.

"This must've come off the *hombre* who got shot's shirt. With luck he'll still be wearing the same shirt when we catch up with these sons of bitches. If so, we'll be able to make a match, putting him here on scene."

"Not to mention the bullet wound," Flanders said. "That'll damn sure pin him to the crime."

"Right, Mark," Jim agreed.

He hit the speed dial for D.P.S. Dispatch.

"Dispatch, Ranger 810," Jim said, as soon as the phone was answered. "I've got updated information for you. It appears one of the suspects may have been shot and wounded during the firefight. He's also possibly wearing a green checked shirt. Advise all agencies. Also alert all medical facilities and physicians between here and El Paso."

"10-4, Ranger 810."

"10-4. Out."

Jim scraped the bloody sand into baggies.

"What's next, Jim?" Flanders asked, once he was done.

"We've still got a long night—or, I guess I should say 'rest of the morning'—ahead of us," Jim answered. "I'd like your deputies to scour this entire area. I want every last bit of evidence they can find, especially the bullet that went through Baldwin."

"All right. What about the shell casings?" Flanders asked. "Do you want to get those yourself?"

"Nope. Your deputies are plenty capable of doing that, without compromising the evidence or the scene. Just make certain none of them tramp on any footprints or tire tracks until Casey gets his casts made and photos taken. Right now, I want to get a look at Baldwin's and Garland's truck. Have you called for a hook to haul it out of the water?"

"I have," Flanders confirmed. "Hale's Auto Body should be arriving any minute. I told them not to hurry, since I knew it would be a while before we could release the truck to them, on top of which they can't get to it without driving over the scene. They'll have to wait until we're finished. Of course, they won't mind that, since they'll be getting paid by the hour for sittin' and doing nothing until we release the truck to them."

"Good. Soon as we get your people to searching, we'll check that truck."

A short while later, Flanders led Jim down a one lane dirt road that paralleled the bridge, to where the brand inspectors' truck had been driven or shoved into the Blanco.

"There it is, Jim."

Flanders shone his searchlight onto a dark red Ram pickup, which had come to rest just underneath the bridge, about fifteen feet from the riverbank. The vehicle was nosed into the river, submerged almost to thc doors. Water lapped at its frame.

"Damn!" Jim exclaimed. "It's in deeper than I figured. How'd they manage to get it out so far?"

"My guess is it was in drive, and stalled when it hit the water," Flanders said.

"Yeah, but this river isn't usually more than a couple of feet deep, at most," Jim objected. "Most of the time, it's not even a foot deep."

"That's still true for the most part, but those Memorial Day floods back in 2015 dug out some deep holes in soft spots along the riverbed," Flanders said. "In fact, that's probably why no one who lives around here was aware of what was goin' on tonight. Quite a few of the houses closest to the river that were washed away still haven't been rebuilt. Some of 'em probably never will be. So, the bridge is more isolated than it was before it got washed out a couple of years back. The state DOT did one helluva job rebuilding it as fast as they did."

"Well, I damn sure can't wait for the hook to get here," Jim said. "It's been raining upstream for a few days now, some pretty heavy gullywashers every afternoon. That means this river's gonna keep rising, and I can't take a chance on any evidence in that truck being contaminated when water gets into the cab, or even worse, rises enough so it floats that truck downstream. I'm gonna have to wade out there and go through that truck *pronto prontito*. Hell."

Jim sat down on a large piece of concrete, a piece of the remains of the old bridge that had been left behind after the new one was built. He started to pull off his boots.

"Aren't you gonna go back to your truck and get your muck boots and BDU?" Flanders asked.

"No." Jim shook his head. "First, I don't feel like climbing all the way back up the riverbank to my truck. Second, I can't tell how fast the dang river's rising, which means I don't know how much time I have to get out to that truck before any evidence it contains is ruined. Third, the water's deeper than my boots, anyway. Fourth, I was out so long dealin' with that other bunch of rustlers last night I just fell into bed when I got home. I took my BDU out of the truck a couple of days back to clean it, and I plumb forgot to throw it back in the truck before I headed over here tonight. It'd only get waterlogged and weigh me down, anyway. Besides, it's just river water. I'm not so sweet that I'll melt."

"You're damn sure for certain right on that last one," Flanders agreed, with a laugh. He watched as Jim pulled off his boots and socks, then rolled his pants legs up to his knees.

"Man, you've got some damn ugly feet there, Jim," Flanders said, chuckling. "Your legs ain't much to look at either."

"Mebbeso. I never paid much attention to 'em," Jim answered. "Right now, I wish they were duck's feet."

He put his boots and socks on the chunk of concrete, then removed his hat and gunbelt and placed those alongside them. Finally, he took his fingerprint collecting kit, along with a few other items he felt he might need, from his evidence collection case. He put those in a waterproof sack, along with his phone, and tied that around his neck.

"Well, here goes. Keep your light on me,

63

Mark," he said. He shone his flashlight onto the water's surface and stepped into the river.

"Be careful you don't slip," Flanders called after him.

Jim worked his way carefully out to the truck. While the riverbed was mostly sand, there were still a good number of rocks under the surface, along with rubble left behind from the old bridge. He yelled and cursed more than once when he stubbed a toe on an unseen rock.

"You're almost there!" Flanders shouted encouragement after the Ranger. "Only a few more feet. Better hurry. The river seems to be rising pretty fast."

Jim turned his head to say something in return. Whatever that was, the words never were uttered, for he stepped on a moss covered, slick rock, and went down on his back with a splash. Flanders started in after him, but Jim quickly got back up, cursing both himself and the rock.

"You all right?" Flanders called. "I didn't know you planned on taking a swim."

"Ask me that when I'm back on dry land," Jim answered. He gingerly made his way the last few feet to the truck. Using just one finger, to avoid damaging any latent prints, he eased open the driver's door.

"Mark, the keys are still in this thing, and it's a diesel. Since the exhaust pipe's still out of the water, with any luck it'll start for me. If it does,

I'm gonna try'n back it outta here. The river's risen another couple of inches since I started. It's about to wash into the cab. If that happens, I'll lose any evidence that might be in this truck. Wish me luck."

Jim got into the pickup, touching as few surfaces as possible to avoid disturbing any fingerprints. He took a moment to dust the keys, ignition, and steering wheel for prints, then shifted from neutral to park and switched on the ignition. The engine caught, sputtered for a moment, then settled to running smoothly. Jim shifted from park into reverse, and stepped on the accelerator. The Ram's wheels spun for a moment, then obtained purchase on the river bottom. The truck shot out of the water. As soon as it was on the bank, Jim stepped hard on the brake pedal, which was spongy under his bare foot. The waterlogged brakes had little power to stop the truck. It crashed into a stand of cottonwoods, which brought it to a halt. Jim shoved the vehicle into park, shut off the engine, and got out.

"Damn, that was some display of driving," Flanders said. "They teach you that at State Trooper school?"

"No, I learned that playin' bumper cars on the highways around Dallas–Fort Worth," Jim retorted. "By the way, it was in neutral, not park. Which probably means they pushed it down the bank. With any luck, those *hombres* left us some nice, clear hand and fingerprints on the tailgate."

"Now that you've got that thing out of the river, what're you gonna do? Wait for the hook to take it out of here?"

"No, I'll process it right here on scene, as I normally do. Besides, the cab's all damp. I'm gonna give it a look through, pull out any evidence I can find, and dust it for prints before the moisture smudges them. I'll have Hale's take it back to their lot for impound in case I want to check it again later."

"You want me to try'n find you some dry clothes? One of my deputies might have something you can borrow. It's still kind of chilly. You don't want to be working while you're soaking wet."

"No, but thanks for the offer. I'll be fine. I'll just retrieve my boots and socks. I don't want to walk around on this jagged gravel in my bare feet any more than I have to." Jim paused, and looked at the eastern horizon, where a streak of gray was brightening to soft yellow. "The sun'll be up—"

He stopped when his phone rang.

"Hold on a second. With any luck, this is dispatch calling to tell us our suspects have been located, and stopped."

"Ranger 810."

"Dispatch, Ranger 810. I have Luna County Sheriff Jorge Calderon on the line. Hold on while

I put him on speaker. Sheriff Calderon, I have Ranger James Blawcyzk on the phone. Go ahead, Ranger 810."

"Howdy, Sheriff. I appreciate your calling me back. Sorry I had to bother you this time of the mornin'."

"No problem at all, Ranger. My deputy gave me a quick explanation of why you called. I understand you'd like my office to search the Slash P Ranch, in connection with a cattle theft and homicide?"

"That's correct, Sheriff. From what the evidence I have indicates, a trailer load of cows was stolen from the Circle Dot Ranch over here. Two brand inspectors must've stopped the rig, and both got killed for their trouble. One of 'em managed to scratch out a message in the dirt before he died. It seems to say those cows are being taken to the Slash P. I've had roadblocks set up on all the main routes from Texas to New Mexico, and also of course had your state police and ports of entry notified, as well as the Border Patrol and U.S. Customs. With any luck, we'll get those *hombres* before they ever reach the Slash P. However, I'd like you to be ready in case we don't. I know the evidence I have so far is a bit flimsy, but if you can get a search warrant—"

"You don't need to say another word, Ranger. My office has been suspicious of the Slash P for quite some time now. We know they're running wet cows down into Mexico. We just haven't been able to get any proof. We'll help you any way possible. Don't worry about a search warrant. Obtaining one shouldn't be a problem."

"*Gracias*, Sheriff. I'm obliged. I already gave what information I have about the men and vehicle we're after to your office. I'll get back to you when I come up with more. Is there anything else you need right now?"

"Not that I can think of. If there is, I'll get right back to you."

"That'll be fine. Let me give you my cell number. It's 512-483-8528."

"Got it. Mine's 575-934-3695."

"Got yours, too, Sheriff. I'll get in touch with you if those boys are rounded up before they get into your territory."

"And if they do make it this far, we'll keep 'em hog-tied for you, until you can pick 'em up and haul their sorry butts back to Texas to get the needle. *Adios* for now."

"*Adios*, Sheriff."

"I take it that was the Luna County sheriff," Flanders said, once Jim hung up.

"It was," Jim answered. "Seems the Slash P has been on his radar for some time. We'll have full cooperation. Now, as I was starting to say. The sun'll be up in about an hour. I'll process this truck, while your deputies keep working at finding every bit of evidence they can. Soon as it's light, I'll want to go over this scene again, tryin' to figure out the sequence of events, and make certain nothing was missed."

"All right, Jim. I'm gonna have one of my deputies run over to Wimberley and pick up some breakfast. Do you want anything?"

"Coffee'll do. Black and strong. I've got plenty of Dr Pepper and cashews in my truck. They're all I need to keep goin' for two-three days."

"I'll have him bring you something back, anyway. You need more than soda and nuts to keep goin'."

"All right, Mark. Meantime, I'm goin' to work on this truck."

Jim spent the next hour and forty-five minutes processing the brand inspectors' truck. He dusted it for fingerprints, and removed several items of possible evidence, which he bagged and labeled for further examination. He was halfway up the riverbank when Mark Flanders met him.

"I was just comin' to see what was keeping you," the sheriff said. "You find anything in that truck?"

"Quite a bit, I hope, which is what took me so long," Jim answered. "I got some nice, clean prints, too, especially off the tailgate. Those'll help nail those *hombres*, once they're finally caught."

"Still no word they've been sighted?"

"Not one jingle on my phone, so I'd say not yet. I sure hope they didn't slip past the roadblocks, or worse, that I guessed wrong, and they didn't head for New Mexico at all."

"It'd be pretty hard for them to get by any roadblocks or checkpoints," Flanders answered. "There's hardly any roads goin' west once you get past Fort Stockton, and even fewer that can handle an eighteen-wheeler. Oh, I heard back from my deputy at the Circle Dot. Seems your hunch was right. Just a quick count told them that at least seventy or so head have just wandered off. They haven't sold off any beef for more than two months."

"Yeah, wandered off with a little help," Jim answered. "It could be the *hombres* who helped them leave home just might've outsmarted us, and worked their way around. Say they did somethin' like pick up U.S. 67 west of Fort Stockton, took that south to U.S. 90 west, then either took 90 back to I10 at Van Horn, or possibly took Texas 118 north out of Alpine and back to the interstate. Either one would get 'em around the roadblocks."

"But every law officer in west Texas is lookin' for that rig," Flanders pointed out. "And those cow thieves can't get into New Mexico without goin' through a Port of Entry, so worst case scenario is the New Mexican authorities will grab 'em for us. That is, unless they dropped down 67 all the way to cross into Mexico at Ojinaga, but that's pretty unlikely. Even if they did, U.S. Customs or the Border Patrol will get them. You set as tight a net as you could, Jim. It's just a matter of waitin' until it closes in on those bastards. They won't get away with killin' those two men. Here. My deputy just got back with breakfast. There's a couple of egg, bacon, and cheese sandwiches in this sack, along with a large black coffee. You'd better take a couple of minutes to rest and chow down before you do any more. Pardon my sayin' so, Jim, but you look like hell."

"Thanks, Mark," Jim said, as he took the sack and opened it. "I'll be fine, once I can get outta these wet clothes. Now that the sun's up, they should dry out pretty quick, anyway."

"It's still pretty nippy, especially for this time of the year," Flanders answered. "You'd better hope you didn't catch a chill, and come down with pneumonia."

"At least that'd give me some time to rest. Hey, this isn't half bad," Jim said, as he took a bite out of his sandwich. "Where'd your deputy get these?"

"A little place called Mama Pajama's, over to Wimberly," Flanders said. "It's been open for a couple of months, now. The place is always busy, since she makes a mean breakfast."

"She sure does," Jim said. "I'll have to keep it in mind."

Despite Flanders's urging him to take his time, Jim wolfed down the sandwiches.

"Let's get back to work," he said, after draining the last of his coffee. "I'd imagine you and your deputies have collected quite a bit of evidence."

"We have. I took a quick look at the shell casings. They didn't come from the same weapons. There were some nine millimeters, and a couple of .38s," Flanders confirmed. "Your guess about more than one shooter was right. Where would you like to start?"

"Soon as I put what I've got so far in my truck, I'll want to see the casts Deputy Thorne made."

"He's already waiting at your vehicle. Since the casts were set, I had him lift them, mark their locations, and bring them up there. I figured you'd rather have them ready to look at than having to lift them yourself."

"You figured right, Mark. Casey's really good at gathering evidence, very thorough. I've tried, more'n once, to talk him into joining the Highway Patrol and hopefully, in a few years, try out for the Rangers, but he'd have none of it. Said he likes being a county deputy, who's home most every night, just fine. Who can blame him for that?"

"No one, I guess," Flanders answered. "I know I sure can't. Besides, I'd hate to lose him. As you said, he's one of my best officers."

• • •

"Mornin', Ranger Blawcyzk," Thorne said, when they reached Jim's Tahoe. "It's been a long night, hasn't it?"

"It sure has been, Casey," Jim answered. "I appreciate your helping save a bit of time by making the casts. What'd they tell you?"

"I've got them lined up right here, alongside your truck," Thorne answered. "And yes, they did tell me quite a bit. Here. Take a look."

"All right."

"This first set is the treads from the tractor-trailer," Thorne said. "I was able to distinguish between the steering tires, the drive tires, and the trailer tires. The trailer has several mismatched tires, so once the rig is located, it'll be a cinch to place it here at the time of the killings."

"Great work, Casey. Excellent, in fact. I still wish you'd reconsider joining D.P.S., and working up to the Rangers."

"Not a chance," Thorne said. "My wife would divorce me, and I like bein' home for my kids at night. I'm not finished. The next set of casts is the boot prints. The first matches the boots worn by Baldwin, then next those worn by Garland. Alongside those you'll see three different casts. That indicates to me there were three men involved."

"I'll agree with everything you've deduced, Casey," Jim said. "Or maybe I should start callin' you Sherlock. Nice work. Mark, I'll need to borrow five of your deputies now. While you're roundin' them up, I'll make a couple of calls."

"Sure, Jim. Thorne, you're one of them. Get Munson-Lopez, Herrera, Stone and Karpinski. Bring them back here."

"Sure thing. It won't take me long, Sheriff."

Jim pulled out his phone to call dispatch.

"D.P.S. Dispatch."

"Dispatch, Ranger 810. Have there been any possible sightings of the suspect vehicle?"

"None at this time, Ranger 810. All roadblocks are still in place."

"10-4, Dispatch. Additional information, apparently there are three suspects in vehicle. Unknown if tractor has sleeper, but any officer approaching or stopping vehicle matching description should be aware one person will probably be riding or hiding in bunk. Also, Circle Dot Ranch reports loss of approximately seventy head, have not sold any cattle recently. Any cattle from Circle Dot discovered definitely stolen."

"10-4, Ranger 810. Will pass along new information to all concerned Texas and New Mexico agencies."

"Thanks, Dispatch. Ranger 810, out."

"Dispatch, out."

Jim hung up, then dialed Sheriff Calderon.

"Sheriff Calderon."

"Sheriff, Ranger Blawcyzk. I don't suppose

there's been any sign of a load of cattle approaching the Slash P."

"No, there sure hasn't, Ranger. I gather they've managed to elude the manhunt."

"So far. Listen, here's an update. There are most likely three suspects in the vehicle. Also, the owner of the Circle Dot Ranch says it appears about seventy head are missing, and he hasn't sold any cows for quite some time. If those *hombres* do make it to the Slash P, there's no question the cows are stolen."

"I see. If those *hombres* do make it into New Mexico, do you want the Port of Entry to pass 'em on through, so we can nail 'em at the Slash P?"

"If this weren't a murder case, that's exactly what I'd ask you to do. However, since it is, we can't take any chances. Once they're located, they have to be stopped. Besides, having forged papers showing stolen cattle consigned to the Slash P should give you enough probable cause to execute that search warrant. I'm certain, once you do, you'll find enough evidence to shut down the operation for good."

"I understand, Ranger. If they do somehow make it into my state, they won't get away."

"I'm obliged, Sheriff. I'll call you if I have anything further."

"And I'll do the same. Talk to you later."

"Later, Sheriff."

"I see you've got everyone together, Mark," Jim said, once he hung up.

"We're just waiting for your orders, Jim."

"We're going back to where Garland and Baldwin were shot. I need some stand-ins for the shooters and victims while I try to determine the order things happened. Casey, Karen, since you were the first ones to examine the bodies, you can be the victims. Casey, you'll be Baldwin; Karen, Garland."

"Thanks a lot, Ranger," Thorne said.

"You didn't even let me tell you I'm gonna want you to lie down like you'd taken the slugs Baldwin took," Jim answered. "Stan, Julianna, Chuck, I want you to take the positions where our suspects apparently stood. Mark, you'll tell me if you think I'm right, or if I might've made a mistake."

"Sure, Jim."

Boot prints and the markers where the shell casings had fallen indicated where the rustlers had been standing at the time of the shooting.

"Do you want me and Casey to lie down now?" Munson-Lopez asked.

"Not quite yet. It looks like you're all in the right places. Stan, sorry, but from where you're at, that man couldn't have been one of the shooters. From that spot, he wouldn't have been able to aim at the victims. Plus, there weren't any shell casings over there. Not that I'm saying he couldn't have picked them up, if he did fire, but it's highly unlikely. You can just stand there and take it easy."

"Julianna, from where you're standing, it appears you'd be the shooter who got Baldwin. Casey, turn your back to her."

"All right, Ranger."

"Julianna, lift your hand and point it at Casey, as if you were aiming at his back."

"Don't tempt me, Ranger," Herrera said, with a grin, as she complied.

"Perfect," Jim said. "Casey, act like you've been hit low in the back, then the hip. Start to drop, twisting as you do."

"Here goes."

Thorne jerked as if he'd been hit by a bullet, then stumbled for a step. When he turned to face Herrera, Jim called to him again.

"You just took another slug, this one in the belly, Casey. Drop down within the outline. Don't worry if you mess it up a little. We've already got photos."

Thorne finished his fall.

"Good. Now Karen," Jim said. "Use your hand as if you were gonna try for the shooter. Turn toward Chuck while you're pulling your weapon."

"Okay, Ranger."

"Chuck, you're the one who plugged Garland. Go for it."

"Gladly. I've been waitin' for a chance like this."

Stone repeated the actions of Thorne and Herrera. Once Munson-Lopez had twisted sufficiently, Jim stopped them.

"That's it. Karen, he just got you right in the middle of your gut. Chuck, she managed to get a shot off and wound you before she went down. Karen, put yourself inside the outline. Chuck, you can stumble a bit, then walk toward Stan."

"That's how I see things went down, Mark. Baldwin got hit first, then Garland. Garland shot his killer before he fell. The foot prints give us the positions of all three rustlers. What do you think?"

"I wouldn't figure it any different, Jim."

"Okay. Deputies, thanks for your help reenacting the crime," Jim said. "You can get up and dust yourselves off now. I'd like to say it's time to go home, but we've still got more to do. First thing is to take some measurements."

Jim pulled off the tape measure clipped to his belt.

"The next step is to take figure the distances between shooters and victims. I want to know exactly how far apart everyone was. Hold on a minute."

Jim's phone was ringing.

"Ranger Unit 810."

"Ranger 810, this is Dispatch. I have Sergeant Camarillo of the New Mexico State Police on the line. I'll put him through to you. Sergeant, I have Ranger Blawcyzk for you. Go ahead."

"*Buenos dias*, Ranger Blawcyzk."

"*Buenos dias* to you, too, Sergeant. I hope you're going to tell me something that really *will* make it a good day."

"Indeed I am, Ranger. The three men you are after were stopped and arrested at the Port of Entry in Anthony. They've been taken to the Dona Ana County Jail in Las Cruces. We'll hold them on fugitive from justice warrants until the paperwork is done to send them back to Texas. They've also been charged with bringing stolen livestock across state lines, of course."

"That's great news, Sergeant. Did they give you any trouble?"

"They thought about it, but decided that wouldn't be such a good idea."

"What about the wounded man?"

"He was shot in the left leg. The wound is serious, but not so serious it couldn't be treated at the prison infirmary."

"Tell your people I'm much obliged, Sergeant. I appreciate their fine work. Have you notified Sheriff Calderon over at Luna County?"

"He's been notified. I think he was rather disappointed he didn't get the chance to grab them. Listen, I'm still making out my report. Do you want the names of those *hombres* right now?"

"No, I'm still on scene, gathering evidence. Just send everything through to my email. That's JamesCBlawcyzk@Rangers.Texas.Gov. Blawcyzk is spelled b-l-a-w-c-y-z-k. Should have been c-z-y-k, but somewhere along the line one of my ancestors reversed the y and z, and it stuck. Send along the mug shots, too."

"Will do, Ranger. Glad to have been of help."

"Thanks again, Sergeant. If you ever need anything on this side of the state line, just get in touch. *Adios*."

"*Adios*."

"Good news?" Flanders asked, as soon as he hung up.

"No, *great* news. New Mexico has those bastards in custody. As soon as the arrangements are complete, they'll be transferred back to Texas. In the meantime, there's still plenty to do here. I don't want one speck of evidence missed. Those killers damn sure ain't gonna go free because we missed something."

By the time Jim finished gathering evidence, analyzing it, then requesting arrest warrants and completing paperwork, plus working with the county prosecutor to start the process for extraditing the three suspects back to Texas, the sun had long since set before he returned home. He took just a moment to say goodnight to Copper and the other horses, then went straight into the house. Frostie came bounding out of the living room to greet him. Jim bent down to rub the dog's head.

"Kim, I'm finally home," he called.

"We're in the living room," his wife answered.

Kim and Jim's mother, Betty, were both on the couch, watching a movie. They looked up when he came into the room.

"Jim, what in the world happened to you?" Kim exclaimed, when she saw her bedraggled husband. His shirt and trousers were wrinkled and stained, and, despite his having washed up a bit at his office, there were still streaks of dirt on his face and chunks of mud in his hair.

"It was such a pleasant evening last night, I decided to go for a dip," Jim answered.

"Jim, will you be serious for just once in your life?" Kim answered. "What really happened?"

"The murders I went to investigate turned out to also be a case of cattle rustling. Two brand inspectors must've tried to stop the thieves, and got gunned down for their trouble. Then, their truck was rolled into the Blanco. With the summer thunderstorms, the river was rising fast, so I couldn't wait for a hook to pull the truck out of the river. I had to wade in and drive it out myself. When I did, I slipped on a rock and took a tumble into the water. It was worth the dunkin', though. There was plenty of evidence in the truck. Even better, in case you didn't see it on the evening news, the three suspects were caught at the New Mexico Port of Entry. Now it's just a matter of bringing them back to Texas for trial. I'm still cold, though. I didn't have any clean clothes to change into, and the unplanned swim chilled me to the bone."

"I hate to sound like a worried mother, Jim, but you look exhausted," Betty said. "You should take a nice hot shower, then head straight to bed."

"Well, you *are* my mother, Ma, so I reckon I can't complain too much about your frettin' over me. And you're right. I've only had about four hours sleep in the last three days. I'm going to find something to eat first, though. I haven't had anything but nuts and Dr Pepper since this morning, so I'm starving."

"I stopped by the deli this afternoon," Kim said. "There's cold cuts in the fridge, and ciabatta rolls in the bread drawer."

"Chips?"

"God forbid I should ever run out of potato chips in this house," Kim said. "You'd never survive. There's three full bags in the cupboard, mesquite barbeque, sour cream and onion, and plain."

"Great. I'll make a couple of sandwiches, then take a soak in the tub before I turn in."

"Are you sure you wouldn't like to watch the rest of the movie with us?" Betty asked. "That might help you unwind a bit."

"Another one of those impossibly evil male, only-too-perfect female gets revenge chick flicks? Not a chance," Jim answered, laughing. "G'night, Ma. G'night, Kim, I'll most likely be sleeping by the time you come to bed. C'mon, Frostie, I'll give you a snack."

Jim went to the kitchen, where he made himself two maple honey baked ham and Swiss cheese sandwiches on ciabatta rolls, dry, with no lettuce, tomatoes, or condiments. He took two Dr Peppers out of the refrigerator, along with a bag of mesquite barbeque chips from the cupboard. Frostie, as usual, sat expectantly by the table, knowing Jim always had some ham and cheese slices to toss him. After finishing his supper with a pint container of tapioca pudding, topped with whipped cream, Jim, with Frostie tagging along, headed for the master bathroom. He undressed, filled the whirlpool tub with water as hot as he could stand, then settled into the steaming liquid. With a long sigh, he leaned back, allowing the jets of water and streams of bubbles to ease his aching muscles, and chase the chill from his body.

Jim soaked for well over an hour. By the time he finally got out of the tub and toweled off, his mother had already gone home. Kim was lying in their bed, covered only by a sheet. Jim slipped alongside of her. He slid a hand under the small of her back and began rubbing it, his hand gradually working its way lower. Kim shifted away from him.

"Kim, you're not trying to turn the other 'cheek' on me, are you?" Jim whispered.

"No, but you said yourself that you're worn out. You need sleep more than anything else," Kim answered.

"There's one thing I need more than sleep," Jim said. "Besides, even after soaking in the tub, I'm still feeling a little chilled. When a person has hypothermia, and is in danger of dying from his core temperature dropping, the fastest way to warm him up is skin-to-skin contact, under a blanket or in a sleeping bag."

"You're making that up," Kim said.

"I am not. Don't forget, I'm a Texas Ranger, trained in survival skills. You wouldn't want me to perish of hypothermia right in our own bed, would you?"

"You're not that cold."

"I am. I'm about to start shivering. Plus, my ears are numb, and about to fall off. I'd better do something drastic, right now."

Jim buried his face in his wife's cleavage.

"That feels better already," he said, his voice muffled. "Nice and cozy."

"Jim, you . . ." Kim stopped short when Jim started laughing.

"What's so funny?"

"Nothing."

"Then why are you laughing? There must be something, and you'd better tell me what it is, right now."

"All right, but you'll be awful mad."

"I'm already mad."

"Okay, here goes. I just realized your breasts remind me of your license plate." Jim laughed even harder.

"What?" Kim shouted. "You'd better have a good explanation for that, mister, or it's about to get a lot chillier for you. I sure hope you're not trying to say my chest is flat and hard. You'd better not be."

"No, it's not that at all," Jim said, his laughter subsiding a bit, as he tried to get out his explanation. "But, for some reason, the letters on your plate just popped into my head. B-Z-M. If you say those three letters phonetically, they sound out 'bosom.' And you have a lovely bosom, my dear."

Kim glared at him in disbelief.

"Either you banged your head on a rock when you fell, or the river water somehow seeped into your brain. Only you, Jim."

She started chuckling, despite herself.

"Are you still angry?" Jim asked.

"Does this answer your question, cowboy?"

Kim pressed her lips to his, then reached down to his groin, gently massaging his most sensitive spot.

"It sure does," Jim answered, molding his body to hers.

3

Dawn had always been Jim's favorite time of day. He loved the peace and quiet, the soft, pastel light, and having some moments to relax and unwind. This was the only time he could truly call his own, when the demands of family and job were pushed to the background, if only for an hour or two.

As usual, Jim started this Saturday by going out to feed the horses, his paint, Copper, Kim's bay Morgan gelding, Freedom, and Slacker, his mother's chestnut quarter horse gelding. Frostie always accompanied him, starting his day by barking at the three barn cats, then digging through the hay and straw, looking for any rodents they might have missed.

Jim paused on the back patio to look over his land, the land which had been in his family for generations, but which had nearly been lost after the murder of his Texas Ranger father, during an attempted terrorist attack on the Alamo. Jim's father had stopped the attackers before they could carry out their plot, killing four of them before being gunned down by the two survivors. Jim avenged his father's death by tracking down and killing his murderers in a fierce gun battle along the Mexican border.

Afterward, two unscrupulous county commissioners attempted to swindle Jim's grieving mother out of the family property, intending to build an upscale, gated community, cynically named Ranger Estates, on the acreage. They'd almost succeeded, but instead were now serving long jail sentences. Once the case was settled, Jim cleared out the overgrown brush, built a house for himself and Kim, and a smaller one for his mother. He'd also moved the remains of all his paternal grandparents to the small family cemetery where the first Texas Ranger James Blawcyzk and his wife Julia rested. His last step was to make certain the land would remain in the Blawcyzk family in perpetuity. If the family died out, the Blawcyzk homestead would become a county historic park.

"C'mon, Frostie, let's go," Jim said. As he headed for the barn, he took a quick glance at his mother's house. Since her husband's murder, she sometimes had difficulty sleeping. On those nights when slumber refused to come, she often worked on stained glass windows or suncatchers, in the small studio behind her home. This morning, though, there were no lights on in either building.

"Looks like Ma got a good night's rest, Frostie," Jim said. When he reached the barn and slid open the door, the dog bounded down the aisle, while the horses whinnied a greeting.

"All right, all right, I'm gettin' your breakfast," Jim said to them. "Just hold your horses. I've gotta feed the cats first."

Copper pinned back his ears and snorted.

"You don't like my jokes, bud, no peppermints for you later," Jim told the paint, giving him a pat on his velvety muzzle.

Copper snorted again.

Jim spent the next two hours feeding the horses, brushing them, turning them out into the corral, then mucking out their stalls and spreading a fresh layer of shavings. With the sun now up, the day's heat was already starting to build. His T-shirt was soaked with sweat, as was the old Stetson he wore around the barn. He removed the hat to shake the sweat from its inside band, then pulled the bandana from around his neck to wipe his dripping brow and face.

"C'mon, Frostie, time to head in to get ourselves some breakfast," he called. "You want some, or would you rather stay out and hunt?"

Frostie came racing out of the brush. He ran straight to the back door, not even hesitating as he shot by Jim.

"All right, I reckon we're both hungry," Jim said, laughing. "I'll rustle us up some grub."

Kim and Josh were still sleeping, so Jim worked as quietly as he could while frying up a mess of bacon, scrambled eggs, and hash browns, along with a pot of coffee. This was another thing he loved about Saturday mornings, the chance to relax over a leisurely breakfast, rather than having to gulp down a stale convenience store pastry and weak coffee while rushing on his way to yet another crime scene. By the time he ate his meal, rinsed the dishes, and put them in the dishwasher, Kim had awakened, fed Josh, taken her shower, and dressed.

"Good mornin', Kim," Jim said when he walked into the bedroom. He kissed her on the cheek, and tickled Josh's chin. "I'm going to take my shower. Do you need anything first?"

"Good morning," Kim answered. "No, Josh is fed and dressed, and I'm just going to have coffee, if you left any in the pot."

"You want some of *my* coffee? You hate how strong I make it."

"Just this once. I don't have time for anything else. You haven't forgotten you're watching Josh today, while your mother and I go shopping for the things for Rosa's baby shower, have you? We'll have breakfast at the diner."

"No, I sure haven't. I've arranged with LaTonya Quarles to cover for me today, just in case, so you don't have to worry about my being called out for a case. I'm looking forward to spending the day with my little pardner."

"And keeping out of trouble?"

"Do *I* ever get into trouble?" Jim said, with a laugh.

"Only every time I leave you home alone in this house," Kim said, with a laugh of her own. "Go ahead and take your shower. Your mother will be here any minute, and we want to head right out. We've got a long day of shopping ahead of us. And you smell like horses and sweat."

"You say that like it's a bad thing."

"It is, Jim. Trust me, it is."

"Okay, I can take a hint," Jim said, as he headed for the bathroom.

Forty minutes later, Kim and Betty were getting ready to leave.

"Are you certain you'd prefer to stay home, rather than come with us, Jim?" his mother asked.

"Stay home and play with Josh, maybe watch a movie or catch a Rangers game on TV, or tag along while you two ooh and aah over all sorts of cutesy little frou-frou baby dresses and things? I'd rather have a root canal without Novocain first. I'm stayin' right here, thank you very much."

"I think he means 'no,' Betty," Kim said. "We'd better get started. We'll stop at Daisy Babies first. Jim, have a good day."

"I will," he assured her.

Holding Josh, Jim stood on the front porch and

waved as he watched his wife and mother drive off.

"Let's see, Josh, what should we do first?" he said. "I know."

He carried Josh into the kitchen and began rummaging through the cupboards.

"I'll have to pick up a few things, buddy," he said. "Looks like you and me are gonna need to make a trip to the grocery store."

"We certainly accomplished a lot today, Kim," Betty said, when they pulled up in front of the house around four that afternoon.

"We sure did," Kim agreed. "We got almost everything we needed, except for the food, and it's too soon for that, anyway. The shower is still three weeks away, but this was the only day we both had free. I wonder what happened here while we were out."

Kim put her Equinox in park and looked around the yard.

"Let's see. Jim's old truck is still here, and so is his Ranger truck. The horses are all in the pasture, and Frostie's not running around barking. Could it possibly be Jim really did spend a quiet day with Josh, and didn't try anything silly or crazy?"

"I suppose it's possible, but not probable," Betty answered. "After all, there *is* a tornado watch out for this afternoon. If Jim really didn't do anything but watch Josh, that would upset the balance of nature. In that case, those tornadoes are guaranteed."

"We'd better go inside and find out," Kim said. "We can get the car unloaded faster if we have him help us."

Once they got inside the house, there was no sign of Jim or Josh.

"Jim, we're home," Kim called. "Where are you?"

"We're in my office," Jim answered. "C'mon and join us."

"I'm almost afraid to," Kim half-whispered to Betty.

"We'll find out what he's been up to sooner or later anyway, Kim. There's no point in putting it off."

They went down the hall and into Jim's office. Josh was crawling along the floor, with his father on his hands and knees above him, scooting along with the baby.

"You're home earlier than I expected," Jim said.

"We got all our shopping done," Kim answered, "Would you mind helping us unload the car?"

"Not at all," Jim answered. "C'mon, pard, time to get to work."

He picked up Josh and stood up, then handed the baby to Kim.

"What did you do all day?" Betty asked.

"Not much, Ma. A little of this and that. We

watched *El Dorado* on the Blu-ray. Josh likes watching the horses and listening to the gunfights in Westerns."

"Plus, you think you're John Wayne," Kim said.

"Not really," Jim answered. "I just wish it was as easy for me to clean out the bad guys as it was for the Duke in his films. Well, let's get the car unloaded. I've got supper all ready for us. Just have to heat it up."

Kim happened to glance into the kitchen when they walked by it on the way back outside.

"Oh, my Lord!" she screamed. "Jim, what in the world did you do to my kitchen?"

Dirty pots and pans covered the counters, with dishes piled high in the sink. The batter-spattered mixer was next to the microwave, which had spots of batter and speckles of sauce coating its door. Soiled potholders hung from a cabinet door handle, while a stained dishtowel was draped over the faucet.

"I wanted to surprise you with supper," Jim answered.

"You did a hell of a lot more than just surprise me," Kim answered. "How . . . how could one man make such a mess?"

"It didn't start out that way," Jim tried to explain. "You see, I got a hankering for real banana pudding, not the kind that comes in a box, but the real thing, made from scratch, with bananas and vanilla wafers and whipped cream on top. Not aerosol whipped cream, either, but heavy, sweetened cream that I whipped myself."

"And which is just one of the things you got all over the kitchen, even the floor," Betty said.

"Just some. Anyway, I had to go to the store to get the fixin's. While I was there, I decided we'd have Mexican tonight. So I got the makings for chicken and beef quesadillas. Just like the cream, I didn't want anything canned, so I got fresh peppers, onions, tomatoes, scallions, and chili peppers to chop up. And you can't have Mexican without nachos, but I sure didn't want salsa from a jar, so I bought the ingredients to make it fresh, too."

"Which explains the food processor, or what's left of it," Kim said. She sighed.

"Then, I decided banana pudding isn't authentic enough for a Mexican dessert, so I made flan," Jim said. "Then I decided just flan wasn't enough, so I made some filled dessert churros, vanilla, chocolate, and butterscotch. And strawberry cheesecake burritos. I also got vanilla ice cream so we can have Dr Pepper floats with supper. Josh helped me. We licked the bowls and beaters."

"Which also explains this pot," Betty said, holding up a burnt sugar encrusted saucepan. "And the food stains all over Josh's shirt."

"Jim, how could you?" Kim said, almost in

tears. "You know I've asked you to let me do the cooking inside, except for when you have to make breakfast. Just look at this disaster. And you let Josh have batter that contained raw eggs? You know better than that."

"I've always eaten raw batter, and never gotten sick," Jim said. "As far as the mess, you wouldn't have seen it if you hadn't come home early. I was going to clean it up earlier, but I got sidetracked. I played with Josh, then when I put him down for his nap, I took one, then after he woke up and I fed him, we watched the movie, then he was having so much fun crawling around I couldn't bring myself to put him in his crib so I could clean the kitchen."

"The least you could have done was gotten everything in the dishwasher," Kim said.

"I did, as much as I could. It's full," Jim answered, chagrined. "But supper's all ready. Everything is in the fridge. Once the nachos and quesadillas are heated up, we can eat. I'll clean the kitchen once we're done with supper."

"No one is eating until this disaster is gone," Kim yelled. "James Charles Blawcyzk, get out of my kitchen, and I mean right now! Go unload the car, and put everything in the spare bedroom. Then just stay out of my sight!"

"But, Kim . . ."

"Don't you 'but Kim' me, Jim. Get out. Out!"

"All right. I'm sorry, but I wanted so badly to

surprise you. I promise not to try'n cook, not ever again."

Shoulders slumped, a hang-dog expression on his face, Jim went outside.

"Betty, would you mind giving me a hand cleaning this mess?" Kim asked.

"Of course not," Betty answered. Silently, she picked up a mixing bowl to rinse it out, then set aside until the first load of dishes had been washed.

"Sometimes I just don't understand Jim," Kim said, shaking her head as she looked around the kitchen once again. "I can't imagine what got into him, thinking he could cook anything more complicated than bacon and eggs, or steaks and burgers on the grill."

She turned on the dishwasher and sighed.

"Betty, do you think perhaps I hurt his feelings more than I realized? Do you think I was too hard on him? What would you have done?"

Betty shook her head.

"I honestly don't know the answer about Jim's feelings. I do know he'll get over his hurt, sooner or later. As far as what I would have done, had it been my husband, or what you should do, I'm not going to answer that. I swore I would never interfere in my son's marriage. I love you both, and the last thing I want to do is say the wrong thing, and make either of you angry at me. I'll just remind you that both Jim's father and I warned you what you were getting into, and that being married to a Ranger is probably harder on a spouse than almost any other type of marriage. We also warned you that you would never know what to expect with our son as your husband. He can be a little . . . different.

"I'll tell you what. Let's get to work and clean this kitchen as fast as we can. The sooner we get Jim back in here to eat, the sooner this whole thing will be forgotten. You know how he loves to eat. Once he's working on his supper, he won't be worried about anything else."

"I hope you're right, Betty. Right now, I feel just awful."

"Jim probably does, too, knowing how unhappy seeing this mess made you. He'll come around, don't you worry."

An hour-and-a-half later, the kitchen was sparkling clean.

"Let's see what we have in here," Kim said, as she opened the refrigerator door. "Oh, my Good Lord!"

"Let me guess," Betty said. "Jim made enough food for a dozen people."

"More like a dozen armies," Kim answered. "How are we ever going to eat all this before it spoils?"

"Well, Jim will eat a lot of it tonight," Betty answered. "I can take some and put it in my freezer. What's left can go in yours. Perhaps there will be enough leftovers we can freeze some for Rosa's shower. Why don't you go get Jim while I start heating things up?"

"Supper isn't the only thing I'd like to heat up," Kim said, her anger flaring again.

"TMI," Betty said, laughing. "Although I wouldn't mind another grandchild."

"That's not the kind of 'heating up' I meant," Kim retorted. She went out the back door.

Jim was in the back yard, playing a game of fetch with Frostie, who was always eager to chase down a tossed toy.

"Jim, supper will be on the table in a few minutes," Kim called. "I thought you might like to wash up a bit first."

"All right," Jim answered. "C'mon, Frostie boy, time to eat."

After saying grace, Jim and his family dug into supper.

"Jim, this is really good," Kim said, halfway through her first quesadilla. "When did you learn to cook?"

"I really didn't," Jim answered. "I can only make a few things. Mexican food is one. And as you found out, a neat cook, I'm not."

"I would say so, to both," Kim answered. "Only you made way too much."

"Not really," Jim answered. "There's enough

for tonight, and perhaps there'll be enough extra to freeze two meals for when we're both too busy to cook. As far as the burritos and churros, what you and Ma don't eat, I'll polish off tonight."

"You won't!"

"He will," Betty said. "I'm surprised you haven't noticed by now, your husband's sweet tooth is insatiable, and his stomach is a bottomless pit."

"Oh, I have," Kim answered. "But it seems every time I think I've discovered the bottom, Jim manages to surprise me again. For example, Jim, which of the desserts *will* you be having tonight?"

"What do you mean, which?" Jim answered. "I'll have some of all of them, of course."

"Naturally," Betty said. "Kim, you'd better hope Josh hasn't inherited his father's appetite. If he has, you'll have to find a place to buy your groceries wholesale."

"Or buy a farm," Kim answered. "Perhaps a restaurant."

"I could help by cooking," Jim said, laughing.

"Not a chance," Kim said. "From now on the only place you cook is on the grill, or if I'm here to help."

"Deal," Jim said. "Now, pass me another quesadilla, please."

Jim's offer to help clean up after supper was roundly vetoed by both his wife and mother.

Instead, he took Josh out to the back patio to play with him while the ladies took care of the kitchen.

"Oh, that son of yours is just so damn infuriating, Betty," Kim said, once he was out of earshot.

"What do you mean?"

"He's doesn't seem even a tiny bit angry. He *never* stays angry. It's like my upset over the mess he made never even happened. Just once, when I'm angry and in the mood for an argument, I wish he'd fight back."

"I could have told you that, Kim, but I knew you'd figure it out for yourself, sooner or later," Betty said. "His father was the same way. He'd always just listen to me, agree with me, say he was sorry, whatever upset me wouldn't happen again, and that would be that. It used to drive me crazy. I wish I could tell you how to deal with it, but I can't. The only reason I can give is Mike used to feel so guilty for being away so much, and so tied up in his work, that he couldn't bring himself to argue with me. I believe that's why Jim does the same thing. They're men, so who knows what they're thinking?"

"That's what men say about us women," Kim answered.

"True," Betty agreed. "However, as the French would say, '*vive le difference.*'"

101

4

Tuesday morning, Jim was in his office, going over the autopsy reports on Bobby Lee Garland and Joe Baldwin, when his telephone rang.

"Ranger Blawcyzk."

"Ranger Blawcyzk, this is the Hays County Sheriff's Department. We need your assistance at an apparent hostage situation, with possible shots fired."

"What's the location?"

"14702 Ranch to Market Road 150 in Driftwood. That's just south of the junction with Elder Hill Road, County 170. Landmarks are the Stonehouse Villa wedding facility and the Driftwood Baptist Church. Location is about a quarter-mile south of those."

"On my way. ETA fifteen minutes."

"10-4, Ranger Blawcyzk. Will notify personnel on scene you are *en route*."

When Jim arrived at the given location, several Hays County patrol cars were on scene. The residence was a small cinder block farm house, its yard littered with junked vehicles, old appliances, and other debris. The Hays County police units surrounded the property, while two ambulances and a fire rescue truck were standing by, a bit farther up the road. Deputies were crouched behind their cars, or the junked vehicles and discarded appliances in the yard. All had rifles pointed at the house. Jim pulled up next to the county unit which was closest to the driveway, parked, and took his rifle from the back of the Tahoe. While he was putting on his bulletproof vest, Hays County Sheriff Mark Flanders walked up to meet him.

"Howdy, Jim. Glad you were able to get here so quickly," Flanders said.

"I was in my office, so I wasn't all that far away," Jim answered. "What, exactly, is the situation here?"

"We're not certain." Flanders pointed to a driver standing next to a brown parcel delivery van. "That driver was dropping off a package, when he heard what sounded like gunshots. He also heard a scream, and thinks he saw a person fall, but he's not certain about that. We've been trying to establish contact with someone inside the house, but so far no luck. Someone inside did shout, 'Don't come in here, or I'll gun all you no-good lawdogs down,' " but that's all. The San Marcos SWAT team is on its way, but I'd rather not break into the house unless there's no other options."

"Any more gunfire since your units got here?"

"None that we've heard." Flanders shook his head. "You know hostage or domestic situations are among the toughest we have to face. That's why I sent for you. Perhaps you'll be able to talk whoever's in there into giving up."

"Do you happen to know who lives here?" Jim asked.

"I don't, but Tammy does," Flanders said, then called to a deputy.

"Duvall! Come here a minute."

"All right, Sheriff."

One of the deputies left her position from where she was crouched behind her car, and came over.

"Deputy, this is Ranger Blawcyzk. He needs to know about who lives here. I told him you could supply that information."

"Sure. This is the Holsclaw farm, or what's left of it. Bonnie Holsclaw owns it. She lives here with her father, George Dingle, and her son, Ronny. He's her only child. Howard, Bonnie's husband and Ronny's dad, died three or four years back when the tractor he was driving rolled over, and he got crushed under it. Since then, the place has pretty much gone to hell, as you can see. George is an old man, crippled up and confined to a wheelchair. He's hard of hearing, and gets confused sometimes, too. As far as the boy goes, Ronny's always been a little off."

"Off in what way?" Jim asked. "Has he ever shown any signs of a temper, tendency to be violent, or ever threatened anyone?"

"No, nothing like that," Duvall answered.

104

"He's just a bit . . . slow, is the way I'd put it. He got picked on some in school, never had many friends, but never caused anyone any trouble, either. He's got to be about eighteen or so now, but I'd say he's got the mental development of a ten- or eleven-year-old. The whole family pretty much keeps to themselves. I only know them because I was the investigating officer on Howard's accident."

"How are they getting by?"

"Barely, is what I understand. George gets his Social Security, and Ronny Social Security Disability. Bonnie works as a cashier at the Gas 'n Go station up on 290 in Dripping Springs. I've already called her workplace, but she's off today. There's no car in the yard that's registered, or even runs, so I don't believe she's home. The last I knew she drove an older Pontiac Grand Prix. We've put out a bulletin on it."

"So, unless someone got into the house, it appears only the grandfather and grandson are inside," Jim said. "Mark, is there any sign someone might have broken in, or otherwise gained access?"

"Nothing that would suggest it," Flanders answered. "Of course, we haven't attempted to get near enough to the house to check that out. I won't let my officers become sitting ducks."

"That's why I'm here," Jim said, with a rueful smile.

"I didn't say that," Flanders protested.

"No, but that's what you're thinking," Jim answered, with another grin. "Well, let's see what I can do. Deputy Duvall, I'd like you to remain here with me, since you have at least a passing knowledge of the family."

He opened the driver's door of his Tahoe, turned on the ignition, flicked on the switch for the P.A. loudspeaker, and picked up the mic.

"Anyone inside the house. This is Texas Ranger Jim Blawcyzk. Can you hear me?"

He was met with silence.

"Hello the house!" He tried again. "Can any of you hear me? Mr. Dingle?"

Again, no answer.

"Ronny! Ronny Holsclaw! Are you inside? Can you hear me?"

"I can hear you just fine, Ranger," came a voice from inside the house. "I've been waitin' for one of you Rangers to show up. C'mon and try to get me. I'll shoot you down just like I gunned the sheriff down."

Jim glanced at Flanders, who merely shrugged.

"Ronny, the sheriff's out here with me. What sheriff did you shoot?"

"The Dry Gulch sheriff. Got his deputy, too."

"Something's really wrong with that damn kid, Jim," Flanders said. "We've got to do something, and pronto."

"Just let me keep talking to him, and see what

I can figure out," Jim answered. To Ronny, he continued, "Son, is your grandpa in there with you?"

"Yup, he's here, all right."

"Is he okay?"

"He's just fine."

"Can I talk with him?"

"No, sir, Ranger. He's watchin' the back of the cabin, in case you brought more Rangers along, and they try'n sneak up on us from the back yard. He'll plug them if they do, like we did the first one who tried."

"There's no other Rangers with me," Jim answered. "Just the sheriff and his deputies."

"Don't lie to me, Ranger. Another one already got in the house. He done kilt my brother, but then me'n Grandpa nailed him. He's deader'n a doornail, just like the no-good sheriff and his deputy. We dunno how you found our hideout, but you'll never take us outta here alive."

Jim turned to Duvall.

"Didn't you say Ronny was the only child?"

"That's right, Ranger. He's the only one Bonnie and Howard ever had."

"Do you reckon somebody else got inside, and the boy and his grandpa killed him?" Flanders asked.

"I don't know." Jim shook his head. "Deputy, you said Ronny was mentally challenged. Do you think he'd even know how to use a gun?"

"I can't say for certain, but I doubt it," Duvall answered.

"You can't take a chance that he doesn't know how to use one, Jim," Flanders said. "It seems to me the only way out of this situation is to blast our way into the house. Here's the San Marcos SWAT unit pullin' up now. Once they get in position, we can end this real quick."

"Let's not jump the gun, as it were, Mark," Jim answered. "I want to work this out a bit more, before we do anything drastic."

"It'll be on your head, Jim."

"Usually is." Jim shrugged. He turned his attention back to the house.

"Ronny, why don't you come outside, and we'll talk things over?"

"Uh-uh. We ain't got nothin' to talk about, Ranger. Tell you what. You come in here, and we'll settle this man to man, just you'n me, over leveled guns."

"I don't want to die today. Do you, son? Let's try and settle this peaceably, without gun-play."

"I ain't worried about dyin', because there ain't no lawman alive faster'n on the draw than me. Only man who might be faster is my grandpa."

"Mark, I believe this kid thinks he's playin' cowboys, or perhaps acting in an old Western movie," Jim said to the sheriff. "The million-dollar question is, does he have a real gun on him? And if he does, did he kill his grandfather?"

"And if he does, and you guess wrong, you'll likely wind up dead," Flanders replied. "What're you gonna do?"

"Talk to him a little more, see if I can get a hint from what he says. I really don't believe he killed his grandpa. He talks as if the grandfather's in on the game with him. Damn, I wish his mother would turn up. She might be able to tell us something."

"Ronny," Jim called again. "If I come in there, do I only have you to face, or is your grandpa gonna try'n get me too?"

"Only if you somehow plug me first, Ranger. If you get me, then he'll get you."

"Sure sounds like the grandfather's still alive," Jim said.

"Which means if he is, and also has a gun, you'll be facing two men if you go in there alone," Flanders said. "I still say, now that the SWAT team's arrived, we let them bust their way into the house."

"Sorry, Mark, but as the Ranger, I'm in charge of this operation. I'm not going to take a chance on killing a crippled, senile old man, and his teenaged, mentally challenged kid, both of whom my gut tells me aren't armed. We can wait the situation out, at least until Mrs. Holsclaw gets back. Have one of your deputies tell the SWAT team they're to remain on standby until I have a good handle on this. I don't want them moving any closer to the house, and maybe panicking the boy into doing something reckless."

"But how come the grandfather hasn't responded?" Flanders asked. "The boy might already have killed him. I still say we need to get inside that house as quick as we can."

"Damn it, we're gonna wait. No argument," Jim said, losing his patience. "While we are, I'd like to speak with the delivery driver. Have one of your deputies bring him behind my truck. That way, I can still keep an eye on the house, and he'll be safe behind my vehicle while I question him."

"All right. You've made it plain this is gonna be your call, Jim," Flanders said. "But I want it on the record you went against my advice, and I won't be responsible for what happens."

"You've made that pretty clear already," Jim said.

"I'll get that driver for you myself."

Flanders stalked away, shaking his head.

"Hey, Texas Ranger," Ronny called from the house. "Are you gonna come in and see who's the faster man with a gun, or not? Maybe you're just yellow."

"Now I *really* feel like I'm playin' the lawman in a bad B Western," Jim muttered to himself.

"I'm just waitin' for a few more folks to show up, that's all. You don't want to gun me down without anyone seein' how fast you are, do you, kid?"

"Nah, I reckon that makes sense, Ranger. I want a lot of people to see me put a couple of bullets in you. The whole town, in fact. Then everybody'll know I'm the fastest gun in all of Texas. Especially after I gun down a stinking Texas Ranger."

"Ranger, I think you're doing the right thing," Duvall said. "Like you, I'm almost positive the boy doesn't have a real gun. As far as his grandfather, he's probably too scared to say anything, with all the police here. Or, he might not even be home. He could be out with his daughter. Ronny can take care of himself for a short time, as long as he's not left alone for more than a couple of hours."

"Thanks, Deputy," Jim answered. "I've gotta give the kid credit for being smart. He's not showing himself at any of the windows. If he hasn't done anything, I'd hate to see him get picked off for no reason. Here comes the sheriff and the driver."

"Mr. Cassidy, this is Ranger Blawcyzk," Flanders introduced the driver, once they reached Jim. "Jim, Robert Cassidy. Mr. Cassidy, Ranger Blawcyzk would like you to tell him exactly what you found when you arrived here."

"Take your time, Mr. Cassidy, and try to recall every detail you can," Jim said. "With your permission, I'm going to record your statement."

"Of course you can record me. I'll do my best, Ranger," Cassidy said, as Jim switched on his recorder. "I was delivering a package, when I heard what sure sounded like gunshots from inside the house. Then I heard a man scream, like he was in pain. I wasn't close enough to a window to see for certain, but I'm pretty sure I caught a glimpse of someone falling down. I immediately went back to my truck, called 9-1-1, then called my dispatch office to let them know what had happened, and that I would probably be here for quite a spell."

"I see," Jim said. "Which window were you looking at?"

"The one at the right front corner of the house. I was walking past it to leave the package at the front door. I was so startled, I dropped the package. Then, I ran back to my truck and called 9-1-1."

"Could what you heard as gunshots possibly have been another noise, say a vehicle backfiring somewhere nearby, or perhaps a door slamming? Something like that?"

"I suppose it could be possible, Ranger, but I doubt it. I'm a hunter, so I know gunshots when I hear them."

Flanders's hand-held radio crackled to life.

"Hays County Unit 419 to Sheriff Flanders."

"Unit 419, stand by."

"Hold on just a minute, Jim," Flanders said.

"Let's hope one of my people has found Mrs. Holsclaw."

He keyed his mic.

"Sheriff Flanders. Go ahead, 419."

"I've located Mrs. Holsclaw at the Driftwood Recycling Center. Am escorting her home now. Will be at your location in less than five minutes."

"10-4, 419. Sheriff Flanders, out."

"You heard that, Jim. Maybe we finally caught a break."

"Let's hope so," Jim said. He resumed his questioning of the delivery driver.

"Mr. Cassidy, am I correct in assuming you didn't attempt to look more closely into the house, or try the door to see if anyone was home?"

"No, sir, Ranger. I wasn't going to take a chance on getting shot."

"That was a wise decision. That's all I have for now. Thanks for your cooperation."

Jim handed the driver a business card.

"Here's my card. If you think of anything else, get in touch with me. I'll get your contact information from the sheriff. Thank you again for your cooperation, Mr. Cassidy. Unless the sheriff has any more questions for you, you're free to leave."

"I don't have anything else," Flanders said. "I'd also like to thank you, Mr. Cassidy."

"I'm happy to have been of help," Cassidy answered. "I hope everything turns out all right."

"We appreciate that," Jim answered.

As soon as they were out of their vehicles, the deputy who had located Bonnie Holsclaw brought her right over to Jim and Sheriff Flanders.

"Mrs. Holsclaw, this is Ranger Blawcyzk," the deputy introduced him. "He'll explain the situation to you."

"Ranger, what's wrong?" Mrs. Holsclaw asked, her voice trembling with worry. "All I was told is that there was an emergency at home, and I needed to return as quickly as possible."

"Howdy, ma'am," Jim said. "I'm sorry to meet you under these circumstances. A package delivery driver believes he heard gunshots inside your house, then someone scream as if they'd been shot. He also thinks, but can't be positive, he saw someone inside fall after the shots. I understand your father and son are in the house. I've been trying to speak with them, but only your son has answered, and he refuses to come out. He says he wants to shoot any lawman who tries to take him."

"Is *that* what all this is about?" An expression of relief crossed the woman's face. She gestured to the police officers and vehicles surrounding her home.

"Beggin' your pardon, ma'am, but yes," Jim

answered, puzzled by her reaction. "The witness gave a credible report of a shooting taking place inside your home. We have been unable to contact your father, and your son insists he'll shoot anyone who comes in after him. He's mentioned several times that he'd particularly like to take down a Texas Ranger. It almost seems as if he thinks he's in a cowboy movie."

"That's because he does, Ranger," Mrs. Holsclaw answered. "He won't actually shoot anyone. In fact, he can't."

"You're going to have to explain what you mean."

"It's like you said, Ranger. Ronny thinks he's playing cowboys. He and my father watch Westerns or war movies on television or DVDs almost all day long. They both just love them. When my dear Howard, Lord rest his soul, was still alive, he did, too. He and my dad would play shoot-'em-up with Ronny whenever they had the time. My son might be practically a grown man, but his brain still functions like a little boy's. He won't hurt anyone. He's just fascinated with playing a cowboy or soldier."

"But, Mrs. Holsclaw, what about the gunshots the delivery driver heard?" Flanders asked. "And the person he heard yell, then saw fall down?"

"That would be Ronny pretending he got shot," she answered.

"Or another imaginary person, such as his brother," Jim said. "He claims that another Ranger had shot his brother, then he and your father killed the Ranger, along with a sheriff and deputy."

"That sounds about right, Ranger," Mrs. Holsclaw said. "You must remember when you were a boy, and played war or cowboys with your friends. You'd get shot, fall down, then after playing dead for a minute, get right back up and start shooting again. Ronny and my father must be playing the bad guys today."

"What about the gunshots?" Flanders pressed.

"That's just a recording my husband made for Ronny, a few months before he passed. He shot off his rifle a few times, and recorded the sound because Ronny enjoys hearing the shots while he's playing. Or, those could have been cap guns. Sometimes, my father and son play with cap guns, sometimes with foam swords or rubber knives, but most of the time they use those foam dart guns that seem to be so popular nowadays. That way they can actually shoot each other without anyone getting hurt."

"But why hasn't your father answered us?" Jim asked.

"My poor father's afraid of strangers since he's gotten old, and been confined to his wheelchair," Mrs. Holsclaw explained. "He's most likely too frightened to answer you. Plus, he seems to lose a bit more of his mental capacity every month. Sometimes, I think playing with Ronny is the only thing that keeps him from complete senility. Add in his loss of hearing, and it should be plain why he hasn't answered you."

"I don't know, Jim," Flanders said. "Mrs. Holsclaw, your story sort of makes sense, but what if your boy did get his hands on a real weapon?"

"He couldn't have, Sheriff. After my husband died, and my father began to slip into early dementia, I sold all their guns. I didn't want them in the house, where Ronny might accidentally get his hands on them. The only guns left in the house are those foam dart and cap guns I've already mentioned."

"You're absolutely certain Ronny couldn't have gotten his hands on a functional weapon somehow?" Jim asked.

"I'm positive," Mrs. Holsclaw answered. "Ronny never goes anywhere except with me. Same for my Dad. Neither one can leave the house without my help."

"So you're saying, if I do have to go in the house to get your son out, I don't have to worry about being shot, Mrs. Holsclaw?" Jim asked.

"Not at all. The most Ronny might do is punch you, if he decides he wants to have a fist fight with a bad guy. Or maybe stab you with a foam sword."

"He says *he's* the bad guy, don't forget," Jim said.

"Then if he wants to have a fist fight with a good guy. Other than that, the worst that can happen to you, Ranger, is my son shoots you with a foam dart."

"I'd much prefer he not shoot me at all," Jim answered. "Also, I don't want to chance frightening, or perhaps hurting, your boy or your father. Do you think you can talk your son into coming outside?"

"Why don't I just go in and talk to him myself?"

Jim shook his head.

"I'm sorry, ma'am, but I can't take that chance. I believe everything you've said, but there is still the possibility, no matter how slight, that your boy found an old, working gun somewhere on your property, or somehow obtained one. I can't let you go in there. I'm the one who will have to do that. Unless you can convince Ronny to come out, I have no other choice."

"What if he does? One of these deputies might shoot him."

"I promise you, that won't happen." Jim tried to reassure her. "These officers are all under strict orders not to fire, unless they are fired upon first. So, unless your son comes out of the house shooting, nothing will happen to him."

"There's no other way?"

"I'm afraid not, ma'am. Here's the mic to my

truck's P.A. system, if you'd like to see if Ronny will listen to you. Just key the button on the side of the mic to talk, then release it to listen."

He handed the mic to Mrs. Holsclaw, who reluctantly took it.

"Ronny," she spoke into the mic. "This is your mother. It's time for you to stop playing this game, and come outside. You're frightening everyone, so please, listen to me and come out of the house. No one's going to hurt you."

She was met with silence from the house.

"Ronny, do you hear me? Please answer me."

"I'm sorry, Mom. I can't come out. Not until that Ranger out there comes in and faces me over our guns. I'm gonna show him there ain't anyone faster on the draw than me."

"Ronald Gordon Holsclaw! You listen to me. You come out of that house this instant. If you don't, you'll be in big trouble."

"I'll come out as soon as I finish that Ranger, Mom. I promise you."

Mrs. Holsclaw handed the mic back to Jim.

"I was afraid of this, Ranger. Sometimes, when Ronny is playing a game, his mind tricks him into really believing he's actually the character he's pretending to be. There's no telling how long that will last. I'm afraid I won't be able to convince him to come out."

"So you're saying I'll have to go in there and get him?" Jim said.

"I'm afraid I am, Ranger. I'm sorry."

"Mrs. Holsclaw, why haven't you ever done anything about this before?" Flanders asked.

"Because Ronny's never hurt anyone, or caused any trouble," she answered. "I don't want to take charity, and I surely don't want the state to take my boy from me, nor to tell me how to care for him. As I've already said, he's got the mind of a child in the body of a man."

"Mrs. Holsclaw, I do have to warn you, once the dust settles here, I'm going to request a visit from Hays County Social Services," Jim said. "You can either allow that to be done with your voluntary cooperation, or if necessary, I'll obtain a court order. As you say, it appears your son hasn't hurt anyone . . . yet. However, it's obvious he's not receiving the proper care and counseling he needs, and could well become a danger to himself or others in the future. It also appears you could use some assistance caring for your father.

"Now, that said, there's no sense putting this off any longer. I'm going in there to get your son. I promise you, Mrs. Holsclaw, no harm will come to him, nor your father, as long as you're telling the truth, and neither one tries to shoot me. In that case, I will have to fire back in self-defense, to protect both myself and everyone out here, including you. However, that will be a last resort."

"I understand, Ranger. You do whatever you need to. As far as sending someone from the county here, we can talk about that later."

"Thank you, ma'am."

Jim turned to Flanders.

"Mark, I'm going in there . . . alone. Unless you hear gunshots, and I don't come back out, no one is to make a move. Not a damn one of you. That includes you, your deputies, and the SWAT team. Is that clear?"

"Jim, just what the hell do you think you're doin'?" Flanders answered. "For all you know, that kid could have a damn AR15 in his hands, ready to blow your head off the minute you show it."

"I don't think he does," Jim answered. "I'm almost one hundred per cent certain he's just a young man who sometimes loses his grip on reality, like his mother says."

"Then what about the grandfather? Did it ever occur to you the kid might only be actin' as a decoy for the old man, who's just itching to put a dozen bullets through you?"

"In which case, Bonnie Holsclaw is a damn good liar. However, I've got no reason to doubt her word. What's your take on her, Deputy Duvall?"

"None of the family's ever been in trouble, until today," she answered. "I'm certain Bonnie's telling the truth."

"Then it's settled. It's time to end this," Jim said.

"Jim, if anything does happen to you, I'll turn the SWAT team loose," Flanders said.

"If anything does happen to me, that'll be your prerogative, since then it'll be your operation," Jim answered.

"I still think you're making a mistake, but good luck," Flanders said.

"I appreciate that."

Jim laid his rifle on the hood of his Tahoe, then pulled his Ruger SR 1911 from its holster on his left hip.

"Ronny, I'm comin' in. You're not gonna try and plug me while I'm crossin' the yard, are you? It's just gonna be you and me, face to face, right?"

"That's right, Ranger. Only the two of us, over our gunsights. I'm waitin' for ya, sidewinder. C'mon."

"I'm comin'."

As he started toward the house, Jim made the Sign of the Cross and murmured a silent prayer. Despite the confidence he'd tried to project to the sheriff, he knew he was taking an awful chance. His guts felt as if they were tied in knots, with a large chunk of ice sitting in the pit of his stomach. If he'd miscalculated, he could well be shot dead before he made it halfway across the yard.

When he reached the front door, Jim exhaled a huge sigh of relief.

"So far, so good," he muttered. Standing to the side of the door, in case Ronny Holsclaw was waiting to ambush him on the other side, he slowly turned the knob, then carefully opened the door and stepped inside. There was no sign of the young man in the living room, nor the kitchen. Unlike the debris-strewn yard, the inside of the house was meticulously kept. While the furniture, electrical fixtures, and appliances were outdated and worn, everything was spotless, except for foam darts scattered on the floor.

"Ronny, where the heck are you?" Jim called.

"I'm in the back bedroom now, with my grandpa," Ronny answered. "I want him to see me shoot you down."

"I'm comin' in there," Jim warned him. He walked down the hall to the far back room. In there was an elderly man in a wheelchair, who looked at Jim blankly. He had a foam dart rifle lying across his lap. Off to his right, holding a foam dart pistol leveled at Jim's chest, stood Ronny. He was younger, taller, heavier, and more powerfully built than Jim had expected, about six-and-a-half feet tall, and weighing about two hundred and twenty pounds. He was wearing a black T-shirt, jeans, black cowboy boots, and black Resistol. His dark brown eyes glared malevolently at Jim from under the pulled-low hat.

"I was beginnin' to think you were too yellow to show, Ranger," he said.

"I said I'd be here, so here we are, face to face, just the two of us," Jim said. "Now that I'm with you, it's time to end this game, son. You're not in a movie, and you're not a gunslinger. Your mom's waitin' for you. She's really worried about you and your grandpa. So, let's make this easy on both of us. Come outside with me, so your mom can see you're both safe."

Ronny shook his head.

"Uh-uh, Ranger. I said I was gonna kill you, and that's exactly what I'm gonna do. I'm gonna put a bullet right through your lousy guts."

"Son, please listen to me," Jim urged. "This gun I'm holding isn't a toy, like yours. It's real, and the bullets it shoots are real. If you force me to use it, you'll be dead. Do you understand me?"

"The only one who's dying here today is you, Ranger. If it takes more'n one slug to kill you, so much the better. Now, are we gonna holster our guns, then draw, or would you rather I gunned you down right where you stand?"

"I don't want either one of us to die, Ronny," Jim said. "I don't want to hurt you, or make this harder than it has to be. Why don't you simply give me your gun, and then everything will be just fine?"

"Just like I figured, you're yellow. If you take one step toward me, I'll shoot. At least I'm givin' you an even chance, if you're smart enough to take it. Once you're dead, then I'll go see my mom."

"If you try'n go outside, those law officers out there will shoot you to bits, the minute you show your face, son. Now, give me your gun, or I'll have to take it from you."

"No! I said I was gonna have a gunfight with you, Ranger, and that's just what I'm gonna do. This is your last chance to holster your gun so you'll have a fair chance to get me before I get you."

What the hell am I gonna do? Jim thought. *I know this damn kid can't hurt me with that dart gun, but the only way I can see him givin' up is if I take him by force. If I try that, someone's liable to get hurt, because he looks like one helluva scrapper. On top of that, I'm not even certain I can outmuscle him. I'd bet my hat if he landed one good punch he'd send me from here clear to Sunday. Mebbe I'd just better . . .*

Jim sighed. Violating every principle of police procedure, he holstered his gun. When he did, Ronny did the same.

"All right, kid. You win. Whenever you're ready, grab for your gun. Just remember, I'm a lawman, one who's been fightin' outlaws like you for years. Not once has any *hombre* ever outdrawn me. You don't have a chance of beatin' me to the draw."

"That's where you're wrong, Ranger."

With that, Ronny yanked his gun from its holster. Jim also went for his gun, deliberately moving more slowly than he could, making certain the loaded weapon never left its holster. Ronny pulled his pistol's trigger, and a foam dart bounced off Jim's stomach. Jim yelped as if in pain, and clutched his middle, doubling over slightly.

"Told ya I'd get ya, Ranger," Ronny shouted. "Plugged you right in the belly, just like I said I would. Ya never even cleared leather."

"You . . . you nailed me solid," Jim gasped, as he staggered toward Ronny. "Reckon I'm . . . done for."

"Not quite yet," Ronny said. "You're still standin'."

He triggered his gun again, bouncing another dart off Jim's gut.

By now, Jim had gotten close enough to reach for Ronny's wrist. Hoping his trick would work, he made a lunge at the boy, who took a step backward, amazingly quickly for his size.

"You're supposed to be dead! What are you doin', Ranger?" Realizing Jim had tricked him, Ronny took a wild swing at his head, which Jim easily ducked. He then sent a vicious punch of his own into the boy's gut. Ronny's eyes bugged out, he gasped as he lost all the air from his lungs, and doubled over. Not giving him a chance

126

to recover, Jim grabbed the boy's right arm and twisted it behind his back. He took the handcuffs from their holder on his belt, clamped one around Ronny's right wrist, then grabbed his left arm, pulled it behind the boy's back, and cuffed his hands together.

"I didn't want to have to do that to you, son, but you didn't give me any other option," Jim said, as he pulled the boy upright. "Time to go talk to your mom."

He looked at Ronny's grandfather, who had thrown his rifle to the floor and held his hands raised shoulder high.

"Don't worry, Mr. Dingle," Jim tried to reassure him. "Everything will be all right, now. Someone will be here to take care of you in a minute."

The old man just gave him another blank stare. Jim had no idea whether he'd understood his reassurances or not.

"C'mon, Ronny, let's go."

As he took the boy by the arm and started walking toward the door, Jim keyed the mic on his hand-held radio.

"Sheriff, everything's under control. No one's been hurt, and I've got the boy in custody. We're coming out now. Make certain everyone understands there's no danger, and they can stand down. I don't want anyone getting nervous and taking a shot at us."

"I've got that, Jim," Flanders answered. "I'll pass the word."

When they reached the door, Jim looked out before exiting the house, erring on the side of caution.

"Does everyone know they're not to shoot?" he radioed to the sheriff.

"Yes, they've got the order," Flanders radioed back.

Now satisfied it was safe, Jim walked Ronny out of the house. They were about five feet into the yard when the boy suddenly stopped.

"No. I'm not givin' up without a fight," he screamed. He slammed his shoulder into Jim's side, breaking the Ranger's grip on his arm, and knocking him to the ground. Jim caught a glimpse of a SWAT officer raising a rifle to his shoulder.

"No! Don't shoot!" Jim lunged for Ronny, pushing him off his feet just as the officer pulled the trigger. A spray of blood hit Jim, and something stung his left cheek. Ronny yelled in pain, then crumpled to the ground.

"Ronny! Ronny!" Jim yelled. Blood was spreading over the right side of the boy's shirt, just under his shoulder, and spurting from a severed artery in his right arm.

"Get those paramedics down here *now!*" Jim shouted. He pulled the tie from his neck and used it as a tourniquet around Ronny's arm. "Who the hell fired that shot?"

"I guess you win, Ranger," Ronny said, struggling to get the words out. "One of your pards plugged me."

"That wasn't my pard," Jim answered. He shook his head as he realized that, despite being shot, Ronny still thought he was an old West outlaw. "Let me see how bad you're hit." He lifted the boy's T-shirt, to reveal the bullet hole in Ronny's chest, as well as a gaping exit wound in his side. He pulled the handkerchief from his back pocket, stuffed it into the wound in Ronny's side, them jammed his hand into the hole in the boy's chest, pressing hard to stanch the flow of blood, as much as possible. In what seemed an eternity, but was, in reality, less than a minute, two of the Hays County paramedics were at his side.

"We'll take over now, Ranger," one said.

"All right. He's bleedin' bad. Let me take the cuffs off him so you won't have to cut 'em off. Do your best for the kid."

"Always do," the other answered. "You might as well take your tie, also." He removed the tie from Ronny's arm and handed it to Jim.

While the paramedics worked on Ronny, Jim got to his feet and looked around. Sheriff Flanders rushed up to him.

"Jim, how bad is it?" he asked. "Are you all right?"

"Yeah, I'm fine. I dunno if the boy's gonna

make it. He took one in the chest. The slug apparently came out between his ribs, hit his arm, and severed an artery in that, too. I just hope the paramedics can stop the blood before he bleeds out. Who the hell fired that shot, Mark?"

"One of the damn San Marcos SWAT officers," Flanders answered. "He shouldn't have. I made certain everyone, and I mean *everyone,* knew they weren't to fire unless they were fired upon, that you had the boy in custody."

"Mark, I need one of your people to go in the house and bring Mr. Dingle out," Jim said. "He's in the back bedroom. I'd say he should be taken to the hospital, just to be checked out. Where's Mrs. Holsclaw?"

"She's with Deputy Duvall, who had to restrain her. She wanted to run right to her son, of course."

"I'd better go talk to her, let her know her boy's still alive," Jim said. "And I want you to tell that San Marcos son of a bitch I'm going to make certain he's suspended, at the least. He had to see the boy was cuffed. Tell the whole bunch they're not to leave here until I talk to them. I'd also appreciate it if you'd have one or two of your deputies try'n find that bullet. You know there'll be an investigation into what went wrong today, and that slug'll be evidence."

"You've got it. And I'm sorry for what happened."

"There's no need to apologize to me. You did everything I asked for, despite not agreeing with me. Now, let me go talk to Ronny's mother."

"Hold on a minute," Flanders said. "You'd better get yourself patched up first. Your cheek is bleeding pretty bad."

"What do you mean?"

"It looks like you got grazed, and *way* too close for comfort."

"I don't even remember gettin' hit," Jim answered. In the adrenaline of the moment, he'd forgotten the sting on his cheek. Now that Flanders had mentioned the wound, he could feel his cheek throbbing, and the blood running down it and over his neck to soak his shirt collar. He touched his hand to the wound. It came away sticky with blood.

"This ain't all that bad. It can wait until after I speak with Mrs. Holsclaw. All it needs is a bandage from my first-aid kit. I can't figure how I took a bullet. I only heard one shot, and the slug that hit Ronny sure didn't get me too. The angle wasn't right."

"I dunno." Flanders shook his head. "You're still bleeding. Tell you what. I'll send one of the paramedics over to you."

"Okay, that'll be fine."

Jim walked over to where Bonnie Holsclaw was standing, too shocked to cry. Tammy Duvall had an arm around her shoulders, attempting to comfort the distraught mother.

"Ranger! You bastard!" Mrs. Holsclaw screamed, when she spotted Jim. "You killed my son!"

She tried to lunge at Jim, but the deputy held her back.

"You don't know that for certain, Bonnie," Duvall said. She tightened her grasp on the woman. "Give Ranger Blawcyzk a chance to speak."

"Mrs. Holsclaw, first, let me assure you that your son is still alive," Jim said. "However, he has been shot, as you know. I can't tell you how serious his injuries are. As far as what happened, one of the local officers on scene failed to follow orders, and shot Ronny when he pulled away from me. He or she did so despite being warned not to fire unless fired upon, or if I had been shot. Sometimes, a law officer's instincts kick in during a tense situation, as today.

"I'm not excusing the officer who fired the shot at all; however, if Ronny had not pulled away from me, he wouldn't have given the officer a reason to think I, or any of the other officers present, were in danger. In that case, it's probable no shots would have been fired. Now, I have no authority over the officer in question, but I am going to request his or her department to place the officer on suspension, or

132

at least administrative leave, until a complete and thorough investigation is completed.

"I also, of course, apologize to you and your family. As for your father, he is safe, and unharmed. One of the Hays County deputies will be bringing him out shortly."

"I don't care. You promised me no harm would come to my son if he listened to you. Just leave me alone, Ranger. Get out of my sight."

"If that's what you'd prefer, Mrs. Holsclaw. Right now, my main concern is seeing that your boy gets the medical care he needs. I'll ask the paramedics working on him to allow you to ride in the ambulance with him to the hospital. I'll have Sheriff Flanders make arrangements for your father, also. I know you're too upset and angry to believe me at the moment, but what happened is almost as upsetting to me as it is you. Again, I apologize."

"Your apology means nothing, you damn son of a bitch."

"That's enough, Bonnie," Duvall said. "You can't blame Ranger Blawcyzk. What happened here today was not his fault. I hope you'll come to understand that. I know he must feel terrible how things went awry. From what I saw, Ranger Blawcyzk did everything he could to keep your son, and father, from harm."

"Thank you, Deputy, but it's all right," Jim

said. "She's no more upset than any other mother would be. I can't really blame her."

"Ranger, here's a paramedic now," Duvall said. "Mrs. Holsclaw, I'm going to recommend she give you a mild sedative, to help your breathing and heart. It wouldn't do for you to become so upset you can't go to the hospital with your son."

"Ranger, I'm Michelle Minor, from Hays County EMS," the paramedic introduced herself. "Sheriff Flanders told me you were injured, and need some medical attention."

"Mark's just an old fussbudget. I only got a scratch," Jim answered.

"You just let me be the judge of that," Minor said. "To be blunt, you're a damn bloody mess. It can't hurt to have me check you over."

"All right." Jim gave in. Reluctant as he was to admit it, the wound on his cheek was still oozing blood, and he was feeling a bit flushed. "However, first, I need to ask you two favors."

"Of course."

"I'd like you to radio the other paramedic team, the one working on Ronny Holsclaw. I'm requesting his mother be allowed to ride to the hospital in the ambulance with him."

"I can handle that. What else?"

"Deputy Duvall believes Mrs. Holsclaw needs a mild sedative. If she agrees to take one, would you administer that to her first, before you treat me? That way it will start to take effect before she gets into the ambulance."

"All right, Ranger. Mrs. Holsclaw, would you agree to taking a small dose of paroxetine? It's not as fast acting as Valium, but will not make you as drowsy, just help settle you a bit?"

"All right, as long as this Ranger gets out of my sight."

"I'll tell you what, Bonnie," Duvall said. "As soon as you receive the sedative, I'll take you to the team working on your son. Michelle, if you could call them right now, get that permission, and perhaps see how Ronny is doing?"

"Of course."

Minor moved out of Mrs. Holsclaw's earshot, radioed the other EMS unit, and explained the situation. Once she had an answer, she returned to Ronny's mother and the others.

"I have some good news, Mrs. Holsclaw," she said. "Your son has been stabilized. He's being loaded into the ambulance right now. They'll pick you up as soon as they're done. Let me give you the sedative, so you can be ready. You'll be going to Seton Medical Center Hays in Kyle, since that's the nearest hospital with a trauma center. Unfortunately, none of the medical choppers can fly today because of the high winds."

"So he'll be all right?"

"I can't say that for certain, since I'm not with him, nor am I a doctor," Minor answered.

"However, the fact the medical personnel working on Ronny were able to stabilize your son is a very good sign."

Jim had walked away from the distraught mother. He waited until the ambulance carrying her son had picked her up and was on the way to the hospital before he returned to Minor and Duvall.

"All right, Ranger," Minor said. "Are you going to let me care for your wound now?"

"I suppose you're not gonna leave me alone until I do, are you?"

"That's right. I can be just as stubborn as you seem to be. Sit down on the tailgate of that old pickup over there, and I'll take a look at you."

"All right."

Jim followed the paramedic the few yards to the pickup she had indicated, and sat down.

"Please take off your hat, so I can get a better look at your injury," Minor requested, as she placed her first aid bag on the tailgate alongside Jim. "Unbutton your shirt, too."

"Why the hell do you want me to unbutton my shirt?" Jim asked.

"You know the protocol, Ranger. I've got to check your heart, blood pressure, and pulse rate." Minor laughed before concluding. "And if you don't behave, I'll insist on taking your temperature, too. I'll do that by ramming a thermometer up your butt. Do you get my drift?"

"It's pretty plain," Jim said, also laughing. "I promise, I'll be good."

"That's a good little Ranger."

Minor opened the bag, and donned a pair of sterile nitrile gloves while Jim removed his hat and opened his shirt.

"Since the bleeding has almost stopped, I'll take your vitals before working on you," Minor said. She proceeded to check his heart, pulse rate, and blood pressure.

"So far, so good," she said, as she removed the blood pressure cuff from Jim's arm. "Everything's normal. Now, let's see what we have, here."

Minor opened a packet containing a large antiseptic wipe and used that to clean most of the blood from Jim's cheek. Jim winced as the antiseptic bit into his raw wound.

"You've got a pretty nasty gash here, Ranger," she said. "It could probably use a few stitches; at least, that's my recommendation."

"Do you think it can be closed without using stitches?"

Minor looked critically at the wound before answering.

"I'm not certain. I would advise against that. However, if you wish, I can clean the wound out, treat it with antiseptic ointment, and push the edges together. Then I'll put a butterfly bandage over it, and finally tape a gauze patch over that. It could work."

"Then let's try it. It'll save me a trip to the ER."

"All right, but remember, you may end up needing to go for stitches anyway. If that happens, it will leave a worse scar than if you had stitches in the first place."

"I'll take the chance," Jim said. "Who knows? A scar could make me more rugged looking."

Minor had to laugh.

"You're a mess, Ranger, you know that? And I'm not talking about your cheek."

"So I've been told," Jim said.

"Let me get to work."

Minor cleaned out the wound once again, then sprayed more antiseptic into it, causing Jim to grimace.

"I know, that had to hurt," she said.

"You've got that right," Jim answered. "More'n whatever hit me in the first place."

"I don't have much more to do."

Minor closed the wound, taped the edges together with a butterfly bandage, then put a good amount of triple antibiotic on a gauze pad. She placed that over the wound and taped it in place.

"I'm all finished, Ranger. Just keep in mind, you'll need to change those bandages after two days, and every two days thereafter. Make certain to keep that wound clean. And I shouldn't need to tell you this, but if the wound becomes hot, red, or inflamed, or if you develop a fever, get to a doctor pronto. It's too close to your eyes, nasal passages, or sinuses to fool around with it. An infection could easily travel to your brain and kill you."

"I'll be careful," Jim said, then grinned. "Of course, lots of folks tell me that's not where my brain is located."

"I can just imagine," Minor said. "Well, I'd better see if I'm needed elsewhere. Nice meeting you, Ranger. You take care."

"You too, Doc."

Minor laughed, then waved him off. Jim stood up, buttoned his shirt and tucked it back in, then put his tie and hat on. He started walking toward the house. Sheriff Flanders met him halfway there.

"You don't have to go to the ER, Jim?" he asked.

"Nope. Just a bandage was all I needed. Did your men have any luck findin' that bullet?"

"They sure did, although there wasn't much left of it. We also found this."

Flanders handed Jim a plastic baggie holding a small chunk of cinder block, with a slight reddish-brown stain on its jagged, pointed edge.

"This?" Jim said, puzzled for a moment.

"Yup. After the slug tore through the kid, it ricocheted off the house. It knocked off that piece of block, which is what must've hit you. You can see the blood stain on it. Jim, I knew you were a blockhead, but I never realized until now that was literally."

"And this here's a chip off the old block," Jim said. "Where's the bullet?"

"Right here."

Flanders handed Jim another baggie, this one containing a hunk of metal, so battered it was unrecognizable as a bullet.

"Good work, Mark. Tell your deputies I said so. How are things coming along? What arrangements have been made for Mr. Dingle?"

"The second ambulance is taking him to Seton in Kyle to be checked out, just as a precaution. I would imagine they'll keep him for a few days. From what I can see, the old man really should be in a specialized dementia facility."

"I agree with you there. The boy needs more help than his mom can give him, too. If his mother had asked for help sooner, none of this would have happened today. I'm counting on you to make certain someone from the county social services follows up with the family, once the dust has settled."

"You know I'll do just that," Flanders said. "Jim, if you don't mind, I'd like to make a suggestion."

"Sure, go ahead."

"Unless there's something specific you need,

why don't you let my office finish up here? You've had a rough day, and I don't just mean physically. Seeing that boy shot just when you thought the situation was under control would be hard on anyone. I don't care how tough they are, or think they are, it's bound to affect them. There's not much more to do here but secure the scene. We can handle that all right. You need to go on home and get some rest."

"I'm doin' all right," Jim answered.

"No, you're not. Whether you want to admit it or not, you nearly had your eye taken out, or worse, by that piece of cinder block. Plus, I can tell just by lookin' at you that you're really shaken by what happened. It's in your eyes, and you're not walking too steady. Just get on home to your family."

"All right, I'll go along with you. I've got a lot of soul-searching ahead of me. If I'd done a better job, that kid wouldn't be fightin' for his life right now. His getting shot is on my head."

"No, it sure is not!" Flanders said. "You did every damn thing you could. Don't go beating yourself up over what might or might not have been. You're too good a lawman for that. Hell, if you'd listened to me, the kid would most likely be dead by now, maybe his grandpa too, and their house all busted up, besides. Don't go layin' a guilt trip on yourself, especially when it isn't warranted."

Jim managed a rueful grin.

"I can't help it. I'm Catholic," he answered. "We're real good at guilt trips."

"I'm Jewish. You think we're not?" Flanders answered, with a laugh of his own. "So, from one expert to another, there's not one reason I can think of for you to put the blame on yourself. And at least you're smiling again."

"Yeah, but not inside. Today's gonna eat at me for quite a spell. You too, even if you're tryin' not to admit it. I'll concede you're right, Mark. Soon as I talk with the SWAT team, I'm gonna head for home. I'll write up a quick report, then crash for the rest of the day."

"Now you're talkin' sense. Do you mind if I come along while you talk with the San Marcos SWAT people?"

"Not at all. Maybe when I'm through chewing 'em out, you might want to lay into 'em yourself. If that's the case, be my guest."

"Y'know, that's not a bad idea, Ranger. I'm more than a bit ticked about that boy being shot, just like you. Let's go get 'em."

When Jim and Flanders reached the SWAT unit, there were only three men standing outside it. Whether from sheer exhaustion or pure disgust, most of Jim's anger had subsided, replaced by what he could only describe as a mixture of frustration and worry over how severe Ronny

Holsclaw's wound was. He could only pray it wasn't fatal.

"Who's the person in charge of this unit?" he asked. "And where are the others?"

"I am," one said. "Captain Jonathan Culpepper. This is my second in command, Lieutenant Lucille Cardones. The other officer is Peter Cannon. He's the one who fired the shot which hit the suspect. As far as the other members of the team, they're inside the van, staying out of the heat. I didn't feel they needed to be part of this."

Jim's anger came flooding back.

"Not just the suspect. Officer Cannon, your bullet ricocheted off the house after it went through that boy's chest. It took off a chunk of concrete which just missed taking out my eye, or worse. What the hell were you thinking?"

"I thought he was going to shoot you, when I saw him push you down," Cannon answered. "I feel that I acted appropriately. If he'd gotten his hands on your gun—"

"Stop right there. You damn sure *didn't* act appropriately. I'm certain you could see that boy was handcuffed, behind his back. It would have been impossible for him to even grab my weapon, much less fire it. He damn for certain wasn't going to run anywhere, not with this place surrounded by half the law officers in Hays County. *If* he had somehow managed to get my

143

gun, that would have been the time to fire, not when he was just trying to run away. You and your team also were ordered not to fire unless fired upon."

"Hold on a minute, Ranger," Culpepper said. "Those were your damn orders, not mine. I told my people if that kid made one wrong move, to shoot the hell out of him. I wasn't about to take any chances with a damn lunatic."

"Oh, really? Well, Culpepper, you'd better listen, and listen to me good. When the Texas Rangers are called in, they have complete charge of a case or situation. That means any orders issued by a Ranger supersede any given by a local or state officer, oftentimes even a Federal official. I was going to request you place the officer who fired that shot on suspension until the investigation into what occurred here today is complete, as per standard police operating procedure. Now, I'm going to contact *your* commander and insist you also get placed on suspension, or desk duty. Mark, did you know about this?"

Flanders shook his head.

"I sure the hell didn't, Jim. I would have told you if I had."

"Which is why I didn't tell you, Sheriff," Culpepper said. "I protect my men and women, no matter what."

"You also may just have taken the life of an

innocent, confused boy. Not to even bring up the fact that, if Cannon had missed, his bullet could just as easily have hit me," Jim said. "Mark, let's get outta here, before I say or do something I shouldn't. Besides, suddenly I'm getting sick to my stomach. Culpepper, you'll be hearing more about this."

Jim spun on his heels and stalked away, with the sheriff at his side. Flanders had a look of concern on his face.

"Jim, maybe you should swing by the hospital, if you're feeling like you're gonna puke. It could be a reaction from the wound."

"No need. The only thing making me sick to my stomach was Culpepper. I can't believe him."

"Sadly, I can," Flanders said. "I've had dealings with him before. He's a stubborn son of a bitch. Kind of like Custer at the Little Big Horn."

Jim had to laugh.

"And we know what happened to him. Thanks, Mark. I'm headed for home."

"That's the best thing you can do right now. Talk to you soon."

"Later."

Once he reached his Tahoe, after taking off his gear, Jim got behind the steering wheel and started it. Instead of leaving immediately, he took a few minutes to enter a brief report into his laptop, and more importantly to him at this point, unwind a bit by downing almost a full can

145

of cashews and two cans of Dr Pepper. Finally, he put the truck in gear and left, planning on going by the hospital to get an update on Ronny Holsclaw's condition, then swinging by his office to complete a full report. He gave a sigh of relief when the deputy manning the roadblock at the Elder Hill Road intersection waved him past. A number of television satellite trucks were parked on the shoulder of the road, but the deputy had done a good job of keeping them well back from the Holsclaw farm. When several of the reporters and cameramen attempted to get Jim to stop, the deputy held them back, while Jim accelerated away.

Jim arrived home about three thirty in the afternoon. As usual, Frostie came bounding off the front porch to greet him, then followed him inside the house.

"Jim, is that you?" Kim called from her office.

"Yup, it is," Jim answered.

"You're home early for once."

"Now that you mention it, I guess I am. Something sure smells good."

"I'm making chili for supper," Kim answered. "It should be ready in about an hour. Your mother made a strawberry cheesecake for dessert. Why don't you come take Josh off our hands, then perhaps we can get our work done a bit early, too?"

"All right."

Jim opened the refrigerator to get a bottle of beer. He removed the top and took a good swig before he went down the hall to Kim's office. When he walked in, she looked up and gasped when she saw the bandage on his face, and the dried blood staining his shirt. Betty put a hand to her mouth in shock.

"Jim! What happened?" Kim exclaimed.

"A big fiasco, that's what happened," Jim answered, shaking his head. "As far as me, I'm fine. This bandage just covers a cut I got on my cheek, from a piece of flying cinder block. It's not much, and I'll be healed up pretty quick."

"But how did you get it?" Betty asked.

"From a SWAT officer's stupid mistake," Jim said. "I got a call from the Hays County Sheriff's Office about a possible shooting and hostage situation, just outside Driftwood. I'm not gonna rehash everything that happened, but it turns out there was no shooting, nor any hostage situation. What there *was,* was a senile old man and his mentally slow grandson, who evidently spend a lot of their time watching cowboy or war movies, and also playing cowboys or soldiers. Of course, their house was already surrounded by Hays County deputies, and Sheriff Flanders was there, when I arrived. Flanders had also called the San Marcos SWAT team.

"I tried to talk to the boy, who's about eighteen

or so, to come outside, but he wouldn't. When his mother arrived back home, she also tried, but he wouldn't listen to her, either. She explained that sometimes her son's mind would really convince him that he was the character he was playing. She also assured me there were no weapons in the house, except for some foam dart guns and a couple of cap guns. So, after warning everyone not to begin shooting unless they heard shots fired, and I didn't come out of the house, I went in to bring the boy and his grandfather out. It turned out the grandfather was wheelchair-bound, and had no idea what was really happening.

"The boy wouldn't give up. He was absolutely convinced he was an old West outlaw, who'd just killed a sheriff, deputy, and Ranger who had discovered his hideout, and that he was going to kill me next. Since he only had a soft dart gun, I let him shoot me, pretended I was really hurt, then grabbed him and handcuffed him. Before coming back outside, I radioed that I had the boy in custody, everything was under control, and for everyone to stand down, and that especially no one was to fire. I even looked around outside before bringing the boy out."

"But something went wrong," Kim said.

"It sure did. The boy's a big kid. Even though I'd cuffed his hands behind his back, he managed to pull away from me and knock me down. I yelled 'Don't shoot,' but it was too late. One of the SWAT officers had already pulled the trigger of his rifle. I lunged and knocked the boy down, but a moment too late. The bullet hit him in the chest, came out his ribs, and severed an artery in his arm. After it hit the boy, the slug ricocheted off the house. It knocked loose the piece of block that hit me. Most of the blood on my shirt is the boy's."

"Was he killed?" Betty asked.

"No, he's still alive, but it's touch and go. I stopped at the hospital on my way back, but he was still in surgery. His mother's a wreck, of course, plus his grandfather was also taken to the hospital as a precaution."

"How about you?" Kim asked. "Besides the cut, I mean?"

"Me?" Jim answered. "I'm just sick about what happened. The damn SWAT officer shot that poor kid when the boy was right alongside me, with his hands cuffed behind his back. He had to know the boy couldn't do anything, not even get far if he tried to run, since the house was surrounded. He had no reason to pull the trigger. I wouldn't be surprised that he'll be charged with reckless endangerment at the least, assault or even attempted murder at the most. And if the boy dies, involuntary manslaughter. I've been goin' over and over the entire situation in my mind, attempting to figure out how I could have prevented the boy from getting shot.

There has to be something I missed. There has to be."

"Jim, perhaps there wasn't," Betty said. "From what you just told us, it appears you did everything you possibly could to prevent such a tragedy. And if the Lord is willing, that boy will survive. Either way, and I know this is a lot harder than I'm making it sound, you can't keep stewing on it. You're a law officer, and you know that. Your father taught you that, too. There are so many ways things can go wrong, even when just pulling someone over for a traffic violation. The best thing you can do right now is get some rest, and realize that nothing you do at this point will change anything."

"Your mother's right," Kim added. "Worrying won't change anything, and it won't do you any good. It won't help that poor boy, either. His life is in God's hands. Now, instead of taking care of Josh, leave him with us. Go take a nap before supper."

"No, I'm too wound up to be able to sleep," Jim answered. "I'll get out of these bloody clothes, then feed the horses. I'll take Josh with me. After that, I'll take a quick shower before supper. Doing some work will help me far more than any nap."

He took Josh out of his play pen.

"C'mon, little pard, let's go see your big buddies in the barn."

• • •

Supper was eaten mostly in silence, Jim clearly not in the mood for conversation. Sensing how deeply troubled he was, Kim and Betty also kept their small talk to a minimum.

"Jim, you only ate two helpings of chili, half a loaf of Italian bread, and just one piece of cheesecake," Kim said, as he pushed back from the table.

"I know," he answered. "I guess I'm not really hungry. Hold on, and I'll give you a hand with the dishes."

"Don't even think about it," Kim said. "I love you dearly, but you're more clumsy in the kitchen than the proverbial bull in a china shop. Why don't you take Josh out on the patio and let Frostie play with him? Your mother and I will clean up, then we'll join you."

"That sounds like a good plan," Jim agreed. He took Josh from his high chair and glanced at the dog. "C'mon, Frostie, let's go."

Forty minutes later, Kim and Betty came outside. Jim was sitting in his favorite porch rocker, with Josh sleeping in his lap. Frostie was running around the yard, occupied with tossing, then catching, one of his toys.

Kim carried a cooler holding six cans of beer. She sat down next to her husband, opened one, and handed it to him, then took one for herself.

"Thanks, honey, but I've already had a couple, so I'm not all that thirsty," Jim said.

"Trust me, Jim, you'll need that beer," she answered.

"Why?"

"You'll know when you see this," Betty said. She handed him her laptop, which was paused, and set to the website of one of the local Austin independent television stations. She touched the on-screen button to resume play, starting the story which had been streamed earlier.

"Good evening, this is I-Team reporter Brandon Logan with a follow-up to a story we reported on earlier today. Once again, there has been an apparent unjustified, deliberate shooting of an unarmed civilian in the greater Austin area. This one took place in Hays County, outside the small village of Driftwood. From what I have been able to determine, despite stonewalling from the Hays County Sheriff's Department, the San Marcos Police Department, and the Texas Rangers, the victim is a mentally challenged, autistic boy, who is only eighteen, and whose identity this station is not revealing, to protect the family's privacy. This station has obtained exclusive drone video footage showing a Ranger bringing the victim, already handcuffed, out of his home. Once they emerge, a San Marcos SWAT officer shoots the boy. Worse, it appears from the video that the Ranger purposely led the boy into an ambush. You can see the Ranger push the boy away from him, just before the shot is fired. This reporter has been refused comment by all three departments involved. However, it is plain . . ."

"Damn troublemaker. I've seen enough," Jim said. He turned the laptop off. "He's got no idea what the hell he's talking about. If I run across him—"

"You won't do anything stupid," Kim finished.

"Don't count on it," Jim said. "This is one of those times I wish you and Ma wouldn't watch the damn news. Listen, I'm going to sit by the pond for a while. I need some time to think."

"Would you like me to come with you?" Kim asked.

"Not right now. I promise I won't stay out there too long. Don't worry."

"Of course," Betty answered. "You take as long as you like."

"Do you want the beer?" Kim asked.

"No," Jim said. "Getting drunk is the last thing I need. I want to think through everything that happened today. Tomorrow morning, I'll call Lieutenant Stoker to see how he wants to handle that bastard Brandon Logan. That son of a bitch has been trying to build his reputation on the backs of the police, bordering on slander, for too long now. It's time to put a stop to it."

Jim walked over to the corral, got Copper, led

him out, and jumped on the horse's bare back. He sent the paint trotting toward the pond.

"Betty, do you think I should go after him?" Kim asked.

"Not quite yet. I'd give him an hour, then, if he hasn't returned, that's when *I'd* follow him, if he were my husband. By then, he might want someone to talk to, and you'll be there if he does."

"That's what I'll do," Kim answered. "Would you mind watching Josh?"

"Not at all. Why don't I go inside and pour us some wine? We'll stay here and sip our drinks until we see what Jim does."

"All right," Kim said. "But I'm only giving him an hour. Not one minute more."

5

Three days later, Jim, having worked far beyond the limits of his endurance, had fallen asleep in his office, with his head on his desk, when the phone rang. He jerked awake and grabbed the receiver.

"Ranger Blawcyzk."

"Jim, it's Lieutenant Stoker. I'm on my way back to San Antonio from Waco. I wanted to make certain you were in the office. I need to stop by and talk with you for a few minutes."

"I'll be here. I'm just going over the files on the Thompson murder cold case, trying to see if there's something everyone missed. I'm gonna track down whoever killed that young woman—you can bet your hat on it."

"Keep digging deeper and you will. I've got plenty of confidence in you, Jim. I'm passing through Temple right now, so I'll see you in little more than an hour."

"I'll see you then."

Jim hung up the phone, picked up his mug, and went for the coffee pot.

"I'd better down a couple more cups to make certain I'm wide awake when the lieutenant gets here," he muttered, as he filled the mug yet again with the bitter black brew.

Jim was leaning back in his chair when Lieutenant Stoker walked in.

"I see you're goofing off on the job again, Ranger Blawcyzk," he said, with one of his rare smiles.

"Why not?" Jim answered, with a grin of his own. "It's not like I have a heavy work load or anything."

"Of course you don't," Stoker said. "No Ranger ever does. Say, the coffee sure smells good."

"It is," Jim said. "I finally took your advice, and replaced my old coffeemaker. I just brewed a fresh pot. Pour yourself a cup."

"I don't believe it. You actually got rid of that old thing?"

"I had to. It finally gave out. Sample a cup from my new pot."

"I don't mind if I do. Thanks."

Stoker turned to the dorm size refrigerator, on which Jim's coffee pot sat.

"What the hell is *that?*" he exclaimed.

"It's a percolator, like almost everyone used before the drip machines and pod brewers came along," Jim answered. "My grandpa had one. When I was a kid, I always loved to watch the coffee perking in the glass dome on the cover. In fact, I've even got an old 45 r.p.m. record at home from 1962, titled *The Percolator Twist.* Plus, the aroma is really soothing, but it'll wake you right up first thing in the mornin'. I found this one at an antique shop in Boerne. It makes the finest cup of coffee you ever tasted."

Stoker looked doubtfully at the pot, which was still percolating.

"I'm not so sure about that. I've had your coffee before, I'll remind you."

"Yeah, but that was from my old coffeemaker, don't forget."

"All right, I'll take a chance."

Stoker picked up a mug from alongside the percolator, and filled it to the brim. He took a swallow, then spluttered, and spit the coffee back into his mug.

"Damn you, Jim. This is even worse than the stuff you used to make. I think I've been poisoned. How old is this crap?"

"Like I told you, Lieutenant, I just brewed a new pot. Of course, the grounds have been in there for three days. They're just about perfectly aged. When the coffee starts to get weak, I just add more grounds to the pot."

"You've *got* to have guts made of iron," Stoker said, shaking his head. He put the mug back on top of the refrigerator and sat down. "Well, before your so-called coffee kills me, I'd better tell you why I'm here."

"I knew you didn't stop by just for the coffee," Jim said. "What's up, Lieutenant?"

"First, although I realize you're already aware

of this, I merely want to state, for the record once again, you are in no way responsible for what happened to the Holsclaw boy. I know the investigation is still ongoing, but everything indicates you did all you could to protect that boy. You're damn lucky you didn't take that bullet."

"I would have, if it had kept that poor kid from being shot."

"I know you would have. Any of us would. And you did save his life by shoving him out of the way, so he wasn't hit dead center. And although he's still got a long road to recovery ahead of him, he is going to pull through. Of course, his mother's already gotten a lawyer, who intends to sue the pants off everyone involved. You're not to worry about that. Let the state's attorney's office handle it. Let them handle that son of a bitch Logan, too.

"Now, that said, I know you've been beating yourself up about what happened, and still trying to find some way to blame yourself. That won't do you or anyone else any good. In fact, stewing about it too much could lead to your making a real mistake in another hostage situation, and possibly cost you your job . . . or even your life."

"I'm doin' all right," Jim objected. "You don't have to worry about me."

"You're not," Stoker said. "I talked to your wife, and your mother."

"Blabbermouths," Jim said. "Besides, they worry too much. Both of 'em are like a couple of mother hens, watchin' over their chicks."

"It's not just them," Stoker replied. "Just about everyone you work with at D.P.S. has also noticed there's something wrong. You've been quick to argue, and you barely speak to anyone. Hell, Mary Huggins told me you haven't even been telling any of your awful jokes. That was the clincher. If you're not making bad jokes, something's definitely wrong."

"I hope you're not saying I'm being put on administrative leave, Lieutenant."

"No, not at all. I conferred with Major Voitek, and we did consider ordering you to take a medical leave, and a complete physical and mental examination before you were allowed to return to duty. However, both of us feel that isn't necessary; at least, not yet. You'd only worry yourself to a frazzle if we put you on leave, and probably make yourself feel even worse. Luckily, a solution was dropped right in our laps."

"I'm almost afraid to ask what it might be."

"I have it right here."

Stoker pulled a thick manila envelope from his briefcase and plopped it on Jim's desk.

"Do I dare look?" Jim asked.

"No," Stoker said. "It's a bit of good news, and a bit of bad news. The extradition process for those three sons of bitches who murdered the brand inspectors is completed. These are the papers authorizing us to bring them back to Texas."

"I assume that's the good news. What's the bad?"

"The bad news is, New Mexico refuses to transport them for us, which means we have to go pick them up. Also, no airline is willing to allow three accused murderers on a plane, plus there's no good connections between Las Cruces and Austin, anyway. A flight would take almost as long as driving there. That's where you come in."

"I'm sorry, Lieutenant, but I'm not following you. Maybe I *do* need some time off, because you've totally lost me."

"I'm asking you to go get them, and transport them back here. I know Rangers don't transport prisoners all that much nowadays, but in this case, we have no choice. It's a two-day drive, ten hours or so each way—well, probably less, as fast as you drive, so while you'll technically be working, the first day all you'll be doing is driving, and I know you enjoy that. Then you can get a good night's sleep. It'll be a bit tougher bringing the prisoners back, but you can handle it. I figure you can leave on Thursday morning, be back by Friday night, and then take the weekend off. The drive should give you enough time to think, and by the time Monday rolls around, you should be fit for full duty once more. It's not the ideal situation, but it's better than being forced to take a medical leave. We're short-handed enough as it is without losing you for a month or more."

"You'd have one helluva fight on your hands if you attempted to put me on medical leave, Lieutenant."

"Don't I know it. Now, before you agree, there's a bit more I have to tell you."

"You mean it gets even better?"

"It sure does. You won't be going alone."

"You mean you're sending another Ranger along with me? That doesn't seem necessary, just for a prisoner transport," Jim objected.

"Of course it is," Stoker replied. "You'll be transporting three vicious killers, who, when they were caught in the act of stealing cattle, gunned down two men without compunction. There's no possible way you could keep an eye on all three of them for the entire trip, which I don't have to tell you is over seven hundred miles each way. That means you'll have to make a couple of stops for gas, food, and bathroom breaks. Besides, you'll also be taking a prisoner *to* New Mexico."

"Now this is getting interesting. Keep talkin'."

"Collin County has an escaped bank robber and killer, name of Antonio Pedro Morales, in custody. He stuck up a bank in Santa Fe, then, while he was being taken to prison, he somehow got his hands on a deputy's gun and shot him in the back, then stole his car. When he dumped the deputy's car, he shot and killed another man

161

while carjacking his. New Mexico has agreed to reimburse Texas for the cost of bringing that man back to their jurisdiction. You won't have to take him all the way to Santa Fe, however. You'll leave him at the Dona Ana County Prison in Las Cruces, where our men are being held. New Mexican authorities will take him the rest of the way to Santa Fe. You'll pick up our suspects, and bring them back to Hays County. Having a second man along means he can share the driving, too."

"That's too bad. Santa Fe's a mighty pretty town. I wouldn't have minded spending some time there."

"Don't push your luck, Ranger. I trust you'll accept the assignment."

"That depends. Who's goin' with me? It better not be you, Lieutenant, with all due respect."

Stoker laughed, something he seldom did. Jim was one of the few Rangers in Company F who could break through the usually stoic lieutenant's reserve.

"Twenty hours stuck in a truck with you, listening to your awful jokes and cowboy music? There's not a chance of that. I'd be the one ending up going *loco*, instead of you. No, since the prisoner you'll be taking to New Mexico is in the Collin County jail in McKinney, Bruce Sherman, one of the two Company B Rangers assigned to that city, will be going with you. Since you and he have worked together before, he was the logical choice, even though Reuben Marquin, the other Ranger stationed in McKinney, made the capture. Do you have any other questions, or objections?"

"None at all," Jim answered. "Bruce is a good man, even though he hasn't been with the Rangers all that long."

"Good, then everything's settled. I'll contact Major Hough at Company B and see what time Ranger Sherman can meet you at the prison."

"There's no need for that, Lieutenant. I'll call Bruce myself, and just pick him up at his house. He lives in Rockwall, so it's not that far out of my way. There's no sense in him driving to McKinney, since I'll be going right past his place. When we get back, I can take him home after we drop off our suspects." Jim hesitated, grinned, and concluded, "Besides, we wouldn't want to get the major at Company B in a Hough."

"You're suspended. That's one of your worst jokes yet," Stoker said. "However, I agree that it's logical for you to meet Ranger Sherman on your way. Now, let's go out and get some decent coffee, and some lunch. There's not a chance I'll ever drink a cup of your coffee again. We can iron out any minor details over our meal."

"That sounds good to me. I'm plumb starved."

"Now *that* sounds like the real Jim Blawcyzk," Stoker said, laughing. "Let's go. I'll even drive."

6

Jim originally intended to leave for Rockwall early on Thursday morning. However, since the drive from his place to Bruce's was over two hundred and fifty miles, and more than three hours under the best traffic conditions, he would have had to start out around three in the morning to beat the horrendous Dallas–Fort Worth metroplex rush hour traffic, which began as early as five a.m.

Instead, at Kim's urging, he drove to Rockwall late Wednesday afternoon and obtained a motel room for the night. His wife's foresight proved prescient, as around four-thirty in the morning, three tractor-trailers collided on the I20 causeway over Lake Ray Hubbard, one of them jumping the center divider and overturning, the others jackknifing and catching fire. The crash closed all lanes in both directions, backing up traffic for miles, with the Highway Patrol estimating the interstate would be closed until at least noon.

One advantage of being a Ranger was, having to be away from home overnight so often, meant sleeping well in a bed other than your own. Jim slept soundly and awakened refreshed, a bit later than usual, since it was only a few minutes from the motel to Bruce Sherman's house, a one-story brick residence in a typical Dallas area subdivision. He pulled up in front shortly before 7:30.

When he rang the bell, the door was answered by two little blue-eyed boys, a blonde of about three, who had suspenders holding up his jeans, and his sandy-haired older brother of five. The older boy wore an enormous black cowboy hat much too large for his head, and jeans held up by a belt which sported a big oval silver buckle, and was emblazoned with a brass outline of Texas.

"Hey, Dad," the older one hollered, "There's another Ranger here."

Bruce Sherman came rushing out of the hallway, knotting his tie around his neck. Like his older boy, he also had sandy hair, and eyes the same shade of blue.

"How many times have you boys been told, never answer the door unless your Mom or I are with you? You can never be sure who's on the other side."

"You mean like a dinosaur, with big teeth to eat us?" the younger boy asked.

"I don't think a dinosaur would know how to ring the doorbell," Bruce answered, laughing.

"Besides, Dad, we were right here by the door," the older boy said.

"Never mind where you were. You don't answer the door unless me or Mom are with you. Sorry, Jim," he continued. "C'mon in. You're just

165

in time for breakfast. I hope you haven't eaten."

"You told me not to, so I haven't," Jim said. "Good thing I came up last night, though, with 20 closed."

"Yeah, I heard about that accident," Bruce said. "That means 66 goin' toward Dallas will probably be jammed up for miles, too. We might have to take the back way, 205 up to 78 around Lavon Lake, then shortcut by way of 550 to U.S. 380 West into McKinney. It's a bit farther around, but it'll sure beat sittin' in traffic. Doesn't really matter, because we can't pick up our prisoner until after nine o'clock. Anyway, I hope you're hungry."

"Always am."

"Good. Kelle's in the kitchen. These two little outlaws are my sons. The older one's Wyatt, and his brother is Marshall. Boys, say hello to Ranger Blawcyzk."

"Hi, Ranger Blaw . . . Blaw . . ." Marshall stumbled.

"Don't worry about my name," Jim said, laughing. "Even grown-ups have trouble with it. Just call me Ranger Jim."

"Okay. Howdy, Ranger Jim," Wyatt answered.

"Howdy, boys," Jim answered. To Bruce he said, "Wyatt and Marshall, huh? Two good names for a lawman's sons."

"So I've been told, more than once," Bruce said. "Let's get to breakfast."

Bruce led Jim to the kitchen, with Wyatt and Marshall trailing behind.

"Good morning, Jim," Kelle said, when they walked in. "It's good to see you again, and this time not in a hospital bed. How's Kim?"

"She's just fine," Jim said. "She told me to say hello, and that she'll call you in a few days."

"I'm looking forward to hearing from her. We're going to arrange a get-together."

Two other couples, older, were also in the kitchen.

"Jim, these are my parents, Bubba and Becky Sherman," Bruce said. "And Kelle's mom and dad, Kay and Larry Chambers. Folks, this is Jim Blawcyzk."

"Pleased to meet y'all," Jim said, removing his Stetson.

"You also, Ranger," Larry said.

"Call me Jim."

"Sure thing," Bubba agreed. They shook hands all around.

"We're goin' to the zoo with our Papaws and Memaws today," Marshall said. "We're gonna see the dinosaurs. Mom's comin' too."

"Real live ones?" Jim asked.

"Are they, Memaw Sherman?" Marshall asked her.

"You'll just have to wait and see," Becky answered.

"He'll sure think they are," Kay said. "Those

animatronic figures the zoo put up purely do look and sound life-like."

"I want to see the lions and tigers," Wyatt said. *"Roooaaarrr!"*

"Then you'd better sit down and eat your breakfast," Kelle said. "Jim, the chair at the end is yours. We've got pancakes, bacon, eggs, sausages, and hash browns. Biscuits, gravy, and grits, too, if you're of a mind for those."

"You didn't have to go to all that trouble," Jim said.

"I had help from my mother and Bruce's," Kelle answered. "It's not all that often the whole family can be together for breakfast, so adding one extra plate was no big deal. As soon as you and the boys sit down, we can eat. Since you're our guest, Jim, would you mind saying the blessing?"

"Not at all," Jim answered. "I know you're Baptists, but I hope you don't mind if I say the Grace I always say. It's the one I was taught in Catholic school."

"Of course not."

Once everyone was seated, they bowed their heads.

"Bless us, O Lord, and these Thy gifts, which we are about to receive from Thy bounty, through Christ, our Lord. Amen." Jim prayed.

"Amen."

"Now let's eat!" Wyatt shouted.

With everyone eager to be on their way, it didn't take long for the meal to be devoured.

"Bruce, we'd better get goin', especially with the highway closed," Jim said, as he took his last swallow of coffee. "We can help clean up before we leave, but then we've really gotta get on our way."

"There's no need to help," Kelle said. "I'll put the dishes in the dishwasher and let them get cleaned while we're at the zoo. Besides, your wife warned me never to let you help in the kitchen. Boys, say goodbye to your father, then get your things."

"All right!" Wyatt shouted. He and Marshall kissed and hugged their father, then raced for their bedrooms to gather their backpacks.

"Bruce, please be careful," Kelle said, as they kissed.

"I will be. You know that," Bruce said.

"Kelle, there's really nothing to be concerned about, at least not this time," Jim said. "Prisoner transfers are fairly routine. The only thing different about this assignment is D.P.S. has two Rangers doing the transfer, rather than state troopers or sheriff's deputies. We've just got a long drive ahead of us, a night in a motel, then another long drive back. Bruce will be home tomorrow in time to tuck the boys in for the night."

"See, there's nothing to worry about," Bruce

said. He picked up his duffel bag. "Which vehicle are we taking, Jim? Yours or mine?"

"Mine," Jim answered. "It's fueled up and ready to go. Besides, I enjoy driving. We'll switch when we stop for gas, anyway, if you want to take over for part of the trip. Nice meeting all you folks. Have a good time at the zoo."

"Yeah, while we deal with another kind of animals," Bruce said. "Let's go, Jim."

Due to the accident which had closed I20, even the back roads were jammed with traffic. The trip from Rockwall to the Collin County Jail, which normally ran between forty-five minutes to an hour, took Jim and Bruce nearly two hours. It was almost ten-thirty when they reached the Collin County Jail. After checking their identification papers, the guard in the entrance booth opened the gate. Jim drove through the gate and across a small parking lot. A second guard opened an overhead door for Jim, so he could back his Tahoe into the sally port.

"Well, we're late, but we finally made it," he said, as he shut off the engine.

"Yeah. Let's just hope this isn't a sign of things to come," Bruce answered.

A third guard checked their identifications once again, then unlocked the armored door to the hallway, and led them to a small, locked office. He unlocked the door. Three men were inside, one a guard. The man behind the desk was in a suit and tie, the other in an orange prison jumpsuit, his wrists and ankles shackled. He glared at Jim and Bruce.

"Warden, these are the Rangers, here to pick up Morales," the guard said.

"Thanks, Morton. Please, remain here while the paperwork is completed, then you can escort the Rangers and prisoner back to their car."

"Of course, sir."

"Rangers, have a seat. I'm Assistant Warden Homer Travis. This is the man you'll be taking to New Mexico, Antonio Pedro Morales."

"Rangers Bruce Sherman and James Blawcyzk," Bruce answered, as he and Jim sat down.

"You're a bit late," Travis said.

"Traffic," Bruce answered. "We had to take the back way around, with the interstate being shut down."

"We can make up the time, Warden," Jim said. "Once we get past Fort Worth, it's a straight shot to Las Cruces. I can shave at least an hour off the trip, easy."

"You'll have to do some mighty fast driving, Ranger," Travis said.

"Trust me," Jim answered, with a grin.

Travis shook his head.

"I don't want to know."

"I'm not certain I do, either," Bruce said. "I've never ridden with Jim before."

"Well, as soon as I turn Morales over to you, that's neither here nor there," Travis said. "Once he passes through the gates, he's you Rangers' responsibility. I have the transfer papers right here on my desk. All we need do is sign them, then you can be on your way."

"Let's get it done," Jim said.

He, Bruce, and Travis signed the papers. Travis gave Jim two copies.

"Good luck," he said, as they shook hands.

"Thanks, Warden," Jim answered. "C'mon, Mr. Morales, let's go. I'd like to get you to your new home before dark."

"I ain't in any damn hurry, Ranger," Morales said.

"I'll bet you're not," Jim answered.

"Just keep shut and get moving, Morales," Morton said. He took the prisoner by an elbow and pulled him out of the chair. "Move, mister."

Morales shrugged. Hampered by the shackles restraining his movements, he shuffled along, with the guard pushing him as quickly as possible, Jim and Bruce just behind. When they reached the sally port, Jim unlocked his truck and opened the right rear passenger door.

"Get inside," Morton ordered. Jim stopped him.

"Not quite so fast, guard," he said. "I want his

handcuffs taken off, then his hands cuffed behind his back before he gets in my truck."

"You must be damn crazy, Ranger, thinkin' I'm gonna sit with my hands cuffed behind me for over seven hundred miles," Morales protested.

"Guard, do it, then shove him in the truck. Belt him in once he's sitting down," Jim said. "Morales, it doesn't matter to me what you want. You're not getting the chance to try'n wrap those cuffs around me or my partner's necks. You give either of us the least bit of trouble, and I mean one bit, and I'll hogtie you and toss you belly-down in the back of my vehicle. Or even better, tie you to the roof like a damn trussed up wild hog."

"You wouldn't dare," Morales said.

"Try me," Jim snapped.

Morales started to frame a retort, then thought better of it. He meekly allowed the guard to cuff his hands behind his back, then ease him into Jim's truck and fasten his seat belt.

"He's ready to go," Morton said. "Have a safe trip. It's a long way to Las Cruces."

"It sure is. A long way with a lot of desert country, where an escaped prisoner can just disappear and never be seen again. It would be a real shame if that happened to Mr. Morales, here."

"It sure would," Morton agreed. He slammed the back door shut, as Jim and Bruce got into the

Tahoe. "Open the gate," he radioed to the outside guard.

"We're on our way, Bruce," Jim said, as the Tahoe cleared the gate and it closed behind them.

"These are your stomping grounds, Bruce," Jim said, as they drove away from the jail. "Quickest way around Dallas from here the Rayburn Tollway and 121 to 20?"

"Dallas traffic is always a crap shoot, at best, but that's the route I'd use," Bruce answered.

"Then that's what we'll do," Jim answered. "I'm gonna clear the way a bit, until we get on the highway."

He switched on the red and blue strobe lights hidden behind the Tahoe's grille, and gave an occasional quick hit on its siren, until they got off U.S. 75 and merged onto the Sam Rayburn Tollway. Once they rolled past the toll booths, he switched off the siren, but left the strobes flashing as he settled to a steady eighty miles per hour.

"I can see why you told the warden you'd make up the time," Bruce said.

"I'm holding back until we get past Fort Worth," Jim said. "Once traffic thins out, then we can really get movin'. I intend to make Las Cruces before dark."

"At this rate, you'll get there earlier than we left," Bruce answered, laughing. "Don't forget, we do gain an hour when we cross into Mountain Time."

"I know," Jim said. "With all the miles ahead of us, I need some music. You have any preferences?"

"What've you got?"

"Unless you want to try and find something decent on the radio, I've got Mike Blakely, Wylie and the Wild West, Chris LeDoux, Michael Martin Murphey, or Emmy Lou Harris all uploaded and ready to go."

"In this vehicle? It's the state's."

"Yup. Had to get the D.P.S. to let me put in the system, and, of course, I had to pay for it, but since I'm in this thing so much, it was worth every penny. So, any preference?"

"Not really. The only one I've heard of is Emmy Lou Harris. Go ahead and play whatever you want."

"Okay, I'll start with Mike Blakcly. I've got his *Rarest of the Breed* album all uploaded and ready to go. There's a Texas Ranger song on it I think you'll enjoy. You might as well relax and enjoy the music, Bruce. Just don't forget our friend behind you in the back seat."

"There's not a chance of that, Jim," Bruce assured him.

Jim switched on the music upload. After three of Mike Blakely's songs had played, Morales began complaining.

"Am I gonna have to listen to this damn cowboy crap all the way to New Mexico?"

"Yup," Jim answered. "Just wait awhile. You're in for a real treat. Soon as we get past Fort Worth and out of the city traffic, I'll start singing along. My voice has been known to make grown men cry."

"Morales, please, whatever you do, don't make him start singing," Bruce pleaded. "He's right, his voice does make men cry—cry in pain, their ears hurt so bad. I've heard him sing, and believe me, you don't want to. For both of our sakes, just keep shut."

"Now you've hurt my feelings, Bruce," Jim said. "You're too late, anyway. The next song up is *Go Easy*. That's the song about a frontier Texas Ranger, and I can't help but sing along with that one."

"Lord help us. Here he goes," Bruce muttered, as Jim accompanied the music coming from the speakers.

Once they cleared the suburbs of Fort Worth, Jim picked up speed.

"You do realize you're going a hundred miles an hour, don't you?" Bruce asked.

"That's one of the best parts of the job, bein' able to drive fast," Jim answered. He grinned. "I'm holding back a bit, because traffic's a little heavy today."

"Do you plan on stopping at all?"

"Yeah, we'll have to stop for fuel at least once. We'll be at Big Spring in a little under three hours. That's a bit less than halfway to Las Cruces. We'll stop there for gas, a quick bite, and a bathroom break. We'll switch drivers there, too. You'll take over the wheel. After that, it's straight through to New Mexico."

"We're coming up on Big Spring," Jim said, about three hours later. "Our stop's two exits ahead."

"It's about time," Morales grumbled from the back seat. "I need to take a leak so bad, my bladder's about to bust."

"You're lucky I can't make Las Cruces on one tank of gas, or we wouldn't be stopping at all," Jim answered. "I've still got a couple cans of cashews and six or seven cans of Dr Pepper left. That's all I need to make the rest of this trip."

"Well, as much as I hate to agree with our friend back there, Jim, I'm also mighty grateful we have to stop," Bruce said. "My belly's been complaining for the last fifty miles, and I need to pee real bad, too."

"That's good, because *you* get to take Morales to use the men's room while I fuel up, Bruce."

"Me? Why not you?"

"Because he was picked up in B's territory, so he's all yours," Jim answered, then laughed. "Got ya. I wouldn't send you in alone. We'll both go in with him, soon as I fill the tank. Here's our exit now."

Jim pulled off the highway and onto the I20 frontage road. While they waited for the red light to change, he pointed to a building just ahead, in front of which were two signs on one signpost, one for a Conoco station and convenience store, the one below it reading "Tico's Tacos," and which included a large working analog clock.

"Tico's Tacos?" Bruce said, raising an eyebrow.

"Yup. I generally stop here whenever I'm out this way. The food's decent, and the service is fast, plus the place is small. That means we won't disturb many people by bringing a prisoner inside. Also, the bathroom is only one toilet, and has no window, so our friend, here, won't be able to try'n sneak out the back way. We'll be in and out real quick."

"Okay, but what's with the clock on the sign?"

"Simple. American clocks go 'tick tock,' Mexican clocks go 'tico taco.' At least that's what the owner tells me," Jim answered with a laugh.

"But the proper pronunciation is 'teak-o,' not 'tick-o,'" Bruce objected.

"If you want to tell Enrique that, go right ahead," Jim said, as the light turned green and he put the Tahoe into motion. "I'm sure not going to. No secret sauce in my tacos for me."

"You're messed up, Jim. I hope you know that," Bruce said.

"So I've been told, many times," Jim answered. He pulled up to a pump and turned off the truck. "Soon as I fill the tank, we'll eat. Morales, you can order whatever you'd like. The state of Texas is paying, and it's probably the last decent meal you'll have, at least one that isn't prison food, for a long time to come."

Once the Tahoe was fueled, Jim pulled into a space at the side of the lot. After all three men were out of the vehicle, Jim took the cuffs off Morales, allowed him to wave his arms and flex his wrists and fingers, then replaced the handcuffs, with Morales's hands now in front of him, so he would be able to unzip his trousers to use the toilet, and have them free to eat.

"Let's go," he said.

"Ranger Blawcyzk! *Hola!*" the man behind the counter shouted when they walked in. "It has been too long, *mi amigo*. Rosita, look who is here."

"Ranger Blawcyzk," the owner's daughter said. "It's good to see you."

"*Hola*, Enrique, Rosita," Jim called back. "You're both right, it *has* been too long. This is my fellow Ranger, Bruce Sherman. The other man is Mr. Morales. We're taking him back to New Mexico, where he is wanted."

"So I see," Enrique answered, glancing at

Morales's shackles. "Well, if it is permitted, I'll prepare him a delicious lunch to remember Texas by."

"Of course it is, Enrique. The state will even pay for it. We'll use the men's room, then place our orders."

"*Bueno*, Ranger."

Emilio turned his attention to another customer.

"Morales, don't take too long in there, and don't lock the door," Jim warned, as he opened the men's room door. "There's no other way out, and you sure don't want us to have to shoot the lock open to get you out of there."

"Ranger, all I want is to get to Las Cruces and away from your damned cowboy music," Morales retorted. "I never thought I'd say this, but the sooner I'm back behind bars, the better. I'd rather rot in jail than have to hear you sing, ever again."

"He has a point, Jim," Bruce said, chuckling.

"You can always walk home, Bruce," Jim retorted.

Once they had taken care of necessary business, the three men took a booth in the far back corner, where Morales's shackles would not be as noticeable to the other patrons. Rosita came over to take their orders.

"Your usual, Ranger Blawcyzk?"

"Si, Rosita. The Number Three combo, and an extra-large Dr Pepper."

"Do you want me to save you a banana swirl cheesecake burrito? We're almost out."

"*Por favor.*"

"Whipped cream and powdered sugar on top?"

"You've got it. *Gracias*, Rosita. And a couple of bags of Claey's sassafras hard candy to take along. That stuff's not easy to find."

"Bueno. How about you, Ranger?"

"I'll have the Number Six, and a bottle of mineral water," Bruce answered. "No dessert for me, thanks. Just coffee when you bring Ranger Blawcyzk's cheesecake. I'll watch his arteries clog."

Rosita laughed.

"Very good. And you, sir?"

"Is there a limit, Ranger?" Morales asked.

"Not as far as I'm concerned," Jim answered.

"Good. *Senorita*, I'll have a steak quesadilla, fish taco, dos pollo y arroz burritos, a side of nachos grande, and one of those strawberry cheesecake swirls, and a banana one, like the Ranger's having. Plus a pot of coffee, black."

He looked directly at Jim and Bruce.

"Do you have a problem with that, either of you?"

"Don't ask me," Bruce said. "Jim's in charge of this little expedition. Of course, so much for getting out of here quick. It'll take you a while to eat all that."

"I have none, except don't forget we won't be stopping again until we reach Las Cruces," Jim said. "I hope you can hold all that for another three or four hours."

"I'll manage," Morales answered.

"It could have been worse, Jim," Bruce said. "He could have ordered a plate of refried beans, and bean burritos."

"Not while he's ridin' in my vehicle, he wouldn't," Jim said.

Forty-five minutes later, they had finished their meal. Morales's hands were once again cuffed behind his back. Bruce got him into the back seat. When he leaned in front of the prisoner to buckle him in, Morales head-butted him, the top of his skull hitting Bruce directly on his left temple. Stunned, Bruce was still able to recover and drive a vicious right hook into Morales's gut. Morales doubled over, until the shoulder belt locked, holding him half upright. He began gagging. Bruce backed out of the truck, his hat knocked askew and a trickle of blood running from the split open skin over his temple.

"You didn't see that, did you, Jim?"

"See what? I didn't see a damn thing. Are you okay, Bruce?" Jim answered.

"Yeah, I'm all right. You'd better check on Morales," Bruce answered.

"That was pretty stupid, Morales," Jim said. "I warned you not to stir up trouble. You gonna puke up your lunch?"

Still trying to catch his breath and unable to speak, Morales merely shook his head.

"He's all right, Bruce, but if he starts pukin' all over my truck, you're gonna clean it up. That'll teach you not to relax, and get too close to an *hombre*, even one who's shackled."

"Yeah. I screwed up, dammit," Bruce said. He pulled out his handkerchief to dab at the blood running down his cheek.

"We've all screwed up, most of us plenty of times," Jim said. "Don't worry about it. No real harm done. I'd better get the first aid kit, clean out that cut, and bandage it up."

"That's not necessary," Bruce protested.

"I'm not worried about you. I just don't want you to get any blood on my truck," Jim said. "It'll only take me a minute."

He got the first aid kit from the back of his Tahoe, then had Bruce sit on the tailgate.

"This won't take long," Jim said. "All it needs is some antiseptic and a bandage."

He opened an antiseptic wipe, used it to wipe the blood away from the cut, then taped a bandage over it.

"It's already turning black and blue, Bruce. Starting to swell, too. You'll have a nice lump there for a couple of days. You still gonna be

183

able to drive? You're not feeling dizzy, as if you might've gotten a concussion?"

"No, I feel fine, just damn stupid. If you're finished, give me the keys, and we can get movin' again. Just realize I won't drive quite as fast as you've been."

"All right, but if you start to feel sick, you pull over."

"It's a deal, Jim."

Jim handed the keys to Bruce, who got in the driver's seat, and adjusted it to his height, arm and leg lengths. Once he was settled, and Jim got in the passenger seat, Bruce started the Tahoe, put it in gear, and rolled back onto the interstate.

"She's all yours, Bruce," Jim said. He pulled his hat low over his eyes and leaned against the side window. Before five minutes had passed, he was sound asleep.

Bruce glanced in the rearview mirror to check on Morales, who was staring out his window, somewhere into the distance. He then looked at Jim and shook his head.

"And you told me not to let down my guard, Jim," he muttered. "Yet, there you are, sound asleep. Aw, hell, I guess it doesn't matter. And at least I won't have to listen to your caterwaulin'."

Bruce shut off the sound system and pressed down on the accelerator, until the Tahoe reached eighty-five, then put it in cruise.

"Ah, blissful peace," he murmured. "Let's hope he sleeps all the way to New Mexico."

"Jim, wake up," Bruce said, softly. "End of the road. We're pulling up to the Dona Ana County Detention Center."

Jim opened his eyes, pushed back his hat, and blinked.

"You mean to tell me I slept all the way from Big Spring?"

"You sure did, except for a couple of times when you woke up, warned me to watch my driving, then went right back to sleep. You've got a lot of nerve, telling anyone how to drive, considering the way you manhandle a vehicle."

"Sorry, Bruce. I must've been more tired than I realized. I take it Morales didn't give you any trouble?"

"No, he fell asleep not long after you did. I got tied up in some traffic just before El Paso, but that was about it."

Bruce pulled up to the guardhouse at the prison's main gate. When the guard on duty came out, he rolled down his window.

"Howdy," he said.

"Good afternoon," the guard answered. "Please state your business."

"Of course," Bruce said. "Texas Rangers Bruce Sherman and James Blawcyzk. We've got a prisoner for you, Antonio Morales. We'll also

185

be picking up three men to take back to Texas."

"Ah, yes. We've been expecting you, Ranger. If you'll just show me your papers, I'll pass you through the gate."

"Of course."

Bruce took Jim's papers from him, then handed both sets to the guard.

"These seem to be in order," the guard said, after examining the documents. He handed them back to Bruce. "When I open the gate, you'll see another vehicle door, across the courtyard. I'll call the guard at that door and have her open the gate. Honk twice, and she'll let you in. She'll bring you to the warden's office."

"Much obliged," Bruce said. He waited for the gate to open, then drove across the yard. Once he blew the Tahoe's horn twice, the armored door slid open, then closed behind the truck as soon as he drove in. He pulled into a space the guard indicated.

"Here's your keys back, Jim," he said, removing them from the ignition and handing them over.

"You just knew I wanted them back, didn't you?" Jim answered, with a grin.

"Yep. Let's get Morales turned over so we can find some supper and get some rest," Bruce answered.

"That sounds reasonable to me."

"Welcome to Las Cruces, Rangers," the guard

said, once they were out of the truck. "I'm Corrections Officer Sergeant Denise Claxton. I'll escort you and the prisoner to Warden Hernandez."

"Ranger James Blawcyzk, and my partner, Ranger Bruce Sherman," Jim answered. "Much obliged. I'll have him out in a minute."

He opened the Tahoe's rear passenger door, unbuckled Morales, and helped him out of the truck. He handed Claxton three clear plastic, sealed bags.

"Those are Hays County prison uniforms for the men we're picking up, as well as the restraints we'll be using."

"You don't object if I examine the contents, do you?"

"Not at all. We'd expect you to."

"Thank you."

Claxton opened the bags, and went through their contents.

"There's no contraband, not that I expected any," she said. "I'll take you to the warden now."

"Lead the way, Sergeant."

"Follow me."

Claxton led the three men through several sets of locked, armored doors and three hallways, until they reached the warden's office. She slid her magnetic card and entered a passcode in the sensor alongside the door, which granted access to a small, unfurnished room. She pushed the button on an intercom box, looked at the camera suspended from the ceiling, and waited for an answer.

"Yes?" came a voice over the intercom.

"Sergeant Claxton, Warden. The Rangers have arrived with Morales."

"Very good. Bring them in."

Once the lock clicked, Claxton opened the door, and they went into the warden's office.

"Gentlemen, I'm Warden Raphael Hernandez. I'm pleased to see you've arrived safely."

Hernandez came from behind his desk to shake hands.

"Ranger James Blawcyzk, and my partner, Bruce Sherman."

"And Antonio Morales. Welcome back home, Mr. Morales," Hernandez said.

"Yeah," Morales muttered.

"I knew you'd be thrilled," Hernandez said. "Did he give you any trouble, Rangers?"

Jim and Bruce glanced at each other before Bruce answered.

"No, he just got a little carsick, that's all. He slept most of the way."

"That's good. Sergeant, take Mr. Morales to check-in, then his cell. The Rangers and I can handle the transfer papers. He doesn't need to be here."

"Yessir, Warden. Morales, come with me."

"Am I allowed to say something first?" Morales asked.

"As long as it's brief," Hernandez said.

"*Gracias*, Warden."

Morales turned to face Jim and Bruce.

"I just wanted to thank these two Rangers for treating me halfway decently, like a human being. They didn't have to do that, especially since . . ." Morales stopped when Jim shook his head. "Anyway, I've made a lot of mistakes, and I wouldn't have blamed either of you if you'd treated me like dirt. So, I just wanted to say I'm grateful, especially for the meal."

"You're welcome," Jim said. "Least we could have done. And we're obliged you were so cooperative. A lot of men headed for a long stretch in prison, or worse, wouldn't have been. Good luck to you."

"The same from me, Morales," Bruce added. "Good luck."

"You've said your piece, Morales. Get movin'," Claxton said. She shoved him out of the office.

"Gentlemen, please be seated," Hernandez said, once the door closed. "I trust you have the transfer papers."

"Got 'em right here," Jim said. He removed the papers from the manila file folder he held, and slid them across the warden's desk. Hernandez put on a pair of reading glasses, and looked over the forms.

"These seem to be in order," he said. "Once we've signed them, the first part of our business will be completed."

"Then comes the main part," Jim said.

"Yes. Unfortunately, as you know, we won't be able to complete the paperwork on the men we're extraditing back to Texas until morning, when they'll actually be leaving Dona Ana County's custody. However, I have it right here."

Hernandez tapped his finger on three files on the corner of his desk.

"Dean Elliott Suggs, Walter Adams Creighton, and Donald John Tyler. All accused of murder, cattle theft, and various other charges. You men, and the state of Texas, are more than welcome to them. I'll be here in my office at 7:30 tomorrow morning, so you can get a somewhat early start. Now, let's attend to the business of Mr. Morales."

"Okay," Jim said. He, Bruce, and the warden signed the papers, then shook hands.

"There are bunks you can use for the night if you want," Hernandez offered. "Plus, the food in the staff cafeteria's actually pretty decent. You'd be more than welcome."

"Thank you, but I reckon not," Jim answered. "It's been a long day, and tomorrow promises to be an even longer one. We'll get a motel room for the night, and a good supper. But we do appreciate the offer."

"I completely understand," Hernandez said. "I'll summon a guard to escort you back to your car. I'll see you in the morning."

"That'll be fine, Warden," Jim said.

Hernandez pushed a button on his phone, and told the person who answered to send in a guard, who arrived a few minutes later.

"Freeman, these are Texas Rangers Blawcyzk and Sherman. Please accompany them back to their vehicle."

"Of course, Warden," the guard replied.

"Rangers, until tomorrow," Hernandez said.

"*Manana*," Jim replied.

"Do you have anyplace in particular you want to spend the night, Bruce?" Jim asked, as they drove away from the jail. "How about supper?"

"Not really, on both," Bruce answered. "This is the first time I've ever been in this town, except for driving through it on the way to someplace else."

"I don't have anyplace picked out, either," Jim said. "There's a whole bunch of motels and restaurants at Exit 141 off I10. I'll just get off the highway there, and we'll choose one that's decent, but not too expensive."

"And has vacancies," Bruce answered.

"That's a given."

Jim drove the short distance to his desired exit. The state of Texas had arranged discount

191

programs with several of the major hotel/motel chains, since distances across the Lone Star State were so vast overnight travel was often necessary when conducting state business. Jim chose the one of those nearest the exit, and which had a Texas Roadhouse alongside it.

"Bruce, as soon as we check in, I'm headin' over to the Roadhouse," Jim said, as he parked. "I'm gonna pick out the biggest steak they've got in the case, have one of those giant deep-fried onion things they've got, and eat about a dozen of their rolls, drenched with that honey-cinnamon butter that's so good. I could make a meal out of those rolls alone. I'll have a salad and fries with the steak, which'll be smothered in onions. Then I'll have supper."

Bruce looked askance at his fellow Ranger.

"You're kidding, right?"

"Yeah . . . about having supper afterwards," Jim answered. "Let's get our room."

The front desk clerk looked up from the newspaper she was reading when Jim and Bruce walked into the lobby. She gave a slight start when she saw them. It wasn't every day two young, good-looking Texas Rangers, wearing their badges and guns, along with their required white cowboy hats, light colored dress shirts, neckties, neatly pressed slacks, and polished western boots walked into a motel in Las Cruces,

New Mexico. However, the young woman quickly regained her composure.

"Good evening, gentlemen. Welcome to Las Cruces. Are you in need of accommodations?"

"Yes, ma'am, we are," Jim answered. "One room, two beds, if possible on the ground floor with a parking space for our vehicle, right in front of the door."

The clerk checked her computer monitor.

"I have something for you. Room 110, in the front of the building, a few doors down to the right. We are a non-smoking facility. I hope that's not a problem."

"Not at all," Jim answered. "We belong to a non-smoking organization."

"Wonderful. I'll just need your information, including your vehicle description and license plate number, positive photos I.D.s, and a credit card to place on file. The rate is $109.00 per night, plus tax. How long will you be staying with us?"

"Just one night," Jim answered. "Also, your hotel chain has discounted rates for State of Texas employees. I'll be paying with a state credit card."

"All right, let me look that up for you, Ranger," the clerk answered. She typed some more information into her computer. "Here we go. A twenty per cent discount. If you'll just fill out the registration form while I run your card, you'll be in your room in only a few moments."

"Of course," Jim said. He took his credit card from his wallet and handed it to the clerk, along with his Ranger identification card, then began filling out the registration form. Bruce also passed her his Ranger I.D.

"Here's your key cards, Ranger Blaw—" the clerk said, once she had finished checking them in.

"BLUH-zhick," Jim helped. "And Ranger Sherman."

"Thank you, Ranger Blawcyzk," the clerk said. She handed him back his credit card, along with two key cards. "The Wi-fi password is in the envelope with your keys. Vending is just off the lobby. We have a fitness center and indoor pool, if you'd like to take advantage of those. We include free breakfast with the price of your room. We offer scrambled eggs, bacon, sausage, and waffles, along with an assortment of pastries and muffins, plus unlimited coffee, tea, juice, and milk. Our breakfast room opens at six, and remains available until nine. Is there anything else I can do for you?"

"I don't believe so," Jim answered. "We're just looking for a good night's sleep, since we have to get an early start in the morning."

"Well, I can assure you both of that," the clerk answered. "If you do need any assistance, just dial the front desk. And please, have a pleasant stay."

194

"Thank you, ma'am. We'll do just that," Bruce said. "Let's go, Jim."

It only took a moment for Jim to locate Room 110. He backed his Tahoe into the parking space in front of the room, then he and Bruce got their duffle bags from the rear of the truck. Jim unlocked the room and turned on the lights.

"This isn't bad at all," Bruce said as they went inside. "The a/c needs to be turned down, though. It's a bit stuffy in here."

"What did you expect?" Jim answered, with a laugh. "It's the New Mexico desert in summertime. I'll crank it down."

"I'd appreciate that."

"Which bed do you prefer?" Jim asked.

"It doesn't really matter," Bruce answered. "I'm not particular."

"Me, neither," Jim said. "One motel room's pretty much the same as another. You'll learn that when you've been with the Rangers for a while. Tell you what. I'll take the one by the window, you can have the other. That'll give you control of the TV remote."

"That's fine with me," Bruce said. He tossed his duffle on the bed he'd be using, removed his hat and loosened his tie.

"I'm gonna clean up a bit. Soon as I'm done, you can wash up too, then we'll go eat."

"All right," Jim said. When Bruce went into the bathroom and closed the door, Jim stretched out on his bed. He idly flicked on the television, and tuned it to the local news.

"Let's see what's happening in this neck of the woods," he muttered.

When they returned to their room after supper, Bruce took off his hat, tie, gunbelt, and boots, then plopped down on his bed. He turned on the television, and searched the channels until he found a Rangers game. Jim opened his laptop, sat down at the desk, and began working on a file.

"Jim, it's been a long day for both of us, and tomorrow promises to be an even longer one," Bruce said. "Eight or more hours on the road, keeping an eye on three suspected murderers the entire time, isn't something I'm really looking forward to. Why don't you shut that thing off, relax, and watch the ball game? If you're still hungry, although I don't see how you can be after what you ate for supper, I've got the chips, pretzels, and beer I picked up at the Quickie Mart while you were fueling the truck. Whatever you're working on can wait until we're back home."

"Uh-uh." Jim shook his head. "I'm still tryin' to figure out if there was anything I could have done to keep the Holsclaw boy from being shot. I haven't yet turned in my final report, and I won't until I've figured out what I might've missed.

There has to be something more I could've done."

"Jim, you're becoming obsessed with that day," Bruce answered. "I've been told it's starting to affect your work, and now I can see for myself it probably is. You've got to let it go."

"I can't, Bruce. I just can't. What happened is a monster eating at my guts, and it *won't* let go. It's tearing me apart inside. But that doesn't mean I can't do my job. I'm fine. I just need a bit more time to work this out."

"In the meantime, while you try and 'work this out,' it could cost you your job, or even your marriage and family," Bruce warned.

"What the hell are you talking about?"

"Exactly what just happened. I'm trying to be a friend and help you out, here, but you damn near bit my head off."

"Only because I'm tired after the drive, and you're keeping me from getting any work done. I want to go over some more of my cases before I turn in for the night. You go ahead and watch the game. Wait a minute. What do you mean, I could lose my family? And just what the hell do you mean that 'you've been told what happened to the Holsclaw boy is starting to affect my work?' "

"Just what I said. You know Kelle and Kim talk on the phone all the time. They tell each other everything. Your wife's told mine she's at her wit's end, because you spend hardly any time with her or your baby nowadays."

"Don't give me that bull. Kim and I had many long talks before we got engaged. She knew exactly what she was getting into when she married a Ranger. I made it clear to her that I'd be gone a lot, and working crazy hours. She said she understood. Did your wife happen to mention there's plenty of times I've been alone, while Kim's been working late, or off on a business trip or at a conference? I'll bet she didn't. Besides, Kim hasn't said anything to me."

"According to what she's told Kelle, she's tried, but you won't listen. Jim, I know how much time being a Ranger takes away from your family life. As short a time as I've been one, it didn't take me long to learn that. But, you can't let this job take over your every waking minute. It'll end up killing you if you do. I've learned that already, too, but it seems like you haven't. No one is Superman, not even you."

"I'll know when I've been working too hard," Jim objected.

"You already are, and you don't even realize it," Bruce answered. "You're worn out. Look what happened on the way here. First you drive like a madman. Then, as soon as I took over the wheel, you went right to sleep, and basically didn't wake up until I called you. If Morales had somehow gotten loose, he could have strangled you before I could've done a thing about it. You're irritable, you look like hell, and unless I miss my guess, you'll collapse from exhaustion and be in a hospital bed before the month's out."

"I've heard enough," Jim said.

"No, I don't think you have," Bruce answered. "I didn't want to tell you this, but I guess I'd better. I'm not along on this trip just to keep you company. Your boss, Major Voitek, asked my boss, Major Hough, to send me along on this trip, and let them know how I thought you were doing. Hell, you know damn well it doesn't take two men to transport a few prisoners."

"So you're spying on me. All the while, I thought you were a good guy, and a friend, especially after you pretty much solved the murders of those elderly women, which had me stumped. Instead, I find out you're an informant. Thanks a lot, pal. Boy howdy, if that don't beat all."

"Jim, you might find this hard to believe, but I *am* a friend," Bruce said. "Would you rather Major Voitek had sent along another man, one who barely knows you, if he knows you at all? Or maybe someone who doesn't like you one bit, and would hang you out to dry in a minute, just for the hell of it? At least I'll give you every break I can. You know I learned to respect you, and to like you, when we were working together on those murders. However, you've got to try and help me, here. I really want to report you're doing all right, that you're just a bit overtired, along with stressed from seeing the Holsclaw boy gunned down right in front of you, but that there's no need to place you on medical leave. Right now, all I can think of when I watch you is one of the lyrics from the old Hank Snow song *90 Miles an Hour Down a Dead-End Street.* You're like a bad motorcycle with a devil in the seat, headed straight for a crack-up into a stone wall."

"So what do you want me to do? Just up and quit? Or be forced to take medical leave, and have sessions with a psychiatrist? Doin' either one would end my career as a Texas Ranger faster'n any outlaw's bullet."

"You're not listening to me either, Jim, just like your wife says you won't listen to her. As far as I can see, you're still capable of doing your job, but you won't be for much longer, not if you keep goin' the way you are. You *have* to slow down, before you make a mistake that *does* cost you your job, or worse. I'm giving you a chance to do just that, and you can get started, right now. Just turn off that laptop, close it, and have a couple of beers with me while we watch the game. Then get some more sleep."

"I've been a Ranger for more than three years now, and I'm being told what to do by an *hombre*, a rookie who's been one less than six months," Jim grumbled, more to himself than to Bruce.

"That's right. And if you want to be a Ranger for a lot more years, you've got to take my advice, Jim. So what do you say?"

Jim sighed, and his shoulders slumped.

"Jim?"

Jim glared at Bruce, then slammed his laptop closed.

"Hand me one of those damn beers."

"Now you're talking," Bruce answered. He popped open a can and gave it to Jim.

7

Bruce was standing in front of the mirror, shaving. The two men had argued well into the night, not only over Jim's fitness to keep working, without taking a leave of absence, but also whether or not the Texas Rangers baseball team would make it to the World Series. When the tied, fifteen inning game finally ended, they had lost another close one. It was past midnight when Jim and Bruce finally turned in.

"Still friends, I hope," Bruce said through a lip full of shaving cream as Jim came from the shower.

"We were, until you beat me to the shower," Jim answered, grinning. "You forgot protocol, that the senior Ranger has first dibs on the shower."

"Funny, I must have missed that in class, and I didn't see that regulation in the manual, either," Bruce said, laughing. "Listen, Jim, I know things got a little heated last night, but I hope everything's finally settled."

"It is as far as you and I are concerned, Bruce. As far as what happens, I'll just have to wait and see. Unless Major Voitek or Lieutenant Stoker forces me, I have no intention of taking any time off."

"I don't blame you there. Unless something drastic happens before we get home today, my report will say all you need to do is cut back a few hours, and you should be fine."

"But if we don't get to breakfast soon, I won't be," Jim said. "Let's hurry up and get down there so we can eat, then check out and be on our way. I'd like to be back home before it gets too late."

Jim pulled up to the prison gate just before seven-thirty. As the day before, the guard on duty at the gate examined their papers before allowing them to proceed, then another guard let them inside the sally port and took them to the warden's office.

"Good morning, Rangers," Hernandez greeted them. "You're right on time. I hope you got a good night's rest."

"We've got a long drive ahead of us, so we want to get rolling," Jim answered. "And yes, our room was quite comfortable. They had an excellent breakfast spread, too."

"That's good. Perhaps some day you'll be able to return to Las Cruces when you're not so pressed for time, and under more pleasant circumstances. I won't keep you. As soon as the paperwork is completed, your men will be turned over to you. They won't be brought to my office. The guards will bring them directly to your vehicle."

"That'll be just fine, Warden," Jim said.

"Good. Let's get started."

Hernandez opened the first of the three files. He passed that one to Jim, then opened the second and handed that one to Bruce, then took the third one for himself, to recheck it one last time before signing it.

It only took a short while for the three men to make certain the papers were in order, then sign them. Hernandez handed the Rangers' copies to Jim, along with a plastic bag marked "Evidence."

"That's the bullet the prison doc pulled out of Creighton," Hernandez said. "I sure hope it connects him and his partners to the crime scene."

"That makes two of us," Jim said.

"Everything's in order, and you're good to go," Hernandez said, as he leaned back in his chair. He picked up his telephone receiver and dialed an extension.

"This is Warden Hernandez," he said, to the person who answered. "You may bring the Texas transferees down now."

"You're all set," he said, as he hung up the phone. "Let's go."

Accompanied by two guards, Hernandez took Jim and Bruce back to the sally port. Ten minutes later, three prisoners were brought in, now wearing the Hays County prison uniforms and shackles Jim had brought.

"Here's your men, Ranger, and welcome to

'em," the apparent lead guard said. "They haven't exactly been model prisoners during their stay with us."

"We'll have them off your hands in just a couple of minutes," Jim said.

"Good." The guard handed Jim a package. "This is the uniform and shackles your prisoner was wearing. Sorry we didn't have time to clean them."

"That's not a problem," Jim said. "Bruce, would you mind putting these in the back of the truck? Open the rear doors, too, so we can get these *hombres* loaded."

"Not at all, after I check the contents, to make certain no contraband has been hidden in here," Bruce answered. He took the bundle from Jim, who used the remote to unlock his Tahoe.

"Suggs, you first," the lead guard ordered. He took Suggs by the elbow and brought him to Jim's truck. In short order, all three of the accused murderers were in the back seat, shackled hand and foot, as well as to each other, and buckled in.

"Thanks again to you and your staff, Warden," Jim said, as he slid behind the wheel. "We're on our way."

"We're obliged to you, for taking those three yahoos off our hands," Hernandez answered. "Have a safe trip home."

Jim closed his door and started the Tahoe. A short while later, he rolled back onto I10 east, heading for Texas. When his phone rang, he glanced at the number displayed on the dash-board screen, then answered.

"Ranger Blawcyzk. Good morning, Sheriff."

"*Buenas dias*, Ranger," Luna County Sheriff Jorge Calderon replied. "I just wanted to check that you have the prisoners, and also thank you for providing enough evidence for us to raid the Slash P Ranch yesterday. We discovered not only were they dealing in wet cows, the place was also being used to smuggle drugs and illegal aliens. My office is mighty grateful. That's the main reason I called. There were some threats heard about an attempt being made to help those men escape your custody. I wanted to warn you to be careful."

"I appreciate that, Sheriff. Yes, we have them, and we'll keep our eyes open for anything suspicious. *Gracias*. If you're ever around Austin, I'll take you out for some genuine Texas barbeque."

"And if you're ever near Luna County, I'll take you for some real chili, not that weak soup you Texans *claim* is chili."

"Careful how you talk about Texas chili. Them's fightin' words, Sheriff," Jim said, laughing. "But you're on. *Adios*."

"*Adios*, and *vaya con Dios*, Ranger."

Once they were on the highway, Jim glanced in the rearview mirror for a better look at the prisoners, who thus far hadn't spoken one word. All three appeared to be, or at one time had been, typical Texas ranchers or ranch hands. Two were white, one African-American. Even in their prison uniforms and close-cropped haircuts, they looked the part, at least to Jim's experienced eyes. Their faces were still leathery, their tans still evident, even under the prison pallor. Their hands were calloused from hard work.

"How far are we gonna go before you take a break, Jim?" Bruce asked.

"I'm not takin' a break," Jim answered. "Not with three cold-blooded murderers along. We can't take any chances of their making a break for it at a gas station or truck stop, especially after Sheriff Calderon's warning. I'll stop for fuel at either Fort Stockton or Ozona, that's it. We'll switch drivers there, and you can take it the rest of the way to San Marcos."

"You're plumb *loco*, Ranger," Creighton said. "You can't keep us cramped in this back seat for almost seven hundred miles."

"The hell I can't," Jim answered. "You think I'm worried about you *hombres'* comfort, after you killed two men, one of whom had a wife and two little kids? Think again. Besides, it's not gonna take us all that long. Soon as we cross back into Texas, I'll pick up the pace."

"You're going eighty-five already, Ranger," Tyler said. "Any faster and you'll kill us all."

"Besides, you can't go that far without allowin' us a bathroom break," Tyler said. "And you have to feed us."

"You'll get one somewhere alongside the road," Jim said. "We'll pull off onto one of the ranch roads. We'll feed you there, too, even though we really *don't* have to. There's a cooler full of sandwiches and drinks in the back. Picked those up this morning, so they'll still be fresh."

"Trust me, the trip'll be easier on you fellas if you just keep your mouths shut," Bruce said. "Jim, I hope you're gonna slow down, at least a little, through El Paso."

"Depends on the traffic," Jim answered.

Bruce's phone dinged, indicating he had a text. He took it out, read the message, and sent an answer.

"Good news, Jim, at least for you," he said. "Kelle took Marshall and Wyatt down to your place for the day. She and the boys are visiting with your wife and mom. The boys will get to do some horseback riding. Kelle will pick me up at your house, so you won't have to bring me all the way back to Rockwall after we get rid of these *hombres*."

"Another part of the plot to make me slow down, Bruce?" Jim said. "If it is, I just want to let you know—"

"Yeah, Jim?"

"That I appreciate it."

Bruce glared at Jim, laughed, then punched him lightly on the arm.

The first two hours went uneventfully, the only complaint voiced by one of the prisoners about Jim's choice of music. On the long upgrade outside of Sierra Blanca, traffic slowed to a near stop, then moved at a crawl. Jim already had his strobe lights flashing, and now added blares of his siren while he worked his way through the traffic.

"I wonder what the hold-up is," Bruce muttered. "I don't hear any chatter on the radio."

"I dunno, but this is a big mess," Jim said. "It doesn't help that the damn shoulders in this stretch aren't wide enough for me to get by. I'll just have to squeeze through the best I can."

"Don't hurry on our account, Ranger," Suggs said. "We ain't in any rush."

"I don't imagine you are," Jim said. "You mind tellin' me how you got into the mess you're in?"

"The damn banks, that's how," Tyler answered. "We were partners in a decent-sized spread. They took our ranch."

"Don't say anything more, Don," Creighton warned him. "Ranger, once we get into court, and tell our story, we'll walk out free men."

"Not if you're guilty," Jim said. "There was a lot of evidence left at the scene of the killings.

I should know, since I gathered most of it. It all points to you *hombres* being there."

He hit the siren again, at a particularly stubborn driver who refused to move over, hanging on the man's back bumper until he moved aside.

"I can see flashing lights about half-a-mile ahead, Jim," Bruce said. "There seems to be some sort of roadblock."

"Now I know what's goin' on," Jim said. "It's gotta be the damn Border Patrol. They must be checking for illegals again. They're fond of setting up on this hill, since trucks have to struggle up the grade. That makes it easier to stop any big rigs trying to run. Once we're past the checkpoint, we'll make up the time."

Five minutes later, they reached the checkpoint. One of the Border Patrol officers flagged them down. Jim rolled down his window.

"Good morning, sir," the officer said. "Sorry to inconvenience you, but we're checking all vehicles passing through this checkpoint. I can see you're a peace officer, however, I still had to stop you . . ."

"Understood," Jim said. He held up his I.D. "But we're hardly smuggling illegals. We're Texas Rangers, transporting three prisoners back from Las Cruces."

The officer glanced at the men in the back seat, then waved Jim forward.

"Have a good day, Ranger."

"You also."

Jim rolled up his window and jammed the Tahoe's accelerator to the floor.

Once they passed Van Horn, the one-hundred-twenty-mile section of interstate from there to Fort Stockton was mostly a long, straight stretch of road through desolate high desert, flat to rolling terrain interspersed with the occasional mesa or rocky hill. Just beyond Plateau, a townsite which had been established around a Texas and Pacific Railroad section house in the 1880s, had a Post Office by 1907, lost that in 1916, and died by 1940, the Tahoe began to swerve. Bruce frowned.

"Are you getting too tired to drive, Jim? Maybe you should have gotten off the last exit and taken a rest, or let me take over the driving."

"No, I'm doing fine. The wind's picking up, and pushing the truck around, that's all," Jim said, watching a dust devil crossing the highway. "It's getting a bit harder to hold the wheel. As far as stopping back in Plateau, there's nothing there but a small truck stop. The only people who live there own the place. That, and I seem to recollect a hardscrabble farm, which depends on deep well irrigation."

Just as he said this, two high-powered luxury cars, both with New York plates, passed, as if the Tahoe was standing still.

"That's probably why," Bruce said. "You're doing ninety, and those two Lexuses shot by like you were parked. We got caught in their slipstream."

"Lexii."

"What?"

"Lexii, Bruce. Just like cacti is the proper plural of cactus, and crocii is the proper plural of crocus, Lexii is the proper plural of Lexus."

"Jim, you're probably the only person in the world who gives a damn *what* the plural of Lexus is," Bruce said. "And it doesn't matter. Those drivers are in one helluva hurry."

"You want me to run 'em down and ask why?"

"No, I just want you to keep this thing between the ditches. Although you don't reckon they could be part of the escape attempt Sheriff Calderon warned us about, do you?"

"I doubt it," Jim said. "The cars are too flashy, and they're already out of sight. Plus, if they were going to try and run us off the road, this would be the place to do it. It doesn't get any more isolated along this highway than right through here."

"Then just keep this vehicle on the pavement, all right?"

"Okay, if it'll make you happy, I'll do that," Jim said. "Matter of fact, this wind's starting to blow so hard I've gotta slow down. It's giving me no choice." He glanced off to his right, where dust was beginning to rise on the stiffening gusts. "I just hope we're not gonna end up drivin' into a dust storm. It's pretty weird that the wind's blowing this hard out of the south, too, especially this time of year. Usually wind this strong is out of the north or northwest, meaning a dry front is coming through. It's way too early in the year for a blue norther."

"Might be we'll run into some wicked thunderstorms," Bruce said.

"Let's hope not," Jim answered. "With the dust being stirred up, that would mean raining mud. Ah, here we go, time for a tumbleweed demolition derby. I figured one was about due."

The wind was driving scores of tumbleweeds across the highway, which were actually the above ground portion of an invasive plant called Russian thistle, that detached when the plant died, then, driven by the wind, "tumbled," dispersing their seeds. They disintegrated when Jim's truck struck them, the pieces flying away with the wind.

He eased back on the accelerator until the speedometer settled on seventy. They'd gone about another three miles when trouble hit.

Jim was passing an eighteen-wheeler, a moving van that had been struggling against the wind. A strong gust pushed the rig into Jim's lane, then it started to topple, when the full force of the wind hit the apparently empty trailer.

"Jim, look out!" Bruce shouted. "That damn thing's gonna crush us."

Concentrating on keeping his vehicle under

control as it was buffeted by the wind, Jim didn't answer. He swerved hard to the left, at the same time gunning the Tahoe's engine. The big V8 responded instantly, sending the heavy truck rocketing forward like a spooked wild stallion. When Jim drove onto the median, the Tahoe bucked and bounced as crazily as if it indeed *was* a locoed mustang. The truck cleared the front of the moving van just as the trailer tipped completely on its side, taking the tractor with it. Barely keeping the Tahoe from tipping over itself, Jim maneuvered back onto the pavement.

"Ranger, in front of you!" Creighton, who was seated in the middle of the back seat, yelled.

"I see it!" Jim said. Directly in his path was another eighteen-wheeler, this one jackknifing, its tires squealing and smoking as its driver struggled to keep it under control and bring it to a stop. Jim manhandled his truck into the right lane, then had to swerve off the pavement and onto the shoulder. Directly in front of him were several vehicles, including the two New York cars which had blown past him a few miles back. The lead Lexus was braking to a hard stop. The driver of the following one was unable to stop in time, and plowed into the rear of the first. Three more cars and a dually pickup crashed into them, then the tractor-trailer, skidding sideways and blocking both lanes, slammed into the wreckage.

Jim barely caught a glimpse of any of the mayhem as he skirted around it. He was too busy trying to keep the Tahoe under control on the rutted, sandy shoulder, praying that he could get it stopped before it hit a soft patch of dirt or deeper rut and flipped over. Once it had slowed sufficiently, Jim spun the truck in a one-eighty. It came to a stop in a billow of dust, facing the wreck.

"Bruce, you all right?" he asked.

"Yeah, seem to be. I'm just a bit shaken up. Damn, that was too close. That was some driving, Jim."

"How about you men in the back?"

He was answered with a string of curses, some uncomplimentary remarks about his driving ability, and a comment from Tyler about dying before ever getting to prison.

"Good. Bruce, call this in, and keep an eye on our prisoners. I'm gonna go help those other folks."

"Sure thing, Jim."

While Bruce radioed dispatch, Jim grabbed his first aid kit and dashed toward the wrecked vehicles. People were already emerging from them, some bloodied, others only dazed. The eighteen-wheeler driver was already out of his cab. He, two other men, and a woman were trying to wrench open the doors of one of the wrecked vehicles, which was smoking, apparently from a fire under the crumpled hood. One of them spotted Jim.

"Officer! We need help over here. There are two people trapped in this car."

Jim hurried over. A quick look told him there was no possible way to pry the doors of the demolished compact sedan open without the Jaws of Life or a metal cutting saw.

"Stand back!" he ordered. He took his Ruger 1911 out of its holster, wrapped his handkerchief around the gun, and used its butt to smash open the driver's window. After knocking out the last shards of glass, Jim reached in for the elderly driver.

"Are you pinned, or will I be able to pull you out through the window?" he asked.

"I don't think I'm pinned, but could you get my wife first?"

"The fire's starting to spread. There's not enough time to bust out the other window," Jim said. "Ma'am, once I have your husband out, will you be able to crawl across the seat so I can pull you out this side?"

"I believe so. My foot was caught under the dashboard for a moment, but I've worked it free."

"*Bueno.*" Jim pulled the driver out, then his wife. Neither appeared to have suffered any serious injuries, aside from cuts and bruises.

"That was great work, Ranger," the person who had called to Jim said.

Jim gave a nod of acknowledgement. "These folks don't seem to be hurt too badly. Get them to the side of the road, where they'll be safe from any oncoming vehicles, and stay with them until EMS arrives. The rest of you, come with me, while I see how many others need help."

The next hour was complete chaos. It took nearly twenty minutes for the initial state trooper to arrive, followed shortly by the first ambulances, fire apparatus, and rescue unit, which came from Van Horn, the nearest town, more than twenty-five miles to the west. Other help had to come from volunteer departments in small towns such as Balmorhea, with more ambulances and rescue personnel arriving from as far away as the nearest city, Pecos, seventy miles to the east. Until they arrived, Jim was on his own, except for the help from a few civilians who had escaped the wreck unharmed, and a number of passersby who stopped to offer assistance. He had the least injured taken over to his truck, so Bruce could render aid and still keep watch over the prisoners, while he helped extract people trapped in their destroyed vehicles, and treated the more severely injured. He worked until sufficient state troopers and paramedics arrived to take over.

"Sergeant," he said to the lead state trooper. "You've got things well in hand now. Unless you still need me and my partner, we've got to be on our way."

"No, I don't need you, Ranger," the sergeant answered. "However, you won't be going anywhere, at least not for quite a while. We've had to close 10 all the way to its junction with I20. Past that, 20's closed all the way up to Toyah, and 10's closed down to Texas 17 at Saragosa. You can't turn back toward El Paso, either. We've had to shut down the highway from here to Sierra Blanca. The dust is blowin' so bad in some sections the visibility's down to zero."

"You don't understand, Sergeant. We're transporting three accused killers back to Hays County. We can't be delayed any more than we already have been."

"I don't know what to tell you, Ranger, except you'd be a fool to try. It's not just that we were forced to shut down the highways because of the dust, there's also accidents all over the place. A lot of 'em have completely blocked the highway. Several happened on bridges over dry washes or deeper arroyos. That means, just like here, you can't get around the wrecks. You said you saw this one happen, and were almost right in the middle of it. That means you know you're damn lucky to be here standin' and talkin' with me, instead of being buried under a few tons of scrap metal."

"I'll give you that. The Good Lord was

watching out for me and my partner, that's for certain. Did you ever find out what caused this whole mess?"

"Yeah, it seems so. Based on preliminary information, and conversations with the drivers, it appears one driver slammed on his brakes to avoid hitting a tumbleweed."

"That's what caused all this? Who the hell stops for a tumbleweed?" Jim asked. "All they do is break apart if you hit one. Don't even scratch the paint on your car."

"Easterners," the sergeant said, with a shrug. "Or damn Californians."

"Those New York cars that went by us like bats out of heaven, as my mother would say," Jim exclaimed.

"That's right. When the driver of the first one hit the brakes, he lost control, and one thing led to another."

"Why the devil was he goin' so dang fast?"

"Because the people in those two cars are big-time Hollywood types. They're filming a movie here in west Texas, and were rushing to get to Odessa before dark. They were supposed to be shooting a nighttime scene there two days ago, but got behind schedule. The cars are rentals being used in the film."

"Well, they sure won't be doing any filming tonight," Jim said.

"I reckon not," the sergeant agreed. "Won't be

using what's left of those two cars, either, that's for damn certain. Just like you won't be goin' anywhere until the wind lets up and we get the roads cleared."

"Don't bet your hat on that, Sergeant," Jim answered. "If the roads are closed, I'll just have to go cross-country."

"Tell me I didn't hear what I think I just heard."

"You mean that I'll head cross-country? You did."

"Y'know, I've seen and heard you Rangers do some crazy things over the years," the sergeant said. "But this one's plumb *loco*. You can't even try it. It's impossible. This is mighty rugged territory. There's no roads, nothing but a few scattered ranch buildings, mostly abandoned, rattlesnakes, scorpions, cactus and sand for the next fifty miles. Even the Kent store's shut down, and the only other place to get fuel between here and Balmorhea burned down last month. I'm not even gonna mention the dry washes you'll have to cross, and steep hills you'll have to climb. You'll never make it. And if you were thinkin' of detouring all the way around by way of Fort Davis, forget it. A bad storm last week washed out about a mile-long stretch of 118, and a mudslide blocked another section. It'll be at least a week before it's reopened."

"I've got plenty of fuel, plus two five-gallon jerry cans of gas strapped to the tailgate. I've got extra food rations, and I'm drivin' a four-wheel drive SUV that's as tough as they come. There's also lots of old dirt roads that cut through the *malpais*, some of which parallel the highways, that I can follow. It'll take me a while longer, but I'll get through. Then once I hit Saragosa, it'll be smooth sailing."

"I still say it's a crazy idea." The sergeant shook his head. "Just like the movie title says, this is no country for old men."

"Good thing I'm a young one then," Jim said, laughing.

"You try driving through these badlands and you won't *live* to be an old one," the sergeant said, and scowled. "Maybe your partner can talk you out of this fool notion."

"He can try, but it's my truck, and I've got the keys," Jim said, with a smile. "He doesn't have a choice."

"Then all I can say is good luck, and *vaya con Dios*."

"*Gracias*, sergeant. *Adios*. See you down the road."

With that, Jim headed back to his truck. Bruce had all the windows lowered, and was sitting behind the wheel.

"Are we ready to get rollin' again?" he asked Jim.

"Yeah, soon as I grab a can of Dr Pepper and some cashews, we'll be on our way," Jim answered. "There's a slight complication, how-ever."

"Really? I haven't known you all that long, Jim, but I've learned enough to know what you call a slight complication is a major obstacle for most normal people."

"Bruce, you hurt my feelings. I'm crushed," Jim said. "We're just going to get back home a bit later than I'd hoped, that's all. Besides the delay here, the highway's closed from back at Plateau all the way to Saragosa. 20's closed from the 10 junction up to Pecos. Lots of accidents, and a wicked dust storm."

"I've heard some of that on the radio," Bruce answered. "Why can't we get through, though?"

"Most of the wrecks have completely blocked the highway. Some of them are on bridges where there's no way around. So, that means we'll have to go cross-country most of the way. There's only a few stretches of highway we can try, and it'll probably be quicker to just stay off the road entirely until we reach Saragosa. We'll actually be saving a few miles."

"What if we get stuck in a gully somewhere, or this truck breaks down?"

"We've got a radio, phones, GPS, extra fuel, good tires, emergency rations, and this is one vehicle that I haven't been able to kill yet, hard as I've tried on occasion," Jim answered. "I'm not worried. So slide over."

"Well, I damn sure am, Ranger," Suggs said from the back seat. "I sure as hell wouldn't mind seein' you and your partner die out in the middle of nowhere, but I sure ain't hankerin' to die of thirst or starvation. If you're wrong, what happens to us?"

"Well, Mr. Suggs, if we do get hopelessly lost, or stranded and no one finds us until it's too late, it'll save the state of Texas the cost of a trial, and keeping you and your buddies behind bars," Jim said, as he got behind the wheel. He threw the Tahoe into gear, reversed direction, and headed onto the dirt service road paralleling the interstate. Once the truck was rolling, he pressed the steering wheel button for his phone, and told it to dial his wife's business number. After two rings, the call was answered.

"Tavares Consulting, Elizabeth Blawcyzk speaking. How may I help you?"

"Howdy, Ma. It's Jim. Is Kim there?"

"She is, but she's on a conference call with one of her clients. Evidently something urgent came up. The company phone has been forwarded to my cell. I'm actually down at the barn. The Sherman boys are just about ready to take a horseback ride. Can I give Kim a message for you?"

"You sure can. We're going to be later getting home than planned. We're still out in west Texas. We got tied up by a big accident just outside Plateau. There's a nasty windstorm brewing out here. It's kicking up a lot of dust, and caused quite a few bad accidents, so the Highway Patrol has closed the interstates all the way from here to Saragosa and Pecos. That means we'll have to take the back roads to get home. I sure don't want to wait until the highways are opened again."

"I understand, Jim. I'll let Kim know. Do you have any idea when you might get back?"

"I really don't. That depends on where we can pick up the highway once more. I'm hoping by seven or eight o'clock. Once I have a better idea I'll call back."

"All right. You be careful."

"I always am, Ma."

"Liar," Betty said, laughing. "Just like your father was."

"He couldn't fool you, and neither can I. Ma, would you put Bruce's wife on the phone?"

"Sure. Kelle!"

Kelle's voice could be heard in the background.

"She'll pick up in a minute, Jim."

"Thanks, Ma. I'll say good-bye now. Love you. Tell Kim I love her, too. See you tonight."

"I will. Bye, Jim. Here's Kelle."

Kelle's voice came through the speakers.

"Bruce? Where are you?"

"Still a few hundred miles from home," Bruce said. "That's why Jim called. We won't be back until probably around seven or eight."

"What happened?"

"First, we had to stop and help out at a big accident. Now, the wind's blowing so fierce the highways are closed, so we have to circle around by way of the old route. It's either that, or hunker down for the rest of the day, spend the night in the truck, then finish the trip in the morning. Neither one of us wants that, especially with three prisoners on our hands. I guess that means you might as well head on home."

"Hold on a minute, Bruce. Betty wants to tell me something."

A muffled conversation came over the Tahoe's speakers. A moment later, Kelle's voice took its place.

"Bruce, Betty wants us to stay here until you get back. If you arrive too late, she says we can spend the night. Is that all right with you?"

"It is as long as it's okay with Betty and Kim," Bruce answered.

"Betty's already said it is."

"Then it's fine by me."

"Bruce, I'd better go. The boys are anxious to get on their horses. I'll see you tonight."

"Sure thing, see you then. Give the boys a kiss for me. Love you, Kelle."

"And I love you, Bruce. Good-bye."

"Bye."

Once the phone went silent, Bruce gave Jim a look.

"What? What's that for?" Jim asked.

"We're taking the back roads? You know damn well we're not taking *any* roads."

"Sure we are," Jim answered. "We're on one right now, ain't we? When we run out of road, we'll make our own. Besides, this way our wives won't worry as much. Sometimes you need to bend the truth a bit. Anyway, I noticed you didn't tell Kelle any different."

"A bit? You just bent the truth into a horseshoe. And the only reason I didn't say anything to Kelle about what we're really doing is I didn't want her to say anything to Kim, and get you in trouble."

"Uh-huh," Jim said. "Sure." He picked up speed to just around fifty.

"I hope you're not gonna try and go seventy or eighty on this gravel and dirt," Bruce said.

"Nope, not most of it, anyway. This is about tops," Jim said. "Hang on for a second. Cattle guard just ahead."

He slowed to forty. The Tahoe lunged and lurched as it crossed over the guard, vibrating wickedly, as if it were going full speed over rumble strips on the highway shoulder.

"Dammit, Ranger, you're gonna kill us all," Creighton yelled.

"Jim, I've gotta agree with him, much as I hate to," Bruce said. "My teeth just about rattled out of my head, and my butt's gonna be sore for a month of Sundays."

"It's about to get a bit rougher. End of the road," Jim said, with a laugh.

A hundred yards past the cattle guard, the rough road ended, fading into two rutted tire tracks through the scrub, which soon completely disappeared. Jim cut his speed down to thirty-five.

"Now things start getting interesting," he said, as the truck dropped into a shallow dry wash, then climbed out the opposite side. "You done much back country drivin', Bruce?"

"Some, but not a whole lot," Bruce admitted.

"Then I guess I'm stayin' behind the wheel until we can get back on the highway. Dang," Jim said, as he mowed down a patch of dead scrub and withered mesquite. "This could be a bit rougher than I thought."

For almost two hours, Jim worked his way through the badlands, traveling old dirt roads when he could find them, otherwise making his own trail through the arid high desert. In many places, he had to drop the Tahoe into low range four-wheel drive, either to climb a steep slope, or ease down a sandy bank, across a draw, then back out again. More than once, he had to detour around a slab-sided mesa blocking the way, or drive along the rim of an arroyo until he found a place to cross.

"Jim, are you certain we're still going in the right direction?" Bruce asked. "Between the dust flyin' and you zig-zagging all over the damn place, I've got no clue where we're at."

"We sure are," Jim answered. "We're goin' east. We're not all that far past Kent."

"How do you know that?"

"Instinct," Jim said, laughing. "Plus the compass reading on the dash display tells me we are."

"Funny, Jim. Real funny. So, are you gonna try'n get back on the highway soon? We could stop for a break at the Fort Davis rest area."

Jim shook his head.

"Uh-uh. I'm stayin' off the highway until we reach Balmorhea."

"Why the hell would you do that?" Bruce asked.

"Three reasons. One, we don't know whether or not 10's been reopened. Two, 10 starts cutting northeast, until it meets up with 20. Since we're already way off 10, there's no point in going back north to reach it, only to find it's still shut down. From here, it's shorter to go straight across. Third, in case Sheriff Calderon was right, and there's an ambush set up and waitin' for us somewhere, they'll never figure out we've given them the slip."

"What if the ambush is past Balmorhea?"

"I doubt it. Whoever's behind it would wait for us before the junction with 20, since they'd have no way of knowing we might pick up U.S.

190 and take that straight into Austin. Plus, the farther east we get, the more towns there are, and more traffic. They'd want to hit us out here, where things are real sparse." Jim glanced in the rear-view mirror. "Isn't that right, gentlemen?"

"You can go to Hell, Ranger," Tyler said.

"If I do, I'm takin' you three with me."

"So you're gonna jounce us around like this all the way to Balmorhea, Ranger?" Creighton asked.

"Even I'm not that hard-hearted," Jim answered. "I'm fond of my kidneys, too. No, once I find it, I'll pick up Farm 3078 down to Toyahvale, then take Texas 17 north to Balmorhea, and back to the highway. If things time out right, there's a little drive-in at Balmorhea called Matta's Burger Place. It's nothing more than an eight by ten corrugated steel shed with a porch and a couple picnic tables, but they make really good burgers. If you three don't act up, I'll stop and we'll eat there."

"If our stomachs haven't been jounced out through our throats when we finally *do* get there," Bruce said, when Jim hit another particularly deep rut.

"Don't worry. The terrain flattens out for quite a few miles from here. We'll make better time."

"We won't be making any time at all, Ranger," Suggs, who was seated behind Jim, said. "Look to the left!"

Jim looked out his side window, to see a wall of dust boiling up at least a half-mile into the air, a seemingly solid mass of writhing sand and debris, bearing down on them.

"Holy guacamole! It's a monster haboob!"

"That looks more like a derecho to me," Bruce said.

"This ain't the time to split hairs," Jim said. "Either way, it's bad news. That thing's movin' almighty fast, probably forty or fifty miles an hour, and it's gonna catch us out in the open, unless we find something to duck behind real quick. Hang on!"

Jim pressed down on the accelerator, increasing speed to as fast as he dared without tearing the suspension out of the Tahoe. The fierce southerly wind increased even more, buffeting the truck as Jim raced desperately to find shelter.

"It's almost on top of us, and I don't see any place to hide. We're not gonna make it," he yelled, as the wall of dust pressed nearer, and the wind suddenly shifted direction, now coming from the north at almost the same speed. "Hold on. I'm gonna turn tail to the wind."

He hit the brakes and turned sharply to the right, so that the back of the Tahoe was pointed directly into the wind. He had just stopped and turned off the engine when the full force of the storm descended, enveloping the truck in a whirling, blinding dark brown curtain of dust.

"Jim, do you know what the hell you're doin'?" Bruce shouted, to be heard over the howling wind.

"I sure hope so," Jim answered. "Just like horses, we'll try to ride this out with our tails to the wind. Obviously, I can't see to drive, and even if I was fool enough to try, this sand would clog up the engine before we made a mile."

"I've been in one of these before, and I never wanted to see another one," Suggs said. "If it's a big one, it could end up buryin' us alive."

"Then let's hope it isn't," Jim said. "This might be a good time to think about prayin', even if you're not a religious man."

"If I prayed for anything, it'd be a cold beer," Suggs answered. "I'm powerful thirsty, and it's gettin' awful stuffy in this truck, besides."

"There's no beer, but I've got emergency supplies in the back," Jim said. "The only problem is we won't be able to reach 'em until the storm passes. If we tried to open the doors, the wind would rip 'em right off, and fill this thing with sand in no time. That's also why we don't dare open the windows, not even a crack. We're just gonna have to wait it out."

"If the damn wind doesn't flip us over first," Creighton said, when another gust rocked the truck. "Y'know, Ranger, you could uncuff one of us. That's one way to reach the supplies. Or climb between us and into the back."

"Yeah, that'll sure happen," Jim replied. "Not a chance. Besides, I'm keeping myself buckled in just in case this truck does go tumblin' down a draw like a damn tumbleweed. Y'all might as well settle down and relax, best you can. What, Bruce?"

Bruce was giving Jim another exasperated look.

"Holy guacamole? Really, Jim? What's next, 'Auntie Em, Auntie Em, it's a twister'?"

"Could be," Jim answered. "I'm gonna try to raise dispatch on the radio, and let them know what's happening. While I do that, why don't you call Kelle?"

"You took the words right out of my mouth."

Jim picked up the radio mic and keyed it.

"Ranger 810 to Dispatch."

No answer.

"Ranger 810 to Dispatch. Come in, please. Ranger 810 to Dispatch."

Again, no answer. Several more attempts brought the same result.

"It's no use. Either this storm is blocking the signal, or we're in a dead zone. It doesn't seem like you're having much better luck, Bruce."

"I'm not. There's not even a hint of a signal for the phone out here. Why don't you give yours a try, Jim?"

"All right, here goes."

Jim attempted to use his phone both through

the system in his truck and off-system, with no luck.

"All right, we're out of range for both the radio and phones," he said. "We'll just have to wait until the storm breaks, and we can get to a place where there's service."

"You mean if we end up stuck out here, no one's gonna help us?" Tyler asked.

"Oh, they will . . . sooner or later," Jim answered. "It might take a couple of days before they start to search, though."

"So we could die out here."

"We could dic in a wreck on the highway, too. Wait a minute, we nearly just did, not too long ago. Or get hit by a meteorite. It seems to me you're awfully worried about dying for an *hombre* who's facing the needle anyway."

"Only because if I do get convicted, the appeals will take long enough I might die a natural death behind bars. Plus, the needle would be quicker."

"Enough of that kind of talk, Don," Suggs said. "You're givin' me the creeps."

"Jim, if we do die out here, Kelle's gonna kill me," Bruce said. "You, too."

"You don't want to know what Kim'll do to me before Kelle has the chance," Jim answered. "Look, there's nothing we can do about the situation until the storm lets up. Once it does, I'll probably be able to get a radio signal, and as soon as I can see a few hundred feet, we'll be moving again. These things don't usually last much more'n an hour or two. I'm not worried. If it'll raise your spirits, though, I can always sing, or tell a few jokes."

"Anything but that," Bruce said. "You start, and I'm runnin' out into the storm. It would be far less painful."

"All right, then we might as well all settle down. I'm gonna take a quick nap. I suggest all of us do. Bruce, wake me up in an hour, then you can take yours."

"You really think we can sleep through this, Ranger?" Creighton said.

"It's up to you," Jim answered, with a shrug. "But I sure can."

He tilted his Stetson over his eyes, leaned against his side window, and within two minutes was fast asleep.

"He really did go to sleep," Creighton said. "I don't believe it. Ranger, you do realize he's more'n a bit *loco*, I hope? How long have you two been partners?"

"We're not," Bruce answered. "We've just been given a couple of assignments to work on together, that's all. We're not even in the same company. Jim might be a bit *loco*, as you say, but he's one helluva Ranger."

"While he's asleep, maybe I can talk some sense into you," Suggs said. "We've barely been able to move since we left Las Cruces. If these cuffs don't come off soon, I'm liable to lose my hands. I've got no circulation left, and my arms and back are cramping up somethin' awful. I'm sure my partners' are, too. You need to take the cuffs off for a while, so I can stretch a bit."

"Sorry, mister, but you'll have to put up with the situation until we can both keep our eyes on you. How stupid do you think I am?"

"Pretty stupid, to let your partner get us into this fix in the first place," Suggs said. "If anything happens and we all end up dead, it'll be on his head."

"You don't expect me to buy that. Jim didn't have anything to do with the wreck, and he sure can't control the weather. And if you keep on yappin', I'll gag you. That'll shut you up."

"We've all gotta take a leak real bad, too," Creighton added. "What happens when we can't hold it any longer?"

"Then you'll have a mighty uncomfortable ride the rest of the way," Bruce answered. "It doesn't matter what you want, anyway. Even if I wanted to, which I sure don't, I couldn't unlock your cuffs. Jim has the keys in his pocket, and he'd wake up the minute I tried to get them. So, y'all are plumb out of luck, no matter what. The best you can do is hope we ride out this storm in one piece. Until then, just keep shut."

Bruce was answered with a string of curses from all three men, then silence.

• • •

"Jim, you awake?" Bruce asked, an hour later. When he received no response, he shook Jim's shoulder.

"Jim?"

"Yeah, I'm awake." Jim sat up straight and shifted his hat back in place. "I see the storm hasn't let up."

The Tahoe was still being buffeted by the wind. Despite the windows being closed tightly, wind-driven dust was seeping through the weather stripping and vents, covering the interior of the vehicle with a thin, brown film. Bruce had a bandana covering his nose and mouth, while in the back seat, the prisoners had handkerchiefs covering theirs.

"No, it sure hasn't," Bruce said. "Longest dust storm I've ever experienced. And before you even ask, no, I haven't had any luck reaching DPS, or Kelle."

"That's not good," Jim said. He took a bandana from the center console and covered his own face, then looked at his watch.

"Quarter after three, and it looks like twilight," he said. "Guess we won't be home by eight, after all. Kim sure ain't gonna be happy."

"Kelle will be a mite perturbed, too," Bruce answered.

"How about our friends in the back? They been behaving themselves?"

"Pretty much. They've grumbled a little about being cuffed, but that's about it."

"I can't hardly blame them for that," Jim said. He glanced in the rear-view mirror. "As soon as the wind dies down enough, we'll turn you men loose for a while. We'll feed you, let loose one of you at a time to go to the bathroom, then we'll get rollin' again."

"Bathroom? Out here?" Creighton said. He snorted.

"Sure. Plenty of cactus and mesquite for privacy. And prickly pear pads to wipe with."

"Funny, Ranger. Real funny."

"Bruce, you should take a quick snooze, like I did," Jim advised.

"I'll try, but I don't think I'll be able to. I don't know how you managed to sleep through all this."

"A couple of years in the Rangers and you'll be able to sleep anywhere, anytime, too. Even standin' up or in the saddle."

"I'll stick to investigating or forensics work, and leave the horses and cow thieves to you, Jim, thank you very much."

"Good thing it's not a hundred and forty years ago, Bruce. You wouldn't have made it as a Ranger."

"But it's not, so I don't have to worry about it."

A flash of lightning cut through the dust, followed by a loud rumble of thunder. Huge raindrops began spattering on the Tahoe.

"No, but *that's* something we *do* have to worry about," Jim said, as more lightning flashed and thunder rumbled. The rain mixed with the dust, effectively turning into blobs of mud as it fell. "If this turns out to be a real gullywasher, the ground'll turn into sticky gumbo. It'll become such a quagmire even this truck won't be able to get through."

"Or if you try movin' you could drive right into a patch of damn quicksand, Ranger," Tyler said. "No one would ever know what happened to us. We'd disappear without a trace."

"If that happens, we'll become one of the great mysteries of the West, like what happened to Judge Fountain and his boy over in New Mexico back in the 1890s, or maybe Jimmy Hoffa," Jim answered. "We'd be famous."

"We'd also be dead," Bruce pointed out.

"Well, yeah, that would be a drawback," Jim conceded. "The best we can hope for is the rain and wind let up enough so I can see to drive, before it gets dark."

"I'm more worried about the lightning," Suggs said. "This damn truck is the highest point anywhere around here. We're liable to get struck."

"Yeah, but a car is one of the safest places to be in a thunderstorm," Tyler said. "As long as you're not touching any metal parts."

"Maybe so, but not *this* truck," Jim said. "I've

got two five gallon cans of gas lashed to the back tailgate. If we do take a lightning strike, they'll explode for certain. In which case, we'll go out with a bang."

"You're real cute, you know that, Ranger? Real cute," Suggs grumbled.

"Yeah, but look at the bright side. The explosion should be loud enough, and throw off enough light, that someone is likely to notice it, and could give anyone lookin' for us a lead as to about where we're at."

"So they'll find some melted metal and ashes," Bruce said. "You've got a real way of comforting people, Jim . . . *not.*"

"How about I try this, then? The rain seems to be slackening. The wind's finally dying down, too. With any luck, it won't be too long before the worst of the storm blows itself out and I can see well enough to drive."

The words were barely out of Jim's mouth when a bolt of lightning struck less than a hundred yards from the Tahoe. A sharp crack of thunder, so loud it shook the truck, immediately followed. The rain came down even harder, now mixed with hail the size of mothballs, pinging off the truck's hood, roof, and windshield like so many white bullets.

"Jim, please, don't say another word," Bruce pleaded. "I'm beginning to think you're a damn jinx."

"I'll admit we've had a few unexpected problems," Jim conceded. "All part of the job."

"Are you certain you know the way out of here?" Bruce asked.

"Sure. No problem at all," Jim answered.

"How can you be so positive? Do you know this area that well?"

"Yep. I spent my first two years as a trooper stationed out here. I know almost every canyon around here as well as I know my own back yard. Once the weather clears, we'll be back on the highway in no time."

"If you say so, Jim." Bruce shook his head. "Personally, I'm beginnin' to think this rain's never gonna stop."

"Just give it half an hour."

Despite Bruce's skepticism, not to mention the prisoners', the precipitation did indeed slow down to a steady, but moderate, rainfall less than thirty minutes later.

"Told you it would let up," Jim said. He started the Tahoe and switched on the windshield wipers, front and rear. It took four passes before they cleared the mud off the windshield and back window sufficiently so he could see. A glance in the side view mirrors revealed the truck, from the front doors back, was buried almost to the windows in a slanting bank of mud. However, visibility had improved to close to a quarter mile.

"Yeah, but we're buried so deep you'll never get us out, Ranger," Suggs said.

"We'll be out in two shakes," Jim said. "It's only the rear that's buried."

"If you can't get this thing unstuck, *our* rears will be in a sling, once we get back," Bruce said, dryly.

"You're worried about nothing," Jim said. "Watch and learn."

He put the Tahoe into four-wheel drive low, threw it into gear, and pressed gently on the accelerator pedal. The wheels spun at first, then the front tires gained purchase, and inch by precious inch, the truck eased out of the mud.

"We're on our way," Jim said. "Soon as the rain lets up a bit more, and we reach solid ground, I'll stop so we can eat, and take a leak. It's gonna be real slow goin', but at least we're moving again."

In forty minutes, although the rain had slackened to little more than a drizzle, Jim made only about three miles. He was working his way past the sloping base of a mesa when the Tahoe began slipping sideways.

"Jim, the bank's too steep," Bruce said. "You'll never make it."

"That's not the problem," Jim answered. "The ground's giving way."

"It's not just the ground under us, Ranger," Suggs yelled. "It's the whole damn cliff. Look over there!"

241

Suggs pointed to a large section of rain-loosened soil that had detached from the mesa's wall, and was flowing toward them in a fast-moving mudslide.

"Just hold on," Jim said, as he swung the truck hard to the left. "The only chance we've got is if I can outrun that slide." He hit the accelerator, sending his truck jouncing and skidding over the slick ground.

"You'd better hope you don't plow into a rock and take out the oil pan, or break a strut," Bruce shouted, as the Tahoe dropped into a shallow dip, then became airborne when Jim gunned it up the other side. Jim didn't attempt to answer, concentrating solely on escaping the slide. Mud was now beginning to overtake them, within moments surrounding the Tahoe on three sides, then all four, sweeping it along as the mud covered everything in its path. Jim fought the steering wheel furiously, struggling to keep his truck's nose pointed as straight ahead as possible, to avoid it being spun sideways, overturned, and buried.

Several times, it tilted on two wheels; each time Jim was able to bring it back down. For half a mile, he tried to outrace the mud, gradually easing his truck toward the edge of the flow. When the mud spread out once it reached more level terrain, Jim was finally able to drive onto solid ground. He stopped the truck, put it in park, turned off the engine, and sat, shaking, as much from the effort as fear. Sweat poured down his face, stained his hat, and plastered his shirt to his skin. He made a quick Sign of the Cross, then gave a long sigh.

"*Madre de Dios! Gracias.* We made it. Thank you, Jesus. You too, St. Christopher."

"I can't believe you pulled that off, Jim," Bruce said. "I thought for certain we'd be buried alive."

"We were lucky, and someone was watching over us, that's for certain," Jim said. "Plus, when you're caught in a mudslide, as long as you're still able to stay above the surface and keep moving, it's the same principle as escaping a rip current in the Gulf if you get caught in one, or an avalanche in the mountains. You don't fight it, you go with it, and work your way toward the edge until you can swim or ski out of it."

"So now what, Ranger? Are we just gonna sit here until we die, or are you really foolhardy enough to try and keep going?" Creighton asked.

"Neither," Jim answered. "We *are* gonna stay here for the night. The sun'll be down in a couple of hours. With the clouds still hanging on, it'll be dark early. It wouldn't be safe to try'n drive over these badlands. I wouldn't be able to see any soft ground that might swallow up the truck, or draws too steep to cross until it was too late. And of course, with all the rain, flash floods will have turned the dry washes into raging torrents, that would sweep us away if I drove into any before seein' 'em. So, we'll spend the night here, which will give things a chance to dry up some, and start out again at first light."

"I hope you don't expect us to stay hogtied like this the whole damn night," Suggs said.

"Even I'm not that cruel, although, in the old days, you and your pals would've been hangin' from a tree by now," Jim said. "No, we'll take off your shackles so you can relieve yourselves and then eat. There's a tote in the back with toilet paper, disinfectant wipes, and hand sanitizer. There's the cooler with sandwiches and drinks. There's also a couple cases of bottled water. It's not gourmet eating, in fact not even as good as you boys'll get in prison, but we won't starve.

"Once we're done with supper, I'll put the back seat down. You three'll be shackled together again, and chained by your ankles to the back bumper, but at least you'll be able to lie down, although it'll be a mite crowded. Me'n Ranger Sherman will sleep in the front seats. Of course, we'll be alternating watches, so one of us will always be awake to keep an eye on you three. Once it's daylight, we'll have a quick breakfast of jerky and water, then be on our way again. Bruce, why don't you try and reach your wife one more time, while I try to raise dispatch?"

"All right."

Once again, their attempts to make contact by radio or phone were stymied.

"We must still be in a dead zone," Jim said.

"Or it's quite possible the storm knocked out all the nearby cell towers," Bruce answered. "I guess there's nothing we can do but make the best of it, until morning."

"There is one thing I can do," Jim said. "See if I can get the news on the radio, to find out if the highways are reopened."

He turned on the Tahoe's ignition, and fiddled with the radio until he got a weak, staticky signal from an AM station in Pecos. Two commercials played, then the announcer returned to the air.

"Continuing our special coverage of the storm aftermath in west Texas. The state of emergency declared by the governor is still in effect in Reeves, Terrell, Pecos, Brewster, Culberson, and Hudspeth Counties. Interstates 10 and 20 remain closed in both directions from Sierra Blanco to Sheffield and Pecos, respectively. Hundreds of motorists remain stranded by drifted sand, or washed out bridges over normally dry stream beds. In addition, Texas DPS and local authorities are dealing with scores of accidents and missing persons' reports. We will continue to update you on this developing situation."

Jim switched off the radio.

"Seems like things are even worse than I imagined," he said. "10's closed all the way to

Sheffield, now. Well, if we can at least get as far as Fort Stockton, we can pick up U.S. 190 there, take that through Iraan to Texas 137, then follow that and Texas 163 back to the highway at Ozona."

"Yeah, but at least if our wives saw the news, they probably won't be expecting us home tonight after all," Bruce said. "They'll still be worried, but not as much as if they had no idea what we came up against. We might as well settle in for the night."

"You're right," Jim said. He pushed the button for the tailgate, unlocking it. "You get the supplies while I unlock our prisoners."

The next morning, Jim was awakened by rays of the rising sun streaming through the windshield. He tilted his hat back on his forehead, yawned and stretched.

"Good mornin', Jim," Bruce said. He had taken the second watch.

" 'Mornin', Bruce. Any problems from the *hombres* in back?"

"Not a one. All three of 'em slept the whole while."

"No thanks to you two," Tyler muttered. "Cramped in the rear of this thing was almost as bad as being jammed together in the back seat."

"Look on the bright side," Jim said. "In a few hours, we'll be at the Hays County jail. You'll all have a nice, spacious cell."

"You're a million laughs, Ranger."

"Doesn't matter. We'll finish off the rest of the supplies, take a leak, and then we'll finally be on our way again."

"That's if you even have any idea where we're at, Jim," Bruce said. "Or for that matter, are even headed in the right direction."

"We're headed east, all right. The sun's in our faces," Jim answered. "I've got a pretty good idea where we're at, too. We didn't get as far as I'd hoped we would last night, but unless I miss my guess, we're only about ten miles from Farm 3078. If we cut southeast, in a couple of miles or so, we'll come across an old, unnamed dirt road. That'll run us south around East Tank, a lake that's usually dried up, or nothing more than a bed of alkali mud, to another dirt road, Woulfter Ranch Road. We'll pick that up, and it will take us east, straight to 3078. From there, it's an easy shot to Toyahvale, then up Texas 17 to Balmorhea, and back to the interstate. We'll be home in time for supper.

"First, though, let's see if we can raise anyone on the phone, or the radio. With any luck at all, 10'll be reopened at the junction with 20. In that case, we'll be able to just take 3078 back to 10. Bruce, you try'n call Kelle, while I see if I can get Dispatch to answer the radio. Soon as we've done that, we'll eat, then get rollin'."

Yet again, Jim and Bruce's attempts to make

247

contact with the D.P.S. or their families were futile. Neither was able to obtain a signal for their phones, and the only sounds which came over the two-way radio were hisses and static.

"I guess we'll have to try again a little farther along," Jim said. "Might as well eat."

Twenty minutes later, Jim had the Tahoe moving once again. He turned on the radio, fiddling with the dial until the Pecos station came in more clearly.

"It should be time for the news. Let's see if they'll have an update on the roads," he said.

"Good morning, Reeves County and west Texas," the announcer's voice came over the speakers. "We are continuing our special coverage of the historic dust and rain storms which hit the entire Trans-Pecos region yesterday. As of right now, Interstate 20 has been completely reopened from Pecos west to its junction with Interstate 10. Interstate 10 has been reopened from the junction with 20 to Exit 209 near Sheffield in both directions. However, it does remain closed from its junction with I20 to Sierra Blanca. The Texas Department of Public Safety and state D.O.T. are unable to provide a timetable as to its reopening."

"As to the latest count of fatalities and injuries, at least seven people have lost their lives directly as a result of the storms. In addition, four more have perished in accidents at least somewhat attributable to the weather. Nineteen people remain hospitalized in medical facilities throughout the region, while scores more have been treated for lesser injuries.

"Now to the missing. State and county authorities put the number of missing persons at eighty-nine. That number is expected to drop, as more persons are able to make contact with authorities or families. In addition, some of the names on the lists may be duplicates, or persons who are not aware they have been reported as missing."

"Two of the missing persons are Texas Rangers, who were transporting three prisoners, accused of the murders of two brand inspectors in Hays County, from Las Cruces, New Mexico back to the Hays County Correctional Facility in San Marcos. The prisoners are also missing. The five men were last seen yesterday, at the scene of an accident on Interstate 10, near Plateau, where the Rangers had rendered assistance. One of the Rangers told a Highway Patrol sergeant they were going to cut across country, since the highway had been shut down. A spokesperson for Ranger Headquarters in Austin stated that there is no particular concern as to the Rangers', nor their prisoners', safety as of yet. The spokesperson indicated the Rangers, whom they did not wish to identify at the time, had most likely just stopped to wait out the storm, and were out of two-way radio and cell phone range. The spokesperson also said since the Rangers always carry emergency supplies, and are highly trained in survival skills, they would be able to live off the land for several days or more, if necessary. Finally, she said, while there is no reason to believe the prisoners have escaped custody, if anyone should see any man in the state of emergency area wearing Hays County prison jumpsuits, do not approach them, as they would be considered armed and extremely dangerous, but contact your local law enforcement authorities, the Highway Patrol, or the nearest Texas Ranger office, immediately. Two of the prisoners are white, the third African-American. The Rangers' vehicle is a dark blue 2017 Chevrolet Tahoe, bearing Texas license plate CMT 4089. Again, if you see this vehicle, do not approach it, but instead contact your nearest law enforcement agency."

"Damn!" Jim switched off the radio. "Hearing *that* won't get our wives worrying. Not much, it won't. Besides, who says we're missing? We're right here."

"Wherever 'here' is. Maybe they didn't put that piece about us from Headquarters on the local news back home," Bruce said, wishfully.

"And maybe aliens did land back there at Area 51 in New Mexico, we just didn't see them,"

Jim answered. "We'd just better hope we get to a place where we have a cell signal sooner than later. Boy howdy, Kim's gonna tear me apart for fair."

"Kelle won't exactly be happy with me, either," Bruce said. "However, once we explain the situation, our wives will understand. Let's talk about something else to keep our minds off them, since there's nothing we can do until we can reach them, or Dispatch, anyway. You mentioned space aliens. We're less'n a hundred miles from Marfa. You believe in the Marfa lights?"

"I sure do. I've seen 'em a couple of times."

"Do you think they're just mirages, or something more?"

"I'm not sure," Jim said, shaking his head. "I'm certain most of them are mirages, either that or refracted reflections from vehicle headlights. But there was one set I saw I just can't explain. They started off as just one, big white ball of light, then split into about half-a-dozen. Then they started changing colors, and zipping back and forth, up and down, all over the horizon. I still can't explain those. I do know someone wrote an old song about them, back in the sixties. Maybe you've heard your parents or grandparents play it on an oldies station."

"You're not serious."

"I sure am. I'll even sing a line or two to see if you remember it. Here goes. 'I see the lights,

I see the Marfa Lights, they're red and blue, and green . . ."

"Jim, I *have* heard that song, but it damn sure ain't called *Marfa Lights*. The song's name is *Party Lights*."

"Uh-uh. It's *Marfa Lights*," Jim said, laughing. "Ow!"

The Tahoe hit a deep chuckhole, bouncing sideward, causing Jim to hit his head on the side window.

"Serves you right," Bruce said. "Why don't you try'n raise Dispatch again? I'll give Kelle another call and see if it goes through."

"All right."

Jim keyed the mic for his radio, and made several attempts to reach D.P.S. Dispatch, to no avail.

"Jim, I've got a signal," Bruce said, on his third try to call his wife. "Hold on. Kelle's phone's ringing. Damn."

After two rings, the signal was lost.

"Let me try my phone," Jim said. He pushed the Tahoe's button for his phone. There was one ring, then nothing.

"Our luck's still holding," he muttered. "We don't have any."

"We might have some," Bruce answered. "I think I had a connection long enough for it to have registered on Kelle's phone. If it did, she'll know I'm trying to reach her. At least our families will realize we're still alive. And either Kelle or Kim will know to call the Rangers, too, and let them know we've attempted to make contact. We'll just have to keep trying. How much farther to that old road you're looking for?"

"No more'n three or four miles, at most, unless I miss my guess," Jim said.

"Once we hit that, do you reckon we've got a better chance of getting a phone or radio signal?"

"It might could be. If not, we should have service again for certain once we get to Woulfter Ranch Road. The last I knew, that ol' spread was still hanging on, and the only way they'd have phones is by cell or satellite."

"So then it won't be much longer before our wives won't have to worry about us."

"At least not today, Bruce," Jim said, with a rueful smile. He pressed down on the accelerator, picking up the Tahoe's speed to forty.

"There's our road," Jim exclaimed, twenty minutes later. He made a hard right, sending the Tahoe skidding in a cloud of dust, then straightened out its trajectory. "I nearly missed it."

"You damn near rolled us over, too," Bruce answered. "What was that I said about our wives no longer having to worry? I forgot the *loco* way you drive."

"I always have this thing under control," Jim retorted. Over the two-way radio speaker came the chatter of a dispatcher speaking with several Highway Patrol units. "And there's our radio."

He grabbed the mic and keyed it.

"Ranger Unit 810 to Dispatch."

"Dispatch, Ranger 810. Good to hear from you. Your current location and situation?"

"Thank you, Dispatch. We are approaching Woulfter Ranch Road. We'll take that to Farm 3078, follow that to Toyahvale, then pick up Texas 17 through Balmorhea and back to I10. ETA to San Marcos is about three-and-a-half hours. Prisoners are all secure. We were forced to shelter in my vehicle last night when conditions made continuing impossible. Please notify Hays County jail of our approximate arrival time."

"10-4, Ranger 810. Will advise, and also advise Ranger Headquarters you are safe and *en route* to destination."

"10-4. Ranger 810, out."

"Dispatch, out."

"Three-and-a-half hours?" Bruce said. "Are you insane, Jim?"

"It'd be three if we didn't have to stop for fuel, and to get something to eat."

"Aren't you going to let me do the rest of the driving once we're back on the main roads, and get yourself some rest?"

"Yeah, I am. I'd forgotten you drive a bit slower than I do. I reckon I should have told Dispatch an ETA of four-and-a-half or five hours. Never mind about that. Let's try and reach our wives."

Jim tried his phone again. This time, it had a fairly strong signal. After two rings, Kim answered.

"Jim! Where are you? Are you all right? Kelle and I have been worried sick. We were told you were missing."

"We're both fine, and'll be home in a few hours. We weren't lost, just off the beaten path. The storm was so bad I couldn't see to drive, so we had to stop and hunker down until it blew itself out. Unfortunately, we couldn't get a connection to call you, or a radio signal to contact Dispatch, until just now. We're almost to Toyahvale. From there, we'll stop in Balmorhea or Saragosa to get something to eat and put gas in the truck, then be back on the highway. As soon as we drop the prisoners off in San Marcos, we'll be home. I'm sorry I put you through this."

"It's all right, as long as I know you're okay," Kim answered.

"Thanks, honey. Look, we're still on a really rough dirt road, so I've got to concentrate on my driving. Could you put Kelle on the phone?"

"Of course. Kelle! It's Jim and Bruce."

Jim heard Kelle reply, then Kim was back on the phone.

"She'll be right here."

"Good. I'm gonna say good-bye now. I love you."

"I love you too, Jim. Here's Kelle."

"Bruce?" Kelle said.

"I'm right here, sweetheart. The trip's been a bit rougher than we planned. We got caught in that big storm, and had to wait overnight until we could get moving again. We'll be home in five or six hours. I hope you didn't worry too much."

"Not at all. I just couldn't sleep all night, I kept calling you every half-hour, and Kim and I spent the entire night glued to the television, hoping for news. No, I wasn't worried. Not one bit. I was only scared half to death, that's all."

"I'm sorry, Kelle. The damn storm cut off all communications. We just got service back now. We also kept trying to call all night. The minute we got a signal, Jim called. Listen, I've got to go now. We'll be stopping soon, so I can take over the wheel. I love you. Kiss the boys for me, and tell them I love them, too."

"I will," Kelle promised.

"All right then, Good-bye, Kelle. I'll see you this afternoon."

"Good-bye, Bruce."

Jim clicked off the phone. Bruce turned to him.

"Can't you make this thing go any faster?" he asked.

"Just you watch," Jim answered.

The rest of the trip home, thankfully, was uneventful. The only stop they had to make was for food, fuel, and to switch drivers. Once the prisoners were dropped off, Bruce insisted on driving the rest of the way to Jim's house.

"We're almost there," Jim said, as they neared San Leanna. "I guess now we've got to talk about the elephant in the truck."

"You mean what I'm going to report about you to Major Hough, to pass along to Major Voitek. I'm not gonna lie, I'll tell you that much, Jim."

"I wouldn't expect you to. You'd only get found out, and that would cost you your job. You're too good a Ranger to have that happen, just to protect me."

"I'm glad you understand, Jim. After seeing you work these past couple of days, how you handled things at that wreck, and how you got us through the storm, my report's gonna say you're absolutely fit for duty. I will recommend you cut back on your work load a bit, but that's all."

"I'm obliged. I know it must've been hard, being put in the position you were. *Muchas gracias*, pardner."

"Don't thank me yet. There is one other slight matter."

"What's that?"

"Not 'what's that'? It's what's a Matta?" Bruce burped, loudly. "Those burgers at Matta's Drive-In were the best I've ever tasted, but unfortunately I can still taste 'em. That's what's the Matta."

"That's all? I'm proud of you, Bruce. You've learned how to make jokes as bad as mine. That makes the past three days worth every minute."

"That's what you say," Bruce retorted. "I don't think anyone else will appreciate my new talent. Well, here's your street."

Bruce pulled into Jim's yard and turned off the Tahoe. Both his and Jim's families were waiting on the front porch. They rushed up to greet the two men as they got out of the truck. Bruce's boys outran their mother and jumped into their father's arms.

"Dad, you're home!" Wyatt shouted.

"I sure am," Bruce said.

"Did you bring us anything?" Marshall asked.

"I'm afraid I didn't have time," Bruce answered.

"He brought himself back, Marshall," Kelle said, as she gave Bruce a kiss. "That's all that matters. I'm so glad you're home, and in one piece."

"It was an interesting trip, to put it mildly," Bruce said. "But it's over. Time to go home."

Kim had hugged Jim tightly, and now took a step back, looking at him. Betty held Josh, while Frostie bounded around them.

"Jim, you're a mess," Kim said, with a smile. "So's your truck."

"I've just spent three days transporting three killers, got caught in a sandstorm and mudslide, then had to spend the night sleeping in my truck with four other men," Jim answered, laughing. "I'm surprised I look this good."

"You'd look good to me no matter how dirty and disgusting you were," Kim answered.

"Aw, gee honey, thanks . . . I think."

"I was going to hand Josh to you, but I believe I'll wait," Betty said. "You smell worse than one of his full diapers."

"I love you too, Ma," Jim said. "But I don't blame you."

"Jim, I'll give you a call Monday," Bruce said. He handed Jim his truck keys. "Right now, it's high time we got on home. There's a special family service at our church tomorrow, and I promised I'd help with that, so I'd like to get some sleep first."

"Sure thing. Thanks again for helpin' me out."

"Like I had a choice," Bruce said, chuckling. "Kim, Betty, thank you again for having Kelle and my boys over."

"Anytime," Kim said. "The boys loved riding our horses. Bye, Kelle. Good-bye, everyone."

"Jim, you take it easy for a couple of days," Bruce said.

"That's exactly what I plan on doing. You do the same. Talk to you Monday."

The Blawcyzks waved good-bye as the Shermans pulled out of their yard.

"Are you going to take a shower now, or do you

want something to eat first?" Kim asked, as they walked toward the house.

"Actually, I'm just gonna crash on the couch in my office," Jim answered. "I'll take a long soak in the tub after I wake up."

"How about church tomorrow? Perhaps you should skip Mass. I don't think God would be upset if you did. He'd understand."

"No, I'll get up and go," Jim answered. "Then I can sleep some more afterwards. But I've got to thank God for seeing me through the past few days."

"All right. I'll treat you to breakfast at MacPherson's after Mass, then."

"That sure sounds good," Jim said. "I'm gonna hit the hay before I fall asleep on my feet."

"That's the smartest thing I've heard you say in a long time," Kim said. "I'll leave some supper in the fridge, in case you wake up and want to eat later."

"Thanks, Kim."

Jim kissed her on the cheek. Once inside the house, he went to his office, and closed the door behind him. He took off his hat and tossed it on his desk, then removed his gunbelt and holster to hang them on a wall peg. He sat down, tugged off his boots and socks, took off his shirt and tie, then stretched out on the couch. Within two minutes, he was fast asleep.

8

As always, Jim and Kim went to the first Sunday Mass at their parish, St. Patrick's, while Betty watched Josh. Afterwards, Kim drove over to Jock MacPherson's Scottish Lion Bakery, Restaurant, and Gift Shop. She read a new slogan painted on the window, then glared accusingly at her husband.

"Jim, you've been here talking to Jock again, without me, haven't you?"

"I have not," Jim protested.

"Then how do you explain *that?*" Kim pointed at the new slogan. "It sounds just like you."

"Our sausages are the wurst," Jim read aloud, then laughed. "I do have to admit, it does sound like me. I guess some of my jokes must've rubbed off on Jock. Let's head inside. I'm starved."

Jock, the owner, spotted them as soon as they walked through the front door.

"Jim and Kimberly. I knew it was about time for you both to make an appearance. I have a table in the back empty, just as you prefer. Follow me. I'll have Delores bring coffee right over."

He led them to a booth in the rear corner.

"I have some new items on the menu," he said,

once they were seated. "Cranberry orange scones, plus jalapeno sausages. My own recipes."

"I thought you Scotch, for that matter the entire United Kingdom, called sausages 'bangers,'" Jim said. "And jalapenos in a Scottish restaurant just doesn't seem quite right."

"I'll remind you that I'm a Scot, or a Scotsman, Jim Blawcyzk," Jock said. "Scotch is whiskey, or perhaps tape, not a person. If anything, call me Scottish. Now, if you'll let me finish, I just made a fresh batch of haggis. Perhaps you'd like to sample that."

Jim made a face.

"Jock, I'm a Texas Ranger. I'm trained to live off the land. I've eaten jackrabbit, squirrel, snakes, lizards, grubs, and insects. However, even I couldn't possibly down sheep stomach stuffed with sheep guts."

"You don't eat the stomach, Jim," Jock pointed out. "It's just used to cook the contents."

"As if that makes a difference," Jim retorted, with a laugh. "I think I'll stick with your scones, thank you very much. Tell Delores three of those cranberry orange, and three cinnamon."

"Certainly. And for you, Kimberly?"

"Two slices of your date and walnut loaf, Jock."

"Buttered?"

"Lightly."

"Excellent, lass. I'll let Delores know. I'll

put in your order for her, while she brings your coffee."

"Thanks, Jock," Jim said.

Betty met them at the front door when they arrived home.

"Shh," she half-whispered. "Josh has been really fussy this morning. I finally got him to go to sleep. We don't want to wake him."

"No, we surely don't," Kim agreed. "Jim, what are your plans for the rest of the day?"

"Just what I said last night. I'm going to get some more sleep. Unlike Josh, I won't have any trouble falling asleep. Five minutes after my head hits the pillow, I'll be gone."

"I'm glad to hear you say that," Kim answered. "I was afraid you'd change your mind, and try to get some work done."

"Not today," Jim answered. "In fact, I'm goin' to take tomorrow off, too. Maybe then I can finally get everyone off my back."

"What do you mean by that, Jim?"

"You know exactly what I mean. If I'm still asleep, don't wake me for lunch or dinner."

Kim and Betty stared at him as he turned on his bootheels and went straight to his office, then slammed the door shut behind him.

"He seems pretty upset about something," Kim said.

"Yeah. He sure does," Betty agreed. "I would imagine we'll know what before too long."

Sometime later, Jim was awakened by a disturbance from the corrals. Instantly awake, he grabbed his boots and pulled them on, then ran down the hallway and out the back door. Kim came around from the front yard.

"Something's wrong with the horses," she said.

"I know. They're really stirred up," Jim said. "I wonder what's gotten into them. Maybe a pack of stray dogs is prowlin' around."

In the rear corral, Copper, Freedom, and Slacker were milling in panic, whinnying with fear. It was especially unusual for Copper, trained in police work, to be so frightened.

"There's what it is," Jim said, pointing at an object in the sky, which was circling the corral, swooping up and down as it buzzed the horses, chasing them.

"It's a drone!" Kim exclaimed.

"It sure is. I'll take care of it."

Jim ran to his Tahoe, opened the tailgate, and pulled out his shotgun. He hurried to just outside the corral, aimed at the drone, and fired two rounds. The lead shot blasted the drone to bits, the pieces falling to the dirt. Jim put down his gun and went into the corral to calm the frantic horses.

"Easy, boy, easy," he said, when Copper came

up to him, and put his head on Jim's shoulder. "It's all right now. That thing's not gonna bother you anymore."

While he patted Copper's neck, reassuring the paint, Freedom and Slacker also pressed against him, whickering. Kim joined them, taking those two horses by their halters and petting them. Betty came running out of her house.

"What happened?" she asked, once she reached the corral.

"Some idiot was chasin' the horses with a drone," Jim answered. He pointed to the remains of the machine. "I solved the problem, permanently."

"Jim, you can't just shoot someone else's property out of the sky," Kim said.

"I damn sure can, if it's harassing livestock, especially someone else's stock," Jim answered. "I think I know a little bit more about the law than you do, honey. Doesn't matter, I would have shot that thing down in any event. Whoever was flying it might take to spying on you and Josh next. We sure can't have that. If its owner does show up to try and claim it, I'll arrest him faster'n a tornado blows over a single-wide trailer.

"Tell you what. Why don't you and Ma settle the horses in their stalls, while I pick up the pieces of that thing and see if I can figure out who it belongs to. Or, I guess that should be *belonged*."

"Kim, I'll do that, if you want to check on Josh," Betty said. "All the noise from the horses and Jim's shotgun probably woke him up."

"Thanks, Betty."

Kim went back inside, while Betty gathered the horses to put them in their stalls, and Jim picked up what was left of the shattered drone.

"Damn," he muttered. "I was hopin' I missed the camera, but there's nothin' left of it. Looks like I took out the SD card, too. That means I've probably got no chance to figure out who was operating this thing."

"Which is just as well," Betty said. "If you found them, you'd probably shoot them."

"No, I wouldn't, Ma. Give me a little credit."

"When it comes to your horse, you're just like your father was," Betty said. "I never was sure who he loved more, me or his horse. In fact, I'm sure Jonas died of a broken heart when your father never came back home."

"That *is* a tough choice . . . just kiddin' you, Ma," Jim hastened to add, when Betty glared at him. "Since there's nothing I can do with this thing other than dump it in the trash, I'll give you a hand with the horses, then go back to catchin' up on my sleep."

"*Now* you're talking sensibly," Betty said. "Don't forget, you're coming over to my house for supper tonight. I'll see you then."

"If I can make it that far," Jim said. "It's a long

walk across the yard, and as you and everyone else keeps reminding me, I'm too worn out to do much of anything."

"Jim . . ."

"What?"

"Never mind."

Jim slept late the next morning, then decided to take Copper out for a short ride. He was warming him up by longeing him around the corral when Kim came out of the house.

"Jim! Just what do you think you're doing?"

"I'm heading out for a ride as soon as I stretch Copper's legs, like I told you. Why?"

"You're getting dust all over the clothes I just hung out, that's why."

"Oh, jeez. I never thought about that. I'm sorry, honey. Do you want me to wash them again?"

"No, just go enjoy your ride. The wind will take care of the clothes."

"All right, thanks."

Jim unhooked the longe line from Copper's bridle, hung it from the fence, mounted, rode out of the corral, shut the gate behind him, and loped off toward Onion Creek.

Shortly after nine-thirty that evening, with Josh down for the night, Jim and Kim were already in bed, both having decided to turn in early.

"Jim, we have to talk," Kim said, after a few

moments of silence. He had his back turned to her, watching the television while he waited for the ten o'clock news to come on.

"About what?"

"About what's bothering you. You've been moping ever since you got back from New Mexico. You've hardly spoken to me, except when I ask you something, and you're avoiding me whenever you can. Even at MacPherson's, you didn't have much to say. Plus, you've been spending an awful lot of time sleeping in your office, rather than the bedroom."

"Because it seems easier, that's all. I can sleep in there without being disturbed, and that way you can take care of Josh, and get your work done, without worrying about bothering me. You keep telling me I'm working too hard. I would think you'd be happy I was getting more rest."

"It won't wash, Jim. Something's wrong. You can't deny it. Do I have to drag it out of you?"

Jim grunted, and rolled over to face his wife.

"No, I reckon not. You're right, I'm angry. Damn angry, at you, and Ma, and a few others."

"Why?"

"I think you know why. You talked to Kelle, who talked to Bruce, who probably let something slip, even if he didn't mean to. Someone also called Major Voitek, and you're the only one I can think of who would do that, unless it was another Ranger, and I can't think of any who

268

would complain to him without talkin' to me first. Are you trying to get me discharged from the Rangers?"

"No, Jim. Not at all. I was trying to help you, if anything, *keep* your job."

"That's an awfully strange way to go about it. Then you must also know why Bruce was sent along with me to New Mexico."

"Yes, I did know. I'll be honest, I was hoping you wouldn't find out. I should have known someone would talk."

"Not until I forced it out of that someone. Why, Kim? You knew what I was from the first day we met, and that being a Texas Ranger is all I ever wanted, just like my pa, and my grandpa, and all my grandpas before them. That, and a family. Bein' a Ranger is the most important thing to me in my life, besides you and Josh. So why?"

"Because I was worried about you, and you wouldn't talk to me. Every time I tried, you clammed up, disappeared into your office, or buried yourself in your work. I was so frightened, thinking that you'd become so exhausted you would collapse, or make a mistake that would get you killed. I still am."

"You don't think I have sense enough to know when I've reached my limit? Boy howdy, I guess you must really think I'm dumb. It's either that, or you hate me being a lawman, but don't want to tell me straight out, so you've gone behind my back."

"Jim, that's not fair. I'll admit I sometimes wish you weren't a lawman, and that you weren't working late so much, or away from home so often, but I accepted that the day I agreed to marry you. What I *didn't* consent to was your driving yourself so hard you'll kill yourself from a heart attack or stroke. Have you already forgotten it wasn't all that long ago you nearly died after being ambushed? I don't want to be a widow before I'm thirty-five years old. I've tried to talk to you about this, more than once, but you won't listen to me. I was at my wit's end, so yes, Kelle and I talked about what I should do, and we both agreed I should speak to Major Voitek about my concerns. He was grateful to hear from me, since he had been hearing the same from some of your fellow Rangers, that you were pushing yourself way too hard. I only confirmed what he already knew, or at least suspected."

"I'm so glad to know how confident you are in me," Jim said. "I've never complained, not once, about the times I've gone to bed alone because you were working late, or on a call with an overseas client. I never once objected when you and Ma went off for a few days, or even a week, to a conference or business meeting, and I was left to fend for myself."

"That's different."

"Is it? You've come home from those pretty worn out, too, sometimes. Yes, I work hard, but I also know when to back off."

"I don't think you do, Jim. I also think that boy being shot right in front of you is affecting your judgment. You don't want to admit it, but it is. I honestly believe you need to talk to a professional about what happened that day."

"So now it comes out. You think I'm goin' plumb *loco*. Well, I have news for you, Kim. I'm not. Bruce saw that. He's going to report that I'm working a bit too hard, and recommend that I take things a little easier, but that I'm absolutely fit for duty. So that ends that."

"No, Jim, it doesn't. I don't know how you fooled Bruce into thinking you're just fine, but—"

Jim interrupted her.

"Hold it. I've got to hear this."

"See, you still won't listen to me."

"Just gimme a minute, Kim."

The ten o'clock news had just come on, with a "Breaking News" logo. The anchor woman was reading the lead story.

"Jim, don't cut me off."

"I told you, in a minute. This could be trouble."

Jim turned up the set's volume.

"We have a developing story tonight from north central Comal County," the announcer read.

271

"There has been a report of a police involved shooting, just outside the Sattler area of Canyon Lake. Details are still coming in, but from what we have learned so far, a deputy sheriff and a civilian have both suffered gunshot wounds. We have no information as to their identities or conditions at this time. We have a crew *en route* to the location, and will provide more details as they become available."

"In other news, the Austin City Council . . ."

"Jim, are you going to listen to me, or not?" Kim said.

"I'm listening."

"No, you're not. You've still got your eyes on the television."

Jim picked up the remote and clicked off the set.

"There. Are you satisfied now?"

"No. I can tell you're hearing what I'm saying, but you're not paying one bit of attention."

"I am so, but I'm not even considering what you're suggesting. You complain I never open up, that whenever you're angry, or we have a fight, I just agree with you, say I'm sorry, and that's that. Well, you're about to get your wish. You want me to open up, so I will. I'm not cutting back on my work load, I'm not quitting the Rangers, and if my work starts to become too much, I'll be the one who decides that. Not you, not my mother, not Bruce Sherman, not Lieutenant Stoker or

Major Voitek. It's my decision, and mine alone. There, I've said it. I hope you're satisfied. I'm communicating. Now good night!"

Jim turned off his bedside lamp and burrowed under the sheet, his back to Kim.

"Jim, I'm not finished."

"Well, I am. Good night."

"Jim, you're just like your mother warned me you'd be, as damn stubborn and thick-headed as your father. Look where that got him."

Jim sat up, his face red with anger.

"It got him a place in the Texas Ranger Hall of Fame, that's where it got him. How could you even bring his death up? I still miss him like it was the day he died. Yeah, he was killed, but he saved an awful lot of lives by givin' up his own. He died a hero."

"I'd rather be the wife of a live coward than the widow of a dead hero," Kim answered.

"Then we have a real problem," Jim said, "Because I'd rather die than live as a coward."

"Jim, when we first met, you told me Rangers did mostly investigative work, that being a Ranger was far safer than being a state trooper or a city police officer. Were you lying?"

"No, I wasn't. We're not necessarily on the front lines, but that doesn't mean we don't get involved with some real bad *hombres*. That's what I do, help gather the evidence that puts the bad guys behind bars, which also means Rangers get into some awful risky situations, especially when it comes to making an arrest. We deal with the dregs of society, the worst of the worst. I never told you my job wasn't dangerous."

"Jim, you weren't—"

Jim's phone rang.

"Hold on, Kim," he said, as he picked it up. "Ranger Blawcyzk."

"Ranger Blawcyzk, this is the Comal County Sheriff's Office. Sheriff Donavan is requesting your assistance at an officer involved shooting."

"I just saw that on the news," Jim answered. "I figured you'd be calling. What's the location?"

"Sheriff Donavan asked you to meet her at the River Road bridge over the Guadalupe, just south of Sattler."

"I know where that is. Tell the sheriff I'll be there within forty-five minutes, sooner if possible."

"Will do, Ranger."

Jim clicked off the phone and got out of bed.

"I'm sorry, Kim. I've gotta go. I told you that shooting would be trouble. The sheriff needs me down in Sattler. I don't know when I'll get home."

"You haven't listened to one word I just said. Go ahead and get yourself killed, Jim. That's what you want, so don't let me stop you. See if I care."

"You don't mean that. I don't mean to hurt you,

either. I dunno, maybe we both need to take some time and step back."

Kim buried her face in her pillow, softly crying.

Jim hurriedly dressed, started for the door, then turned around, leaned over, and kissed his wife.

"No matter what, Kim, I still love you, and I always will. That's one thing that will never change, not even for the Texas Rangers."

9

The sheriff's department had closed River Road at its intersection with Farm to Market Road 2673. The deputy manning the roadblock flagged Jim down.

"Howdy, Ranger," he said. "Sheriff Donavan is waiting for you at the bridge."

"Thanks, Deputy," Jim answered. The county officer waved Jim through. A minute later, the Ranger pulled up to the bridge over the Guadalupe River, which was surrounded by police vehicles, a fire department rescue truck, the sheriff's department dive team unit, and two ambulances, plus a county coroner's van. Portable floodlights illuminated the scene. Comal County Sheriff Rosalie Donavan was waiting for him as soon as he got out of his truck.

"Howdy, Jim," she said. "Sorry to get you out this time of night. Glad you got here so quick."

"This is what the state pays me for," Jim answered, with a shrug. "Howdy, Rosalie. What've you got?"

"One helluva mess, which is why I called for you. One dead suspect, and probably one of my deputies. He fell into the river after being shot, then another of my men ran down and killed the shooter, in the camping resort over yonder. We haven't found my deputy, or his body, as of yet, and it's too dangerous to put the divers in the water until we get enough daylight. Right now, we do have a boat in the river, but they haven't had any luck. Where do you want to start?"

"Is the entire scene secured?"

"What do you think, Jim?"

"With you in charge, Rosalie, it's more secure than Fort Knox. How about your deputy? How's he doing?"

"He's in his car, with strict orders not to speak with anyone except me or you, until after we've questioned him. I've gotten a preliminary statement, of course. I've got another deputy with him to make certain he stays put."

"The shooter?"

"Still where he fell. No one has touched the body, or the immediate area around it."

"Then I'll begin there. Just gimme a minute to grab my evidence kit. You can give me the details you've got while you take me to the shooter. Let's start from right where your deputy says things went down. I want to retrace the route. I'll record what you say, of course."

"All right."

After Jim got his collection kit from the back of his truck, Donavan led him to a point about three-quarters of the way across the bridge. A number of markers indicated shell casings or other possible evidence. He switched on his recorder and dictated the date, time, and case number into it before he allowed Donavan to speak.

"All right, Sheriff. Go ahead."

"Luke Carter says he and Herb Solis, the missing deputy, were sitting in their cars in the pull off on the side of the road, back there at the bend. They were taking a break and doing some paperwork. They'd gotten out to stretch their legs, when they both saw a person come walkin' out of the Rio Resort, carrying two big packs or satchels. When they yelled for him to stop, he took off running, onto the bridge. Both of 'em gave chase. Solis caught up to the shooter first. When he did, the man threw whatever he was carryin' into the river, then turned to face my deputies. Solis was right on top of him, according to Carter. They struggled, Carter heard a shot, he saw Solis stagger back, then fall off the bridge. Let's keep walkin'."

"Okay."

"After he shot Solis, the shooter fired a couple or three shots at Carter, jumped over the guardrail, and ran back into the campground. Carter went after him. He caught up to him tryin' to duck around one of the RVs. They exchanged shots. The shooter missed, but Carter didn't. Carter called for help, made certain the shooter wasn't goin' anywhere, then went back to the river to look for Solis."

Donavan nodded to a deputy, who was keeping

a small knot of spectators out of the taped off crime scene, as she led Jim into the campground.

"It's not far now. Just beyond this row of cottages."

"Any witnesses?"

"None that we've found, so far. A lot of these campers belong to Canadian snowbirds, who leave 'em here year 'round, but only use 'em in the wintertime. That means they're mostly empty, which could be the reason the shooter figured it would be an easy haul. It's also Monday night, so all the damn weekenders who clog up the roads and stir up trouble went home yesterday. There aren't a lot of folks stayin' here right now."

"What about the office?"

"It closes for the night at nine. There's only an overnight maintenance man on call, who's got a cottage way down back."

"Surveillance cameras?"

"None. And since my deputies were out of their cars, and the county hasn't funded body cameras yet, there's no video from them, either. Here we are."

Donavan nodded to another deputy, who was guarding the site, then led Jim in between two unoccupied travel trailers. Between them was a flood-lit body, lying on its back, with a pistol in its right hand. Several markers indicated where shell casings had been found.

"Boy howdy, your deputy shot this man to damn pieces, Rosalie."

"What did you expect, Jim? He'd just seen one of his partners gunned down, in cold blood. Any one of us would probably have done the exact same thing."

Jim switched off his tape recorder while he took photographs of the body and the surrounding area, then turned it back on.

"Did any of you recognize this *hombre*?" he asked, as he studied the body more closely.

"Yeah. Cutler recognized him. His name's Randall McPartland. According to Cutler, he worked as a fry cook at Jeffers' Café up the road, until it burned down last year. Since then, he's been doin' odd jobs and handyman work for the resorts and vacation condos around here. He'd have plenty of knowledge of folks' comin's and goin's, and what valuables they might have."

"Speculation, Rosalie," Jim grunted. "Lemme get this over with."

He switched his recorder back on.

"Texas Ranger James Blawcyzk, continuing the investigation into the apparent homicide of Comal County Deputy Sheriff Herbert Solis, then the subsequent killing of the suspected assailant by Comal County Deputy Sheriff Luke Carter. Assisting me is Comal County Sheriff Rosalie Donavan."

"The victim is a black male, approximately in

his late twenties. Per Sheriff Donavan, Deputy Carter identified the victim to her as one Randall McPartland. The shootings took place at approximately nine-twenty tonight, according to Sheriff Donavan. Victim has been shot at least four times, in the chest and abdomen. Condition of the body is consistent with the sheriff's timeline. There is a pistol in the victim's right hand, which I am now removing."

Jim took a pencil from his pocket and a plastic baggie from his evidence kit. He slid the pencil into the gun's trigger guard, then put the weapon into the bag and sealed it.

"Pistol is a Smith and Wesson M&P40 Compact, .40 caliber. Ballistics tests will be made to determine if it is the same weapon used in the shooting of Deputy Solis, and the attempted shooting of Deputy Carter. I am now going to check the victim's pockets, for identification and any other evidence."

The dead man's pockets contained his wallet, some change, a handkerchief, and a set of keys, one an apparent house key, the other an ignition key for a Plymouth.

"Driver's license in victim's wallet confirms his identity as Randall McPartland, age twenty-four, address 11005 Cranes Mill Road, Canyon Lake, Texas. After completing my preliminary examination of the body, I will release it to the Comal County Coroner's office for autopsy."

Once Jim got all the information McPartland's body could give him, he drew a chalk outline around it. He stood up, stretched, and arched his back to remove a kink.

"Rosalie, you can contact the coroner now and tell him he can come get McPartland. Let him know I want to be present during the autopsy. Also, that I want the toxicology reports ASAP. While you do that, I'm going to go over the scene here, and gather what evidence there is. I also need the area searched for a Plymouth, which McPartland was probably drivin', at least that's what this key indicates. If it's located, I don't want it touched. I'll go through it on site, after I interview Carter, then call for a hook to have it taken to the impound. After that, I'm goin' back to the bridge. I want Carter there with us."

"Why, Jim? Are you suspicious of something?"

"No, nothing in particular. I just want Carter there to show us exactly where on the bridge Solis was shot, to the best of his recollection. Merely standard procedure."

"Okay, Jim. You're in charge."

Donavan contacted the coroner and two of her deputies, then assisted Jim as he checked over the area where McPartland had died. After twenty minutes, the sheriff received a call on her radio."

"Sheriff Donavan, this is Deputy Morgan."

"Go ahead, Morgan."

"We've located what appears to be the suspect's vehicle. It's a 1997 dark green Plymouth Voyager. The plates come back to Randall McPartland. It's parked on River Gate Road, just outside the self storage place."

"Good work, Morgan. Stay with the vehicle until Ranger Blawcyzk and I get there."

"Will do, Sheriff."

"Jim, McPartland's vehicle has been located. How much longer will you be at this area?"

"Last thing here, then we can go back," he said. "There's a bullet hole in this trailer. Soon as I dig the slug out, we're finished in this area. I want this whole section, including the entire campground, kept off-limits until daylight, though. I want to go over it one more time, in better light. For anyone staying here, the place is on lockdown until I say it's clear. Naturally, I'll want to speak with any possible witnesses."

"I'll make certain of it."

"I'm obliged."

Once Jim dug the bullet out of the trailer, then dropped it in a baggie for ballistics comparison later, he and Donavan headed back to the bridge, getting Deputy Carter on their way.

Jim took Carter back to the location on the bridge where he'd said Deputy Solis and his apparent killer, McPartland, had fought. He switched his recorder back on.

"Deputy, for the record, would you please state your full name and occupation."

"Certainly, Ranger. My name is Luke Matthew Carter. I am a deputy sheriff with the Comal County Sheriff's Department."

"How long have you been an officer with that department?"

"A little more than seven years now."

"Thank you. Please tell us, as fully as you are able, what happened at this location earlier tonight."

"Of course. Me'n Herb Solis were parked just past the north side of the bridge, in that little turn off at the curve. We'd do that quite often when we had the graveyard shift. We'd meet, do some paperwork, maybe take a little break. The radio record of when I called in will give you the exact time we stopped. We'd walk a bit to stretch our legs, take a look at the river, have some coffee. It's usually a nice, peaceful spot. But tonight, it sure wasn't."

Carter stopped, trying to keep his composure.

"Go on, Deputy. Take your time," Jim said.

"Sure. Sure, Ranger. We'd walked up the road to see how the new restaurant building was comin' along, and were headed back to our cars when a man came walkin' out of the Rio Resort. He didn't see us, but both of us could see him, pretty clear."

"Even with no street lights around here?"

"Yeah. The resort's lights were enough so we could make him out, plus there was some light from the moon. Not as much as if it were full, but still, enough to illuminate the bridge. When we realized he was carrying somethin', we called out to him, identifyin' ourselves as deputies.

"Instead of stopping, the *hombre* looked back at us, then took off for the bridge. We both chased after him, but Herb runs a lot faster'n I can, so he caught up to him first. The *hombre* must've realized he was about to get caught, because he threw whatever he had into the river, then spun around.

"Him and Herb fought for, I dunno, maybe less'n a minute. Then I heard a shot. Herb stumbled back, he was kinda hunched over, then he fell over the side of the bridge. The *hombre* took a couple of pot shots at me, just enough to keep me pinned down until he could make it to the riverbank. He jumped off the bridge and took off runnin', back into the campground. That's where I shot it out with him, and killed the damned son of a bitch. Then I called for help and went back to look for Herb, although I knew there wasn't much chance of findin' him."

"You didn't try to help your partner by firing at the suspect?" Jim asked.

"I didn't dare, for fear of hittin' Herb instead of him. I was still pretty far back, and as I said, while there was light, it wasn't all that good for shootin'. He shot Herb before I could catch up with the two of 'em. And of course, these days, we couldn't shoot him in the back when he started runnin', since we had no idea whether he had a gun, or whether he hadn't done anything, but was just scared."

"Even in the old days, shooting a fleeing man in the back, without good reason, was pretty much frowned upon," Jim answered. "Sheriff Donavan has already walked me from here to where you caught up with the suspect. I want you to walk us along the exact path you took, telling me what happened, where, along the way. Sheriff, if you have any questions, or anything to add, jump right in. Deputy Carter, first, did the suspect ever get out of your sight?"

"No, he damn sure didn't, Ranger."

"So there's no chance you might have mistaken the man you shot for another one?"

"No, sir."

"You're certain?"

"Yes, sir."

"Good. Now, let's get started. This is just about the spot where Deputy Solis was shot, correct?"

"That's correct, right about here."

"Which side of the bridge did he go over, upstream or down?"

"Upstream."

"So he, or his body, would have been washed under the bridge. Maybe gotten hung up under it?"

"That's correct. But that was the first place I looked for him, and didn't find him."

"Fine. Let's start walking. Can you tell me about where the suspect jumped off the bridge?"

"Sure. He got far enough to where it wouldn't be that far a fall, so between the edge of the water and the guardrail at the end of the bridge. He rolled down the bank, then took off runnin' up those stairs the tubers use."

"Do you have any idea what he might have tossed into the river?"

"It looked like a couple of big satchels, or maybe backpacks. I've got no idea what might've been in them."

"Okay, you lead the way from here, Deputy."

Jim made observations and took notes as Carter retraced the route of his pursuit of McPartland, until they reached the spot where McPartland had fallen.

"Stop right there, Deputy. What happened here, when you caught up to the suspect?"

"He was tryin' to get around the back of that trailer on the left. I hollered for him to stop. Instead, he turned and took a quick shot at me. I shot back, and hit him. He got off one more shot, then I emptied my gun into him. I wasn't givin' the bastard the chance to do to me what he'd done to Herb."

"How far apart were you?"

"Let's see. He was at the corner of the trailer,

and I was standin' about here. I reckon that's about twenty-five feet or so."

"Ranger, we've already taken measurements," Donavan broke in.

"That's good, Sheriff. It'll save me some time. I'm obliged," Jim answered.

"Deputy," he continued. "I have just a few more questions for you. First, I'm kinda puzzled why the suspect would run *toward* you after he shot Deputy Solis, rather than away. Any ideas?"

"I dunno, Ranger. There's nothin' much on the other side of the river, so maybe he knew that, and didn't want to take a chance on getting lost in the woods. Maybe he had a car parked around here, or was gonna steal one. He might've figured on breakin' into a cottage or trailer and taking hostages, if he had to. But you're right. Heading for me just doesn't make sense. I don't know why he did that."

"Second, did you look over the edge of the bridge before you took off after the suspect, on the chance Deputy Solis might have survived both the bullet and the fall?"

"I have to admit I didn't. Everything happened so fast, all I could think of was getting the son of a bitch who had just shot my partner and friend."

"But you did search for him once the suspect was out of action?"

"Of course."

"For how long?"

"Until the first units arrived. After that, I helped them until Sheriff Donavan arrived, and ordered me to stop."

"I understand. I'll probably have more questions for you later. Right now, Sheriff, I assume you're planning on putting Deputy Carter on administrative leave, if you haven't already done so?"

"Either that or desk duty, Ranger."

"I'm afraid it will have to be leave, at least until I'm done with the main investigation," Jim answered. "I'll also need your gun, Deputy."

"My gun? Why?"

"You know why. It'll need to be tested, to make certain your weapon is the one which fired the shots that killed Mr. McPartland."

"Give Ranger Blawcyzk your gun, Deputy," Donavan ordered. Carter hesitated, then unbuckled his gunbelt and handed it to Jim.

"Thank you for your cooperation, Deputy," Jim said, as he switched off his recorder. "I'll return your weapon to you as soon as possible." He glanced up at the sky, where the gray light of false dawn was just brightening the eastern horizon.

"Sheriff, it'll be sunrise in about an hour-and-a-half. Soon as there's enough daylight, I want the divers in the water. I also want two deputies on each riverbank, scouring them for any possible evidence, all the way from here to the dam, a quarter mile downriver. What I'd really like to find, in addition to Solis's body, of course, is whatever McPartland tossed off the bridge."

"It'll be done, Jim. That water is mighty murky, though. It could be a while before we find Solis."

"The river is runnin' a bit higher and faster than usual," Jim answered. "If the divers can't come up with Solis, his body'll probably wash up at the dam downriver, before the day is out."

"Here's hoping. What about Deputy Carter? Do you want him to remain here?"

"Yeah, until I've got everything wrapped up. Deputy, you can go back to your car, and write up your report. I'll need a copy, of course. Once that's done, you can get yourself some sleep, if you want. I'll send someone for you if I need you. Sheriff, I'm gonna do some more pokin' around while we're waitin' for sunup. I need to talk with you privately first, though."

"Shouldn't my deputy hear whatever it is you have to say? After all, it's him who was directly involved."

"A bit later, soon as I say it's all right. Don't worry, I'm not trying to hide anything from him."

"It's okay, Sheriff. I'll go get started on my report," Carter said.

"All right, Luke. You'll be back on duty as soon as possible."

Donavan waited until certain Carter was out of earshot.

"All right, Jim, what's the big secret? Am I missing something here?"

"There's no real secret, but there *is* a problem," Jim said. "A helluva big one. You might not realize it, but you're about to be smack in the middle of a prairie wildfire, one that's headin' straight for you at a hundred miles an hour."

"What do you mean, Jim?"

"Do you know who Randall McPartland, the alleged shooter, was?"

"No, I can't say as I do. Should I?"

"Maybe not, but you're about to find out. He's the son of a preacher man. His father is the pastor of the Second Coming AME Church in San Antonio."

"You don't mean Reverend Dean McPartland. That can't be!"

"I do, and he is. It gets even better. His aunt is Dr. DeQuonya Parnell."

"The professor and civil rights activist?"

"Precisely."

"But why would Reverend McPartland's son be working as a fry cook and handyman?"

"I've heard stories, but since I can't confirm them, I won't repeat 'em. However, you'd better hope your deputies didn't make the slightest mistake here. I'm telling you straight out, if either one of 'em did, my report will show that. You know me well enough to know that I don't cover up anything, for anyone. That's not how

291

the Rangers work, and especially not how *I* work."

"Do you think there'll be protests?"

"Rosalie, you can bet your hat on it. Let's just hope and pray they're peaceful. And be grateful Carter didn't shoot McPartland in the back. You're not to breathe a word of this to anyone, especially the media, until I give the okay. Understood?"

"Clearly. Damn, this is the last thing we needed. Did that boy have a record?"

Jim winced.

"He was twenty-four, Sheriff. That's a young man, not a boy. Not to mention calling any black man 'boy' is offensive. Please don't make that mistake again. Something like that could be the match that sets off the powder keg. And no, he had no record, except for a couple of speeding tickets."

"Sorry. It was a slip, and I meant nothing by it. You're saying my department has a problem, aren't you?"

"Pretty much. There's no possible way I can finish my investigation in a couple of days, and if trouble's gonna start, it'll start by then. Right now, I'm going to call Lieutenant Stoker, and have him notify the family. He happens to attend Rev. McPartland's church, so we caught a break there." Jim shook his head. "Boy howdy, your men really stepped into it, pardon me sayin' so, especially for Deputy Solis. Right now, I need two things from you, Rosalie."

"What are they?"

"I want you to find every possible witness for me to question. Even if they think they just heard a cricket burp, I want to talk with 'em. I especially want to talk with the owner of that burnt out café. With any luck, he can tell us more about McPartland.

"The second thing is, you'd better get a written statement ready for the media. Don't say anything specific, just that the matter has been turned over to the Rangers, to insure an impartial investigation. Also, find one of your chief deputies, and tell him or her to wait for a call from Lieutenant Stoker. Whoever it is will have to know how to handle a real delicate situation, since they'll be goin' with the lieutenant when he tells the family their son is dead. They'll also have to explain why you couldn't be there, instead of them, and that you'll call on the McPartlands as soon as possible."

"Understood, Jim. After that?"

"Use the time until sunup to take a break, all of your people, then get the search started. While you're doin' that, I'm gonna call my wife, then get back to work."

"All right."

Jim took out his phone to dial home. After three

rings, Kim answered. Her voice was still heavy with sleep.

"Jim? Where are you?"

"Hi, honey. Sorry I had to wake you, and I'm even more sorry about last night. I said some things I shouldn't have."

"We both did," Kim said. "I'm sorry, too. Are you on the way home?"

"I wish I was, but I'm gonna be here most of the day. I can't tell you much, except I'm investigating the apparent murder of a sheriff's deputy, and the killing of the suspect by another deputy. I've still got a lot of ground to cover, and witnesses to interview. I'll be home for supper, I hope."

"At least that guarantees you won't be here to destroy my kitchen again," Kim said, with a soft chuckle. "If you don't get home in time for supper, I'll keep it warm for you."

"You're a real gem, Kim, you know that? Listen, I've got to get back to work. I'll call you as soon as I'm on my way home. Love you."

"I love you too, Ranger. Good-bye."

" 'Bye, honey."

Once the sun rose, Jim continued studying the crime scene, including going through McPartland's minivan, while the divers were finally able to enter the water, and the deputies resumed searching the riverbanks. He especially concentrated on the bridge, particularly where Carter had said Solis had been shot, and also where McPartland had jumped over the side. It was about two hours later when Sheriff Donavan called him.

"Jim, it's Rosalie. We've found Herb Solis's body. It got hung up on some rocks, about two hundred yards above the dam."

"Don't move it until I get there," Jim said. "Can I drive close to where you found him?"

"Yes. Cross the bridge and take the first right, onto a gravel road. A short ways down that, you'll see a dirt road to the right, just before a big barn on the left. You can take that all the way to the river. I've already contacted the coroner, so he's on his way."

"*Bueno*. I'll be there in a couple of minutes."

Jim got his Tahoe and followed the directions to the riverbank, where Donavan and several deputies were gathered. The divers' inflatable boat was anchored in the middle of the Guadalupe.

"Down here, Jim," Donavan called, when he got out of his truck. "In the rocks."

At this point, the south bank of the Guadalupe was lined with large, jagged limestone outcroppings. Solis's body was wedged between two of those, belly up and partially submerged. Jim took several photos of the corpse while it was still in the water.

"All right, let's get him outta there," he ordered. "But be careful. We don't want anyone else fallin' in and dyin' here."

It took less than half-an-hour for Solis's body to be secured and pulled out of the river. The deputy county coroner, Judd Grey, who was already on scene at the bridge, waiting during the search, arrived while this was being done.

"Judd, how soon do you think you'll be able to do the autopsies on these two bodies?" Jim asked. "They've got to be a priority."

"I wish I could say today, but that probably won't happen," Grey answered. "We're already backed up with two more suspicious deaths, plus a car crash victim, and we're still tryin' to identify a person who died in a fire last week. Soon as I get the corpses back to the lab, I'll draw the fluids to get the toxicology reports started, but the actual autopsies will have to wait until tomorrow. Sorry."

"That'll be okay," Jim answered. "Since I want to be there, that gives me the whole day here. Looks like they've gotten Solis out of the water. Let's take a look."

Solis's body had been placed on the flat sandy patch at the end of the road.

Jim switched his recorder back on.

"I am with Comal County Deputy Coroner Judd Grey. We are doing a preliminary examination of the body of Comal County Deputy Sheriff

Herbert Solis, which was recovered slightly less than a quarter mile below where he fell into the Guadalupe River, off the River Road bridge in Sattler. There is a bullet wound to the upper abdomen, but no exit wound in the back. Solis's gun is still in its holster, and, except for his hat, the body is still fully clothed. As it was submerged in the river for several hours, most physical evidence will have been contaminated, or completely dissolved. The body will be removed to the Comal County Coroner's Office for a complete autopsy and forensics examination, as well as retrieval of the bullet."

He switched off the recorder.

"Judd, go ahead and load him up. Expedite things as much as you can."

"You know I will."

"Obliged. Sheriff, how have you done finding witnesses?"

"My chief deputy on scene tells me he's rounded up all those he can. There aren't too many, less than a dozen, but one of them is old Clyde Jeffers, who ran the café where McPartland worked. He's probably gonna be able to tell you more about McPartland than anyone else."

"Good. I'll question them while your people finish up searching the riverbanks. If they haven't found any large objects that might've been thrown off the bridge, I'll need the divers to drag the river, to see if they can snag something. They might even have to go in the river and search the bed, if they don't have any luck otherwise."

"My team won't miss a pebble that's out of place," Donavan assured him.

"Good. Let's go see those witnesses."

The crime scene was cleared shortly before five-thirty P.M. On his way home, Jim stopped at a florist to pick up a dozen roses. Next, he stopped at the Walmart near his office for their most expensive bottle of Riesling.

"Ranger, I'm sorry," the cashier said, as he checked out, "but I have to card you. You sure don't look forty."

"That's 'cause I'm not," Jim said, laughing. He pulled his driver's license out of his wallet and handed it to the cashier.

"Thanks, Ranger."

She rang up his purchase, then he was on his way. He pulled into his yard shortly before seven.

"You're home right when you said you would be when you called," Kim said, when he walked into the kitchen.

"I promised you I would be. Where's Josh?"

"He's sleeping, which of course means around eleven he'll be wide awake. Supper is just about ready. If you'll set the table, I'll get it out of the oven. I made roast beef, baked potatoes, and we have some fresh tomatoes from the garden."

"Oh, no. I brought you these." Jim produced

the bouquet of roses and the blue glass bottle of Riesling from behind his back. "White wine with beef. How gauche. We'll never be able to show our faces in high society again. I'm so embarrassed. Here I thought the flowers and wine would help make up for our fight last night."

"Jim, we've never, ever been able to show our faces in high society, especially you," Kim said, laughing. "The roses are lovely, and I'm certain the wine will be fine. Before you start setting the table, I've also got a little something for you."

She took a silver-wrapped box, tied with a blue ribbon, from atop the refrigerator, and handed it to him. Jim looked askance at the package.

"This looks mighty fancy."

"Go ahead, open it," Kim urged.

"All right."

Jim opened the box to reveal an amber bottle, which had a "Jodelle's Parfumerie" label.

"Cologne?" he said. "I've never worn cologne. I've tried a couple, but I just don't like any of the scents."

"I think . . . no, I'm *positive* you'll like this one," Kim said. "Go ahead, open the bottle."

"All right."

Jim unscrewed the cap, and took a tentative sniff.

"I do like this. It smells like leather, and something else I can't quite put my finger on."

He took another, deeper whiff.

"Horse sweat. It smells just like saddle leather and horse sweat. I love it. Finally, a men's cologne I'll wear. Where in the world did you find this?"

"At Jodelle's, the little perfume shop in the San Marcos historic district. That's where your mother and I get our scents. Jodelle says she is able to make up almost any scent, so I asked her to compound the two scents I knew you'd like. It was a challenge for her, but she did it."

"She sure did. Thank you, honey."

He leaned over and kissed her.

"Now, let's eat. I haven't had a thing all day, except for coffee and Dr Pepper."

"Sure, I just knew you hadn't eaten. The murder was on the news, but except for the names of the poor deputy, and his murderer, they didn't have many details, so you can tell me about your day over supper."

"That's because we haven't given the media much, yet. I've still got a lot of follow up to do before we release more information. This is gonna be a tough one."

"I gathered that, just from learning who the murderer's father was. You can tell me whatever you're able to over supper, then I think we should make up for last night. I promise never to have another argument with you again, well, not like that one, and not about your job."

"I promise the same thing. It was hard working

and thinking about how I hurt you. How do you propose we make things better?"

Kim gave him a wicked smile, her eyes glittering.

"For starters, you can wear your new cologne . . . and nothing else. Well, nothing else but your cowboy hat, and a bandana. Oh, and your gun, of course. Also, no shower first. We'll be going to the hayloft. You'll be a cowboy who just rode into town, and I'll be a saloon girl who promised you a good time."

"As long as I don't have to undress until we're in the loft. And what will you be wearing?"

"The same outfit, without the cologne, hat, or bandana. I just might try on your gunbelt for size, though."

"I'll get the plates. This may be the quickest supper we've ever eaten."

10

The nest morning, Jim had been in his office for just about thirty minutes when the telephone rang.

"Ranger Blawcyzk."

"Good morning, Jim. It's Lieutenant Stoker."

"Mornin', Lieutenant."

"I trust you've been following the news since last night."

"As much as I can, while tryin' to put two and two together on the Sattler killings."

"That's why I'm calling. Since you've seen the news, you're aware that Randall McPartland's family, the Black Lives Matter folks, the NAACP, and several other organizations are demanding an independent investigation into the matter, not by D.P.S. or the Rangers, but by the United States Justice Department and the F.B.I. They've requested a public hearing with the Comal County Commissioners. That has been granted. The meeting is scheduled for tomorrow night, seven o'clock at the high school auditorium, since the crowd will probably be too large for any of the conference or court rooms. We'll both need to be there, especially since Major Voitek is still recuperating from his emergency gall bladder surgery. We don't want this case handed over to the federal authorities. To that end, I'd like to meet with you sometime today."

"Sure, that'll be fine, Lieutenant. I was just leaving for the coroner's office, down in New Braunfels. I want to see the autopsies performed, which should answer a couple of questions I have. Would you want to meet me there?"

"I suppose you'll suggest having a spaghetti dinner afterwards."

"No, I won't. I don't understand why everyone jokes about spaghetti after an autopsy. The dissection looks more like lasagna to me."

Stoker gave one of his rare laughs.

"It would. No, thank you. I've seen plenty of autopsies in my career. Why don't I just meet you at your office at five?"

"That'll be fine. I'll brew a fresh pot of coffee."

"Don't bother, Jim. I'll bring my own, rather than drink that poison you brew. See you this afternoon."

"See you then, Lieutenant."

Thirty minutes later, Jim was in the county morgue. Judd Grey handed him a white lab coat, face mask, safety glasses, and pair of nitrile gloves.

"Soon as you put those on, we'll get started," he said. "Which one would you prefer I do first?"

"If it's all the same with you, I'd like you to start with Solis," Jim answered. "I'm a mite curious about how he died."

"You don't think it was the bullet?"

"Oh, I think the bullet was *supposed* to kill him, all right. I'm just not certain it did the job."

"Okay."

Grey removed Solis's body from its compartment, slid it onto a gurney, and rolled it into his examination room. He dictated the name, date, and case number into his recorder, noting that Jim was present, then continued talking as he began the autopsy.

"Here's your bullet, Jim," he said, a short while later. "It penetrated the stomach, and came to rest in the latissimus dorsi muscle. It's still in pretty good shape, since it doesn't appear to have hit any bone."

"Fatal wound?" Jim asked.

"Possibly, even probably, but usually not immediately so. The man might very well have survived with prompt medical attention. However, let me keep digging."

"What are you, a gold miner?"

"The only gold I've ever found is in a dead person's teeth," Grey answered, with a grim laugh. "However, I have dug out a lot of lead in my time." He took out a bone saw to begin cutting through Solis's breast bone and ribs. A short while later, he had Solis's chest cavity open. He carefully examined the dead man's lungs, then sliced into one.

"Just what I suspected," he said. "There's water in the lungs. Deputy Solis didn't die from a gunshot wound. He drowned."

"Are you certain, Judd?"

"You can have a closer look if you want."

"Nah, I'll take your word for it."

"I thought you would. I'll finish this autopsy, then move on to Mr. McPartland. Not that I expect to find anything unusual. It will just be a matter of getting the specifics."

Jim returned to his office with enough time to add the results of the autopsies to the rest of his files on the Solis and McPartland shootings before Lieutenant Stoker arrived. He was leaning back in his chair, taking a brief break, when the lieutenant walked in.

"Are you that tired, Ranger?" Stoker said, unusually for him, jokingly. He handed Jim a manila envelope.

"That's the transcript of my interview with Randall McPartland's parents. It's not going to be much help. Neither one has any idea why their son would be involved in a shooting, let alone kill a deputy sheriff. I've still got the rest of his family and friends to speak with. They're all taking this hard, of course. I'll get those reports to you as soon as they're completed."

"You don't want to ask me if I'm tired a second time," Jim said. "Yeah, it's been a long two days. I think there'll be some even longer ones before I figure out exactly what happened on that bridge. I do appreciate your helpin' me out by questioning McPartland's friends and family for me. That'll save me quite a bit of time right there. I'm obliged."

"This situation needs to be settled as quickly as possible, so I'm doing myself a favor, as much as you. With the major still laid up, this hot potato has been dropped right in my lap. You sound like you feel this isn't a cut and dry case," Stoker said, as he sat down, and took a sip from the paper cup of convenience store coffee he held. "What isn't adding up?"

"Nothing major, just a whole lot of little things that don't match Carter's story."

"Such as?"

"First, McPartland supposedly threw a couple of large backpacks or duffel bags over the bridge while he was runnin' away, before he shot Solis. Yet, there hasn't been any found, not even after two days of searching the river by dragging its bed, and sending divers down, even though it's not that deep. If there was something of any size tossed into the water, we should have found it."

"Could be someone saw them and took them before the search team did. What about on the banks?"

"Just some trash, a ripped-open float tube, and two items that may or may not mean anything. One was Solis's hat. That's probably nothing. The other was a latex glove, which hadn't been in the water all that long."

"That could just be a coincidence. Maybe a kid blew it up like a balloon and threw it into the river to float."

"It wasn't tied shut."

"The knot might've come undone."

"I know, but there weren't any wrinkles where it would have been tied. Still, I've got to wonder why it was there."

"Anything else?"

"There's more. Try as I might, I couldn't find any sign of a struggle on the bridge. Supposedly, McPartland and Solis fought before McPartland killed him. However, there were no scuff marks on the bridge, the sand and gravel on the road weren't disturbed, neither man's clothes were torn. No bruises, swelling, cuts, or discoloration, as if a punch had been landed, either. Even more—and this is why I waited for the autopsies, just to confirm what I found—there was nothing on either body to indicate a fight. No bruised, scraped, or broken knuckles, no skin scrapings, no rips in either man's clothing."

"Maybe they just wrestled a little, then McPartland shot Solis before he could throw a punch."

"I suppose that could be," Jim conceded. "But hear me out. I've got more questions. Why wouldn't either deputy have pulled a gun and fired a warning shot? For that matter, why didn't either one of them even have his gun out, apparently? Solis's was still in its holster when his body was pulled out of the river. When McPartland spun to face him, why didn't Solis tackle him? After he shot Solis, why did McPartland run *toward* Carter, not *away* from him and into the woods, where he'd have had a better chance of shakin' him off? That doesn't make any sense at all."

"All good questions, those. What about McPartland's vehicle?"

"That only adds to the mystery. It was half-filled with things a burglar would take, computers, large screen TVs, coins and jewelry, so forth. Stuff that would be easy to get rid of for quick cash. And yes, his fingerprints were on most of the items. Yet, no one in any of the cabins and cottages along the river has reported their place being broken into or stuff missing, and none of the vacant buildings and RVs seem to have been broken into, either."

"Those things could have come from some-where else."

"Of course they could have. That was one of my first thoughts, that McPartland was stealing the stuff in another part of Canyon Lake, then stashing it in a unit at the self storage place, where his vehicle was located. However, he didn't have a unit rented there, and the manager didn't recognize his picture, so it doesn't appear McPartland had rented a space under another name."

"Perhaps that's why McPartland ran toward the other deputy, rather than away from him. He was trying to get back to his car."

"That's logical, except for one thing. Carter stated that when he and Solis first saw McPartland, he was walkin' *away* from them. That means he was also walkin' away from his car. If he was, in fact, carrying two bundles of stuff he'd stolen, he should have been walking toward his vehicle, not away from it. So he's walking away from his vehicle, until he's confronted by the deputies, then after he shoots one, he heads *for* the other one? Makes no sense at all."

"Maybe he panicked. People do unexpected things when they're dealing with law officers, especially if they have reason to be worried about them."

"I can't disagree with you, Lieutenant. However, there's still more. Carter claims McPartland jumped off the bridge and rolled down the bank alongside the river, then ran up the stairs into the resort. I couldn't find any sign of damage to the grass, and no disturbed soil, anywhere along that whole riverbank, between the railing and the stairs Carter says Solis ran up. There should have been some indication a man went over it, but there wasn't even a bent blade of grass. No footprints where a man landed, either."

"If the grass was still green, it might've sprung back before you looked at it. If the ground was hard, McPartland might not have left any footprints."

"Now you're goin' around in circles, Lieutenant. If the ground was hard, that means the grass would be at least partway dried up, so it would have been smashed down, and shown where a man went over it. If the grass was green, which it was, the ground would be soft enough to show footprints, at least at the spot where McPartland jumped the rail."

"I'm merely playing devil's advocate here. Is there anything else bothering you?"

"Yeah, there is. Solis didn't die from the bullet in his gut. He drowned. That means he was still alive when he went into the water. Now, that itself doesn't concern me. I'm not surprised he was still breathing. What does bother me is the path the bullet took through Solis, where it stopped, and its condition."

"What do you mean?"

"Follow along with me here, Lieutenant, and I'll explain. Carter stated Solis and McPartland were still struggling when he heard one gunshot. After that, he stated Solis stumbled backwards, kind of hunched over, which is consistent with being gut-shot, then fell into the river. There's a couple of problems with that scenario. If Carter's statement is accurate, McPartland shot Solis at point blank range, maybe even with the barrel of his gun pushed right up against the deputy's stomach. That means the bullet should have gone clean through Solis and exited out his back, unless it hit bone, which it didn't, judging from its only minor deformation.

"Instead, the slug was still in him, stuck in his back muscle. Also, the bullet's trajectory through Solis isn't consistent with a shot being fired from close up, and during a struggle. Its path through Solis's abdomen was straight, or nearly so, until it stopped. Most likely, if that shot had happened while the two men were fighting, it would have angled upward or downward. It seems to me that bullet was fired from a distance, not from a gun pressed right into Solis's belly."

"What you're saying makes sense, Jim, but we both know bullets can do funny things once they get inside a person. What about powder burns on Solis's shirt or flesh?"

"It's gonna be hard to say, because of him bein' in the river for a few hours. Judd Grey's doing some more testing, which he'll get to me as soon as he can. I will say the hole in Solis's shirt doesn't appear to be from a close-up shot, but I have no way to prove that, at least not without a reasonable doubt. Neither does the hole in his gut. Saying more about the bullet's trajectory, the pistol in McPartland's hand was a Smith and Wesson M&P .40 Compact. The ballistics tests confirmed it was the same gun that was used to shoot Solis, and to try and shoot Carter. For its size, that's a damn powerful gun. That .40 caliber slug, at close range, should've gone clean through Solis like a hot knife through soft butter. It didn't."

"Did you test McPartland's hand for powder residue? I know we don't perform that test all that often, because it's highly inaccurate."

"In this case I did, and as I expected, it came back positive. As you know, Lieutenant, that could very well be a false result. Someone who actually shot Solis, with that gun, could've placed that pistol in McPartland's hand, after he was already dead. And if they did, they made certain McPartland's fingerprints were all over that pistol.

"There's one more thing about that gun. I haven't been able to trace it back to McPartland. The serial number was filed off. I'm still checking with all the gun shops in the area, to see if they sold a pistol like that to an *hombre* matching McPartland's description. So far, I've had no luck.

"I also attempted some acid etching to see if I could bring out at least part of the serial number, but it didn't work. Whoever filed off that number did a thorough job of it. From what I've learned of McPartland's background, I don't believe he'd have the skills to erase it so completely. Of course, he could have bought it from someone who does, but why?"

"So what're you sayin', Jim? You think *Carter* shot Solis? Why?"

"I'm not ready to say that, not yet. I still need more proof before I can accuse anyone. Maybe McPartland did kill Solis, and I'm just readin' the evidence wrong. Maybe he and Solis were farther apart than Carter recalls. Seein' his partner and friend shot might've shaken him enough his mind recalls what happened differently than the facts. Maybe someone else shot Solis, and for some reason, Carter doesn't want us to find out whom that is. I just don't know. This is a real puzzler."

"Again, why would Carter kill his fellow deputy?"

"Let's get back to Crime Investigation 101, Lieutenant, the basics. Means, Motive, and Opportunity. Carter certainly had both the means, and plenty of opportunities, to kill Solis, if he, in fact, did. The motive is the question. I've still got some more background checking to do, on both men, but so far, there's nothing to indicate Carter would have any reason to kill Solis."

"What about McPartland? What have you uncovered about him?"

"About what you got from his parents. Everybody around here liked him. Every single person I've talked to said he was a good, real happy-go-lucky young man, who always had a smile on his face. He was always ready to help someone, but other than that, pretty much kept to himself, except when he had a gig at one of the bars or honkytonks around here. He was quite an accomplished guitar player and singer, from what I've heard tell."

Jim took a sip from his own cup of coffee, then continued.

"McPartland was so well liked by his boss, Lester Jeffers, that when Jeffers' café burned down he allowed him to stay rent free in the little bungalow he rented from Jeffers, until the place was rebuilt. Told him he didn't want to lose him to another restaurant. And, of course, you already know McPartland's record, except for a couple of old speeding tickets, is clean as a whistle. Do you happen to know why he left home? Knowing the reason may shed some light on what happened. I've heard some stories kickin' around, but they were mainly rumors."

"Yeah, I sure do. You mentioned McPartland . . . um, Randall, was known around here as a guitarist and singer. He was also a really good cook. In fact, so good he applied to one of the most prestigious culinary institutes in the country, up in Connecticut. He was accepted, and even got a partial scholarship. However, his daddy wouldn't hear of it. He was determined that Randall follow him into the ministry, and hopefully take over his church one day. Randall was just as determined that he had no desire to be a preacher. Since his father wouldn't help with the tuition, Randall couldn't afford to go to the school. They had a huge argument, Randall left home, and hadn't spoken to his father since. The last thing he told him was that he'd become a chef at a fancy, high-class restaurant one day, with or without his father's help. Then he stormed out. It's a real shame his father wouldn't allow him to follow his dream. Even though Reverend McPartland is the pastor of my church, this time, he was wrong."

"And his son ended up dead, from all appearances possibly as the killer of a deputy. Sad ending, for everyone involved."

"Damn," Stoker said.

"You can say that again," Jim answered. "There's just too many loose ends to wrap this case up, not without a lot more diggin'."

"No, I meant damn, what you've just told me is exactly what I didn't want to hear, Jim. You're aware rumors have been circulating about protests. I've learned those are more than just rumors. McPartland's aunt, Dr. Parnell, applied for a permit to hold a march on Saturday, followed by a vigil and rally Saturday night, in front of the county courthouse in New Braunfels. Those will be followed by another march and rally on Sunday. The county commissioners had no choice but to grant the permit, of course.

"I'd hoped you'd have a definitive answer to what happened in Sattler before then, so we'd have a better chance of defusing the situation. I'm not concerned about the legitimate marchers, but you know there's bound to be some troublemakers show up. There'll probably be a counter-march and rally, too. On top of that, the businesses in town are already worried about losin' money, and if things get out of hand, damage. I don't need to tell you how much New Braunfels, particularly the water parks, depends on weekend tourist dollars. On top of that, Solis's funeral is Monday, and McPartland's Tuesday. I'm worried tempers might flare at those, too."

"I'm sorry, Lieutenant. I'll work on this day and night, but there's no possible way to figure this out in forty-eight hours. I assume the New Braunfels police and county sheriff's office are getting ready for any trouble?"

"Yes, all leaves for both departments have been cancelled, and of course the Highway Patrol will have troopers in place, also. I don't expect you to be in New Braunfels, since you've got enough to do, trying to get to the bottom of this mess. Even though it's your county, I *would* like to have some Rangers on location, in addition to the local officers and state troopers."

"That's not a problem, Lieutenant. Sounds like we'll need everyone possible there."

"I'm afraid you're right. I also have a suggestion for you, Jim. This isn't an order, so please don't take it as one."

"All right. What is it?"

"I want you to concentrate only on this case, until you've got it cleared up. To that end, I'll have the Rangers from adjacent counties cover anything new that crops up in your area. If you have anything you're working on right now that can't wait until this one's closed, I'd appreciate it if you'd turn those over to me, so I can pass them along to another Ranger."

Jim hesitated before answering.

"I'm not too keen on the idea, but I reckon it'll save me a whole passel of trouble, 'specially at home. Having to worry only about this mess will make things easier for me. You've got a deal, Lieutenant."

"I'm glad you agreed, Jim. I would have hated to get into an argument with you when I *made* it an order."

"I figured on that, too. I do have a couple of cases you can take along."

Jim got up, went to a file cabinet, removed two folders, and handed them to Stoker.

"That's the rape case from down near Spring Branch, and the attempted murder up at Round

Mountain. Everything else can wait a few days, or I can let you know if something changes."

"All right, Jim. I *will* need you with me at the hearing tomorrow night. Let's meet at, say, six-thirty, at the courthouse."

"That's fine with me, Lieutenant."

"Good. As far as the funerals, I'm going to attend Randall's, of course, since I know the family. I expect you'll be going to Deputy Solis's."

"Yeah, I will. I've known him for a long time. He was a good man. Left a wife and two teenage boys, too."

"I know. If there's nothing else, I'd like to get on home. Tomorrow promises to be a long day."

"And a rough one."

"That goes without saying. I just thought of one last question, Jim. What do you think of Luke Carter, as a deputy, and an individual?"

"I haven't had too many dealings with him, but he's a competent lawman, from what I've seen. He's got no blots on his record, no reprimands, nor any instances of excessive force or civilian complaints. What he does have are a couple of commendations. He seems decent enough, too. Certainly no indications he would gun down another deputy in cold blood."

"Okay, that answered my question. I'll see you tomorrow night, Jim."

"See you then, Lieutenant."

11

The auditorium at New Braunfels High School was packed to overflowing. A closed-circuit television link to the school stadium's scoreboard had been set up, so the people who couldn't get into the hall were able to watch the proceedings. Jim and Lieutenant Stoker were seated at one end of a table on the stage. Sheriff Donavan and Howard Wolf, the New Braunfels police chief, were at the opposite. In the center was Simon Kleiner, the Comal County Judge, who was the head of the county commissioners. Flanking him on either side were the four precinct commissioners who, together with Kleiner, made up the County Commissioners' Court. At eight minutes past seven, the judge gavelled for order. After taking the roll call of the commissioners, he started the proceedings.

"Good evening," he began. "For those present who may not know me, I am Simon Kleiner, the Comal County Commissioners Judge. First, I realize we are here to discuss a very tragic, emotional, and sensitive issue, the death of a young man at the hands of a Comal County deputy, as well as the death of a Comal County deputy, allegedly committed by the same young man. To ensure everyone's safety, any person,

I emphasize *any person,* who disrupts these proceedings will be removed from the premises and arrested for disorderly conduct.

"Also present tonight, in addition to myself and the county commissioners, are Comal County Sheriff Rosalie Donavan, along with Texas Ranger Lieutenant Jameson Stoker of Ranger Company F, and Texas Ranger James Blawcyzk, who is in charge of the investigation into this unfortunate incident. I will start with a brief statement, followed by Sheriff Donavan, then Lieutenant Stoker, and finally Ranger Blawcyzk. After those statements, we will take questions, first from the general public, then the media. This meeting will not be adjourned until everyone who wishes has had a chance to speak. With that understood, and emphasizing once again that I expect a peaceful assembly and civil discourse, I will start this meeting.

"The people, government, and law enforcement officials of Comal County, and its communities, are committed to fair, impartial justice for everyone, regardless of race, creed, color, ethnic origin, gender identity, age, disability, or any other reason. To that end, even before notifying this commission, Sheriff Donavan contacted the Texas Rangers to initiate an independent investigation into the tragic events of earlier this week. All of us on the commission wholeheartedly agree with her decision. Deputy

Luke Carter, who fired the fatal shot which killed Randall McPartland, has been placed on administrative leave, and will remain on leave until the Rangers' investigation is completed."

"The unfortunate deaths of Mr. McPartland and Deputy Herbert Solis have left a dark blot on our county. Differences of opinion are expected and welcome, as are peaceful, lawful protests, which are the rights of every American citizen. However, threats of violence and destruction are not what Comal County is about, and will not be tolerated. Anyone, whether a resident of this county or an outsider, who attempts to foment violence, or deepen fissures amongst the residents of our communities, will be dealt with severely, and subject to the harshest penalty of the judicial system. We will not allow the deaths of Mr. McPartland and Deputy Solis to be an excuse for violence and destruction of property. Personnel from the New Braunfels Police Department, the Comal County Sheriff's Department, and the Texas Rangers are prepared to deal with any untoward occurrences. In addition, I have asked the governor to place units of the Texas National Guard on standby, in the event they are needed. The governor has granted my request.

"Finally, I wish to extend my deepest sympathy to the families and friends of Mr. McPartland and Deputy Solis. My thoughts and prayers, as well as those of all the county commissioners, the Comal County Sheriff's Department, and the people of Comal County are with you. Together, we will make it through this dark time, heal, and move forward once again. I will now turn the microphone over to Sheriff Donavan for her statement. Sheriff Donavan."

"Thank you, Judge Kleiner. As I cannot comment on any ongoing investigation, I will only say that I fully expect the Texas Rangers will do a complete and thorough investigation into the circumstances leading to the deaths of Mr. McPartland and Deputy Solis. To that end, I have pledged the full cooperation of everyone in the Comal County Sheriff's Department. All of us at the Department extend our sympathies to both families, especially the family of Deputy Solis, who died in the line of duty."

"Order," Judge Kleiner shouted, banging his gavel, as a murmur of protest swept through some of the spectators. "Please continue, Sheriff Donavan."

"Thank you, Judge. That's all I have to say at this time. I'd like to turn the microphone over to Lieutenant Stoker."

"Of course, Sheriff. Lieutenant Stoker."

"Thank you, Judge. Ladies and gentlemen, I am here on behalf of Major Arthur Voitek, the Commanding Officer of Texas Rangers Company F. Major Voitek is still recuperating from emergency surgery, and so was unable to be present here this evening. He and I both wish to assure you every possible lead, no matter how small, no matter where it takes us, will be followed up in this incident. To that end, I would urge anyone who might know anything at all about Mr. McPartland, Deputies Solis and Carter, or possibly have any information about what happened that night in Sattler, please contact Company F immediately. I am now going to ask Ranger James Blawcyzk, whose territory includes Comal County, and who is therefore the lead Ranger on this case, to provide an update as to his progress. Ranger Blawcyzk."

"Thank you, Lieutenant, Sheriff, Commissioners. I'll give a brief recap of my investigation to this point, where it is going, and possibly when it will be completed.

"I was called to the scene of the shootings, the bridge over the Guadalupe River in Sattler, by Sheriff Donavan, as soon as she realized her department was faced with a difficult situation. While the sheriff and her deputies had begun the investigation, she ordered it halted until I arrived on scene.

"I don't need to rehash the details of what had occurred, the gunshot deaths of Mr. McPartland and Deputy Solis. So far, I have not reached a definite conclusion as to the exact sequence of events that night. While all the evidence indicates, as Deputy Carter has stated under questioning, Mr. McPartland was observed by both Deputy Carter and Deputy Solis crossing the bridge, carrying two large bundles, attempted to flee when confronted by the deputies, fatally shot Deputy Solis, and was, in turn, fatally shot by Deputy Carter, there are still several details of the events that night that have not been corroborated by either evidence or eyewitnesses. My investigation will continue until all those details have been clarified to my satisfaction.

"To that end, as Lieutenant Stoker has already requested, if anyone here has knowledge of, or knows of anyone who can shed further light on what happened that evening, please contact me as soon as possible, either directly at my office in Buda, or through Company F.

"This is all the information I am able to share with the public at this time. Due to the sensitive nature of this investigation, divulging anything more would compromise it, so nothing more can be revealed, either as to evidence, possible witnesses, or any other details. I realize this will not be satisfactory to many of you; however, I give you my word I will keep all interested parties informed of my progress, as much as possible. I will now give the microphone back to Judge Kleiner, who will take your questions. Thank you."

"Thank you for your candor, Ranger Blawcyzk," Kleiner said, as he took the mic.

"Before I take questions from the public, I must request no shouting for attention. Just raise your hand, and I will call on you. I assure you, everyone who has a question or statement will be allowed to speak, no matter how late we are here. To that end, I again ask members of the media to refrain from asking their questions until every member of the public has had their opportunity to speak. If anyone, including the reporters present, does not abide by this simple rule, they will not be called upon, and if disorderly, will be escorted from the room. I will now take the first question. When I call on you, please state your name and city for the record. Dr. Parnell, I will grant you, along with Reverend or Mrs. McPartland, the opportunity to offer the first question or make the first statement."

"Thank you, Judge Kleiner. My name is Dr. DeQuonya Parnell, of San Antonio. I will be speaking for my brother, Reverend Dean McPartland, and his wife Linda, as they are both too distraught to speak in public at this time.

"While we appreciate Sheriff Donavan's asking the Rangers to investigate the events of last Monday evening, we feel strongly that the Texas Rangers, due to their rather questionable record of dealing with members of the black and Latino communities, will not be able to perform a fair and impartial investigation. The family is requesting—no, we are demanding—

the investigation into our son's and nephew's death be turned over to the Federal Bureau of Investigation. We are also demanding a violation of civil rights investigation be initiated by the United States Department of Justice, against the Comal County Sheriff's Department. We feel this is the only way the true facts will come out, and justice will be served. Thank you."

"I appreciate your concern, and understand the reasoning behind your requests, Dr. Parnell," Kleiner answered. "If and when the commissioners at this table feel federal authorities should be involved, we will contact them, and advise you of such. However, any such request this soon would be, we feel, premature. We would rather the Rangers finish their investigation, then, if the results aren't satisfactory to this commission, yourself, the McPartland family, or any other party with a valid interest in this case, then and only then would we entertain your request. Lieutenant Stoker, would you care to elaborate on my response?"

"Yes, I would, Judge. Thank you. Each and every one of us in this room is aware that, in the history of the Texas Rangers, there have been times, unfortunately too many times, when members of the organization were prejudiced in their views and actions, particularly against minorities, including African-Americans and Hispanics, especially Mexicans and Mexican-

Americans. This led to many injustices against non-white citizens of Texas. As an African-American myself, I can certainly understand, and sympathize with, the cynical views of the Rangers held by many present here tonight. However, those days are in the past. I will personally vouch for the integrity of each and every man and woman in Company F, as would Major Voitek, if he were able to be here with us. There is no need to request Federal intervention. Ranger Blawcyzk's investigation into the events leading to Mr. McPartland's death will be complete, thorough, and impartial."

"Judge Kleiner, am I correct that you are refusing our request? As are the Texas Rangers?" Parnell questioned.

"No, Dr. Parnell, I am not refusing it. I am merely asking it be deferred until the Rangers have finished their investigation, and the results are known. Next question. You, sir. The gentleman in the third row."

"Thank you, Judge Kleiner. Daryl Robertson, Austin. I am the district chair for the Black Lives Matter Chapter of Greater Austin. With all due respect to Ranger Blawcyzk, we as a group feel a white man cannot possibly do a fair and impartial inquiry into the death of Mr. McPartland. We insist that Ranger Blawcyzk be removed from the investigation, and that he be replaced by a person of color."

"Lieutenant Stoker, would you care to answer the gentleman?" Kleiner said.

"Damn straight I would," Stoker said, obviously fighting to keep his temper in check. "Mr. Robertson, as you can see, I also am a 'person of color,' as you put it, although I prefer African-American or black. I have been one of Ranger Blawcyzk's supervisors since he first became a Texas Ranger. His integrity and determination to find the truth, no matter where it may lead or whom it might hurt, is second to no man's or woman's. Ranger Blawcyzk applies his high ethical and moral standards, and sense of justice, equally to everyone, man or woman, white, black, brown, or any other color, no matter their background, creed, sexual orientation, or position in society. In addition, he is one of the best investigators I have ever had the privilege to work with. I will not cut Jim off at the knees by handing his investigation to another Ranger, just because of the color of his skin. That would be an insult to him, and an affront to the Texas Rangers. I throw *not one* of my people under the bus, for you or any other person. Understood?"

"No, Lieutenant Stoker. Your loyalty to, and desire to protect Ranger Blawcyzk, is understandable, perhaps even admirable. However, your personal feelings must be set aside in the interest of full justice for the late Mr. McPartland, his family, and the non-white citizens of Texas.

After all, Ranger Blawcyzk is the same man who has been involved in several deadly shootings, most notably that of two of the men who allegedly killed his father, who were members of an ethnic minority."

Stoker exploded with rage.

"Mr. Robertson, how dare you! How dare you impugn the honor and reputation of a man whose family has dedicated their lives, for over a century, to serve and protect the people of Texas? At least two members of that family died in that service, including Ranger Blawcyzk's father, who saved countless lives when he foiled a terrorist plot to destroy the Alamo. I will not allow you, or any person, to stand up in front of this audience and besmirch Ranger Blawcyzk's reputation. There's a word for a person like you, sir, but I will not say it for respect of the others in attendance here tonight. You are undoubtedly one of the lowest—"

Jim broke in. "Perhaps you'd better let me respond, Lieutenant."

"You, Jim?"

"I think it might be best."

"Are you certain?"

"I sure am, sir."

"All right. Go ahead."

Jim kept his voice calm, his face expressionless, as he spoke.

"Mr. Robertson, Dr. Parnell, and those here

329

who are in agreement with them. I understand your concerns, and assure you they will be taken into consideration as my investigation into the deaths of Mr. McPartland and Deputy Solis proceeds. However, and I thank him from the bottom of my heart for sticking up for me, as Lieutenant Stoker just stated, more eloquently than I ever could, nothing or no one will prevent me from doing my job, which includes coming to an honest conclusion as to what happened on the Guadalupe River bridge in Sattler last Monday, based on the facts, and nothing else.

"I would also like to point out to you that, a short while back, I testified for the defense in the case of a poor, young black man, who was accused by a wealthy white woman, a prominent member of Johnson City society, of sexually assaulting her. I uncovered several discrepancies in the woman's story, as well as errors made by the arresting officer and the district attorney. My testimony resulted in a not guilty verdict, preventing an innocent man from going to prison. If that can't convince you of my impartiality, I reckon nothing can.

"Y'all are requesting the F.B.I. be brought in to take over the case. You have the right to request that, and I certainly won't object if you do. However, I must advise you, this is *my* investigation, and mine alone. I will not tolerate any other law enforcement agency, local, county, state, or federal, interfering with me in any way whatsoever. I will not turn over any evidence to them, and I will not cooperate with them, until my investigation is completed, and my report filed. So, go ahead and invite the F.B.I. down here, but until my work is finished, they'd better stay the hell out of my way, or I'll run right over them."

The audience burst into a cacophony of boos and cheers.

"Order. Order or I'll clear the room," Kleiner shouted several times, banging his gavel for emphasis. "Order!"

It took several minutes for Kleiner to calm the spectators.

"We may now resume this hearing," he said, once he could again be heard. "Ranger Blawcyzk, thank you for clarifying your viewpoint."

"I'm sorry if I stirred things up, Judge Kleiner," Jim said. "I just wanted to make certain everyone knows where I stand."

He handed the mic back to Kleiner.

"Understood, Ranger. Next question. The lady in the seventh row, a few chairs in from the right. Please state your name and city, then proceed with your question, ma'am."

"Thank you, Judge. My name is Marjorie Wilkins, from right here in New Braunfels. I have a two-part question. First, what is the plan to protect the citizens of this city from the professional outside troublemakers who will be descending upon New Braunfels? Second, why is what happened even a matter for discussion? It's plain what happened. A law officer was gunned down by a young black man, who was then killed by another deputy. Break the law, pay the consequences."

Kleiner had to shout to be heard, as the crowd erupted into a chorus of boos and catcalls, along with an undercurrent of cheers for the woman.

"Ms. Wilkins, you are out of order, and your comments are not helping matters—"

Here we go, Jim thought, as the shouts from the spectators grew until they were almost deafening. *Nothing good's gonna come of this.*

The meeting finally ended well after midnight. The police kept everyone moving, and opposing sides apart, until they had all left the area. Jim and Lieutenant Stoker were standing alongside their vehicles.

"Jim, I never thought I'd see the day when you were the calm one, and I was the one who got out of line," Stoker said. "I appreciate your stepping in and keeping me from making an even bigger fool of myself."

"I figured I'd better. Making a fool of oneself is *my* job, not yours. Boy howdy, this night went worse than I expected, and I didn't expect much. I'm gonna head on home and hit the sack.

Since you've got to be in Waco in the morning, Lieutenant, would you like to spend the night at my place, instead of going all the way back to San Antonio? That'd at least save you a little bit of drivin'."

"I appreciate the offer, Jim, but I've got to decline. I promised my wife I'd take her to work, since her car's in the shop."

"Okay. Drive carefully."

"Look who's talking," Stoker said, laughing. "G'night, Jim."

" 'Night, Lieutenant."

Kim was sitting up in bed, reading a magazine, when Jim came home. He leaned over and kissed her.

"Sorry I'm so late, honey."

"It's all right, Jim. I watched the news, so I knew you'd be late. Did things go as badly as the reporters made them appear?"

"If anything, worse. Taking those two bullets in the back was less stressful, for me, than going through that meeting. I'd honestly almost rather get shot again, instead of facing that crowd. I'm really worried about what's going to happen during those marches and rallies. At least I won't have to deal with those."

"You won't? I'm certainly relieved to hear that, but why not?"

"Because I'll still be doing nothing but tryin' to

figure out what the hell happened on that bridge," Jim said, as he took off his tie. "Plus, since I'm kinda the flash point for this whole problem, if I were to show up, just my presence could set off some hothead. Right now, both sides are screamin' for my head on a platter. Believe me, I'm not complaining about havin' to stay as far away from those rallies as possible. Right now, I just want to get some sleep."

"Would you like me to fix you a late snack before you come to bed?"

"I appreciate that, but I'm not all that hungry. I'm just gonna take a quick shower, then call it a night, or I guess I should say morning. I'll probably sleep in a little."

"You? Sleep in?"

"Yup. I'm not going to my office tomorrow."

"Today."

"Yeah, I guess you're right. Today. Anyway, what I have to do right now I can do from right here at home. Then, tonight, I'm going back to Sattler. I want to look over the crime scene at the same time it happened, night. I need to see as much of what they were able to see as possible, in order to piece more of this puzzle together. The moon'll be a little brighter, but everything else should be the same. I need to see how the lighting was, what was visible and what wasn't, the shadows, all that in the same light the deputies and McPartland had. Hopefully, that will shed more light on the subject, pardon my pun."

"Don't give me that, Jim. You *never* ask to be pardoned from your bad jokes, particularly the awful puns. Go take your shower, and soak your head for that joke, and your fib. I'll keep your side of the mattress warm."

"All right. I can't refuse an offer like that. You're the best."

"Don't tell me what I already know," Kim said, laughing. "Get in that tub."

"Yes, ma'am!"

12

Just before nine that night, Jim stopped at the Stars and Stripes convenience store in the center of Sattler, to pick up a six pack of cold Dr Peppers and two chocolate bars. Two men standing at the counter, working on scratch off lottery tickets, nodded to him.

"Evenin', Ranger," one said. "Still lookin' into how that McPartland fella got the drop on those deputies? Damn shame a good man like Herb Solis died at the hand of a no-good son of a bitch like McPartland."

"Howdy, fellers. Yup, I am," Jim answered. "Just have a few more details to follow up on, and everything'll be wrapped up. I take it you knew McPartland, and didn't like him much?"

"I only met him a couple of times, but I never trusted him. He wasn't one of the town, you understand? Kind of an outsider. I don't know what Lester Jeffers ever saw in him."

"How about you?" Jim asked his friend.

"Never liked him either. Found him carryin' off some scrap wood and metal one time. Said he had permission to clear it off the riverbank, but the folks who own that piece of land were up north for the summer."

"Maybe he was doin' some work for them while they were back home," Jim said.

"Mebbe, but I doubt it. You can't trust McPartland's kind. You probably know that from dealing with 'em all the time."

Jim forced a wan smile.

"Yeah, I reckon you're right, at that. In this case I'm not so certain, though. I haven't been able to uncover any reason why he'd shoot that deputy. The more I look into what happened, the more there seems to be that doesn't fit the picture. Yessir, it sure is a puzzlement. Well, nice talkin' with you fellers. Have a good night. Hope you've got luck with those tickets."

"We've already won ninety bucks, Ranger. Thanks. You have a good evenin' now."

"You too, men."

After paying for his purchases, Jim drove to the bridge. He left his Tahoe in the same turnout where Carter and Solis had parked. Taking his flashlight, he walked onto the bridge.

"Let's see," he said. "Carter said McPartland and Solis were standin' right about here. McPartland spun, he and Solis struggled, then McPartland plugged Solis, right in the belly at point blank range. Solis falls off the bridge. So why the hell isn't there any sign of a struggle? Why no sign of where McPartland supposedly jumped off the bridge? And if McPartland *did* shoot Solis with his gun shoved into his gut, there should have been at least a trace of blood on McPartland's gun hand, but there wasn't. All the lab tests came back negative. There should even have been some blood spots on the bridge, or at least might've been, but there weren't any. Hell, none of this makes any sense."

Jim looked toward the resort and RV park.

"Now that I can see this road and bridge without the floodlights from the other night, it's almighty dark out here. The lights from the campground don't shine on this bridge at all. There's plenty of shadows, too. The moon wouldn't have been as bright on Monday, so it would've been even darker, with more, deeper shadows. I've got my doubts that Carter could see as well as he claims he could. Looks like I'm gonna be here a while."

Jim spent nearly two hours going over the scene of the shootings yet again, looking for the least little clue he might have missed, but found nothing, except one spot that he would have to investigate in the daylight. One or two cars went by while he was in the campground, but other than that, he was the only person out and about. He returned to his truck, tired and frustrated. He hit his key fob to unlock the SUV. As soon as he opened his door, another vehicle, a green Toyota Tundra crew cab pickup, came out of the side road behind the turnout, then pulled up alongside his Tahoe, blocking it in. Four men emerged from the pickup. Jim recognized two of them as the men he'd spoken with in the convenience store.

"Howdy again," Jim said. "What can I do for you now?"

"This ain't exactly a social call, Ranger," one of the men said. "We came to make certain you come to the right conclusion. We were beginnin' to get tired of waitin' for you."

"And just what would that conclusion be?"

"That Herb Solis got killed by a son of a bitch drug dealer."

"You got any proof of that?"

"We don't need any. He was a black boy, living high on the hog in the middle of all these good white folks. He killed that deputy, sure as me'n you are standin' here. And where else would he get the money but dealin' drugs, and robbin' folks' houses and trailers while they weren't around?"

Jim shook his head.

"I haven't found any firm evidence to prove that yet. As far as him livin' high, he had a run-down shack Jeffers let him live in, and drove an old van. If he *was* selling dope, he sure kept that fact well hidden. Now, you boys just back off, peaceable like, and let me be on my way."

"I guess you didn't understand our meaning, Ranger. That boy killed a good deputy, and we're gonna make certain your report says so."

"You don't wanna try that," Jim warned.

The man nearest to Jim took two steps forward, then swung a right-handed punch toward the Ranger's jaw. Jim ducked the punch easily, and sunk his left fist deep into the man's gut, jackknifing him. Before he could turn to face the charge of the next man, another clubbed Jim across the back of his neck, stunning him. He pitched to the ground face first, unable to move.

"Pick him up," he heard one of the men say. Two others grabbed his arms and dragged him to his feet. Jim was slammed against the side of their truck, the two men holding his arms keeping him pinned there.

"I guess you didn't understand us, Ranger," the apparent leader said. "Maybe this will help make our meaning clear for you."

He slammed his fist into the side of Jim's jaw, then punched him in the belly.

"Understand now?"

"You're . . . you're just makin' things . . . worse for yourselves," Jim said, gasping.

"I guess you need to be taught a lesson, Ranger."

Once again, a fist smashed into Jim's belly. After several more blows to his gut, Jim's knees buckled, and his head drooped. Only the two men holding him upright kept him from sagging to the dirt.

"I reckon he's had enough," the leader said. "Toss him over the bank."

Jim was dragged to the edge of the turnout, where he was kicked in the ribs, sending him over the edge of the riverbank. Before he tumbled all the way to the river and a possible drowning, a tree stopped his fall.

He heard the men laughing on the bank above, one of them saying something about Jim having been taught a lesson, then walk away. Somehow, he found the strength to unholster his gun, and crawl back to the top of the bank. The Tundra was just pulling away. He got off one shot, which struck the pickup, punching a hole through its tailgate. Jim heard the impact of lead against steel, then he blacked out.

Jim was only out for a few minutes. As soon as his head cleared, he pulled himself the rest of the way up the bank, then rolled over on his back. He lay still for a few minutes, until his head stopped spinning and he was able to catch his breath. He got back on his feet, picked up his hat from where it had fallen and shoved it on his head, found his keys and flashlight, and opened the tailgate of the Tahoe. He got his shotgun from the back, then slid behind the steering wheel and started the engine. He waited for another few moments for his head to clear again, then put the truck in gear and headed back to the Stars and Stripes.

The clerk was the only person in the store when Jim walked in. He stared at the Ranger as Jim walked over to the frozen food case, pulled out a bag of frozen peas, and pressed it to his swollen jaw.

"You need help, Ranger?" the clerk asked, when Jim approached the counter.

"Yeah. How much do I owe you for the peas?"

"A dollar twenty-nine."

"Okay."

Jim took out his wallet, handed the clerk a dollar bill, then took two quarters from his pocket and handed the coins to the clerk.

"Put the penny in your penny dish," he said.

"Sure. Is there anything else?"

"Yup, there is. Those two men I was talking with earlier. You happen to know their names?"

The clerk hesitated before answering, then shrugged.

"I do. Bubba Emerson and Larry Nelson."

"They friends of yours?"

"No, sir. Just regular customers."

"You happen to know where I might find 'em?"

"This time of night you'll generally find them at the Sattler's Gorge Saloon. They like to hang out there, drink, and shoot pool."

"I'm obliged." Jim took a fifty-dollar bill from his wallet and tossed it to the clerk. "Thanks for the information. Now, don't you get any ideas about callin' that bar, and warning those boys

I'm comin', y'hear? 'Cause if you do, I'll know who called, which means I'll be back for *you*. I don't imagine you'd enjoy bein' put in jail for obstruction of justice."

"No, sir, Ranger, I wouldn't like that a'tall."

"Good man. Now, where is this bar?"

"Only a minute away. Get back on River Road, take the first right on Sattler, and it's just about a half-mile down, right across the street from the pet funeral home and cemetery."

"Thanks again. You've been a big help."

Before leaving the store's lot, Jim made a call to the Comal County Sheriff's Department.

"Comal County Sheriff Dispatch, how may we help you?"

"Comal, this is Ranger Blawcyzk. I'll need one of your units for assistance at the Sattler's Gorge Saloon on Sattler Road in Sattler. I'll also need a hook at that same location, flat bed, if available. I need a vehicle towed to impound. What's the ETA of your closest unit?"

"Let me check for you."

Jim could hear the dispatcher call several units to ascertain their locations. In a moment, she was back on the phone.

"Ranger, our nearest unit is about twenty minutes away."

"That's fine. I don't want it on scene for at least half-an-hour. Tell your deputy to take his

343

time. Same for the hook. I don't want it for thirty minutes."

"Understood, Ranger. Will advise."

"Thanks, Dispatch. 10-4 and out."

"Comal County Dispatch, out."

As the clerk had said, Jim arrived at the Sattler's Gorge Saloon in less than a minute. There were four cars in the front of the building, one of which was the green Tundra. One other vehicle, parked behind the bar, most likely belonged to the bartender or saloon owner. Jim parked behind the Tundra to block it in, then took his shotgun from the seat alongside him and headed inside.

The four men who had accosted him were the only customers. Two of them were at the bar, nursing drinks, while the other two were at a pool table. They started when Jim pushed through the doors, stared at him for a moment, then went back to their drinks and game. Jim locked the front door, then walked up to the bar.

"Can I do anything for you, mister—I mean, Ranger?" the bartender asked.

"You happen to have any Dr Pepper?"

"Sure."

"Good. I'll have a large one."

Jim took a handful of peanuts from a bowl on the bar to munch on, while the bartender filled a beer mug with his soda and placed it in front of him. Jim picked up the mug and took a long swallow, then set it back down with a bang.

"You four *hombres* are under arrest," he said, his voice barely audible, but his meaning plain. "Which one of you is Bubba Emerson?"

"I am," one of the men shooting pool said.

"Larry Nelson?"

"That'd be me, Ranger," the other player answered.

"And I'm George Fontaine. The man next to me is my buddy, Yancey Reynolds," the man closest to Jim, the one who had taken the lead at the bridge, said. "And if you think you can take all four of us, you're plumb *loco*, Ranger. I guess you need another lesson."

He turned and lunged at Jim, who reversed his shotgun, drove its butt deep into Fontaine's belly, then clubbed it over the back of his neck when he folded. Fontaine collapsed to the floor, all the fight out of him.

"You can't do that, Ranger," Reynolds yelled. "You've got no call for it."

"I can, and I just did," Jim retorted. "He resisted arrest. Seems to me like you are, too."

He swung the shotgun in a wide arc, catching Reynolds on the side of his head, smashing his left ear. Reynolds fell back against the bar, howling in pain. He pressed his hand to his crushed ear, in a futile attempt to stanch the blood dripping from it and running over his shoulder.

"Ranger, you—" The bartender stopped short.

"Stay out of this," Jim said, not taking his eyes off the other two men as he warned the bartender not to interfere. "It's none of your affair."

The bartender lifted his hands and backed away from the bar.

Emerson and Nelson, wielding their cue sticks like clubs, charged at Jim. He used his shotgun to knock the cues out of their hands, tripped up Emerson to send him sliding along the floor, then put the barrel of his shotgun under Nelson's chin.

"You want me to pull the trigger and blow your brains clean through the top of your skull?"

"No. No, Ranger, please don't," Nelson pleaded.

"Then sit down next to your sleeping partner."

"Yessir, Ranger."

Nelson sat alongside the still-unconscious Fontaine.

"You two, get over here where I can keep an eye on all of you," Jim ordered. "Sit with your friends."

Reynolds and Emerson scrabbled along the floor, until they reached their partners.

"You," Jim said to the bartender, "Call the Comal County Sheriff's Office and tell them Ranger Blawcyzk is ready for his backup and the hook. Do it!" he ordered, when the man hesitated.

"You might want to send for EMS, too. These *hombres* could use some patchin' up. Unlock the door while you're at it."

"All right, Ranger. I don't want any trouble."

While the bartender dialed the sheriff, Jim picked up his Dr Pepper and poured it over Fontaine's head. The cold, sticky liquid shocked Fontaine back to his senses. He rolled onto his back, spluttering. Jim jabbed his shotgun into the man's gut.

"Just lay quiet there, and don't move a muscle. Don't even twitch. That goes for all of you, or this thing's liable to go off. I'm still a mite shaky from that beatin' y'all handed me back at the river, so I can't guarantee my finger won't slip. Besides, I just had to waste a perfectly good soda to bring you around, Fontaine. I'm not too happy about that. Wait a minute, I just realized spilling my Dr Pepper on you made you a soda Fontaine."

"Ranger, you are one sorry son of a bitch," Fontaine muttered. "Just wait'll we report you for police brutality. You'll lose your badge for certain. With any luck, *you're* the one who'll end up behind bars. Then we'll sue you for every penny you've got."

"Bartender!" Jim called.

"Yeah, Ranger?"

"I didn't see any police brutality here, did you?"

347

"No. No, Ranger, I sure didn't. All I saw was you tryin' to arrest these four men, who put up a fight."

"That's good, because I'd hate to call the state liquor commission down here on you. I can promise they'd find enough violations to suspend your license for at least a year."

"You don't have to worry about that, Ranger. I run a clean establishment. A deputy will be here in a few minutes. So should the EMTs."

"I'm certain you do," Jim said. "Let's keep it that way. And I'm obliged to you for callin' the sheriff."

"Listen up, you four," Jim continued to his prisoners. "All of you are under arrest. You're being charged with breach of peace, inter-fering with a peace officer in the performance of his duties, obstruction of justice, assault on a peace officer, hindering a criminal investigation, resisting arrest, and attempted murder of a peace officer."

"Attempted murder? We didn't try'n murder you, Ranger," Emerson protested. "We just wanted to rough you up a bit, to make you get off Luke Carter's back."

"Shut up, Bubba," Fontaine warned.

"You might want to listen to him, at least until I've read you your rights," Jim said. "And I can make the attempted murder charge stick. After you were done beatin' on me, you shoved me over the bank, intending for me to roll clean into the river and drown. That's attempted murder. Now, you have the right to remain silent. If you do choose to speak, anything you say can be used against you . . ."

The men sat sullenly until Jim finished reading the Miranda.

"You've got no proof of any of this, Ranger," Fontaine said, once Jim was done.

"I've got plenty," Jim said. "For starters, there's a bullet in the bed of your truck, that I put there. Second, when I process that truck, I'm certain plenty of my DNA is all over it. There's also a piece of my shirt that tore off, stuck in a door handle. Your knuckles are scraped up. I can match the blood on my clothes to you *hombres*. I'll take casts of the footprints you left at the turnout, as well as casts of the tire prints your truck left. Some video of you attacking me might have been captured by my dashboard camera, too. All that's just for starters. Are you such good friends of Luke Carter, that you're willing to go to jail for him?"

"No, we ain't, except for seein' him around town, maybe sayin' howdy to him," Emerson answered. "We just didn't want to see a good man like him railroaded, only because he shot the bastard who killed his partner."

"Keep your damn mouth shut, Bubba,"

Fontaine warned again. "Ranger, we're not sayin' another word, until we have a lawyer."

"That's smart," Jim said.

"The deputy just pulled up, Ranger," the bartender said. "So'd the ambulance."

"Obliged."

A moment later, Deputy Juan Medina entered, trailed by two EMTs.

"Howdy, Jim," Medina said. "What's goin' on?"

"Howdy yourself, Juan. These four yahoos took it upon themselves to try and talk me out of continuing my investigation into the Solis/McPartland shootings. The only problem is, they did their talking with their fists. As if that wasn't stupid enough, when I tried to arrest 'em, they resisted. I've already read them the charges, and the Miranda. As soon as they're patched up, I'd appreciate it if you'd haul 'em down to the county lockup, until I can get the booking papers completed."

"I'll be more than happy to," Medina said. "I'd better call for another unit. The hook's also on its way."

"That's great. As soon as I process these boys' pickup, it has to go to the county impound."

"Jim, it looks like you can use a little patchin' up, too."

"Nah, it's just a big bruise," Jim fibbed, not letting on about the pain in his ribs and gut. "I've put a bag of frozen peas on it already. I'm fine.

Listen, let's cuff these boys, then if you wouldn't mind, could you keep an eye on 'em while I call my wife, to let her know I'll be home later than planned?"

Once the prisoners were secured, Jim called home.

"Hello, Jim," Kim said, as soon as she answered. "Is everything all right?"

"Everything's just fine, honey. I'm calling because I did discover something I have to check out. However, I can't do that until daylight, so I won't be home tonight. Don't worry, like I said, everything's fine. I did have a run-in with a couple of men, but that's all taken care of. I'll sleep in my truck until the sun comes up, then it won't take me all that long to figure out whether I've found something that might shed some light on the case. I'll be home by ten tomorrow morning, at the latest."

"You promise me you'll get that sleep, like you just told me?"

"Promise."

"You'd better. I'll see you in the morning. Love you."

"And I love you, Kim. Good night."

"Good night."

"Okay, Juan, let's get back to work," Jim said. "The sooner I can finish up here, and you haul these *hombres* off to jail, the sooner I can get some sleep."

Since Jim couldn't start his search until the sun was at least an hour over the eastern horizon, he bought some doughnuts and a large coffee at the doughnut shop next to the Stars and Stripes. He then returned to the turnoff at the bridge, where he ate his breakfast while he waited for the sun to climb high enough to cast its light over both riverbanks.

Once both sides of the river were bathed in sunlight, Jim got out of his truck, carrying his evidence kit. He first looked over the bank where he had been dumped alongside the river, taking several photographs to use for evidence against the men who had attacked him. After that, he walked across the bridge.

On the east bank of the river, at the south end of the bridge, there was a low hill, which was covered with trees and brush. What had caught Jim's eyes the night before was a spot where some of the vegetation had turned brown since his first examination of the scene. In addition, it was now plain that some of the brush had been bent and broken, apparently where someone had walked into the woods.

Jim climbed over the guardrail, to find tracks which confirmed two persons had indeed walked off the road and walked along the base of the hill at this point. In several places, the ground was soft enough to show their footprints. He took a moment to mix some dental stone and pour it into several of the footprints to make casts, then began following the broken brush as the makeshift path started to climb the hill.

The trail made by the two persons only ascended for a short way, then turned to parallel the river. Jim gathered several pieces of potential evidence along the way, a button, a scrap of cloth that was probably torn from a shirt, a cast of a handprint where one of the persons had braced himself against the sloping ground.

After a couple of hundred yards, the trail stopped, in a small, open grassy area. A patch of crushed grass and weeds indicated where one of the persons had fallen. Several brown, dried blood stains also marked the spot. Beyond that, a path of bent and broken grass through the field showed where a body had been dragged.

"Maybe I'm finally gettin' somewhere," Jim muttered to himself. After photographing the area, he opened his evidence kit to gather some of the blood-stained grass and soil.

"Let's see where this leads," he said, once he was done.

He followed the path, now consisting of one set of footprints, and drag marks from the body being pulled, as it worked its way back down toward the Guadalupe. Just before it reached the river, the path ended. A wider spot and several footprints showed where the body had been dropped, then the footprints, now deeper, continued to the riverbank.

"I'd bet my hat this is where Solis was killed, not on the bridge," Jim said. "Guaranteed the blood turns out to be his. I'd also wager it wasn't McPartland who killed him. Solis walked into these woods with someone, whether voluntarily or at the point of a gun I have no way of knowing. Whoever he was with shot him back in that little field, dragged him down here, and threw him in the river. They mustn't have realized he was still alive, or they damn for certain would have finished him off before gettin' rid of his body. But I still need more proof. It'll be a real stroke of luck if the casts I made, or those few things I picked up, can be tied to Solis's killer."

Jim took some more photographs, made some more casts of the prints, then began carefully searching for more evidence. A patch of light yellow at the base of a redberry juniper, which had its roots half in the river, caught his eye.

"If this ain't the mate to that glove which was found along the riverbank, I'll eat a double helping of Jock MacPherson's haggis!" he exclaimed. "Whoever killed Solis must have misplaced this glove, and figured no one'd ever find the place where he'd dumped the body. They got careless, and didn't bother to take the time to go back and find the missing glove. Either that, or they didn't realize it had dropped before it got into the water."

Jim took out a baggie and tweezers.

"I just got another break. This glove's not inside out. With any luck, I'll be able to get some fingerprints or DNA samples off it. I'll need to get the tests done pronto. I just hope they nail whoever killed Herb Solis."

13

"There, Jim. That's perfect," Kim said to her husband. Jim was standing on the top rung of a stepladder, hanging a *"CONGRATULATIONS! IT'S A GIRL!"* banner over the living room fireplace.

"It's about time," he muttered.

"What did you say, Jim?"

"Nothing. Nothing at all."

"You'd better not have."

Jim tacked the banner in place, then descended the ladder.

"I know I'm being fussy, Jim," Kim said, "But since this is Rosa's first baby, I want everything for the shower to be just perfect."

Jim winced when Kim kissed him on his still swollen jaw.

"I really wish you'd have let Doctor Goldman look at you," she said.

"There was no need," Jim answered. "My jaw's still a bit sore, but it's almost healed up. The man who gave me this lump is in far worse shape."

"So you told me. That still doesn't make me feel any better."

"But it was worth it. With any luck, when the DNA tests from the glove I found come back, they'll match whoever shot the deputy. What else do you need me to do?"

"Nothing. We're finished. The only thing left that has to be done is putting out the food. Your mother and I will take care of that. If I let you. you'll eat most of it."

"Why don't we relax on the patio for a few minutes, with some iced tea?" Jim suggested.

"I'd love to, but I have to finish wrapping Rosa's present."

"*Now* who's the one who won't take it easy for a bit? Could it be the certain someone who is always telling me I need to slow down? No, it couldn't possibly be her."

Kim laughed.

"I get the hint, Jim. You go outside. I'll make the tea."

"I can do that."

"And get into the cupcakes for the shower, or the icing bowl? Not a chance, mister. I'll bring you some cookies along with your tea."

"That sounds good."

Once she finished brewing the tea, Kim joined her husband on the screened-in patio.

"Here you are," she said, handing Jim his glass.

"Thanks, honey." Jim took a long drink. "This does taste good. There's nothing quite like a tall iced tea on a hot day."

"Jim, I appreciate you taking the time to help me today," Kim said. "I know trying to find whoever shot that deputy is really frustrating you, and you'd rather be working on that."

"Which is another reason why I wanted to help you. Besides needing to take a day off, this gives me a chance to step back for a while, and clear my head. Perhaps getting the case off my mind for a day or so will help me think of something I've overlooked."

"Jim, please don't take this the wrong way, but what are you and my brother planning to do for the afternoon?"

"I'm not certain. I assume you don't want us at the shower."

"I don't imagine it would be your glass of tea, if you'll pardon my stealing one of your jokes, Jim. Honestly, I was hoping you'd find something else to do, besides staying in your office and watching a ball game like you and Russ usually do."

"What's wrong with that?"

"Nothing, except there will be a lot of laughing and giggling from the girls, that could be loud enough it might make it hard for you to hear the TV. There will be some talk about men you wouldn't appreciate, either. Plus, you'll both get hungry and thirsty. I wouldn't want you wandering into the kitchen looking for something, and having any of the guests see you dressed like that."

"What's wrong with the way I'm dressed?"

Jim was wearing a tattered Texas A & M T-shirt

with the arms cut off, riddled with so many holes it looked like it had been hit with a full load of buckshot, faded denim shorts, and sneakers, with no socks.

"Nothing, if you're working around the place," Kim answered. "But you're certainly not dressed for company."

"You're just afraid your girlfriends will get all excited over my hot bod. You're jealous."

"Hardly. I'm afraid they'll think you're a slob. Besides, when you and Russell get to watching sports and drinking beer, the two of you always get into an argument."

"Hey, I can't help it if he's a fan of the wrong teams. How anyone can root for the Astros instead of the Rangers, the Texans instead of the Cowboys, and the Spurs instead of the Mavericks is beyond me. Besides, we don't argue. We just have very pointed discussions."

"Which is exactly what I don't want my guests to hear."

"Well, this is one time you don't have to worry. Russ called me the other day and said he had something planned."

"Did he say what?"

"No. I don't have a clue what he has in mind, except he said he'd keep me busy all afternoon."

"Knowing my brother as well as I do, I'm not certain whether that should make me relieved, or scared to death," Kim said, shaking her head.

"Look at it this way. At least we won't be underfoot. You and Ma, and your mother and sisters, and all your friends, can laugh and squeal, tell jokes, and complain about men as much as you want, and we won't be around to hear you."

"I suppose that *will* be a blessing," Kim conceded. "Rosa and Russ will be arriving in less than an hour. I'd better get dressed, and I still have to wrap her present. Are you going to change?"

"Not unless you lasso me, hog-tie me, and force me to," Jim answered. "I purely hate having to wear those damn dress shirts and ties for work all the time. This is one of the rare chances I get to dress comfortably. Before you go, are you certain you don't want me to watch Josh for the afternoon?"

"No, I promised everyone they would get to play with him. What could be more appropriate for a baby shower than a baby?"

"I can think of something."

"That's for a bridal shower, not a baby shower, Jim!"

"Could work for either."

"And I can think of something else, too, which I promise you *wouldn't* appreciate. Why don't you go play with the dog or your horse until Rosa and Russell get here?"

"That's not a bad idea. I'll give the horses their lunch hay. Soon as your brother and his wife get here, I'll give Russ a hand unloading the car."

"They're not bringing much. The shower is *for* Rosa. She's not giving it."

"I dunno. Russ said he was bringing something. I guess we'll just have to wait and find out what."

"Honey, Russ and Rosa just arrived," Jim called. "Looks like your mother came with them, rather'n driving herself. I guess your father decided to stay home. I'll be outside with them."

"Dad said he was going bowling with some friends. Tell them I'll be right there," Kim answered from Josh's room.

Jim went outside to greet his in-laws.

"Howdy, Russ, Rosa. You too, Mama Sofia. Good to see y'all again. Hit much traffic?"

"Just the usual construction mess on 35 at the ring road," Russ answered. "Other than that, no problem."

Russell Tavares, Kim's brother, was a World History teacher at St. Juan Diego Catholic High School in San Antonio. He also was an assistant football coach, as well as the head wrestling coach. His wife Rosa was a guidance counselor at the same school.

Kim joined them, carrying Josh. She kissed all three, then looked at her brother, critically.

"I see you got dressed for the occasion too, Russell, just like Jim," she said. Russ was also dressed in camouflage patterned shorts, a sleeveless Juan Diego wrestling T-shirt, sneakers, and white athletic socks.

"Hey, I wanted to be comfortable. It's not my shower."

"Would you mind if we went inside?" Rosa asked. "The baby's kicking. I don't think she likes the heat any more than I do. We can talk in the house."

"Of course, Rosa. I didn't mean to keep you out here," Kim said. "Mom and I will get you inside. Jim, will you help Russ unload the car?"

"Sure," Jim said.

"There's not much," Russ said. "Just a present for Josh, and Mom's gift for our little girl. They're in the back seat. If you can grab one of the boxes, Jim, I'll get the other."

"You've got it."

Jim picked up the larger of the boxes, Russ the other, then they followed the women into the house. Soon they were all settled in the living room, holding glasses of iced tea.

"Kimberly, the decorations are just lovely," Sofia said. "You did a wonderful job,"

"Thanks, Mom. Jim helped some. Mostly by climbing the ladder to hang them. I know it's unusual to have the guest of honor arrive to a shower before the guests, but since we've had so little time to get together lately, I wanted some time alone for just the three of us, before the others get here."

362

"That sounds like a hint for us to leave, Jim," Russ said.

"No, not at all. Stay and finish your drink," Kim said. "The shower doesn't start for another hour, so I'm not hurrying you out."

"Don't worry, Sis," Russ said. "I've got a long afternoon planned for your husband. I'm gonna keep him real busy."

"I've got to admit, you've piqued my curiosity," Jim said.

"Then finish that tea and let's go."

Both men drained their glasses in one swallow, then went out to Russ's car.

"New car?" Jim asked. "Nice. It sure is red. Really red."

"Yeah, it's a Mazda CX-5. With the baby coming, we needed a bigger vehicle than Rosa's old Corolla. I'm still driving my Ford pickup, though. It gets me where I need to go."

"That sounds fair enough," Jim said. "All right, enough stalling. What's this big surprise you've been talking about?"

"This."

Russ slid a tarp off the cargo in the back of his car, to uncover what it concealed. There were two large coolers, along with two unopened boxes which held high capacity, long range foam dart guns.

"This, my dear brother-in-law, is what we'll be doing all afternoon. The first cooler is filled with beer, the second is stuffed with sandwiches and chips. We won't be eating those dainty little finger sandwiches and baby greens salads the ladies will be having. A man could starve to death on those."

"All right, but what about those dart guns?"

"You and me are gonna have a good old-fashioned war," Russ said. "We'll spend the afternoon tryin' to gun each other down."

"I dunno." Jim shook his head. "I'm not certain I like the idea."

"Why not? I know you've been under more pressure than usual at your job, which is bad enough anyway."

"I guess the entire state of Texas must've heard that tale by now. I'd like to find just one person who *hasn't*."

"That doesn't matter, Jim. What *does* matter is you work off some of that tension. This is your chance. You can't tell me there haven't been times you just wanted to blow a bad guy to Kingdom Come. So have I. Not any criminals like you have to deal with, of course, but sometimes the kids get to me. There's days I'd like nothing better than to smack some of 'em right upside the head. Same with some of the other faculty. I'd never do that, of course, but there are a few of us who get together occasionally, either after school or on weekends, and blast away at each other with these guns. It's a good way to blow off steam.

There's even a new facility being built in Alamo Heights, just for adults who want to play war games, but don't like paintball, which is messy, and the equipment costs a lot more. Having mock battles with foam dart guns is one of the latest things in team building for big corporations, since you get to take out your frustrations, maybe get even with a co-worker who's irritated you. You can even shoot your boss, and not worry about repercussions.

"Trust me, it's good for your nerves, and plenty of exercise, too, not to mention a whole lotta fun. So c'mon. What d'ya say?"

"I say maybe you're right. Gimme one of those guns."

"Good. It's your choice, Jim. Do you want the Exterminator or the Eliminator?"

"The Exterminator."

"You've got it."

"Let's put this stuff in the back of my pickup," Jim suggested. "We'll head out by the pond. There's no sense in getting your nice, shiny, new car all scratched up."

"Okay."

The coolers and guns were tossed into the bed of Jim's old Silverado. Since the air conditioning in the truck had long since stopped working, both men took off their T-shirts and tossed them on the seat before climbing into the cab.

"I see this old heap's still running," Russ said,

when Jim turned the key and the engine came to life, rattling in protest. "It's a wonder."

"Hey, don't insult my truck," Jim said, laughing. "This baby's got at least another hundred thousand miles in her." He pushed in the clutch, the transmission groaning and grinding when he forced it into first gear.

"Hang on. It's gonna be a bumpy ride."

"Where do you want to set up the field of play?" Russ asked, when they arrived at the pond.

"I figure in that patch of land behind the pond, that I haven't cleared," Jim answered. "I purposely left it that way for the birds and wildlife. That means there's plenty of brush and trees we can use for cover. We might get scratched up a little, though."

"That sounds like the spot, all right."

For the next three hours, Jim and Russ raced through the brush, shooting at each other, stopping on occasion to have a beer, then going right back to their mock battle.

Finally, Russ lowered his gun.

"You want to stop for another beer, or keep playin'?"

"I can't stop for a beer now. It'd leak outta the pretend hole you just blew clean through my gut. Let's go a couple more times, then we'll stop for another beer."

"Sounds good to me. We'll stop for lunch here in a bit and then take a swim to cool off." Jim got to his feet, and followed Russ as he ran back into cover.

Jim and Russ ate their lunch, then downed three more beers each. They were sitting in the grass alongside the pond when Russ spoke.

"Jim, I've got to apologize," he said. "I should have realized gettin' you into a shootin' match with dart guns would bring back bad memories of what happened to that kid. I'm sorry."

"There's no need to apologize. I'm pretty much over that day. I need to be, or I'll have to quit the Rangers. Actually, playin' today helped a lot."

"I'm glad to hear that. And you know if you ever need to talk, call me. I won't say a word to Kim or Rosa if you do."

"I appreciate that. Another beer, Russ?"

"Sounds good."

On the way back to the house, Jim looked at Russ and laughed.

"Now it's my turn to ask what's so funny?" Russ said.

"Kim said I wasn't fit for her guests to see. Just wait'll she gets a look at us now."

Both of them had fresh scrapes and scratches, and were streaked with dirt.

"I guess we are a sight," Russ conceded.

"Yeah, but it was worth it. You were right. I did get rid of a lot of stress. Today did me a world of good."

"I'm glad to hear that. You want to take me on again sometime?"

"Sure. Anytime. But now it's time to face the music."

14

Lieutenant Stoker walked into Jim's office carrying two bags containing bacon, cheese, and egg on bagel sandwiches, along with a cardboard tray holding two extra large cups of black, unsweetened coffee. He placed those on Jim's desk, then pulled up a chair and sat down.

"Good mornin', Jim."

"Good mornin', Lieutenant. I appreciate you meeting me so early this morning."

"I'm glad you called. As you're aware, the situation with the protest marches and rallies in New Braunfels is close to getting out of control. The Deutschland's Höchste Wasserfälle water park and Schwarzwald theme park were forced to close for the entire weekend because picketers blocked their entrances. The business owners in New Braunfels, and the city's Chamber of Commerce, are demanding the National Guard be deployed. That's the last thing we'd need. I have to call the governor after we're done and let him know exactly where you are in progressing with your investigation."

"That's why I called you, Lieutenant. I want to run everything I've got by you, and let me have your opinion. Maybe between the two of us we can figure out our next step."

Jim picked up one of the cups of coffee and took a swallow. He grimaced.

"This stuff's pretty damn weak," he said.

"The store said they were fresh out of used motor oil and red pepper to add to your coffee, and they were sorry."

"I'll get by with it."

Jim handed two manila folders to Stoker, then grabbed one of the sandwiches and took a bite.

"The first file contains Deputy Luke Carter's statements, including his version and the timeline of what happened that night, and also what I noted when I examined the crime scene. The second holds what I've discovered since then. I'd like you to keep them side by side, and compare them as I explain my findings."

"Sure thing."

"Okay, here goes. Deputy Carter claims he and Deputy Solis confronted Randall McPartland on the bridge over the Guadalupe River. He states McPartland was carrying two large bundles or satchels. When they ordered him to stop, he threw those into the river and ran. They pursued him, Solis caught up with him first. Solis and McPartland struggled for a minute, then McPartland supposedly shot Solis. McPartland then ran *toward* Carter, not away from him. Carter alleges McPartland then jumped off the bridge, up the bank, and ran into the Rio resort, where Carter caught up to him, in the campground area.

He and McPartland shot it out, and Carter killed him. Are you with me so far?"

"So far."

"Good. One of my first questions when I started my investigation was why did McPartland run toward Carter, not away from him. The only logical explanation, which is a weak one, is that McPartland was trying to reach his vehicle, which was parked outside the self storage place, even though trying to lose Carter by running into the brush would have made more sense. McPartland's vehicle was loaded with apparently stolen goods; however, so far, none of the owners of those goods has been located, and as of yet, none of the serial numbers on the items appear on any lists of stolen goods.

"In addition, no large satchels or backpacks were ever recovered from the river. More importantly, there are several problems with Carter's story of how the killing of Deputy Solis and the shooting of McPartland took place.

"First, despite Carter's claim, there was absolutely no evidence of a struggle on the bridge.

"Second, the bullet wound to Deputy Solis, and the bullet's path through his abdomen, are not consistent with a shot from point blank range, as Carter stated happened.

"Third, there was no indication anywhere in the grass and dirt alongside the bridge that anyone, meaning McPartland, jumped off the bridge and ran to the stairs leading up from the river.

"Fourth, while I was unable to recover any good footprints from within the resort, since the alleged pursuit took place over paved or gravel roads, I did locate a couple of partial, barely discernable footprints along the supposed pursuit path. I was unable to confirm those matched McPartland's running shoes. The shallowness of those prints, and the spacing between them, indicated whoever made them was walking, not running. While the evidence does indicate that McPartland was killed on scene, the more I go over this case, the more doubts I have that Deputy Solis was even on the Guadalupe River bridge, or that he was shot by Randall McPartland."

"Let's say I agree with you, Jim," Stoker said. "Where does that leave us?"

"I'm about to tell you."

"I'm waiting."

"When I returned to Sattler to take another look at the crime scene, at approximately the same time the shootings happened, I again found nothing to indicate there had been any kind of a fight or shooting on the bridge. I did, however, notice on the south side of the bridge that some of the vegetation had turned brown, which it hadn't been when I first investigated the alleged crime scene."

"Why do you say 'alleged,' Jim?"

"Because I've got almost enough evidence to

prove Solis *wasn't* shot on the bridge. I followed the broken brush through the woods. The path went up the hill for a short distance, then turned and paralleled the river. I collected casts of footprints, one of a handprint, a button from a shirt, and a torn piece of cloth.

"But the damning evidence is the bloodstains I found. Luckily, it hadn't rained, so they weren't too deteriorated to be of any use. They match Herb Solis's blood type. Solis was shot in a little clearing along the side of the hill, then he was dragged to the river and dumped in a short distance upstream from the bridge. One other question is why there were no footprints returning from the river."

"That's still pretty shaky, Jim. It's quite possible Solis and Carter were checking those woods for criminal activity. Solis merely cut himself. That's what Carter will say if he's questioned about what you found, anyway."

"There's still more, Lieutenant. The button and scrap of cloth came off Solis's shirt. The handprint was his, as were one of the sets of footprints. Most important, do you remember the glove that was found along the riverbank?"

"Sure."

"I just happened to find the mate to that glove. It was lying against a tree, where I believe Solis was dumped into the river. Whoever it belonged to either didn't realize he'd dropped it, or thought he had thrown it into the river along with the other one. Would you like to make a small wager as to whose fingerprints I found on that glove?"

"I don't believe I would, because I'm positive you're about to tell me they were Luke Carter's."

"They sure were. I didn't need a search warrant to match those, since of course his fingerprints are in his personnel file at the Comal County Sheriff's Department, as well as in the state's database. What I'd really like to obtain is a DNA sample from Carter, as well as the boots he was wearing that night, so I can go for a match on his DNA and footprints. However, if he is lying, I doubt he'll cooperate, so I'll need a search warrant, both to obtain the DNA sample, and search his residence. You can see it all in the second file, including the photographs I took in that scrub."

"All right, I agree you've come up with a possible alternative scenario for that night," Stoker said. "You've made a very convincing argument. However, let's just step back for a minute and see what you've really got.

"First, as you say in your report, the gun found in McPartland's hand was the same weapon used to kill Deputy Solis, and a bullet from that same gun was recovered, by yourself in fact, from the side of an RV where Carter states he and McPartland shot it out. McPartland's fingerprints were on the gun, as was powder residue. The electron microscope scan you performed confirmed that. I know, it could very well be a false positive, and that gun could have been placed in McPartland's hand by the real shooter.

"You've also got McPartland's van, which was full of allegedly stolen goods. I'm assuming the only fingerprints or DNA traces on that van belonged to McPartland."

"They did."

"So while your theory is plausible, Jim, I'm afraid you still need more proof. Carter could refute just about every piece of evidence you've got."

"Even if it's plain he's lying?"

"It'd be a stretch, but yes. He could say he was so traumatized by seeing his partner shot down his mind had blanked out, and now that he's been shown the evidence you gathered, he recalls that he and Solis chased McPartland into the brush, where McPartland shot Solis, then dragged him to the river and threw him in. Then he dove into the river himself, and splashed his way across it to the campground, where Carter caught up to him and killed him.

"I'll admit, it's far-fetched, but when you put a white deputy sheriff in front of a jury, and they listen to his story, about a poor black man getting caught stealing, and shooting another deputy, the odds are ninety-nine to one that jury will believe the deputy, no matter what the evidence, and your testimony, might show. Also, what about motive? Why would Carter kill his fellow deputy? You haven't shown a reason he would."

"I know it, Lieutenant. Everyone I've talked with says there would be no reason for Carter to commit murder. That's why I'd also like to obtain a court order allowing me to access his telephone records, and search his computer. Maybe I can turn up something . . . anything."

"Those four men who attacked you didn't talk?"

"Oh, they did, in exchange for having the attempted murder charges dropped, but their story that they only wanted to stop my investigation seems to be the truth. There's no indication any of 'em actually knew Carter, except in passing."

"So, it seems to me the only chance you have of getting enough evidence to convince a prosecutor to take a case against Luke Carter to the grand jury is getting those warrants. Does that sound about right?"

"I guess so, much as I hate to admit it. I had hoped you'd agree I've got a solid enough case to proceed without those."

"You could try, but I'd prefer you wait until you uncovered a bit more. Maybe try putting a little more pressure on Carter, see if he cracks. In the meantime, I'll try to convince the governor to hold off on sending the National Guard down to New Braunfels, at least for a few more days."

Jim's phone rang.

"Hold on a minute, Lieutenant," he said.

"Ranger Blawcyzk."

"Is this Ranger James Blawcyzk?" the elderly woman on the other end of the line asked.

"Yes, ma'am. This is Ranger Blawcyzk. How may I help you?"

"I believe *I* can help *you*, Ranger. I've been too afraid to call you until now. I still am afraid. But I can't keep silent any longer."

"What do you mean, ma'am?"

"Are you alone, Ranger? Is there anyone else with you?"

"My lieutenant is here. He's the only one. I can put my phone on speaker if you'd like, so you'll be able to speak with him at the same time as me."

"I . . . I'm not certain."

"May I have your name, ma'am?"

"Yes. It's Mildred. Mildred Grimmell. I know what happened on the Guadalupe Bridge in Sattler. I mean, I *saw* part of what happened."

"Please hold on one moment, Ms. Grimmell."

"It's Mrs."

"Certainly. Mrs. Grimmell."

Jim covered the phone's mouthpiece with his hand.

"Lieutenant, this might just be the break we needed."

He returned to the phone.

"Mrs. Grimmell, I'd like to ask your permission once again to place you on speakerphone. I promise this conversation is totally confidential. It won't go beyond this office."

"All-all right."

Jim hit the speaker button, and nodded to Stoker.

"Mrs. Grimmell, this is Jim's supervisor, Lieutenant Stoker. I gather you have something important to tell us."

"I believe so."

"Mrs. Grimmell, we'll need to speak with you in person," Jim said. "Where are you located? We'll meet you there."

"No. No, not here. Someone might see you."

"Would you prefer to come to my office? Are you afraid someone might follow you?"

"No, that should be fine. I believe I'll be safe until I arrive there."

Stoker spoke up.

"Mrs. Grimmell, if you're worried about your safety, we can arrange protection for you. I can have a state trooper guarding you around the clock. I would also like to offer you a state trooper in an unmarked car to bring you here. Or myself or Ranger Blawcyzk can come get you, since our vehicles are also unmarked."

"I appreciate the offer, but I don't want to take the chance that someone sees me getting into a strange car," Mrs. Grimmell answered. "I'm in a tight knit area, where someone might notice. All I need is the address where Ranger Blawcyzk's office is located."

"I'm in the Hays County Justice of the Peace building and sheriff's department substation in Buda, on Jack Hays Trail," Jim said. "Do you need directions?"

"No, I have a GPS in my car. I'll find you. I'm afraid I'm not a very fast driver, though. It will probably take me an hour to arrive."

"That'll be just fine, Mrs. Grimmell. We'll both be here waiting. If you have any trouble at all on the way here, call us immediately."

"I shouldn't, Ranger. Thank you for taking the time to listen to an old lady. This is a great load off my mind."

"No, thank *you,* from both of us. We'll see you in about an hour. Good-bye, and drive safely."

"Good-bye, Ranger. Good-bye, Lieutenant."

"I wonder just what she saw—or, at least, thinks she saw," Stoker said, once Jim hung up the phone.

"I dunno, but I sure hope it's something useful," Jim answered. "Do you think we should look up her motor vehicle records, to find out what she drives? We could have a trooper pick her up on 35 and follow her until she gets here . . . discreetly, of course."

"That's not a bad idea," Stoker agreed. "I'll

get on that right now. Then, while we're waiting for Mrs. Grimmell, we can dig into these files more deeply, to see if there's something we both overlooked."

"There's a shiny new black Cadillac XTS pulling into the lot right now, Jim," Stoker said, almost ninety minutes later. "There goes the trooper, right on past. This has to be our gal."

They watched as an elderly woman got out of the car and crossed the parking lot. They were both standing up when she walked into Jim's office.

"Mrs. Grimmell? I'm Ranger Blawcyzk, and this is Lieutenant Stoker," Jim said. "Thank you for coming. The chair in front of my desk is yours. Would you like some coffee?"

"Yes, I believe I would."

"I'll pour you a cup."

Stoker raised an eyebrow, worried about how this tiny old lady would react to Jim's wretched brew. Mildred Grimmell was at least eighty years old, stood no more than four-feet-eight inches tall, and couldn't have weighed ninety pounds. Her feet barely touched the floor when she sat down.

"Here you go. Do you need sugar or cream?" Jim asked.

"No, black is fine. Thank you."

Mrs. Grimmell took a sip of coffee and smiled.

"My, this is good. I haven't had coffee like this in years. Thank you, Ranger."

"You're welcome."

"Do you really like Jim's coffee, Mrs. Grimmell?" Stoker asked.

"I certainly do."

Stoker just shook his head.

"Mrs. Grimmell, if you don't mind, I'd like to get started," Jim said. "Do you mind if I record our conversation?"

"Not at all."

"Thank you."

Jim turned on his recorder, and narrated the date and time.

"All right, Mrs. Grimmell. Would you please state your name and address for the record?"

"Certainly. My name is Mildred Grimmell. I live at 10 River Run, in the Sattler section of Canyon Lake. My late husband, Irving, and I moved there from Dallas when he retired."

"Now, take your time, and we can pause or stop whenever you need," Jim said. "You say you have information about the shootings that occurred on the Guadalupe River Bridge."

"Yes, I do. You see, after my Irving passed away, we'd been married for fifty-six years, I needed something to do. My son lives in New York with his family, and my daughter in Seattle with hers. They don't seem to have time to visit their mother. Most of my friends have also passed on, so I get lonely. I decided to take a photography class at the high school. It keeps me busy."

"Are you saying you took some pictures that night?" Jim asked.

"I'll get to that, Ranger. Anyway, Irving passed nearly three years ago. I haven't slept well since. I like to walk along the river at night. I listen to the water and the night birds, and the breeze rustling through the trees. Sometimes, a fish will jump and splash. It's very peaceful and soothing, at least most of the time. After a nice long walk, I can fall asleep and sleep soundly until late morning. However, the night that poor deputy got killed, and the other young man, was anything but peaceful."

"Would you care to rest before you go on, Mrs. Grimmell?" Stoker asked.

"No, I'm fine. I'd like to tell my story and get this done with."

"Then please continue."

"Of course. I was walking along the river when I heard what I thought was a car backfiring. I didn't realize until later what I'd heard was a gunshot. At first, I didn't pay it any mind. However, while I was standing alongside the river, a little ways upstream from the bridge, I heard a commotion on the opposite bank. I aimed my camera where the sound seemed to be coming from, thinking I might catch a shot of a deer or javelina in the moonlight.

"Instead, I got the shock of my life. I think I lost five years that night, and those are years I can't afford to lose."

"It seems to me you have plenty of years left," Jim said.

"Thank you, Ranger." Mrs. Grimmell took another sip from her cup "My, this is good coffee."

"I'm glad you like it. Most folks think I make it too strong. Please continue."

"Certainly. I kept my camera focused on the other riverbank. Two men came out of the woods. They were carrying a body. Luckily, I was hidden by some bushes, and I had on dark clothes, so they didn't see me. I couldn't move, though. If I'd made a sound, I'm sure they would have heard it, and discovered me. Anyway, while I watched, they threw the body into the river."

"Mrs. Grimmell, you said you heard a shot? Did it come from the bridge?" Jim asked.

"It most certainly did not. It came from the woods. I never saw anyone on the bridge."

"Looks like you were right, Jim," Stoker said. "There was never any fight on the bridge, and Solis was shot where you said."

"Mrs. Grimmell, could you identify the two men if you saw them again?" Jim asked.

"I'm not certain. They were pretty far away, and the light wasn't good. However, one of them was dressed like a sheriff. The other was a black man."

"What happened after they threw the body into the river?"

"They had a rubber raft tied up to a tree, right by a little set of stairs that leads to the river. They got into that and floated downstream. As soon as I was certain they were out of sight, I hurried home, locked my doors, and hid under the covers. I was so afraid they might have seen me, I didn't know what to do. Finally, I realized I couldn't live the rest of my life worried they'd come kill me. That's when I decided to call you."

"McPartland must have put that raft in the river, then waited in the woods for Carter," Jim said. "That explains why there were no prints coming back to the road."

"Mrs. Grimmell, think very carefully. Did you hear any more gunshots, later that night, from your side of the river?" Stoker asked.

"No, Lieutenant. I had my air conditioner on high. It's pretty noisy, so it drowns out most outside noise."

"Can you tell us anything else?" Jim asked.

"Only that I'm willing to testify in court if need be. Would you like to see the video I took of those men? I have a very high quality camera, with an expensive zoom lens. The picture quality might be better than you'll expect."

"Please."

Mrs. Grimmell removed a Canon EOS 5D Mark IV from her purse and placed it on Jim's desk. She clicked the "Play Video" button.

"You'll see those men in a minute," she said.

Jim and Stoker watched intently as the image came into focus.

"That's Carter!" Jim exclaimed, as soon as the two men came into view.

"Are you certain, Jim?" Stoker asked.

"Absolutely. And I'm almost certain that's McPartland with him. Our lab people should be able to enhance the images so we can tell for certain."

"Do you mean I've helped you?" Mrs. Grimmell asked.

"You certainly have," Stoker said. "Jim, I believe it's time to get a warrant issued for Luke Carter's arrest. There's no question that you've got sufficient evidence, now. Mrs. Grimmell, we will need to hold your camera until we can copy and process the video. We'll return it as soon as possible, I promise."

"Don't worry about that, Lieutenant. I have three more. I also copied that video onto a flash drive."

"Mrs. Grimmell, I know you don't believe you were seen that night," Jim said. "I don't believe you were either, or you would have been murdered by now. However, until we can take Deputy Carter into custody, you shouldn't go back home, and you shouldn't be alone. Do you have anyone you can stay with? Or if you prefer, we can put you up in a hotel, with a state trooper guarding you."

"I wouldn't want to trouble anyone, and I'm certainly not going to be cooped up in any hotel room, unless, of course, you promise me a *good-looking* state trooper."

Jim and Stoker laughed.

"I wish we could," Stoker said.

"Mrs. Grimmell, I've got an idea. You could stay at my place. We've got an extra room, and so does my mother, in her house right behind ours. She and my wife would love the company, and I've also got a baby boy you can play with. No one will even know you're there."

"You're married, Ranger? Damn, that's a helluva disappointment. But that does sound like a fine idea. I didn't bring any extra clothes with me, though."

"That's okay. My wife and mother love to shop. I'll call them and let them know you're coming."

"I'll contact the Highway Patrol to arrange for a trooper to escort you to Jim's house, Mrs. Grimmell," Stoker said. "That officer will be your protection until we have our man behind bars. We'll need a more detailed, written statement from you, but that can wait until later. We'll make those calls now."

"Might I use the rest room while you do that?"

"Of course. And I must say, Mrs. Grimmell, you are one plucky lady."

"I don't suppose *you're* single, Lieutenant?"

"No. I'm also married."

"Worse luck. Well, perhaps your mother knows some eligible man she can introduce me to, Ranger Blawcyzk."

"She just might," Jim said, with a grin.

15

Jim, Lieutenant Stoker, and Sheriff Donavan were outside Luke Carter's house, just before midnight.

"Looks like he's still awake, watching television. I would have preferred to make this arrest come morning, but didn't dare wait until then, on the off-chance Carter got suspicious, and decided to leave town tonight," Jim said. "He's bound to know something's wrong when we ring his bell this time of night."

"This is your play, Jim," Stoker said. "How do you want to make it?"

"I'll take the front. With any luck we'll take Carter by surprise, and he won't put up a fight. Rosalie, you'll take the back, in case he does make a run for it. Lieutenant, you'll be my backup out front, in case Carter somehow gets past me. We'll go in five minutes."

"All right."

Exactly five minutes later, Jim rang Carter's bell. He waited, then rang the bell a second time.

"I'm comin'," Carter yelled. A minute later, he swung open the door, to find himself staring down the barrel of Jim's Ruger, which was pointed directly at his chest.

"Ranger! What's this all about?"

"It's about placing you under arrest for the murders of Deputy Herbert Solis and Randall McPartland, that's what," Jim said. "Don't try anything stupid. Sheriff Donavan is out back, and I've got backup with me."

"You're crazy, Ranger. This is insane. You've got nothing on me."

"I've got enough to put you in Huntsville until you get the needle, Carter."

"That'll never happen, Ranger." Carter turned and began to run down the hallway. Jim dropped to one knee, aimed at the fleeing deputy's back, then put down his gun and tugged at the end of the hallway runner, pulling the carpet out from under Carter's feet. The deputy went down hard, sliding face first on the freshly waxed hardwood floor, and crashed into the kitchen door frame, knocking himself out cold.

"Lieutenant, Sheriff, it's all over," Jim shouted. "C'mon in. I've got him."

He pulled Carter's arms behind his back and cuffed him.

Stoker came inside, his gun drawn.

"What happened, Jim?"

"He tried to run. I pulled the rug out from under him. Soon as he comes to, we'll get him to the sheriff's office for booking, then in a cell. There's still a lot of questions that need to be answered."

16

"Jim, once again, good job," Stoker said. It was two days after Luke Carter's arrest. They were in Jim's office.

"It might not have turned out so well, if it hadn't been for Mildred Grimmell," Jim said. "Boy howdy, the old lady sure is enjoying the spotlight."

Mrs. Grimmell had made appearances on all the local news and talk shows, and was booked for an appearance on two of national network Sunday morning news programs, as well as all of the late night shows.

"You mind telling me again what all this was about, Jim? I'm still a bit uncertain."

"Not at all. Luke Carter had two motives. First, he was dealing drugs. Herb Solis got suspicious, but before he could go to Sheriff Donavan, or us, Carter caught on to him. He knew he had to get rid of Solis, but make it appear as if someone else had done it. That's where McPartland came into the picture. Carter had ties, under another identity, to several white supremacist groups. He bragged about how he was going to kill a black man. He and McPartland had crossed paths before, when Carter pulled him over and searched his car, for no reason. The electronics that I found in McPartland's van were stolen, all right, by the users Carter was supplying, when they couldn't come up with the cash for their fix. Carter would sell those down in San Antonio. He also hoped he'd start a race war, and damn near succeeded."

"But how did he get McPartland to help him?"

"He convinced McPartland he'd kill his father and mother, if he didn't help him take care of Solis. Of course, he also had him framed by putting all those stolen goods in his van. He told McPartland once Solis was dead, as long as he left Texas, there'd be no more problems for him, and his parents would be safe. Sadly, McPartland must've felt he had no choice. It's too bad he didn't come to us, or Sheriff Donavan. After killing Solis, Carter went to McPartland's van with him, ostensibly to get the stuff out of it and put it in storage. Instead, he shot McPartland, and tried to make it look like he was the one who'd killed Solis, then gotten gunned down by Carter. Carter wanted to make himself look like a hero."

"He was no hero. What he was, was a real sorry bastard, the kind who give all law enforcement a black eye," Stoker said. "A good man, and an innocent one, died because of him. It's a real shame."

"You can say that again, Lieutenant. However, at least he didn't get away with it, and folks have calmed down. Things are back to normal for the businesses in New Braunfels, so this entire situation worked out as well as we could hope for."

"Thank the Good Lord for that. Now that this is over with, Jim, what do you have planned?"

"I've still got a few loose ends to tie up. Once those are taken care of, I'm taking two weeks off. I've rented a beach house down on the Gulf. I'm not doin' anything for those two weeks but swim, sleep, ride my horse, and soak up the sun."

Stoker smacked his hands against his ears.

"Could you repeat that, Jim? I don't believe I heard you right."

"Oh, you sure did. I'll be on the beach for two weeks, my cell phone turned off, and no computer, radio, or television. Come a week from Saturday, me and my family will be incommunicado."

"Ranger, that's the best news I've heard since my first wife filed for divorce. We're gonna call it a day. I'm buying the beer. That's an order."

"I sure don't want to be charged with dis-obeying a superior officer and insubordination, Lieutenant. Let's go."

17

"Jim, renting this beachfront house for two weeks was the best idea you've had in ages," Kim said. Jim and his family were on South Padre Island, enjoying the sunshine and warm waters of the Gulf. "Now, roll over so I can do your front."

Jim sighed. Kim had slathered his back and shoulders with so much sunscreen he felt like a greased piglet.

"I thought it was, but I didn't realize you'd put so much sunscreen on me if I go in swimming the EPA will declare a major oil spill."

"Oh, hush with you, Jim. You don't want to get a bad sunburn. Your skin can't handle the sun like mine."

"She's right, Jim," Betty said. She and Josh were under a bright, rainbow-hued beach umbrella, its shade protecting the baby from the sun's rays. "You know your skin is so fair you never tan, just burn. Just like your father's and grandfather's."

"You too, Ma? I can't win."

"No, you can't," Kim answered. "Besides, you can't tell me you don't enjoy this."

She had finished coating Jim's chest with the lotion, and was now rubbing it on his belly. Jim broke into a fit of laughter.

393

"What's so funny, Jim?"

"It tickles, that's what's so funny," Jim answered, gasping.

"If you think *that* tickles, wait until you feel this."

Kim dug her fingernails into his ribs, running them up and down his side. Jim doubled up, convulsed with laughter, helpless.

"Kim, stop it . . . Please!" he pleaded.

"Only if you promise to go souvenir hunting with me tomorrow."

"I promise. I promise," Jim said. "Anything. Just finish greasing me up so we can go for our swim."

"All right."

A short distance north of the house the Blawcyzks were renting was the South Padre Equestrian Center. Jim had insisted on bringing the horses along and boarding them at the facility, so he and his family could enjoy riding along the beach. It was late in the afternoon when they left Josh and Frostie with a babysitter, while Jim's wife and mother joined him for a gallop along the beach. Jim was wearing only swimming trunks, his wife and mother swimsuits. They were riding bareback, feeling complete freedom as Copper, Freedom, and Slacker pounded through the surf. They galloped for over a mile, then pulled the excited horses down to a walk.

"I wish we could live here all the time," Kim said.

"You'd have to divorce me and marry a multi-millionaire," Jim answered, chuckling.

"That's not a bad idea," Kim retorted.

"What?"

She leaned over from her horse to give him a kiss on the cheek. "I'm just teasing you, Jim."

"Where shall we ride next?" Betty asked.

"I've got an idea," Jim said. "Let's ride over to the ice cream stand. We can get sundaes for ourselves, and cones for the horses. I know I'm ready for a nice, big hot fudge sundae, with plenty of whipped cream, nuts, and a cherry on top. Then again, hot butterscotch would be good, too."

"That's a great idea, but I'll probably just settle for a double scoop cone," Kim said. "Vanilla and chocolate."

"And a strawberry ice cream soda is what I'd like," Betty said.

"Good, then let's go."

They let the horses set their own pace, ambling along the beach until they reached the ice cream stand. The lines for the frosty treat were long, but the horses, tired from running through the soft sand, were content to stand patiently while waiting for Jim to return. Of course, having a passel of children petting them and offering them bites of their ice cream cones made them more than willing to stay right there.

"Here we are," Jim said, when he came back to where his wife and mother were waiting with the horses. He carried a cardboard tray which held his sundae, Betty's soda, and Kim's cone, as well as a vanilla cone for each horse.

"So, what did you finally decide on, hot fudge or hot butterscotch?" Kim asked, when she took her cone from Jim.

"Both. There's a good dollop of each on my pecan praline crunch ice cream," Jim answered. "You just can't see 'em under all the whipped cream."

"Did you really need to ask, Kim?" Betty said.

"No, but I thought for once he might fool me. After all, he *did* take this vacation."

"Well, that has got to be the biggest sundae I've ever seen," Betty said. "Jim, you might break poor Copper's back when you get on him after eating that monstrosity."

"Nah, he'll be just fine. Won't you, boy?"

Copper answered by shoving his nose into Jim's sundae, covering his muzzle with so much whipped cream he appeared rabid. His long tongue licked the cream from around his mouth and nose, then he whickered for more.

"Oh, no you don't, horse," Jim said, holding his sundae at arm's length, while Copper stretched his neck as far as possible, trying to get at it, and the bystanders, including Kim and Betty, laughed. "This one's yours."

He held a cone to Copper's lips. In three bites, it was gone.

"There," Jim said. "You go back to nibblin' on the grass, while I finish what's left of *my* ice cream."

Copper tried once more to bury his muzzle in Jim's sundae, then gave up the effort, and settled for pulling at the grass along the edge of the parking lot.

After finishing their ice cream, the Blawcyzks mounted up once again, for the ride back home. They had their horses trotting along the beach when Jim pulled Copper to a halt.

"Hold on! What's goin' on over there?" he said.

From a short distance down the beach came the sounds of an elderly woman, who was calling for help. A man, most likely her husband, was lying alongside her, where he'd apparently been shoved to the sand. A young man was running away from them, clutching the woman's tote bag under his arm.

"Someone stop that man! He just robbed us!" the woman yelled.

"Kim, Ma, you stay here," Jim ordered. "I'll be right back."

He put Copper into a dead run, intercepted the thief, leapt off Copper and tackled the man, pinning him to the ground.

Betty looked at Kim and shrugged.

"I know," Kim said, with a sigh of resignation. "Here we go again."

About the Author

Jim Griffin became enamored of the Texas Rangers from watching the TV series, Tales of the Texas Rangers, as a youngster. He grew to be an avid student and collector of Rangers' artifacts, memorabilia, and other items. His collection is now housed in the Texas Ranger Hall of Fame and Museum in Waco.

His quest for authenticity in his writing has taken him to the famous Old West towns of Pecos, Deadwood, Cheyenne, Tombstone and numerous others. While Jim's books are fiction, he strives to keep them as accurate as possible within the realm of fiction.

A graduate of Southern Connecticut State University, Jim now lives in Keene, New Hampshire when he isn't travelling around the west.

A devoted and enthusiastic horseman, Jim bought his first horse when he was a junior in college. He has owned several American Paint horses. He is a member of the Connecticut Horse Council Volunteer Horse Patrol, an organization which assists the state park Rangers with patrolling parks and forests.

Jim's books are highly reminiscent of the pulp westerns of yesteryear, the heroes and villains are clearly separated.

Website: www.jamesjgriffin.net

Center Point Large Print

600 Brooks Road / PO Box 1
Thorndike, ME 04986-0001 USA

(207) 568-3717

US & Canada:
1 800 929-9108
www.centerpointlargeprint.com